Revolution

Chris Helvey

Revolution

On top of the taller refrigerator an ancient black radio blared mariachi music, interrupted now and then when the announcer came on and babbled excitedly for a minute. Occasionally, a commercial blasted. Everyone in the kitchen had to shout to be heard above the radio. When the conversation at the tables ebbed, the people in the restaurant could hear the songs.

Once a serious voice broke in over the music to make an announcement concerning a military action taking place in the north. In the kitchen, the people were quiet while the serious voice spoke. People in the restaurant hushed their voices for a few seconds, then resumed their conversations. Most could understand very little of the language, usually words or phrases they had heard in movies, or perhaps they knew a few numerals. Those who understood more grew silent, finding their appetites significantly diminished.

From his table by the window, Bartlett Samuels looked at the people in the dining room and shuddered inside. Spicy eggs, yellow rice, and tortillas were not his idea of breakfast, even with half a grapefruit on the side. He missed his café latte and Danish, not to mention his computer, the stock market reports, and his office. He actually missed the hard-to-get cabs and the surly cabdrivers he usually despised. Certainly, they were better than that stupid yellow bus he had been held captive in for the past week that felt like a month. Bartlett Samuels jabbed his spoon into his grapefruit half. Juice squirted. Seconds later, his brains splattered a Rorschach across the window.

In the aftermath there was only silence. Then a tinkle of falling glass razored a narrow slit in the silence. Maria let the coffeepot slip from her fingers and it shattered against the wooden floor. A woman shrieked, and suddenly the room was full of screams and shouts and the discordant sounds of chair legs dragging on the wooden floor and breaking glass.

As though the wall of sound had broken whatever invisible barrier held the people entranced, they began to run as quickly as they could, staying as low as they could, praying as hard as they could. Gunfire broke out in a spontaneous benediction to the morning.

Revolution

Chris Helvey

A Wings ePress, Inc.
Literary Fiction

Wings ePress, Inc.

Edited by: Jeanne Smith
Copy Edited by: Brian Hatfield
Executive Editor: Jeanne Smith
Cover Artist: Trisha FitzGerald-Jung
Images

Wings ePress Books
www.wingsepress.com

Copyright © 2024 by: Chris Helvey
ISBN 979-8-89197-969-70

Published In the United States Of America

Wings ePress, Inc.
3000 N. Rock Road
Newton, KS 67114

Dedication

To Gina H and Jeanne S, two individuals who helped make *Revolution* a reality

Once, when driving down old Frankfort Pike, I heard a song on the radio with a line that implied you would always remember where you were when the revolution started. It didn't say which revolution; and I have never thought that mattered. The truth was there, simmering inside those words, and the sun was burning the top off a high blue enamel sky, with the sunlight streaming through the open sunroof burning the words, and the images were spinning into my brain. That momentary radiophonic blast was the genesis of this work; that, and nothing more. All characters and scenes are totally fictitious, existing only in my mind. Any resemblance to any person, alive or dead, is purely coincidental, the result of random chance in this random universe.

—Chris Helvey

One

Toucan shit slid down the bottom half of the window like the last dirty snow of spring. Kron stirred restlessly on the cracked leather of the bus seat. He'd been riding since before daylight, and now the late afternoon sun was slicing through the windows, rendering him half blind. Golden-headed flies droned around his head.

Kron despised the bus. Even though the tour was only four days old, he felt as though he had been living in it for most of his life. Another ten days on the tour from hell filled him with dread. It was a struggle to recall why he had ever considered taking such a trip.

Material, he had told himself, material for the novel that he was always on the verge of writing. God, the amazing lies a man told himself when the temperature hovered below freezing for twenty-two straight days. Kron looked around the bus. His fellow passengers were a depressing lot. Leaning to his right, he stuck his head out the open top half of the window. The air was warm against his face, only slightly cooler than the stale air drifting feebly around the bus. Bastards had lied about the air conditioning. That wasn't the only thing they'd lied about.

It was an ancient bus and it had once been painted bright yellow. Now, it was the color of a goldfinch that had been dead for twenty-four hours. It smelled like something dead, too, a combination of diesel fumes, burnt oil, sweat, and stale perfume, tinged with the scent of dead animals rotting by the side of the road and human excrement, with something even more fetid and primeval swirling through it – the jungle that was always there; the great green, alive jungle.

Throughout the day the jungle seemed to be on the march, crowding the road with vines, stretching tendrils onto cracked asphalt, sheltering monkeys who screamed at the bus when it slowed in the snakebelly curves. The jungle curled away from the road when it passed through a dusty village or crossed a ramshackle wooden bridge, the water shining thin and flat and blue in the gorge below, only to reappear beyond a curve that made the passengers regret eating breakfast. Even in the dark, you could hear it murmuring to itself when the wind blew through the canopy. Without a doubt it was alive. Many natives swore it had a spirit.

El Cartero was one. El Cartero drove the bus. He had driven many buses. For eight years he had been driving this particular bus. El Cartero was his nickname. Friends called him that because he delivered the passengers with the same care and dedication the postman delivered the mail. His given name was four names long, but only his mother had ever called him by all of them together, and she had been dead for ten years. El Cartero liked his nickname.

Flicking his eyes to the rearview minor, the driver scanned the tourists, not trying to remember their names. There were so many and they came and went so quickly it seemed meaningless to clog his brain with names he would use only once or twice. Remembering their faces to nod at them frequently during the two-week tour to ensure a good tip was enough. Besides, he needed to dedicate most of his brain to noticing what was happening around him. Rumors of rebels had been flowing like the Sulaco in the rainy season. Then there was always the road, twisting and curving, then twisting again, curling back on itself like a viper striking its own tail. The pavement, where there was pavement, was cracked and rutted, spotted with potholes too numerous to totally avoid. Half lost in thought, El Cartero shifted his eyes back to the road just in time to see the asphalt snake begin to curl to the left. Under his sweating left palm, he turned the wheel as a foot found the brake and he began to downshift.

The bus swerved and the passengers slid across their cracked vinyl seats, pressing their shoes against the floor, bracing themselves against the shell of the bus where they could, sliding into other passengers when they couldn't.

On the last row of the bus, the one that was a single seat running the width of the vehicle, Lady Dianna Threlkeld grimaced as she slid against her husband. Drinking again; she could smell the alcohol on his breath. She glanced at his face. A fine glaze already coated his pale blue eyes. When they had first met, she'd thought those eyes were the most beautiful she'd ever seen. The color of a pale, high Devonshire sky during the final warm spell of October. Now, they disgusted her. The sun wasn't down and Lord Threlkeld was sinking toward his usual evening stupor.

Threlkeld The Soused – it had a certain ring. Wrinkling her nose, she squirmed back across her seat, distancing herself. Ignoring the wind against her face, she stared into the massed, verdant jungle. It looked impenetrable. She wondered what lay beyond the emerald barrier. Shuddering, she turned her face away and shut her eyes, focusing on the swaying of the bus and the fires rising inside her.

One row up, the Reverend Thomas Malloy sighed as he rested his head against his seat back. For him, the tour was a homecoming. Twenty years ago, he had served a year as a missionary in Yuscarana. Ancient history, yet the reverend still remembered the curving blacksnake road, the screaming jungle, and the hollow-eyed, hungry people. He wondered if any would remember him. Always, he had tried to help them. Leaving Yuscarana had not been his idea.

Across the aisle, Trevor Samuels looked up from his book of poems by Bukowski and studied the smile on the reverend's face. At fifteen, Trevor Samuels didn't find much to smile about. His line of sight rotated to the back of his sister's head. She was in the seat in front of him. Trevor knew she was floating. The angle of her head always gave her away. When she was high, her head perched on her neck like a bird balancing on a feeble reed. Shaking his head, the boy dropped his eyes and read

"like the Garden of Eden

except no snake would dare enter

here."

~ * ~

There was a song circling in her head. She could hear notes rising and falling but the refrain only echoed and the words blended together, no matter how hard she listened.

Kristin Samuels opened her eyes enough to let a faint golden light filter in, but only enough to illuminate one darkened corner of her mind. Her body swayed in rhythm to the movements of the bus. It was like floating down a smooth, hot river in a large, fast boat, she thought. Kristin had always enjoyed moving; moving on to the next house or car or boy or drug. Destinations didn't matter. It was the movement that counted. The movement and the chance, albeit quite small, that one more high would produce meaning. Meaning about what, Kristin wasn't clear, but she definitely knew meaning was essential. She had to find it, and find it soon. Focusing on the golden light, Kristin Samuels let the ceaseless river of music flow through her mind, muddied words vibrating off the canyon walls until they were the cries of a thousand hawks, red tails glistening like fresh blood in the sunlight. She was totally unaware that her mother's eyes were fixed on her face.

~ * ~

Where had she gone wrong? That was what Sharon Samuels wanted to know. Homecoming Queen of Bridgeport High, sorority chapter president at a small, but prestigious eastern college, two years with *Vogue* before marrying Bartlett Samuels, who was handsome in his Armani suit and impressive with his drive for success. Marriage to a rising performer on Wall Street hardly seemed a poor career choice.

The first two years had been fun, if hectic. Then Kristin came and the world changed. Daiquiris then accompanied diapers more often than dinner at Chez Richard's; the stars of the *Today Show* grew more intimate than Jolene at the gym; routine household chores replaced roulette on the weekends. But she had tried. She'd read Dr. Seuss books, baked homemade cookies for the daycare, and watched more soccer than should be allowed by law. Bartlett became an astute stock picker. Money flowed like warm amber honey, sweet, yet a touch sticky.

Somewhere, however, the whole damn train had jumped the tracks. Bartlett started working longer hours and golfed with clients on the weekend. Sweet baby Kristin had grown up and discovered boys, along with other vices, then drifted away to a world that wasn't large enough for more than one. Trevor, born two years after Kristin, had always been a different child, loving to read, paint, and play stringed instruments. Remembering her early love for Baudelaire, Sharon had hoped.

What sort of rooms would they find in Yuscarana? So far, Morazon had yielded only small dirty rooms that smelled of stale sweat and cigarette smoke and, occasionally, a fetid odor that hinted at death. Remembering sent a chill through her body and she reached out and touched her husband's bare arm, the hairs on it quite pale in the late afternoon sunlight.

Without looking up from his cell phone, Bartlett Samuels arranged a smile on his face. He didn't look up for three reasons, all of them perfectly sound. First, he was getting an early look at proposed SEC regulations. Forewarned equaled forearmed.

Second, he didn't want to be interrupted. With all the tours of crumbling churches, ancient Morazonian Indian villages, and dusty museums packed with chipped pottery, tourists, and natives positively reeking of sweat, he hadn't really had a good chance to catch up on the messages Brian had been sending him.

Brian was co-manager of their boutique mid-cap fund. Being a co-manager in this market was a real challenge. Being sole manager for two weeks had to be overwhelming. Bartlett felt a twinge of guilt.

Third, he wasn't interested. Not in his wife, nor his kids, nor this damn tour. He got enough of the family at home, and the tour was turning into the tour from hell. Bartlett asked himself how he had let himself get coerced into this stupid vacation. Vacation, shit; it was a living nightmare. Keeping his eyes on the small screen, Bartlett Samuels ran his free hand down his wife's left thigh. Damn, the woman needed to shave her legs again. She was growing hirsute in her maturity. He returned his attention to the proposed language on trading arbitrage regulations.

Late afternoon sunlight poured into the bus like a great golden river, dammed too long before finally breaking through. It grew hot in the bus and sweat rolled down faces and spines, pooled under armpits, dampening chests and running down ass cracks. El Cartero squinted against the light that was blinding, even with sunglasses tinted deep green. Keeping his line of vision a few degrees below the angle of the sun, he focused on the road, ignoring the passengers and the jungle that crept nearer the road with each mile.

~ * ~

Iwakura Tyshimoda sat in the seat directly behind El Cartero. He kept his eyes on the jungle and his face as smooth as an Ohio farm pond on a calm day. Experience had taught him that other people worried about him less when he kept his face and demeanor placid. When he remembered to do this, they ignored him, asked no questions, made no advances toward the fabricated friendship that Iwakura despised. Phoniness he recognized easily, and abhorred. Americans pretended to be so honest and friendly and caring, when actually they were greedy, fronting emotions solely to obtain what they wanted. And as for all super patriots who were ready to crush smaller countries that possessed limited military capabilities, as long as they didn't have to fly the choppers, or drop the bombs, or launch the missiles or, God forbid, actually go in on the ground and face sand fleas, cold rations, land mines, belligerent guerrillas, and hostile native populations, they were all mouth – ignorant. Ignorant of war's realities. Ignorant of the ways of a warrior, of honor, of courage, of death; ignorant of Bushido. Iwakura Tyshimoda reminded himself he wasn't here to judge. He was on vacation to please his wife, who was going to please her sister, who had been forced to back out of the tour at the last minute due to an emergency appendectomy. Iwakura sighed, keeping his eyes on the jungle.

Beside her husband, Akko Tyshimoda sat quite still, sensing, in a subliminal way, her husband's uneasiness, worrying. He thought she wasn't aware of his mood changes behind his fixed face. She knew that from the way he held his body and the angle of his head, even from his controlled breathing. She never told him; she was afraid of his reaction. She had seen his workouts, had seen the damage his hands and feet could do. No, he had never struck her, not physically, but she had felt the mental blows. Iron bars flung from a great height. But it was the ice that really bothered her, drove her to the edge of screaming. Between one breath and the next, Iwakura could turn cold. A cold so deep it hurt; a gigantic icicle thrust into her breasts, stabbing again and again, her strength bleeding away with each heartbeat.

The yellow bus struggled up a long slow rise, hung at the crest for a moment as if to catch its breath, then began the long descent into a valley crisscrossed with dark, moving shadows. Pressing a foot on the brake, El Cartero downshifted. This mountain he knew well. Over the years it had claimed many victims and he had no desire to add his name to the list. El Cartero had never truly had an accident, not one that could be judged his fault. A seriously inebriated English woman had once smashed into his bus while it was parked and a judge in too great a hurry had sideswiped the bus he was driving one night, but otherwise his record was clean. El Cartero planned to keep it that way.

~ * ~

The jungle grew quite close to the side of the road now and wayward tree branches stretched out above the cracked pavement, scratching one side of the old bus.

This jungle reminded him of Vietnam, Joe Moby thought, and the remembering began, images flashing like a newsreel on overdrive. Long-dead friends and enemies, and officers who were almost enemies, and bright green jungles and rain you thought would never end, and fire roaring up around him like a blazing orange shroud, and naked girls of the night, and old women with no teeth, and old men with no children, and howling dogs and dead monkeys and crying babies all whirled in the memory.

Shivering involuntarily, he shifted his mind back into the bus and the woman sitting beside him on the cracked vinyl seat. He loved her very much. Willing his lips into a smile, he stroked her smooth arm. She lifted her face, closed her book, and smiled at him.

Silver lined her hair now, streaking through the black in wide, curling swaths, and wrinkles prevailed on a skin that had once been as smooth as polished stone. Crow's feet expanded out from violet eyes. Beyond the great divide now, she was still beautiful. Amy Moby still felt young and strong and as full of life as when she had been a girl on a Nebraska prairie farm. Still able to teach chemistry to high school students all day, then grade papers, read novels, chair church circles, and make love to Joe Moby late in the night. Age was a relative thing, a sense about oneself that one created in her own mind; that is what Amy Moby believed and what she told herself each morning at 5:30 when she woke without an alarm, lying quietly for a moment, allowing her eyes to adjust, listening to Joe's rhythmic breathing, planning out her schedule, letting the day come to her.

White adobe building blocks rose up out of the shadows. Amy wondered what this town held. She retained enough adventurer's spirit to wonder and fantasize about what each day and night might hold.

El Cartero pressed the brakes harder and limbs scratched the old bus as the asphalt cracked and shifted beneath it. Tour 24 rolled on toward the shadows gathering at the edge of the greedy jungle and Yuscarana. Sunlight glinted off the old bus like visions of Beelzebub.

Two

Yuscarana squatted a quarter mile beyond a wide left-hand turn at the bottom of a steep hill. The town sprawled clearly before you from the crest of the hill, but as you descended, the road curved away from the buildings and the streets, the hillside rose thick and tree covered, and Yuscarana disappeared as though an invisible hand had swept it from the earth. People rounding the curve for the first time were quite surprised to suddenly find themselves face to face with the adobe buildings, gleaming white in the sun like bleaching dinosaur bones.

One paved street wound like an asphalt vein through the heart of Yuscarana. A dozen side streets spread out from the main road, strands of a spider's web, capturing small houses, cafés, and shops. All these streets were dirt, packed smooth and hard over the years. In the dry season, they were better roads than the paved, but heavily-cracked highway.

Awnings hung from cafés and shops like metallic eyelids. At one corner, several small round wood tables were arrayed in front of a café. Most of the tables were empty. However, two old men in peasant shirts and soft, wide-legged pants sat at the one closest to the street. Both were smoking thin hand-rolled cigarettes. Behind them in the shade, with his back against the adobe wall of the café, sat a man in a military uniform. He was wearing an Army cap and sipping coffee. His body was still, but his dark eyes were alive, always moving, even when the street was empty except for an old dog, who walked as though his feet hurt, pausing frequently to scratch at his sores.

Captain Jose Jorge Hernandez Morales heard the bus before it rounded the last curve before Yuscarana. Yuscarana was a quiet town. The only sounds were murmurs of the old men, the faint panting of the old dog and, just at the edge of the village, the whine of a small generator. Captain Morales knew the generator powered the saw that milled the timber a few of the more ambitious residents harvested each year, then sold to a man from the capital who paid them a poor price.

Captain Morales knew a great deal; in fact, he knew almost everything that took place in Yuscarana. Such knowledge was his job. His life depended on it. His life and that of the President of Morazon, Juan Gutierrez.

Known to many as the fortunate one, President Gutierrez had always been a survivor. During his climb to the top of Morazon's political heap, he had survived bullies and sadistic teachers in school, bullets from guards eager to kill during the university riots, women who tried to kill him while they made love to him, and a fistful of would-be assassins. Now, Gutierrez clung to the summit, and loyal men like Captain Morales were critical. Gutierrez had them posted in every village across Morazon because the rebels did not conveniently restrict themselves to a particular town or region. They struck where they chose, without warning, seemingly at random. At first, it had been once or twice a year, then monthly. For the past several months, not a week had gone by without another hit-and-run raid. To date, the raids had been small, but each cost him men, men that were getting steadily more difficult to replace. A major attack was coming; Gutierrez knew this with a certainty that vibrated in his bones. That day he dreaded. For now, however, he relied on men like Morales. They would have to do until he turned the Morazon economy around, or sequestered enough money in his offshore bank accounts to allow him to retire in a style he deemed appropriate.

Captain Morales was especially important. The jungles surrounding Yuscarana were home to some of the most active rebels. In the past month alone, three attacks had been made within a twenty-mile radius of Yuscarana. Reinforcements should have been sent; Gutierrez understood that. The president also understood that if he pulled soldiers from one section of Morazon and sent them somewhere else, he was simply opening up a hole he couldn't fill. Besides, news of such troop movements would be splashed on front pages across the world, damaging the tourist industry that represented one of the few still-profitable sectors of the Morazonian economy. Gutierrez couldn't afford to take that chance. No, Morales would have to hold Yuscarana. No other option existed.

Captain Morales had a vague, smoky understanding of the situation. Details, he did not have, but they were not necessary. The captain already knew what he had to do. Hold Yuscarana. To put it bluntly, he had no choice.

Sipping his coffee, he watched the old yellow bus round the curve. The captain disliked seeing the bus. The bus carried tourists, and tourists were tempting targets to the guerillas who were growing bolder by the day. Morales recognized it was only a matter of time before they moved in from the jungle and struck directly at Yuscarana. Many would die. He didn't want to be there when the attack came. He was too young to die. Morales took another sip of coffee. Way too damn young.

Tipping his cap back, he watched the bus coast to a stop in front of the only hotel in Yuscarana. As the coffee warmed his throat, he recalled his first bus trip. He had been seven, perhaps eight. The morning had been cool. As a boy, Morales had lived in the mountains and each morning a mist the color of steam had enveloped those mountains. Walking with his father through the mist, clutching a big hand, he had wondered, with an intensity that had made his flesh tingle, what the day would bring.

Morales could remember that the seats on the bus were slick and that a bald man sat in front of them, smoking cigars which emitted a heavy smoke and an aroma that was sweet and sour at the same time. Morales remembered his excitement turning to nausea as the bus wound its way down a narrow road more crooked than a deformed snake. Massive walls of green had risen on one side of the bus, while on the other side there had been nothing but air for hundreds of feet above the rock-strewn gorge below. A river ran through the gorge. From the bus, it looked like the trail of a snail. Rocks seemed broken marbles, bleached white under a tropical sun.

Morales had become more and more nauseous as the bus descended. He had tried not to show his misery for fear others on the bus would laugh at him, or that he would be sent home. He had suffered in silence, gradually turning pale and letting intermittent groans slip between pressed lips. Finally, his father noticed and the bus had pulled over to the first wide space by the side of the road. Morales vividly recalled rushing from the bus, the air hot and sticky, taking his breath, smothering him. And then there had been only the bile rising in his throat as he stumbled blindly through the underbrush, followed by the hot rush of vomit burning his throat. Then a merciful darkness.

Captain Morales supposed his father had cleaned him up. Certainly, the trip had resumed. Dimly, he recalled a museum with large paintings of men on horses. More vivid was the memory of an ice cream cone, his first, eaten so quickly it made his teeth hurt. His father had held long conversations with men in suits. Morales remembered his exhaustion as he climbed back on the bus. It was very clear in his mind that the sun had been setting, glittering on a mountain dome, turning it golden. The trip home was blank tape. His father had been dead for a decade.

Shuddering at the memories – they always made him feel as though he were walking through a graveyard – Morales straightened in his chair, tugged the bill of his cap down, and, squinting against the slanting light, carefully observed the descending passengers.

Stumbling down the steps, they stood in the street, blinking against the sunlight. Heads turned as they struggled to get their bearings. A tall man with a mane of silver hair said something to the group. His words were too soft for Morales to catch their meaning, coming to him as murmurs from a shallow stream. The man with the silver mane pointed at the hotel. The tourists began to shuffle toward the Hotel De Cortes. They slogged up the steps like the rearguard of a retreating army.

Captain Morales searched their faces. It was unlikely any guerillas had infiltrated the tourist group. What advantage they might gain from doing so wasn't immediately clear. However, these days it paid to take extra care. Rumors drifted through Yuscarana like jungle rot. From bitter experience, Morales knew the rumors had the nasty propensity to become fact. Only yesterday, he had heard from a half-drunk, but occasionally reliable, source that an attack was imminent. He hoped the rumor was false. A week ago, he had split his garrison, sending half his men under Lieutenant Arroyo to a small village in the northern quadrant of his territory in an effort to quell the attacks that had disrupted traffic, killed the mayor of Arnica, and created great fear and unrest among the local peasants. Nothing had been heard from Lieutenant Arroyo, and Captain Morales was starting to worry.

He was also starting to sense the small nagging worm that crawled around in the muck at the bottom of his brain whenever something was out of the ordinary. Morales liked ordinary. Ordinary was safe. Guerillas were not ordinary.

The man with the long silver hair was causing the nasty little worm to stir. Perhaps it was the way he cocked his head to one side, like a gigantic, inquisitive monkey. Morales was sure he had seen the man before. He never truly forgot a face. He made it his business not to. Although he couldn't immediately place the face, that would come. Captain Morales was certain.

A man stepped out of the front door of the hotel. He stood well over six feet tall, with a head full of black hair that grew wildly from his large, egg-shaped head. A mustache that looked like a small animal curled above his upper lip. Brushing a shock of hair from his forehead, he shouted, "Hello, hello, welcome to my hotel. Come in! Come in out of the sun. Here, let us help you. Manuel, Paco, come, come! Help with the bags."

Two boys, perhaps ten or twelve years old, jumped from the darkness beyond the open door and raced down the stairs. The man, preceded by a substantial stomach, lumbered after them, grinning broadly and shouting in rapid Spanish to El Cartero. The man looked like a happy bear. A girl in a maid's apron stood in the shadowy doorway, staring after the bear. Her face was lovely.

Captain Morales pushed himself off his chair, tossed coins on the table, and began to cross the street. He walked as if he had all the time in the world.

Three

Macaws screamed at spider monkeys who threw rotten fruit at the birds and, when the mood struck them, at other members of the troop. Certain fleshy missiles missed their targets and fell through gaps in the canopy to the jungle floor below.

An overripe plantain splattered on the ground next to a slim, hard-faced man in wrinkled khakis. He stared at the broken fruit, its insides splattered across the jungle floor, and the quick black ants already working, and spat. His spittle struck a large ant and sent him skidding. The man smiled; even with his mouth he was a good shot. Stroking the machine gun in his lap, he glanced up toward the monkeys. Temptation rose in his throat and he swallowed it before he changed his mind. Ammunition had to be used judiciously and, until they were ready, silence was critical.

Restless now in the late afternoon, Carlos Geraldo uncoiled and recoiled his legs, working the stiffness from them. Sitting quietly in the clearing all afternoon with the other men, he had been husbanding his energy, waiting for night. Now that the light was beginning to fail, he sensed the restlessness rising within him. He knew what was coming. The one-eyed boy had delivered the message last night, the message he had been waiting weeks for. Time to attack Yuscarana. He felt the tremor in his left leg and became aware of the tic in his right eye.

All day they had been waiting in the clearing, listening to monkeys and mosquitoes, catching flashes of red and yellow as birds flitted through the thick green canopy, feeling sweat roll down their spines, closing their eyes when their stomachs churned, trying to think of their mothers, or their sweethearts, or anyone who might once have been kind to them, trying to hold on for the night, for one more night.

It was coming now; the light was changing and there was coolness in the air. Carlos let his eyes sweep the clearing, looking at the men. Some he knew as well as he knew his brothers; no, better than his brothers. He had swum and climbed trees and played football with his brothers. With Felix and Jesus the Pig and Tony the Demented, he had marched and fought and killed. Their blood and that of their enemies had soaked into the jungle floor for almost two years, ever since they left their villages in the north and joined forces. In the beginning there had been others: Manuel – killed at San Felipe by a tall man in an army uniform, Rico – found with his throat cut in the dust outside Meriletta, Diego – last seen being marched away with his hands in the air and a rifle against his back. Carlos shook his head, trying to clear the memories. So many were gone, including his older brother, Miguel. A vision of Miguel with his nose and mouth gone and only a gaping bloody hole where they had been flashed through the center of his brain.

Carlos bit his lip and made himself move. He walked across the clearing with a vigor he had not felt all day. For a step or two, Miguel's image clung to his mind, then Carlos was kicking at the feet of a sleeping man and shouting at Jesus to get the men up and moving. Yuscarana was over a mile away and the sun had already slid behind the tops of the tallest trees. Dark would be gathering where the trees grew thick and snakes hung like coils of patterned rope from the limbs, where monkeys howled in the treetops, and the big cats growled from the deep underbrush. Already, Carlos could feel his flesh tingling and the blood singing in his veins.

"Let's go," he called out. Inside his head, his voice sounded loud and high, as monkeys screamed at him from the trees.

Twenty-six men looked up. Some rose immediately; others moved more slowly, as if they were nearly exhausted, or reluctant. A man with a beard and a bandage over his right eye did not move. Instead, he kept his head against a fallen tree trunk and watched the gray line of men file off into the jungle. A week ago, he would have gone with them.

But that was before an unplanned firefight at dusk outside a village whose name he had never learned. Now, he was blind in one eye and gut shot. Not one of the men in the snaking line knew his name. They called him Frijoles because he would eat beans three meals a day if they were available. His mother had always called him Tico. She would never call him that again; Frijoles knew that. He was bleeding inside, bleeding deep in his gut. Life was draining slowly out of him, like daylight fading during a long summer's evening.

He was sad to see the men leave, but glad, too, in a way he couldn't explain even to himself, except that he now wanted to cry for a moment, or two. All afternoon he had been holding the tears, waiting for the men to leave. Now it was almost time; he would count to twenty.

Then the last man in the line, a boy really, looked back. His name was Felix and he lifted a hand and waved goodbye to Tico Frijoles. Gritting his teeth, Tico Frijoles lifted a hand and tried to smile. It was more of a grimace, but the boy smiled before he turned and hurried down the trail.

Tico Frijoles, who would never again see his dog, or his girlfriend, or his padre, or his mother, said a very short, but heartfelt prayer. Then, he closed his eyes and began to count. By thirteen, tears were sliding down both sides of his dirty face.

~ * ~

Felix hustled along the trail. Pausing to wave to his friend had put him behind the others and Felix didn't like being alone in the jungle. It was so alive; full of shrieking monkeys and screaming birds, and a thousand unseen insects that buzzed and hummed and, worst of all, the great smooth snakes that slithered slickly along low-lying limbs. Felix shuddered to think of all the aliveness.

As he jogged, he tried not to think about his friend, Tico. Actually, the man was little more than an acquaintance, but he had been kind to Felix, kinder than the other rebels. Kindness was not friendship, but it would serve.

Until a few months ago, Felix had never stayed even a single night away from his small village and his round, warm mother. For over a year he had thought about joining the rebels. Felix knew of the suffering his people had undergone and he believed in the cause. Being young and uncertain, he had hesitated. Even now, hurrying down the trail, he was not certain why he had slipped away one evening in the gathering dusk and climbed into the wooden canoe waiting along the banks of the Orroce. Perhaps it was the cause moving his heart, or the need to show his courage to his friend, Jorge, who talked of little but the brave rebels who were fighting the soldiers of Gutierrez. Perhaps it was only the impetuosity of a young man.

A mosquito buzzed at his ear and Felix smashed it against his temple. The boat had capsized south of Lavito and Jorge had died of a strange fever in a damp unknown land, sweating and screaming, crying alternately for God, a priest, and his mother. Jorge was a fading memory, his life no more now than the faint scent of an animal that had once passed along a trail.

Now Felix had killed a man, and the image haunted his dreams at night. A curse had settled on him. Inches off the trail something moved in the dense green undergrowth. Felix hurried on, leaving Tico Frijoles behind, along with the last strand of his innocence.

~ * ~

In the middle of the pack, a man waddled, his mouth full of day-old corncakes and his gut preceding him like a wind-filled sail. His clothes were torn and splattered with dried mud and old blood. Only his boots looked even halfway new, and that was because he had taken them off a dead government soldier after the raid on Arnica. He had not shaved or bathed in several days and the stubble grew thick and black, like a swath of burned-over trees, while a nasty, sour odor swirled around him as though his body were rotting fruit. No one walked too close to the man they called Jesus the Pig.

He had been with the rebels so long that the life of a guerrilla seemed to be the only one he had ever lived. Days when he had been a foreman on a small coffee plantation seemed part of another dimension, lived by another man.

Dirt, death, decadence, and disease now seemed the natural order of things to Jesus the Pig. In the early months, he had notched the stock of his ancient rifle in remembrance of those he had slain. After the firefight at the crossroads, where the dead had embraced like lovers, such notching seemed superfluous, and he did not do it anymore.

For a time, he had tried to look like a soldier. It was difficult, though, to find the time or a place to wash his clothes and trim his beard. Jesus was not one to do things the difficult way. Whenever possible, he chose the path of least resistance. He had given up bathing and changed his clothes only when he found a dead soldier close to his own size. The nagging uncertainty of where his next meal would come from caused him to eat all he could, whenever he could. Jesus always ate all his food, along with that of comrades too sick or wounded to eat. Always, he took rations from the dead; they had no use for them.

Killing was now automatic to him. He took no particular joy or pride in it – it was merely his job. He was a rebel against the bastard Gutierrez, a guerrilla who lived in the heart of the jungle, emerging only to kill. That was his job. Who could blame him or hold him accountable? Policemen arrested ordinary men, and jailers jailed ordinary men, and executioners executed ordinary men. Jesus the Pig was a rebel, destined by fate, God, and Carlos, to kill.

Rape, now perhaps one could argue there, if one was a prick who liked to quibble over minor matters. To Jesus, rape was only a word, one that he did not try to fully define even in his own mind. Women, of any age, were spoils of war. He preferred them young and beautiful and pleading for mercy, but he was not overly particular. Not for nothing was he known as the Pig.

Yuscarana was rumored to have many beautiful women. Jesus the Pig swallowed a bite of corncake, farted loudly, and grinned. After the killing, after his work was done, he would enjoy the fruits of his labor.

A small harmless snake stared at him from a branch that curved across the trail like the tail of a wooden horse. Jesus smiled at the snake, nodded politely, then whacked its head off with a single slash of his machete.

~ * ~

Three steps behind Carlos Geraldo a man walked quietly. His face was twisted as if he had grabbed a live electrical wire and been frozen in time. His mustache was thin and black, the stroke of an artist. His eyes were black and moving, always moving.

One of the oldest guerrillas, he was already on the dark side of forty. His body was thin and hard. Light on his feet, he walked like a much younger man, keeping his weight on the balls of his feet, always ready to move quickly and quietly.

As he walked, he thought, as he often did, of his wife. She was dead now, murdered by a man in a uniform they told him; murdered after being raped.

He had screamed at them that day, demanding to know why they hadn't stopped it. With tears in their eyes, they had pointed at the bodies lying in the dusty square, blood still seeping. His children's bodies had been among the dead, their brains splattered against the west wall of the church. They had been six and seven, a boy with bright eyes and a sweet girl who prayed every day. His wife's name had been Maria.

Only the old folks of the village had been spared. No one was sure why. Perhaps it had not been worth the effort for the army men to kill them. Old and toothless, they stank where they had soiled themselves during the attack.

His name was Tony. In his first life he had been a mechanic, working on big trucks in the city, coming home on the weekends and holy days. It had been a holy day when he had come home to the carnage. Never before had he given much thought to politics. Gutierrez had been as good as the next asshole. Then he had come home to find only the old folks still living.

You could have tried to stop them, he had screamed. After the screaming he had gone quiet and his eyes had changed. The old people who noticed the change in his eyes grew afraid.

When he spoke again, it was in a voice that was little more than a whisper. You could at least have tried to save them, he told the old folks. He told them that the second before he slit their throats with the short sharp knife he carried inside his shirt for protection in the city.

After killing them, he had shed no tears. Instead, he left their bodies to rot and buried his wife and children in the clearing behind their small home. Once he finished his final prayer, he had burned the village, one building at a time. Then he had joined the rebels. By now, Tony had killed so many men that he could no longer keep them separate in his mind. Dead faces and bodies all merged into one man; a man he was forced to kill again and again and again. Daily now, the urge to kill came to him like a fever, his mouth gaping open and his eyes growing hot.

Men, even those who marched with him, gave him a wide berth. Something about him made a man step aside. Perhaps his body emitted a special odor, an odor smelled only by the subconscious, the odor of death.

Now he was called, when he was not present, Tony the Demented. No one, except occasionally Carlos Geraldo, spoke directly to him. All the rest of the rebels considered him a devil standing on his hind legs. Death Walking, they called him.

Tony the Demented walked quietly down the trail to Yuscarana, his face as unmoving as stone. Only his eyes were alive.

~ * ~

Carlos kept his eyes focused on the trail. In the gathering darkness it was no more than a pale, jagged wound. He had traveled this path many times before, so he was not greatly worried. Still, there could be no slipups tonight. Too much was riding on the thin ragged line of men that trailed through the jungle like seeping blood.

With his eyes on the trail, Carlos tried to focus on what lay ahead. Troops were stationed at Yuscarana. Informers had told them that much. A man with a patch over his left eye had told Carlos that a significant part of the garrison had been sent north a few days ago. The one-eyed man had passed on information before. Sometimes he was accurate.

Twenty-six men were not enough. Carlos knew that. He should not attack without support, not Yuscarana, not even for the revolution. Morales was at Yuscarana. He knew of Morales – a fighter. That had been proven. Carlos respected Morales as a fighter, even as he despised him as a dog of Gutierrez.

Hatred surged through Carlos Geraldo and he felt his face go flush. He made himself think of the river that flowed smooth and cool and deep beside his village. Losing control of his emotions had proven fatal to the men under his command in earlier battles. Carlos Geraldo did not intend to repeat that error. Never had he claimed to be brilliant. He would show his men and the revolution, not to mention that son-of-a-whore Gutierrez and his bastard Captain Morales that Carlos Geraldo was not stupid. He spat the bad taste out of his mouth and marched more swiftly toward Yuscarana.

Above the guerrillas, the tree canopy grew steadily more dense. Even at noon, daylight had a difficult time penetrating to the jungle floor. Now, with evening settling in, the air had turned a smoky gray and it was impossible to see three feet off the trail. Birds made different sounds as they began to settle down for the night. The howls of the monkeys had faded, but mosquitoes and black flies still hummed, and now there were running sounds in the tangled growth under the trees.

Carlos Geraldo's ears and mind registered the jungle rustlings, but he had heard them thousands of times and, unless they were unusually loud or vigorous, they meant no more to him than his own breathing. Certainly, they were of little importance tonight. Yuscarana was the dominant thought on his mind, eclipsing all others. Twenty-six men marched with him, only enough to aggravate the garrison at Yuscarana, but eighty more men were supposed to be marching toward the town from the north and another forty from the west. Gonzales might spare twenty men from the east, but perhaps it would be a smaller number, or none at all. The men of Gonzales had been in three firefights in the last ten days; fighting had been intense, and in one they had been badly mauled. No, Carlos decided, he would not count on Gonzales. Better to rely on more certain numbers. Stray thoughts worked their way across his mind. Floods, disease, roaming government units might delay or stop the advance of the other rebels. Carlos shrugged. What happened, happened. He had his orders and he would carry them out. Always.

Darkness filled the air now – an ebony curtain. Carlos paused, glanced back. The next man was a dim form emerging from the blackness. Behind him was only darkness.

Carlos wheeled and stepped into the aphotic night. Memories of another such inky night flooded his mind. He wondered if a storm were developing. It had stormed that long ago night. He had been a boy, nine or ten, returning home from visiting his cousins in the next village. His brother, Miguel, who had been two years older, was with him.

They had still been across the river when they heard the sounds. Screams had come first, and they had begun to run hard toward the village, stumbling over exposed tree roots and falling face first into the brush; then rising and running on, fear burning the linings of their throats.

Just as they reached the riverbank, the shots rang out, followed by shouts and more screams. Hunkering down in the tall grasses that grew in the shallows, Carlos and his brother listened to the screams and the curses and the shouts and the shots that howled through the night. Then the sounds had ceased and across the river the world had come alive in a blaze of light. The entire riverbank seemed to be on fire. Firelight reflected on the smooth waters and danced unnamed ballets in the night.

For hours they had watched the fires burn. Surely they would consume the world. Then thunder had rolled and new lights zigzagged across the black sky. After midnight the rains had come.

Dawn had roused them from the sleep they never requested. Across the river nothing moved. Unwilling arms paddled slowly. Only ashes and charred bones greeted them. Skulls stared at them with great empty eye, nose, and mouth sockets. A single mangy dog wandered through the smoldering village. Near the center of the ruins, they found the skeleton of the house they had lived in. Bones were all they discovered. Overarching all was the horrific odor of burned flesh.

They made a blood vow to destroy Gutierrez. Only then did they cry. Carlos had not cried since. Miguel would never cry again.

In the moist darkness, Carlos Geraldo bit his lip and pushed hard for Yuscarana. Thunder rolled in the distance. The air felt heavy and close, a moist blanket clinging to his body and face. Lightning exploded like a humongous flashbulb on the western horizon. Carlos began to walk faster. He did not glance back at his men. They would follow him. The smell of burnt human flesh was strong in his nostrils. Sweat covered his face like silver blood.

Four

Juan Miguel Hernandez Gutierrez stood at the window statue erect, his back stiffened, tightening the cords in his neck, pointing his chin at the window.

Though he was not technically a member of the armed forces, he wore his uniform. Being commander-in-chief, President Gutierrez felt, entitled him to wear a uniform. His uniform had been made to order by a tailor who specialized in personalizing uniforms for officers.

In his small, dimly lighted shop on the corner of Nogales and Vera Cruz, the tailor cut fine cloth to flatter swelling paunches, round out narrow shoulders, or pad bony chests. Working slowly and carefully, he measured precisely and double-stitched. The tailor took a great deal of pride in his work and charged far less than the rate charged by the younger tailors who maintained stores in the newer sections of the capital. His shop was in a part of town that had not been in style since the '30s. Then it had been replete with boutiques that sold silver, lingerie, and perfumes in exquisitely shaped glass bottles, small cafés with green, wrought iron tables and chairs, and restaurants that opened only at night, when they served fine cuisine and vintage wines by the flickering light of candles set in tall gold candlesticks.

Now the area was filled with secondhand stores that sold used furniture and worn clothing, small dirty offices where loans were made at exorbitant interest rates against forthcoming checks, and empty stores with broken glass splattered on the dirty sidewalks outside and plywood jammed in the windows. A few specialty shops, like the tailor's, whose owners were skilled enough to bring in business from throughout the city, still held on. Not that Gutierrez went to the shop himself. A sergeant named Gomez brought the tailor to him. After all, he was *El Presidente*.

President Gutierrez stared out the window. His office was on the top floor of the palace and the grounds unfurled out below him like a painting, no, a photograph – the vista was too realistic for any painter to capture. Palm trees spread gracefully above manicured lawns so brightly green they sparkled like newly formed emeralds. Statues that had been old before Gutierrez had been born were arrayed across the lawn like the vanguard of a marble and bronze army. In the precise center of the verdant expanse, a giant fountain gushed water from the mouths of tigers, maidens, and conquistadors wearing iron helmets and carrying broad swords. From his window, washed daily by an old man who always wore suspenders, Gutierrez could see the people arriving and leaving, seeking favors and offering bribes.

Normally, President Gutierrez enjoyed the spectacle, often watching it for long stretches of time. He felt he had earned it. After all, he had come a long way from his boyhood. His father had been a teacher in a small school in the corner of Morazon that stuck out like a sore finger or an erect penis. Even the finest part of the town he had grown up in had been only a couple of steps up from the current condition of Vera Cruz and Nogales streets.

Yes, he had come a long way and usually enjoyed basking in his reflected glory. Never did he allow himself to reflect on the lies, the torturing; the burnings, and the murders required to get him to his current position. Life was hard. To get ahead, at least in Morazon, you had to be harder than the next man. That was the philosophy of President Gutierrez.

Today, however, he was not happy. In fact, he was downright uncomfortable, perhaps even a degree nervous. That cockroach from Solovision was coming at eleven o'clock to interview him. God how he hated that pissant of a troublemaker.

He hadn't wanted the interview, not any interview really, but certainly not with Ruiz. Why that son-of-a-whore was nothing but a rude, voyeuristic exposer. Ruiz cared nothing for the truth, only for making up the biggest lies his twisted mind could imagine, then splashing them across all the television screens he could – even the largest Spanish language station in the United States. He had ruined Chavez, Del Torio, and that one-armed Chilean general. President Gutierrez could not imagine why he had agreed to the interview, even under threat from his cabinet. Gutierrez shook his head. He could only conclude that he had been drunk.

Turning from the window, Gutierrez gazed at the black telephone on his desk, wondering if there was still time to call his minister of information, who was also his brother-in-law, and cancel the interview. He would look like a coward, but the president wondered if that wasn't better than looking like a fool.

He took one step toward the telephone, then stopped. Footsteps echoed in the hall. Gutierrez stepped back and turned to face the door. Taking a deep breath, he squared his shoulders and fixed an expression on his face he hoped would come across on camera as both friendly and firm. He had not survived as president for all these years without being smart and bold, he told himself. He would simply have to pull it off one more time.

Knuckles rapped on the door, a sharp, vibrant knock. Gutierrez shuddered, then hitched up his pants and reworked his facial expression. He turned the better side of his face to the door. "Enter."

A slightly built man stepped inside, moving with a dancer's gracefulness. Silver hair hung down the back of his head in subtle waves that crested on the collar of a suit exactly the shade of blue that certain women of a certain age tint their hair. His shoulders were slightly bowed, as though for too long they had supported an extraordinarily heavy weight. A smile familiar to millions creased his face.

"Good morning, President Gutierrez," he said in Spanish that flowed as smoothly as water over a round rock.

Gutierrez nodded and said, "Good morning, Señor Ruiz." Already there was something about the man he did not like. Something was wrong with his accent. It had an unfamiliar rhythm, much like a familiar dish will have a surprising flavor when the chef adds a new spice. Gutierrez did not like new things. Different was not good unless he had ordered it. Different had the aura of change, and change for someone in power was not often desired. Gutierrez smoothed down hair that had already been smoothed a dozen times that morning. "Come in, come in."

Jorge Ruiz smiled at the man behind the desk, then ignored him, motioning to his cameraman where he wanted him to set up. He was all business. To him the job was paramount. He had a responsibility to his viewers, millions of them. For years they had been waiting for an interview with Gutierrez. Just hold on, he had been promising them, I will get the interview. Now he was here and he did not intend to waste a single minute. Stalling was a well-known defensive technique. With his hands he made hurrying motions at the cameraman.

"Ready, President Gutierrez?"

Gutierrez nodded slowly, recalling the time when he was still in school and a trio of bullies had beaten him every day for a week after classes and he knew another beating was sure to come. Worse, there had been nothing for him to do except get his back up against the fence and start swinging.

They had beaten him that day, and many more. Yet, he had never surrendered, never run, and slowly, so slowly that it seemed he must be living in a warp of time, he grew larger and stronger, and the trio began to separate like tread from worn tires. Daily he worked on his body, disciplining himself to wait until the time was right. When he was strong enough, and the nights were dark enough, and the members of the trio traveled their own paths, he struck. Struck hard and fast, without mercy. It had not been pretty, but then revenge was often a lonely, bloody evolution.

He remembered it all: the pain and the pleasure, topped by the sweet, sad satisfaction of revenge. Standing up straighter against the wall, he smiled at the silver-haired man with eyes like flashbulbs going off in a Dadaist theatre.

"President Gutierrez, it is said that you are one of the wealthiest men in all of Morazon. Is this true?"

Strong light exploded like a birthing sun. Gutierrez blinked against the light. Black dots danced before him. He could see the outline of Ruiz moving toward him through a saffron haze.

"No, no, Señor Ruiz, I am a man of modest means. Surely, as an important reporter for Solovision you must be aware of this." The president kept his voice calm. At least he hoped it sounded calm. This interview would be broadcast around the world and he had an image to maintain. Mentally, he cursed his brother-in-law. The man was an imbecile. No, he, Gutierrez was an imbecile for listening to a bigger imbecile.

"You say you are a man of modest means, President Gutierrez, yet you own a house that has been valued at over five million American dollars." Ruiz turned and stared into the camera. He wore his eagle's face. "And I have been told by most reliable sources that this is an extremely conservative estimate."

"My home belongs to the people of Morazon."

"Yet the deed is in your name? Here," he reached inside his suit jacket and pulled out a sheaf of papers. "I have a copy of the deed. Would you like to examine it?" He thrust the bundle at Gutierrez like a short sword.

"That will not be necessary. Of course the property is in my name. It will always be in the name of the president of Morazon. I am only holding it for the people, as my successor will after me."

"You speak of your successor, President Gutierrez, yet you have never allowed an election to be held."

"You are mistaken, Señor Ruiz. Only last year a referendum on my presidency was held."

"Yes, and you received over ninety-eight percent of the votes. How do you account for such success?"

Gutierrez could feel sweat forming along his hairline. Fervently, he hoped it didn't show. "I am a popular man," he said.

"Ninety-eight percent is very popular. Christ is not that popular. How could you be that popular?"

Gutierrez shrugged in what he hoped was a humble manner. "You will have to ask the people of Morazon, Señor Ruiz."

"I would be happy to do that, whenever you will allow me to, President Gutierrez."

Gutierrez shrugged as if the comment was somehow an insult. Gutierrez prided himself on his ability to express emotion merely with the calculated movements of his shoulders. He kept his face as smooth as the plaster walls behind him; the smoothness, in inexplicable ways, expressing more than the facial contortions of a circus clown.

Ruiz stared for several seconds at the man behind the desk. He distrusted the man and was glad that he and his crew would be the ones to edit the tape. He held no great expectations for the interview, but it was a foot inside the door of the presidency of Morazon, a door that had previously been shut in his face. He heard the cameraman clear his throat and he forced his mind back into the room.

"You have sons, I believe."

"Yes, two."

"Are they here with you and your wife?"

Gutierrez smiled with his lips. "They are away at school."

"In Morazon?"

Gutierrez looked down at some papers on his desk, then lifted his eyes and stared into the camera. "In the United States."

For an instant, his mind flicked away to his sons whom he had not seen for over a year. It was not safe for them in Morazon. Gutierrez was not an overtly affectionate man. There were some who thought he didn't love anyone, except perhaps himself. They were wrong. He did not love himself. He loved his sons. And, in his own strange, slightly perverted way, he loved Morazon.

Ruiz continued asking questions for several minutes. Gutierrez's responses were brief, full of published facts, occasionally true. He no longer looked into the camera or at Ruiz. What Gutierrez was seeing was not in the room. His aide, Colonel Munuoz, noticed the drifting and signaled the interview was over.

Ruiz was very unhappy. He had waited a long time for an interview that was suddenly in an irreversible death spiral. He signaled the cameraman to keep filming and made certain his microphone remained on. Then he protested loudly and vehemently at the termination, occasionally glancing back over his shoulder to make sure he was on camera.

Slowly, with a strange expression, as though he were waking from a sweet and sour dream, Gutierrez's eyes focused. "The interview is over," he said. Gutierrez spoke very quietly, so quietly that everyone had to stop talking to hear. Still, the cameraman kept on filming. Gutierrez did not speak again, but a small squad of soldiers came quickly into the room. One soldier took Ruiz by the elbow and another put a hand on the back of the cameraman and they escorted the men from Solovision out of the room without speaking.

Colonel Munuoz stayed in the room watching the president, waiting for him to give him the day's orders. After some time, he became aware that his legs had started to ache. He glanced at President Gutierrez. Gutierrez stared back and the colonel felt a chilling of his blood. Turning quickly, he walked out of the room without speaking. He never saluted in private.

President Gutierrez was glad Ruiz and the cameraman were gone. He was especially glad his aide was gone. At times, Gutierrez received the distinct impression the colonel held him in low regard, perhaps even despised him.

For some time, the president thought about his sons. He missed them a great deal, but he was glad he had sent them out of Morazon. They were safer now. He thought of when he had been young and lived with his mother and father in a small village. His parents had been dead a long time and he seldom thought of them. Some days he could not even remember what their faces looked like. When he did remember them, they seemed more like old black and white photographs from the moldy pages of a history book than the faces of his father and mother.

A sharp noise outside the window startled him. He twisted in time to see a large black bird flying very fast. It was flapping its great wings rapidly while six or eight small birds swirled about it in a loose formation. Every few seconds one of the smaller birds would dive at the larger bird. Once, the larger bird screamed and the sound ripped through Gutierrez. He felt great empathy for the larger bird.

Five

The light was beginning to go. Shadows slid down the walls and poured themselves across the floor until they merged. Outside the single narrow window, a remnant of light lingered and dust motes danced slowly, as though the dance had been a long one and they were nearing exhaustion. A few birds called to each other from the trees and a solitary wasp buzzed desultorily at the window sill. Far away, almost beyond hearing, a mother called for a child to come home.

Kron lay on his back atop the striped blanket that covered the single bed. He had been lying on his bed since he had checked into his room. His eyes had never closed. Instead, overtired from the moving bus and the colors that had flashed by like a kaleidoscope on amphetamines, they had flickered relentlessly.

In school, when he had run cross-country, his legs had been like that some nights, especially after a long run over hills on a cool, damp afternoon. He could still remember the way his legs had twitched on and on and on under the covers long after he had turned out the lights. Now, he lay on a bed with sagging springs in a room going dark in an old hotel in Yuscarana, wondering for the hundredth time why he had come so damnably far to be so alone.

Not halfway over, the tour was already stretching out in his mind like a perpetually elastic rubber band. He was tired, not physically, but mentally. A dull, gray tiredness covered his mind like a thick, damp wool blanket. It was the sort of tiredness you felt when you haven't slept for two days; the kind that no amount of eating, coffee drinking, or exercise will alleviate. Kron rolled over onto his left side, facing a wall covered in water-stained, peeling wallpaper. Closing his eyes, he tried to escape from the day that seemed to be stretching to the far side of eternity.

He was intimately familiar with days like these. Days that seemed to have no end. Perhaps they didn't. Perhaps they were only an eternal waking nightmare. He could not total the days he had stayed in his room, curtains drawn against the light, refusing to answer the phone, pretending to write. Only he knew that his writing was so often only make believe.

What writing he managed came in short, irregular spurts, like arterial blood pumping from a wounded, dying animal. A poem someone at a national publication liked, a short story that resonated with an editor of a slick who had grown up in the town the story was set in, a fragment of a novel that his major professor had praised extensively – this pitiful oeuvre was all he had to offer the world as proof of his artistry. However, combined with dark, shaggy-haired good looks and a pleasantly smooth and deceptively casual conversational style, this had often proven enough.

Women liked him, liked to hear him read his poems in small, subtly lighted library rooms that featured Monet and Van Gogh reproductions. Afterwards, they would invite him out for coffee and muffins in quaint corner cafés where they would chat for hours about Eliot and Frost, Whittier and Bukowski. They would talk until she had to pick up the kids from school, or go back to work, or hurry home to fix her husband's supper. They would talk until the coffee was cool and acidic, or the light began to fade, or her nerves failed. Some would give him their telephone number and then he would give them his. Only he never called, and if they called, he never answered. Each reading, and its aftermath, became merely another episode in the poetry game. Kron played numerous games, most of them with his own mind, but then everyone did that. Once, crossing Kansas in a convertible, he had wandered across an oldies station on the car radio and caught a song by a guy named Joe South about the games people played. That was one song which had bubbled over with truth.

Thunder rolled beyond the mountains and Kron turned his face toward the window. Daylight was going quickly now and there was a coolness to the air. Refreshed by the change, Kron sat up on the side of the bed, glanced down at his legs, wondering if he could summon the energy to stand, or perhaps it was courage he needed to rouse.

Kron forced himself off the bed, padded across the smooth wooden floor on his bare feet, and stuck his head out the window. The air was noticeably cooler than when he had disembarked from the old yellow bus, but the humidity was up and he brought his face back with a sheen of sweat on it.

From his window he could not see the main street, only a dusty side street that ran parallel to it. A man in a short-brimmed white hat walked along it, heading south away from the hotel, a gunny sack slung over one shoulder. Behind him, a brown and white dog trotted, its tongue hanging out. A dark wedge of birds flew hard above the bare earth, disappearing in a line of trees that reminded Kron of a row of flag poles with their banners furled against the night. Music drifted to him, floating on the wind. Voices murmured in the hall, and off in the distance, where the mountains were already growing dark, Kron could see dots of moving lights winding down the slopes toward Yuscarana. They looked, he thought, like a strand of Christmas lights.

Christmas made him think of home and his parents. They had been happy to see him off on the tour. They had always been happy to see him off. Off to conservation camp, and Boy Scout hikes, and senior trips to Estes Park, and mission trips to the Bahamas, and college; oh yes, always glad to see him off. When you didn't understand someone, it was easier that way, nicer for all concerned. They hadn't been blatant about it, not cruel, but their quiet pleasure had been easy for Kron to see, even at a quite early age.

Shrugging, he turned his back on the man and the dog and the hard flying birds, and walked across the room with all the determination he could dredge up and slipped on his shoes while still standing. He was reluctant to sit – there was that pervasive problem of getting back up.

Halfway to the door, Kron realized he wasn't wearing any socks. Oh well, he harbored serious doubts that many in Yuscarana were members of the fashion police. Glancing at a cloudy mirror on his way out, he ran fingers through his hair. Since the day would not end, he might as well join in the celebration. Kron grinned at his doubtful self in the smoky glass.

Six

"Damn, it is going to rain, and we're supposed to take a walking tour of the town after dark." Lady Dianna Threlkeld slid her bookmark between pages 66 and 67 of *The Grapes of Wrath* and closed her eyes. The bookmark featured a photograph of the Sistine Chapel, which she had visited the year before with her sister, Pamela. Pamela was too religious for her tastes, but Ascot had been a month away and it had been a dull, slow two weeks since the party at Blenheim and she had been going crazy, so she had taken the Italian tour. Surprisingly, it had been enjoyable. She had met some very interesting people.

Putting the book down, she stood. She was tired of sitting; first the bus ride from hell and then an hour of Steinbeck; it was all too much. Especially when she had been confined to the close proximity of her husband, her dear husband, her dear eternally gently plastered husband, the great Lord Threlkeld. Grapes of wrath indeed; grapes were perfect for him. He had yet to meet a vintage he didn't think was at least passable. And wine didn't hold a flickering candle to his scotch. Vodka was an old friend and schnapps more than a nodding acquaintance.

Stop it, she told herself. You could go on for hours. Besides, she didn't mind a nip herself every now and then. It was his slow, steady drinking from morning to night, when he was never fully sober and never quite drunk, that was driving her mad. That, and his refusal to discuss the situation. A year before, maybe two, he would have become belligerent after a few minutes of polite, if acerbic, discussion and raised his voice and cast blame upon her like an Old Testament prophet. Now, he simply sat there, smiling in a vapid sort of way, sipping from the glass that somehow was never quite empty.

Lady Threlkeld glanced across the room. Her husband was sitting in an easy chair, staring across the rim of his whiskey glass at the middle distances. His eyes, which she had once found so attractive, were unfocused and faintly moist. She started to comment, but the words she wanted to say would only wound them both and she wasn't up to it, not tonight, not after the bus ride through the green-jungle hell. She turned and looked out their window.

Their room was one of the nicer ones in the old hotel. She had insisted on the finest accommodations before the tour had started, and paid dearly for them. So far, their rooms had always been the best the hotels had to offer. The tour itself had been a hot, boring loser, but she had to give them credit for sticking to their promises on the rooms.

Tonight, they were on the second floor, facing the street. A gracefully limbed tree, whose name she had never heard before, draped swatches of green in front of them, screening them from the worst of the noise and dusty sunlight throughout the long afternoon. Dusk had arrived, the air going purple and cool, and she could see lantern lights coming on all along the street as if by incantation. Flickering on sporadically, like a tribe of independent thinking fireflies, they ran like a conga line in the gathering darkness. Dianna Threlkeld felt her spirits rise and she turned and smiled at her husband.

"Think we had better dress, Donald? The party will be starting soon."

Lord Threlkeld brought his mind back into the room. He had been away at Eaton, remembering old Toughy and Bob the Fartcat. What times they had enjoyed!

"What party is that, dear?" He always tried to be pleasant, like that American chap in the movie with the gigantic white rabbit. Arguments always upset his digestion.

"Oh, Donald, don't you remember? I was telling you about it on the bus."

"Sorry."

"It's on the itinerary."

"Never look at itineraries. Bad for your mind. Absolutely full of things some damn fool tour director thinks you must do. And, inevitably, ninety-five percent of them turn out to be the most ghastly bore. Gave up on those years ago. Simply go with the flow now. Works much better that way, I assure you." Lord Threlkeld sipped at his whiskey. It wasn't bad, not for Morazon. Of course, after a bus ride like the one on that old yellow monstrosity, even beer would taste sublime.

He could feel her eyes on him, cool and polished like two fine jade orbs. "You were saying?"

"What?"

"About this party?"

Lady Threlkeld turned from the window. A rising wind lifted the fringes of her hair which hung to her shoulders and she called auburn, although it was streaked naturally with gold and copper and seemed to change colors as the light shifted. Her hair was thick and heavy, but she liked it. Some days she felt that its weight was the only thing keeping her fixed to the planet.

When she was in one of her fanciful moods, she imagined that without her hair she would float away, drifting up to the clouds and the moon, then on to the pale cool stars of deep space. Flipping a wayward bang out of her eyes, she walked with a purpose to the dresser and poured herself an inch of whiskey in a glass that appeared reasonably clean. The amber liquid looked cool, smooth, inviting. She lifted the glass and let whiskey trickled down her throat. It tasted mellow, yet faintly bitter, putting her in mind of an evening gone sadly sour. She emptied the glass. Damn, the man is driving me to drink, she thought as she poured another careful inch.

From the cushioned comfort of his chair, he watched her, slightly bewildered as always by the intensity she projected. This evening the bewilderment was faintly adulterated by a sense of bemusement. She had always been so energetic, so sure of herself, so certain that her way was the correct way, the only way for anyone of sound mind to go, and tonight there was a hairline crack in her façade. Some of the reservoir of imperial self-confidence was seeping out, like pent-up water seeping through an almost invisible fissure in an ancient earthen dam.

Lord Threlkeld's forehead crinkled in amusement. He permitted himself another sip. Discipline was vital to drinking; one mustn't get too far gone too early. Might miss something, and Donald Threlkeld, after waking up one Sunday evening about six, totally unable to recall a single thing from noon Thursday on, had made up his mind never to miss anything again.

Damnation, he had thought, he might have committed a crime – robbed a bank, say – in such a state, and absolutely no telling what he might have said, and to whom. Why he even might have missed some monumental event, like the queen dying, or the discovery of a cure for lung cancer, or the United States dropping the big one on another poor, defenseless country.

He was glad he didn't have to truly live out in the real world. He had no desire, none whatsoever. Bless the old bastard's soul, he'd left him enough filthy lucre so that he would never have to work, nor worry. Still, the old man could have quit with the moolah and left off the title. That Lordship foolishness had always left him cold. He wanted no part of the title and all the tiresome, passé, boring formalities and ceremonies that came with it. Lady Dianna and her ilk could have all that; he preferred being simply plain Donald. A glass of beer with the boys at the local pub, a bet on a friend's horse, a daily ride to work on the underground, a quiet drive in the country in his old rusty Minor. The good life.

Oh, but he was a fine one; all that talk and he had yet to give away the first pound or dollar, or euro, or whatever the hell currency was in vogue. Lord Threlkeld didn't care. He had bankers and accountants and solicitors. Let them attend to the details. He merely wrote checks or, better yet, signed charge slips.

"Donald?"

"Yes?"

"Time to head for the party. We need to make an appearance. Rouse your sodden self from your self-induced stupor and get dressed. We need to be downstairs in ten minutes."

"They can start without us."

"I'm tired of being late. We've been late every night this trip. It's getting old."

"Bad manners, what?"

"Worse than that, Donald; it's downright rude."

"You're beautiful when your nostrils flare."

"Shut up and get dressed." She whirled around and stalked into the bathroom.

Her husband stared at her back. He liked the way it curved down to a narrow waist then flared again. Thunder rumbled as he carefully placed his glass on the small round stand beside his chair. It had a pleasantly-aged marble top. At one time, this had been a nice hotel, Donald thought, smiling in commiseration with the aging structure.

For some time, he stood in front of the window, staring at the dancing lights as tree branches swayed in the rising wind. A smell of rain threaded through the air, faint and far off, but definite. A shower would be nice, cool things off. From out in the alive dark, a man's voice rose, full of long vowels, plaintive. Lord Threlkeld leaned closer to the window, listening for an answer. For reasons he could not explain, it seemed important the voice be answered. He could hear the wind worrying its way among the leaves, and the branches rubbing against the worn hide of the old hotel, and a song as faint as a mother's whisper drifting in from some open window out there in the great growing dark. The words were Spanish and he had never had an ear for languages, but he could catch the meaning in the melody.

The man's voice rose again and this time it was answered by a woman's. Donald smiled; hearing the woman's voice made him happy. Yes, it satisfied a certain equation in him to hear the woman answer. The man's voice had carried in it that seeking-for-love sound. Not that he was much for love, certainly not the roses and chocolates kind, but he did understand the search process. A difficult journey. For a lifetime he had been traveling that curving, unending path.

After the heat of the day, the wind felt wonderfully cool. It crept in at the open window and caressed his face. The long bus ride seemed a hazy, alcohol infused dream. Unbuttoning his shirt, he looked down at his chest hair, somehow feeling quite young, almost a boy. Maybe he would like this god-forsaken country after all. Now, if he could only remember the name of it.

Seven

At night the jungle seemed even more alive. In the faint light that filtered through the thick leaves and snaking vines and trunks that grew incestuously close, there were only quick moving shadows and flickering silhouettes. Red eyes glittered, blinked, disappeared. Sound became the primary sensory perception.

Carlos Geraldo lay on his stomach atop a vine-covered ledge jutting out from the mountain and stared down at the lights of Yuscarana, burning like fallen stars on the valley floor. They looked as far away as the stars in the sky, and as cool and silent.

On the ledge it was far from silent. Monkeys screamed in the trees and there was a constant hum in his ear from the hordes of mosquitoes that swarmed after the men, the whine of the wind rose and fell and rose again, backed by the cry of birds startled from their roosts. In the sudden, hushed interludes,

Carlos could hear the sound of men breathing fast and cursing softly.

Driven by internal demons, he had marched them hard, stopping only to allow them to snatch a cold meal or wash their faces in a swiftly running stream.

Carlos knew the men hated him at this moment. He hoped they were also harboring a grudging respect for him, along with a burgeoning sense of self-pride. As they marched, they had cursed him for a bastard and a prick and a son-of-a-female dog; when daylight came, they would praise him as a warrior, an officer, even a liberator. None of that, the curses nor the praise, meant anything to Carlos Geraldo. Only the attack on Yuscarana mattered. It must not fail. The reinforcements must come, but if they did not, he, Carlos Geraldo, would avenge at least a small share of the great injustices created by that egotistical anus of the civilized world, Gutierrez.

Carlos knew that at times he went a touch loco, but such insight did not bother him. Craziness was essential to any successful revolution. A man simply had to keep it under control, not let the rape and the murder and the torching get to him. Insane, he wasn't. To free Morazon alone was not his expectation. Overthrowing an entrenched psychotic like Gutierrez would take time, an army, a river of blood.

Yuscarana, however, he could take. With the men who were joining him, he could take Yuscarana easily. With great difficulty, he could even take the town with the twenty-six tired, hungry, angry men breathing hard and cursing all around him. One way or another, he would take Yuscarana. In blood, he had sworn an oath. Around him the night screamed.

His eyes flicked away from the starry lights of Yuscarana and searched the darkness of the ledge, focusing on faces; faces he knew and faces only vaguely familiar, even faces he could not recall. In the night all were nervous, like jungle animals. Nerves, he understood. Every day now there was a churning in his stomach. At odd times throughout the day, without warning, he could feel fear rising. Swallowing it got more difficult each day, as though he had a certain reserve of bravery and it was being used up. Used up at a rate he found alarming.

In the old days, before the revolution, he had awakened anxious to begin the day, eager to seek adventures, imagining himself an equatorial Thoreau. Now, fear filled his mouth and he hated to see the day dawn, almost as much as he dreaded the coming of the night. Locking lips with death did that to a man. So much death had passed before his eyes it was difficult to understand how it could still affect him. However, death was not like food or drink, or sleep or sex, by which a man was never satiated. Even a little death was too much.

A thin, white, broken chain of light blinked across the valley floor. Army transports, Carlos guessed. Morales must be moving up reinforcements; it would be just like him, the cagey bastard. Morales was a competent officer, Carlos Geraldo knew that. Even respected him for it, to some degree. Mostly, however, he hated him for it.

Carlos took a deep breath, held it, then expelled air slowly. Control your thoughts, he told himself. Jumping to unsupported conclusions was one of his weaknesses. He recognized he had them – never had he claimed to be perfect – and overly strong reactions were a problem for him. That string of lights could be nothing more than people returning from a visit to the capital.

His part in the revolution—he couldn't bring himself to call it a war—had been going on for almost three years and Gutierrez had lost a number of troops, whether to death or desertion didn't matter. They were no longer available and intelligence reports indicated the remaining reserves had been spread across the country like a thin layer of marmalade. Now that he thought more calmly, it was more likely that over the past few months Morales had been forced to send troops from Yuscarana to fill in gaps in the army's line, rather than truck in reinforcements. Cursing himself silently, Carlos rolled over onto his back.

The sky was a black velvet painting torn into two jagged pieces. One piece was splattered with tiny white star-flowers, the other was layered in swaths of black paint, black on black on black, each layer darker than the one beneath. This slice of sky grew as Carlos watched, consuming the other like a python swallowing a monkey. Jagged lightning sliced through the ebony layers. Thunder grumbled on the western horizon. Rain scents filled his nostrils and Carlos Geraldo smiled. The coming storm would mask the sound of their approach. Provided it was over by daylight, the storm would be a blessing. He would gladly trade a drenching for the element of surprise. Connecting with the other groups would be difficult, but if the connections were not made tonight, everybody would figure out what was going on when the sun came up.

It was clear now his task was not to worry about the others who were coming, or reinforcements from the capital, or even Morales. Only concern himself with getting his men in place for the attack, then making it at dawn – not one minute later. All the rest, including the dying, would take care of itself.

Rolling onto his stomach, Carlos scooted to the edge of the precipice. The lights of Yuscarana burned like candles flung by a careless giant. Carlos concentrated on the image before him, committing the layout to memory; a snapshot he could carry in his mind as they moved down the trail in the dark. He would need it. A few steps down the narrowing, curving trail and Yuscarana would vanish as surely as the Seven Cities of Cordoba.

Carlos looked across the faces of the men on the ledge, seeing the fear spreading across the face of Felix, who was no more than a boy; of Jesus, the animal, unconcerned, except for where his next meal or woman was coming from; the strange quiet unchanging face of Tony, the face of a man-child who had tasted pain and suffering and death, and wanted more. That look Carlos Geraldo knew. He saw it daily in the mirror when he shaved.

He spat into the night and pushed himself to his feet, giving orders, disappearing into the darkness, never looking back. They would obey the orders or he would kill them; that they knew.

Seconds later, he could hear the sound of their footsteps on the trail. Thinking of death and dawn and Yuscarana, Carlos smiled.

~ * ~

He hated the night. Hated the way it closed around him, dark and moist, clinging like an unwanted child. Damp leaves brushed against his face and his arms grew tired of reaching up to brush them away. After a time, he was no longer bothered and it was as though he was in a slow-motion shower in which the water was brushed on with rough cloths.

Animals screamed from the darkness; at least he hoped they were animals and not the zocambie spirits the elders in his village had described as they sat around the ceremonial fires late at night, after the women and small children had gone to bed. Never had he truly believed in the zocambie and their blood sucking, body-invading ways. At least he had never admitted it, even to himself. But always at the back of his brain, wriggling like underground snakes, were fragments of doubt.

In his imagination, Felix could see the smooth-skinned pythons sliding slowly along the limbs above his head, coiling and uncoiling, yellow eyes peering into the darkness, waiting for the coming prey. Always in his mind the snake was on the limb inches above his head, watching him come down the path, waiting for him, eternally waiting.

Other creatures roamed in the dark: jaguars and lizards and scorpions and spiders as big as the palm of a man's hand. He shuddered. He hated and feared them all, but always it was the snakes which lay coiled in the front of his mind.

He could hear thunder now and lightning splashed its reflection on the winding path. Felix stepped more quickly, closing in on the shadowy body in front of him. He did not know the man, not even his name. That didn't matter; any human, even a stranger with blood on his mind, was preferable to the unknown darkness. Ever since he had been a young boy, Felix had been plagued with nightmares, and the worst had always been left alone and dying in the dark, in the monstrous unknown dark.

~ * ~

Jesus burped and tasted the cold tacos he had downed at the last encampment, following up with a fart that popped in the dark like a mini-grenade. Seconds later, the man behind him began to curse in a low voice. Jesus the Pig grinned. This night he would enjoy. Beyond that, well, what man could say? Never was tomorrow truly promised to anyone. Father Alehandro had told him this truth when Jesus had been an altar boy at the small whitewashed church in Novalisto.

Jesus giggled; him, an altar boy? Not one man on the trail tonight would ever believe it, not even if he were drunk. Days passed when Jesus didn't believe it himself. Those altar boy days seemed like a dream that had happened to someone else.

Shivers raced through his body as though he instinctively sensed one of Gutierrez's men had a rifle trained on him. Jesus shook his head, feeling the swinging of his heavy hair as he drifted back into the reality of the night. Think of tomorrow, he told himself. Even though it isn't promised to you, think of it. Nothing is going to happen tonight. No one, except Carlos, knows exactly where we are going and therefore there can be no betrayals. Yes, it was more comforting to think of tomorrow, and Yuscarana.

Thoughts of Yuscarana made him feel better. Women would be there, and he hadn't enjoyed a woman in over two weeks. Even better, no woman in Yuscarana would be able to resist him. Not because of his good looks and suave ways. Long ago, Jesus had learned never to count on those. No, the sub-machine gun slung across his shoulder would do his courting. Yes, the sub-machine gun and the long knife he wore in a scabbard that hung down his back. One sight of either and he had never met a woman who was not immediately cooperative. They might not have been happy about what was taking place, but they were always happy to cooperate.

Certainly there would be women at Yuscarana, and fresh food – and women to cook it – and money and jewels. Death would be there too, with its children: blood and pain. That was only to be expected. No town liked to yield, not to the men of Gutierrez, not to revolutionaries, not to anyone. All little towns had some crazy idea that they could live independent of the struggle, that by sending a few boys off to fight and die for one side or the other they could be free of the conflict. Eventually, they all found out it didn't work that way. Tomorrow would be Yuscarana's turn. Smiling, Jesus the Pig farted again.

The thought that he might die tomorrow flashed across his mind without worrying him. His time would come; everyone knew that. Whether they would admit it even to themselves was another matter; no concern of his. Perhaps in the morning there would be a bullet with his name on it. If there were, he could do nothing about it, so why worry? He had survived many mornings and many battles. Jesus made the sign of the cross; with luck he would survive one more battle, live on to fuck and fart and feed his face. Jesus the Pig imagined a tall, thin, clean-scrubbed woman of Yuscarana, and his teeth gleamed in the dark.

~ * ~

His eyes were on the back of Carlos. The storm was coming, though it was still miles away and not all of the sky was covered by the clouds. Enough light spilled through the leaves so that it was easy to follow the trail. It was wide for a jungle trail and Tony figured at one time it had been used by the men who had come to harvest the timber. He could still remember when men had made their living cutting timber, and the jungle had yet to completely reclaim the trail. Perhaps a few men of Yuscarana still cut the timber, or the trail was used by the drug smugglers. It made no difference to Tony.

His focus was on the man in front of him. Only that man knew the plan, knew what forces were joining them, knew precisely where they were going, knew the exact time of the attack. These were the important things to know, not where the next meal or woman was coming from.

Sheets of lightning smeared the western half of the sky aa the wind began rising. Leaves, larger than the ears of elephants, brushed against his face. The first raindrops fell, tentatively, but heavily, rattling the leaves, the shower stopping as quickly as it had started.

Tony didn't mind the rain. He had never minded rain since that day when he had prayed that it would wash the blood of his children off the wall of the church. Despite his pleas and screams and tears, the rain had not come that day. Perhaps he should have cursed the rain forever. Instead, he imagined that every drop washed another drop of blood off that wall. He had to rely on his imagination. Tony had never been back to that church.

The wind blew a leaf flat against his face and he jerked his head away and glanced at the sky. Only a handful of stars were still visible. He wished they were all gone and that it was morning. He was ready to attack.

Few of the towns they attacked held any memories for him. Yuscarana, however, was different. In his youth he had spent a few months in Yuscarana, beginning his voyage of life. He remembered the hotel where he had worked and the man who had run it. Poncho had been a young man then; he would be on the dark side of fifty now. Tony remembered him well, a handsome man then, tall and slim, with a great sweeping black mustache. A man of great pride. A man who had been decent to a younger, far more innocent Tony. A man to look up to. Yet a man who undoubtedly had not joined the revolution. I will have to kill him, Tony thought, as he brushed aside an overhanging branch, keeping close on the heels of Carlos. Thunder rolled like the backbeat of time, echoing against the walls of his heart. Excitement rose like mercury, the same sensation he received when he killed, a powerful jolt, like electrical current straight to the heart. Hitching up his trousers, he edged closer to Carlos.

Eight

The lobby of the old hotel was dark and cool. Being dark helped keep it cool and helped to obscure the dust. Blinking against the dimness, Captain Morales stepped across the threshold. Boards creaked. Poncho looked up from the counter, smiled, nodded, and turned back to his newspaper. Probably reading about the war, Morales thought. Damn revolution was all anyone thought about these days. He hated the revolution; hated all wars for that matter. For a professional soldier, he had become a rather ardent, albeit silent, pacifist. Never a fan of bloodletting, Morales had reached the point where the sight of blood turned his stomach.

Late afternoon sunlight slanted in through the two large, plate-glass windows that fronted the hotel, striping the floor, adding a golden hue to aged, polished wood. Dust motes slow danced in the swatches of light. Morales walked through the dust motes and sat in a cracked leather chair across the lobby from the massive mahogany check-in desk. Both had come to the establishment in more economically sound times.

Settling into the chair, he propped his feet up on a low-slung coffee table on which a half-dozen dog-eared magazines lay scattered about. They put Morales in mind of fallen soldiers. Thoughts of death, especially of foolishly brave young men who did not know any better, brought sadness to his mind. He would say his soul, but he was no longer certain he had one. The thought kept swirling through his mind that he had seen one too many deaths, and that last one had been the passing of his own soul.

Smiling sourly at his amateur theological philosophizing, Morales picked up a magazine at random, then eased deeper into the chair. The springs were shot and the leather on the arms was cracked, rips running like erosion. Unidentifiable stains dotted the seat. However, the seat curved to the contours of his ass and the chair afforded a panoramic view of the entire lobby and, through the windows, the street outside. Nobody complained if a quarter of inch of ash fell off one of his Cuban cigars, or if he sloshed a few drops of his drink onto the brown leather.

Over the last year, he'd gotten into the habit of coming to the hotel in the late afternoon, smoking a cigar or two and having himself a glass of whiskey, or two, or three. The number depended on the day he'd had and how long the night loomed before him. Nights had developed the nasty habit of stretching towards infinity since his wife had died.

Maria had been so young, at least she had seemed young to him, and she had gone so quickly. Fever, Dr. Quintana had said. He had given it a long name that meant nothing to Morales. No, less than nothing. What mattered was that Maria was gone and a dark ring perpetually surrounded his world. Call it jungle fever, or malaria, or Voodoo Spell Number 9, the only thing that mattered was that she was dead and Morales was alone. Damn her for dying. Damn Quintana for letting her die. Damn his own soul for living.

Voices at the top of the stairs pulled Morales from his waking nightmare and, blinking away the mists, he curled his neck in time to watch four people descend.

Family, Morales decided as they descended, probably American. The mother's eyes were alive and animated as she talked to the boy and the girl. The girl was talking back, saying something about being bored and wanting to find some music. Morales knew enough English to get her drift. The boy rolled his eyes, turned his head, and pushed lank dark hair back with one hand, while peering at Morales as though he found the captain an interesting specimen. Morales wondered how the boy had classified him.

Tall and firm-jawed, the father walked slowly behind the rest of the family, taking care with his footing while he studied a hand-held screen. Morales couldn't get a good look at the device, and he wondered which one of those new electronic gadgets he had read about in the American magazines it was. Perhaps the one named after some sort of wild berry. Gringos in general, and Americans in particular, struck him as strange. He watched the man move with exaggerated slowness down the stairs, half expecting him to stumble and fall.

They all survived the journey, then stood around the lobby arguing in hushed tones, as if they had secrets worth knowing. Morales pulled a cigar out of his pocket, bit off the end and spat. For a moment he simply held the cigar in his mouth, licking it with his tongue, letting the tobacco moisten and flavor seep into his mouth. He liked the taste, and everybody had to die of something.

The girl kept glancing his way, but then she was constantly looking about the room, clearly searching for something, someone. Morales dug a book of matches out of his shirt pocket. Three matches remained. Jerking one from the book, he struck it. Looking over his cigar at the family, he pressed the flame against the tobacco, inhaled deeply, and smiled. The boy was looking his way and Morales winked at him through the smoke. Under the long hair, the boy was clean and his dark eyes appeared intelligent. Morales thought about the son he would never have.

After a moment, he blinked and looked away; he was too old and tough and tired for maudlin sentimentality. The room was growing noticeably darker, yet the evening was not old. The captain peered out the large windows. Dusk was getting assistance tonight. For a second, Morales was envious of the dusk. Then he brushed the thought aside. There would be no aid for the garrison at Yuscarana. Absolutely pointless to delude himself. The captain might fool the citizens of Yuscarana and perhaps, if he tried with great diligence, his troops. No point in stacking such horse manure up in his mind, though. He'd read the reports, seen the numbers. Gutierrez had stretched his army so thin that if anyone truly bothered to look, they would see right through it. If the rebels kept heart and kept probing, they would break through eventually. The breakthrough might come tomorrow, or next week, or next month, or next year. Time and the place were not known to man. The only certainty in the mind of Captain Morales was that the breakthrough would not come at Yuscarana, not while he commanded.

Strange voices spoke in a strange language and Morales turned his head to locate the source. A couple was strolling through the archway separating the lobby from the dining room. They were chant-singing in a language the captain did not know. He could now see they were a middle-aged Asian couple. Morales was not good about recognizing one Asian nationality from another; he had little experience with such races. His sole exposure had been as a young lieutenant stationed in the capital as one of President Gutierrez's staff. One hot sun-filled morning he had accompanied the president to the airport to greet the Japanese ambassador. Now, he remembered only the ambassador's diminutive stature and grave dignity.

Morales watched the couple walk quickly across the lobby, the woman talking rapidly. They might be Japanese, Korean, or Chinese; Morales decided it didn't matter. At the door the couple paused, eyeing the sky, then each other, before stepping out into the night, leaving the air swirling in small eddies, as though they had been debris moving on a swift current.

Captain Morales kept his eyes on the doorway. At any moment, Lieutenant Manuel Escobar was due with the latest messages from headquarters. During the day, the lieutenant commanded the radio shack on the first range of hills west of town. A private and a corporal were under his command. They jotted down all reports from headquarters: battles fought, men lost, supplies that were coming. They also kept an eye out for rebel movements in the hills. Always there were rumors, and Captain Morales felt it prudent to monitor the surrounding countryside. So far, the rumors had proven false, but you never knew. Captain Morales had not survived this long by being an incautious man.

He glanced at his watch. Escobar was due, but frequently he was late. Sometimes he was tardy because an important message was coming through, but more often it was because he was riding his white stallion, Gitano. Gitano meant gypsy, and it was an appropriate name. The horse was a restless creature, prone to be at the far corner of the corral and always difficult to catch. A hard, long ride at least three times a week was essential to keeping the animal under some level of control. Morales could see that, which was why he showed the lieutenant leniency; that, and the fact that since he was a boy he had nourished a soft spot for beautiful horses, and never had he seen a more gorgeous and magnificent animal than Gitano.

Gitano stood at least seventeen hands high, was the color of the alabaster columns that stood in the National Museum of Art, with great dark, alive eyes, a regal way of holding his head, and a truly wonderful way of moving. Morales could watch Gitano canter for hours.

Thunder crackled. Glass in the windows rattled and the mind of Morales swirled back into the room. More thunder, low and rumbling this time, sent a restlessness running through him and he pushed out of his chair and walked across the lobby, sweeping the room with a glance, recording like a security camera. For things he had experienced, Morales had a remarkable memory. Everyone, from his first-grade teacher to the President of Morazon, said so. Yet, he couldn't recall half the words to the most popular songs in the country, or the smell of the huervos rancheros he had enjoyed every morning during his two-year stay in the capital. These days he wasn't even certain of their taste. But he could recall almost everything he had ever seen.

Morales leaned against one of the twin posts that divided the lobby. It stretched from the floor to the high ceiling and the wood was dark and smooth. From his vantage point, with merely a minor twist of the neck, he could see into the dining room, up the staircase, out into the street and, with a slight body swivel, the lobby.

A few tourists and some local regulars were still in the dining room. Just inside the door a couple sat facing him, both on the same side of the table. The man, who looked to be about Morales' age, gazed steadily into the eyes of the captain. His palms were spread out on the table and his face was quite calm beneath close-cropped gray hair. With a small mouth and a broad chin, the man looked like an American to Morales.

Even from the lobby, he could see veins standing out in relief in the man's arms and the smooth cords of muscle. There was a softness around the chin, but the neck looked youthfully thick. A dangerous man to cross, Morales thought, or a good one to have on your side in a fight.

The woman sitting beside the man nibbled at a melon half and lifted her eyes often to gaze around the room. Usually the gaze was accompanied by a smile. A waitress, hardly more than a girl, carried a metal pitcher to the table. She was dressed in a black peasant dress with a white apron on top, and her face was pretty in a plump, dark way. She moved as though the pitcher was heavy. The waitress spoke to the woman and the woman looked up and smiled. The girl poured a stream of dark liquid into the woman's glass.

The girl leaned closer and spoke to the man. He looked up, smiled at the girl as though she were his daughter, then shook his head. Lightning flashed and at the periphery of Morales' sight the world lit up like Carnival. He twisted his head in time to face another flash, one more vicious than the first.

Only after the lightning image faded from his eyes did Morales realize how pretty the waitress had been. He glanced into the dining room, but she was gone. A thin man with dark hair falling down in front of his eyes and a beak of a nose poking out beneath was busing tables. His hair glistened as though anointed with grease.

Across the lobby a telephone rang, once, twice. Thunder rumbled until Captain Morales began to wonder if the rebels had somehow obtained artillery.

A barrage of rain stuck, coming in on a slant, forcefully striking the glass in the large windows that faced the street. The peppering effect put Morales in mind of small arms fire conducted at some distance. Shivering like a wet dog, he rearranged his body against the column. Certainly he had the wind up tonight. And for what? Probably nothing, he told himself. Maybe instinct, his gut whispered. Captain Morales gave his gut an order to shut up and leaned a shade more casually against the smooth wood. He watched the rain and the lightning and the tree branches swaying in the wind while he listened to the clatter of tables being cleaned and the gentle murmur of conversation behind him mingling with the rumble of thunder that seemed to steadily grow more hollow, more distant. He waited patiently for Lieutenant Escobar. The captain was skilled at waiting. He had managed a great deal of practice during his tour at Yuscarana.

Nine

The passage was from Matthew, Chapter 13. It was one that many people, including preachers, often misquoted. The Reverend Thomas Stephen Malloy dug his travel Bible out of his suitcase and flipped it open. As he turned pages, he hummed the refrain from "Leaning On The Everlasting Arms." One of his favorite hymns, it was one of the old standards. As Reverend Malloy aged, he noticed that increasingly he favored the old hymns, the ones he had heard as a boy in the small brown church that sat at the edge of a large oak grove. McClanahan Pike had run only a few yards away in front of the House of God, as his Grandmother Lipsey had always called it. The road had been dirt then and dirt when he left Iowa. But that had been almost fifty years ago, he reminded himself; surely it would now be paved.

Reverend Malloy could still remember the leaving on one hot bright morning in July. His father had passed away in late March, when the wind had been blowing ice crystals between bare tree branches and peppering them against wavy glass window panes. On the day he died, a thin snow lay on the ground, except where the wagons and trucks had worn it away and the frozen earth showed brown.

It had taken his mother time to make up her mind. The Fourth of July had come and gone, and with only one small pack of firecrackers because money was tight. They had traveled to the Malloy farm to eat blueberry pie and say their goodbyes. Grandma Malloy had cried and kissed him. Grandpa Malloy had recited the passage about the "weeping and wailing and gnashing of teeth," patted him on the crown of his head, and gave him a new quarter and an old pocketknife with one side of the bone-handle missing.

The morning Mr. Blankenship hauled them and their suitcases to the train station in his old farm wagon had been withering hot. Sunlight had beaten down without mercy on his bare head and Thomas – his family never called him Tom – had regretted leaving his straw hat hanging on the bedpost (Uncle Joseph was selling the house furnished for them). He had also regretted that Mr. Blankenship hadn't driven them to the station in his pickup, but something had been said about a cracked cylinder head, and that had been that.

They'd caught the train and rolled on for the coast. Thomas, his mother, and his sister Mary were going to live with his mother's aunt in Portland. Reverend Malloy no longer remembered much of that journey; since then, he had made so many they all blended together, like a film montage shown at high speed.

Portland had been followed by Seattle, Salinas, Sacramento, and Santa Fe as they moved from relative to relative, his mother always looking for work, but never a man.

Mary had died coughing up blood in a charity ward in Sacramento. He had found the Lord in a train station on the outskirts of Barstow. Worn out from trials and tribulations, his mother had died in a rest home in Bakersfield, having never found the permanent employment she was seeking, nor ever losing her faith in the Lord.

Thomas had buried them both between classes at a divinity school that no longer existed. Some of the churches he had pastored had been long abandoned, standing empty now, hollow and silent, husks rattling in the hot dry wind. These days, when he was tired, he couldn't name all of them.

Retired from the ministry, he was enjoying life as a tour guide, leading groups to places he had been to, places he had not been to, even a couple he'd never wanted to go to. Yuscarana was old stomping grounds; twenty years ago, he had served as a missionary here for a proselytizing church. He wondered how many people would remember him.

He found the passage he was searching for: "A prophet is not without honor except in his own country and in his own house." Reverend Malloy acknowledged the truth in the statement. The Bible was full of truths: easy to read, hard to live.

Closing the Bible, he placed it carefully back in his suitcase, checked his reflection in the mirror and headed for the door. Time for the Yuscarana assembly.

~ * ~

Pausing for a moment at the top of the stairs, Reverend Thomas Malloy leaned against a railing that gave slightly and gazed down at the lobby, waiting for the optimal moment to make his entry. He liked making entrances that could charitably be characterized as grand. Long ago, he had admitted to himself that he had a bit of the actor in him. 'Stage presence' was how he referred to it when one of his congregation mentioned the attribute. He couldn't see where that was an issue, certainly not a sin. After all, pulpit life was a lonely one, especially after Elizabeth had died. Plus, a man needed something to spice up his existence, and a preacher's options were limited.

So he liked to make a bit of a theatrical entrance. So what? He ascribed it to the theological life; the way the reverend saw things, theology had a great deal in common with the theatrical. In a manner of speaking, both thespians and theologians were interpreters of the written word in an inspirational vein. Granted the stage and screen were full of betrayal and lust and violence and sex, but if you really wanted the nastiest version of all those, you simply had to read your Bible. And it wasn't only the notorious bad guys, the pharaohs and the Philistines and good old Pontius Pilot, but some of the saints and the saved who were the most unrighteous. Why, look at David and Bathsheba, and Paul when he was still Saul, and Peter the Rock who cracked three times before dawn. Yes, the good reverend decided, he knew a lot about life, even if he had lived much of it vicariously.

In the lobby no one seemed to notice his presence. Something outside was attracting their attention. For a moment he stood perplexed. Then a clap of thunder smashed the darkness and he could see lightning through the tall windows. He would be taking second place to a thunderstorm that night. Shrugging, he started down the stairs. The grand entrance would have to wait for another night. Reverend Malloy wasn't overly disappointed. No disgrace to be displaced by the glories of God. In a certain way, he decided as he descended, it was an honor.

He glanced at his Rolex, a gift from a grateful, and well-heeled, sinner come to Jesus late in life, and frowned. The get-together was scheduled to have started seven minutes ago and he couldn't see the punch bowl or cookies that were supposed to be provided by the hotel. They had been paid for and, by all that was holy, he would see that they were delivered. Though his Spanish was rusty, he felt capable of raising a bit of hell.

Not that he was angry, he thought as he trooped down the stairs; more that he was filled with righteous indignation. Yes, that was the proper approach for a man of God. After all, he had cast aside many opportunities to come down here and serve these people, and this was how they showed their gratitude.

Well, he would show them a thing or two before this tour left Yuscarana.

The Reverend Thomas Malloy's lips stretched tightly as he descended the steps with a vigor surprising for a man his age. At the bottom of the stairs he turned, looking for the owner of the hotel. It seemed to Reverend Malloy that he knew the man from his earlier tour in Yuscarana, although he remembered him as a thinner man. I should remember his name, the reverend thought.

The only person behind the counter in the lobby was a young man with greasy hair and a profound case of acne. Recalling his Spanish as best he could, Malloy asked the young man where the *propietario* was.

The young man, really scarcely more than a boy, shrugged and nodded toward a closed door. Reverend Malloy mumbled "*Gracias,*" and headed toward the door. It swung open under light pressure and he walked on in.

Heat and noise flew up like a plague and smacked him in the face. Steam rose as though from hot springs. A man in a spotted white apron and a tall white hat that tilted to one side screamed at a thin-faced woman with heavy legs. Aromas from a dozen spices rose in the steam laden air, mingling with the smells of frying onions, roasting meat, and grease left too long in the fryer.

No one noticed him. Momentarily overcome with the steam and the shouts and the smells, he simply stood silently. Then one of the waitresses saw him and clasped a hand over her mouth, but not before a short yelp escaped. The chef jerked his head up. He held a meat cleaver in his left hand. The blade glittered. Reverend Malloy shivered under the flash of fear. Then he smiled at the man and raised an open palm to show he meant no harm. The chef made a figure eight with the cleaver, then turned back to his work. From behind a large white refrigerator a heavyset man with a large black mustache emerged and walked steadily toward Reverend Malloy, smiling and bobbing his head as if he were a novice in some eastern religion. Malloy peered at the man; he did look familiar. As the man drew closer the reverend was sure. Good, now maybe things would advance.

"*Buenas tardes*. I am Reverend Malloy, from the tour. I am the tour leader. Also, I was here in Yuscarana several years ago as a missionary. You may remember me. You look familiar to me, different, but familiar."

The man looked for some time into the American's face. "Yes," he said slowly, drawing the word out into three syllables, "I remember you. Your hair, it is a different color now and you wear glasses, but I do remember." He wiped a large brown hand on the front of his trousers. "My name is Poncho Herrera. I still own this fine establishment." He swept both arms in wide arcs. "Even after all these years." Poncho smiled, raising his mustache. "Perhaps you recall my hotel?"

Reverend Malloy extended his hand. He was surprised to find that his palms were damp. He blamed it on the steam.

"Yes, of course I remember you, Señor Herrera, and your fine hotel." It was not truly a lie; he did vaguely remember the man's face, albeit a notably younger version, and he was sure he had been in the hotel sometime during his stay in Yuscarana. It was simply that he had stayed in so many hotels over the years they ran together in his mind. Reverend Malloy rearranged his face to show he was going to discuss a serious matter.

"A small get-together for the tour group was scheduled to have started several minutes ago in the lobby. There were supposed to be refreshments: hors de oeuvres and sangria and cakes – little cakes, little cakes with white sugar icing. None of those are out in the lobby where they are supposed to be, none of them." He deepened his frown and spread his arms wide, palms out, feeling a little like he imagined Jesus must have felt when the sinners stood before Him in all their iniquity.

Squaring his shoulders, he thrust out his chest. "Where are my refreshments, Señor Herrera?"

Poncho wrinkled his face into a hundred crinkles. "I am so sorry, but tonight it has been so very busy, the tour and all, you understand." His fleshy face pleaded for mercy.

Reverend Malloy was not in a forgiving mood. He felt vaguely ashamed about it, but not enough to dispel his righteous indignation. The long, exhausting bus ride was to blame, he assured himself.

"Those refreshments have been paid for. The members of my tour are expecting them and if they do not receive them soon, they will be very upset. Upset at me." He fixed his pale blue eyes on the dark brown ones of the hotel owner. "Now, we don't want me to be unhappy, do we?"

"No, no, I want no one to be unhappy."

"Certainly not the person who is responsible for bringing the tour, and all the business, and all the money involved to Yuscarana, to your hotel. You do not want to be known as the man who ruined the tour business, now do you?"

"But of course not, Señor Malloy."

"Reverend Malloy."

"*Sí*, Reverend Malloy."

"Then I suggest that you immediately get all of your people busy on the refreshments. Ten minutes, that is all I will give you. If the refreshments are not out by that time I will move my tour."

Reverend Malloy did not wait for a response. Turning on his heel, he walked quickly. Once he was back in the lobby, he permitted himself a chuckle. As if he could possibly move the tour out at night, especially on a night like this. The man Herrera was a stupid brown peasant for not realizing the shallowness of his threat. And to think that he had ministered to these people. Oh well, he had done his duty. He had labored among the pagans.

No, that wasn't fair and he knew it. Not all of the people of Yuscarana were pagans; many were Christians, good Christians. Reverend Malloy said a short prayer asking forgiveness. Fault finding and blame casting were easy. In his heart he acknowledged that some of the people he had served as missionary were as close to the Almighty as he was. Certain days he wondered if they might not be a little closer. He had to contend with a little sin called pride. Thankfully, his God was understanding.

He stepped forward to greet some of the tour group who had begun to congregate in the lobby. They were milling about, talking quietly. Thunder rumbled like a jazzy percussion session somewhere behind the stage. Lightning rippled on the far side of the windows. An aggravating, nervous tic started in his left eye and his hands trembled slightly.

Putting them in his pockets, he blinked his eyes as though something had drifted in there and become lodged. Rain pounded against the glass. Malloy was grateful to be inside the old hotel. Experience had taught him that the storms of Yuscarana could be brutal. As if a dam had been breached, memories poured down the walls of his mind. He walked through the lobby silent and unseeing.

The long-haired man behind the counter fingered his acne pits and stared with hot brown eyes at the leader of the tour.

Ten

Always there was an almost overwhelming sense of power and well-being, as if he had strategically been placed at this moment in life and nothing could harm him.

Thunder rumbled the air, echoing off hills, reverberating in his ears. Flashes of lightning burnt temporary holes in the blackness, the images lingering briefly on his retinas. There had been a strike close by; the burnt smell was strong. Lieutenant Manuel Jose Rodriquez Escobar leaned forward and pushed his face close enough to the head of his horse to smell the wet hide and feel the roughness of horsehair.

Another lightning strike, even closer. He had seen it slice a large tree in two and the resulting crack temporarily overwhelmed his eardrums. Lieutenant Escobar dug his heels into Gitano's flanks and whispered in his ear, urging the horse on.

The white stallion responded with a burst of speed that left the lieutenant hanging desperately on to the reins and gasping for breath as another rain squall smashed against them.

Already soaked, the lieutenant merely noted the rain. He was enraptured with the graceful power of the animal beneath him. That happened without fail each time he rode the magnificent creature. With each long stride, Escobar could feel the thick cords of muscle rippling beneath him and the wind driving against his face and the long white hairs of the mane brushing against his exposed flesh. They tickled, stung when they flicked against his eyes, but he enjoyed every aspect. The sheer energy created by the creature during a hard run was pure ecstasy to the lieutenant. He loved every minute of each ride, especially when he and Gitano were by themselves. He loved the horse better than he had loved any woman, and there had been many women in the life of the tall, slim, clear-eyed lieutenant.

He loved Gitano's whiteness, as white as the snow that never came to Morazon, and his great, dark, limpid eyes, and the monstrously powerful way of moving that he had, covering huge gulps of ground with each stride. No other horse was like him; there was nothing like him, nothing like his Gitano in this world. The lieutenant was certain of this and he leaned even more forward in the saddle and placed his lips very close to the right ear of Gitano and whispered his name. Perhaps it was only his imagination, and he had an active one – he admitted that without a qualm – but it seemed to Lieutenant Escobar that Gitano responded with yet another dimension of speed.

In his mind's eye he could see them, the great white horse and his tall, lean rider pounding through the night and the storm on the old dirt road from Cedera to Yuscarana that ran narrowly between two ranges of hills rising like women's breasts, dodging the lightning flashes accompanied by reverberations of thunder. Alone in the overreaching blackness, man and horse were racing against an invisible foe, racing against no one, racing only for themselves.

They were rolling powerfully through the night, too quickly for most under the conditions of the road amid the darkness and the storm, but Lieutenant Escobar was not worried. They knew the road well; their communications station lay between the two towns. Gitano was fresh, having not been out of the corral in almost a week. And, with the lightning flashing like it was on amphetamines, the road was often laid white and open against the darkness.

They were racing the storm. There was no vital message to urgently deliver. Rumors were rife: the rebels were heading south, the rebels were on the outskirts of the capital, the rebels had broken through at San Rafael. However, these were only rumors; one heard them in the communications shack, and at the Hotel Universal, and at the *farmacia*. Rumors only, and no more than that, although there was a glint of truth in the old saying of his village that where there was much smoke there had to be a flame. For weeks now they had heard nothing official from headquarters, at least nothing more than mundane lists of supplies that they would be receiving and reports that needed to be completed, announcements of the birthday of General So-and-So, and how the army football squad had fared in the latest match. No, there was no pressing urgency, only the desire to ride hard and fast down a pale dirt road with the rain in their faces and the wind in their hair.

Morales would be waiting. Escobar knew he should have started sooner, but it had been pleasant to sit in the shack with the door and windows open and feel the coolness of the coming storm against his skin, chatting with Ruiz and Delgado about women, football, when and where the rebels would strike next, and what they would have for supper. He had smoked two cigarettes, savoring their harshness as the smoke floated before his eyes like a veil, permitting the remembrances to drift.

The lieutenant often thought of his childhood and his little brother, Chico, who was now a journalist and wrote with admiration of the rebels' principles. Sometimes he reminisced about his mother and father as they were when he had been young. Occasionally he wondered what they were doing now with their hair gone gray, their backs stooped, and their minds greatly unsettled. He thought about women, priests from his childhood, old dogs he had known, the soldiers who served under him now, and how his level of command was a strangely lonely excursion. One could never quite lower himself to the level of the non-coms, yet never quite chin up to the perch the captain occupied.

Speaking of the captain, Morales would probably be pacing the floor of the lobby of the old hotel. Lieutenant Escobar knew that the captain always delayed his evening whiskey until he had received the latest report from headquarters, even if there had not been one of importance for months, and would not likely be one any time soon. Certainly there was nothing tonight, and with the storm there would be nothing tomorrow. Even the loco rebels were not *demente* enough to attack on such a night.

Still, Captain Morales was a disciplined man and he would be waiting. Like all officers, Morales could be a bastard at times, but was basically fair, and had been kind to the lieutenant, letting him stable Gitano behind the hotel on occasion, and signing the pass to visit his mother when she had undergone her operation, even putting in a good word for his brother when the generals at headquarters had wanted to make an example of him over some page three article in an obscure left-wing newspaper. Escobar did not want to disappoint the captain, and the captain was undoubtedly already waiting, so the lieutenant cried to the white stallion and dug his heels in against the horse's flanks and urged him on with the reins. As one, they raced through the night. The rain pounded harder.

~ * ~

By the time he had stabled Gitano and run through the downpour to the back door of the old hotel, he couldn't imagine a dry inch on his body. A shallow porch poked out from the rear of the structure like the tip of a pale tongue and a striped aluminum awning extended above it. The awning was quite old, having been installed before Poncho's time. Although it was rusty along the seams, it did not leak, and Lieutenant Escobar stood under the awning in the light that spilled from the kitchen through the open door, along with smoke, steam, and a conglomeration of aromas, letting rain drip off the brim of his sodden cap and run down the angles of his face.

He could hear rain striking the awning, and in the pools of light cast by the trio of security lights that rimmed the property he could see silver curtains of rain blowing in the wind. He dug a semi-dry cigarette out of the pack he carried in his button-down shirt pocket and wedged it in the left corner of his mouth while he pulled out the aging Zippo his father had given him for a now-forgotten birthday. Flicking the wheel, he touched flame to the end of the cigarette and drew smoke into his lungs with a familiar sense of satisfaction. Smoking was bad for one's health; he had read the reports. However, he had yet to give up the comfort the acrid smoke brought to his mind. Leaning against the metal railing, he stared at the silver rain through the smoke of his cigarette, wondering lackadaisically how damn wet the rebels were getting tonight.

Smiling at the thought, the lieutenant took a final drag off his cigarette and flipped it into the night, its red glowing tip cartwheeling in the rain. Then there was only the dark and the wind and the metallic patter of the rain against the awning. Rolling his shoulders, the lieutenant straightened his cap, turned, and stepped into the kitchen, rain still dripping from his uniform.

Nodding at the busboys and smiling at the waitresses, he strode vigorously across the broad, smooth, handmade tiles. Brown, gold, and red, the tiles had been laid when Yuscarana was still a popular stopping point for European tourists, usually Germans. They were still lovely, in the way that a movie star slipping into middle age retains much of her essential beauty.

"Hungry, Lieutenant?"

Escobar turned his head and nodded at the man in the tall white hat. "*Mucho!*"

"*Bueno*, I have some excellent stew left. Lamb. It was not so popular with the *turistas*, even though it is very good. Shall I fix you a bowl for later, after you have seen the captain?"

"*Por favor*," Escobar nodded, grinned, and flipped a salute in the general direction of the chef. The mention of the captain reminded him he was late and he marched quickly though the kitchen, not stopping off, as he often did, to chat with the dark-haired girl whose waitress uniform fit her snugly across her upper torso. She watched him, however, with eyes so dark and fluid they looked like pools of black water.

~ * ~

Usually the lobby was quiet, a somnolent oasis from the outside world. Often the lieutenant walked softly past a dozing desk clerk. Tonight, however, a large knot of people had formed on the far side of the lobby. Standing around a table, they chattered like parrots. In shirts the color of fresh blood, blouses the color of ripe oranges, trousers the color of the sun at noon, and scarves as many shades of green as the jungle itself, they looked like parrots. *Turistas*, Escobar thought, *turistas* partying in the middle of the revolution. As he had often done, he seriously questioned the intelligence of certain people.

Two large glass bowls, half full of what looked like punch, squatted on the table beside a pair of flat, silver, rectangular trays that now held only crumbs. Six or eight small cakes with white sugar icing sat on an elongated brass tray at one end of the table. Saliva flowed inside the lieutenant's mouth at the sight of the cakes. He had eaten them before. He had not realized how hungry he was.

Turning his head, he searched for Captain Morales. Usually, he was easy to spot. Often, he was the only person in the lobby. Tonight, in the milling crowd of people, it took the lieutenant almost a minute to spot him. The captain was chatting with a tall, silver-haired man whose watch glittered like gold on his left wrist. Escobar studied the side of the man's face that was turned toward him. Certainly, he had never seen the man before. Not knowing who the man was or how important he might be, Escobar circled the crowd, strolling slowly, trying to catch the captain's attention. On the second lap, Morales noticed him and inclined his head. Escobar began to work his way toward the captain and the silver-haired man, using care not to glance at the little cakes with white sugar icing.

Scents of strange, potent perfumes were almost overpowering. Perhaps it was only his empty stomach, but the exotically honeyed mélange made him vaguely nauseous. Lieutenant Escobar was aware several of the *turistas* stared at him as he passed. He wondered what they were thinking. They seemed a strange amalgamation, speaking with diversely accented voices that sounded like alien music. How had they come together and why had they come to Yuscarana? Ignoring the strange perfumes, foreign voices, and small white cakes with white sugar icing, Lieutenant Manuel Escobar soldiered on. In a schoolboy sort of way, he felt rather virtuous.

He maneuvered around a man standing quite erect and very quiet. The man held a glass of punch in his hand while a woman with artificially silver hair talked to him about global warming. She spoke with piquant intensity. The man appeared to be listening closely, but Lieutenant Escobar noticed the man's eyes were as gray and still as stones. If the man noticed the lieutenant, he did not acknowledge him. It struck Escobar that there was something of the soldier in the man.

Lieutenant Escobar sidled behind the silver-haired man who was talking with the captain. When the captain lifted his chin, Escobar made eye contact and saluted. He felt awkward saluting in the middle of the gathering.

The captain casually returned the salute, politely made his excuses, then led the way to a quiet corner where he leaned against an ancient, somewhat dilapidated, black upright piano. Lieutenant Escobar followed, keeping his eyes on the back of his commanding officer, trying to ignore the conversation of a tall woman with an English accent who was saying something about "fucking like a bitch in heat."

Escobar was glad to reach the hushed backwaters. Conversations rippled behind him. The keyboard cover was pushed back. Exposed piano keys grinned at him like aged, yellowish teeth, gaped with great black cavities.

"Running late tonight, aren't you, Lieutenant?"

"The storm, sir; made the going a bit slower."

"On Gitano? Don't joke with me, Escobar. Either you started too late or took the long way home."

Warmth surged through the lieutenant's cheeks. He stared over the captain's head at a dark oil painting of a wooden sailing ship foundering in a storm. Some of the men's faces reminded him of Munch's *The Scream*. He had studied Munch's painting during an art history course the semester before he joined the army. The painting had leaped from the page and branded his mind. For a week he had longed to move to Norway and become a painter.

"Sorry, sir."

The captain nodded. "Don't worry, I have been adequately entertained. Take care of your horse?"

"Yes, sir. Gitano is in a stall in the barn behind the hotel."

"Good, he is a beautiful and valuable animal. Nothing bad must happen to him." The captain massaged his face as though the conversation made his jaw ache. "Storm easing?"

"Perhaps."

"You don't sound sure, Lieutenant."

"It is a very violent storm."

The captain looked across the room. His eyes appeared unfocused to the lieutenant. "When I was a boy, Lieutenant, the old people of my village used to claim a violent storm foretold coming violence." He swiveled his eyes to the younger man's face. "Do you believe that, Escobar?"

The lieutenant shrugged. "It is hard to say with certainty."

The captain threw his head back and laughed as if the lieutenant had told a funny joke. "Yes, that is a comment which could be applied to many things, including our own future. What do you think it holds?”

The lieutenant shook his head. “I do not know,” he said. In truth, he had never given much thought to the future, assuming one day would follow the next, as he followed one order after another. He had daydreamed, of course, but only casual fantasies about women, or Gitano; nothing as formal as the way the future sounded in the captain’s mouth. Perhaps he should begin to think more deeply.

Captain Morales thought Escobar seemed very young tonight, young and, what was the word? Naïve? Yes, naïve. Oh well, once he too had been young and naïve. Clapping his hands, he nodded at the young man before him.

“Well, Lieutenant, what’s the latest from headquarters?”

“They will be shipping us used truck parts next week.”

“Truck parts?”

“Used radiators, batteries, headlights, that sort of thing. All are supposed to be operable,” the lieutenant added in his most helpful tone.

Captain Morales rested one elbow against the top of the black piano. “Why would they send us truck parts? We have only one jeep and two trucks, neither of which has run in a year.”

“Perhaps they want us to repair them.” The lieutenant was trying to atone for being late by being exceptionally positive. His eyes roved across the captain’s face, searching for clues.

“They might well desire it, Lieutenant, but there is one small problem.”

“What’s that, sir?”

“We have no mechanics.”

“True.” Lieutenant Escobar felt rather foolish, juvenile. Conversations with Captain Morales often left him feeling that way. The end of the evening could not come too soon. He comforted himself with thoughts of a final visit to Gitano before turning in for the night. Without warning, the day sapped the back of his neck. Uncontrollably, he yawned, covering his suddenly gaping mouth with a fist. He sensed his cheeks warming again.

Morales smiled. Once he had been in boots very similar to the lieutenant's. However, he reflected ruefully, that had been some years ago.

"I'm hungry, Lieutenant. Have you eaten?"

"No, sir. Ricardo told me he had some excellent stew left. Lamb."

"Wonderful. Lamb stew and a tall glass of good whiskey, I may yet survive to fight another day. Captain Morales nodded toward the kitchen. "Shall we brave the teaming multitudes?"

Lieutenant Escobar nodded and followed the captain, who was making a rapid flanking maneuver. From the sanctity of a large leather couch, Trevor and Kristin Samuels watched them cross the floor. Trevor wondered if there was news of another rebel attack; in a way he hoped so. So far the tour had provided spectacular scenery and some interesting history, but history was history, and after you have seen one jungle...

Kristin thought the older man looked like Coach Hubbard at school, but the younger one was sort of cute, in a clean-cut way. She wondered if he had ever participated in a raid on the drug traffickers who were supposed to travel through the jungle that surrounded Yuscarana. Perhaps, if she played her cards right, he might be induced to confiscate a little something special for her.

El Cartero leaned against the check-in counter, studying the tour group. For several days he had ridden with them, but this was the first time he had seen them without binoculars, fanny packs, sour expressions, and a double handful of inhibitions. It always amazed the bus driver what a loosening effect alcohol had. Not that he minded a drink. Spiked punch in a group setting wasn't his style, though. A quiet bedroom with a bottle of tequila, now that was wonderful; if a pretty woman was added to the mix, all the better.

He blinked against the heaviness that was settling on his eyes. Battling that ancient yellow bus all day on the road to Yuscarana was hard work for an old man. Tequila and bed sounded better with each passing minute. Who could say what tomorrow would bring? Probably only another long, hard, boring day with the never contented passengers from Tour 24. El Cartero took a final glance at his passengers, turned, and began to climb the stairs to Room 26 where bed and bottle awaited.

Eleven

Morning sunlight spilled like yellow paint across the restaurant floor. Coffee aromas mingled with the scents of meat frying in grease, cinnamon starting to burn, and chocolate melting. Murmuring words rose and fell like water flowing over smooth rocks. Maria moved quietly around the room, going from table to table, smiling and pouring coffee for the *turistas*, trying to understand their orders. Poncho leaned against the kitchen doorway and watched the morning unfold.

After the storm of the night before, he was short on sleep, and the room was warm from the sunlight and the stove, and it felt good to lean against the doorframe and allow the world to float by in a golden haze. From time to time, he glanced out the window. A bird, small and blue feathered with a fine black head, swung back and forth on a tree limb. He seemed to be staring at Poncho. Sunlight glittered on the bird's feathers. His eyes were yellow. Now and then a flicker of breeze lifted the bird's feathers until he appeared to be taking flight.

Quiet covered the early morning street. A radio played gently through an open window and a car motor turned over grudgingly, groaning as if it were in pain. Wind sighed in the leaves and an old brown and tan dog barked once, as if to demonstrate to the world that he still could, then fell silent. From the edge of town, the church bell tolled the hour, a deep metallic sound that throbbed in the clear morning air of Yuscarana.

Reverend Malloy walked into the restaurant, rubbing his eyes, trying to pray away a sangria headache. Blinking against the sunlight that seemed too bright to be quite real, he maneuvered through the tables, smiling and nodding like he cared, heading for a small table in a dark corner.

Peering through the steam that rose from his cup of tea, Iwakura Tyshimoda watched the tour guide cross the floor. From the first day, Tyshimoda had harbored doubts about the man. The tour brochure that had come in response to his inquiry had been full of color pictures of spider monkeys, blue parrots, and fish that looked like water-borne rainbows. The words had promised spectacular scenery, exciting adventures, and friendly indigenous peoples. They had sounded good to Tyshimoda, especially after a long day selling toasters and microwaves. Maybe they had sounded a little too good, but then Tyshimoda knew he was a man plagued with doubts. He always had been, even as a child. Doubts were part of him, as much an element of his essence as his black hair, long fingers, and toes that curled up inside his shoes throughout the day.

Knowing his propensity for doubts, he tended to discount them. Ignoring his doubts about the brochure, and his wife's protestations (she had been afraid of the jungle creatures), he had signed them up for the tour. Ever since, he had been having regrets. Disgust rose with the steam as he watched the tour leader ease onto his chair. A man of God, indeed; the God that Reverend Malloy served must be a very strange sort of deity. Tyshimoda lifted his cup. Tea splashed hot and bitter against his tongue.

Across the street from the hotel, the old brown and tan dog lifted his head from the porch of the store that sold hardware, feed for animals, and parts for cars that had not been made for a dozen years. A new smell floated on the air. For a moment, the dog seemed on the verge of rising and going to investigate. Then he closed his yellow eyes and let his head sag back onto the wooden planks sprinkled with dust that resembled dirty powdered sugar. Slanting sunlight cast a halo around the dog's head.

So little was moving on the main street of Yuscarana that the movement of the dog's head caught Kron's attention. Except for one bird that had been going like a bat just released from hell, only shadows were moving in the light breeze.

Kron was jittery this morning. He had slept poorly, not an uncommon experience for him during a journey, and now his left eye ticked like a second hand on a watch badly in need of adjustment, a small sea was churning in his stomach, and his left leg kept trying to rumba solo. He sipped at too hot coffee and poked at his *huervos revueltos* that were starting to go cold, congealing into the consistency of Silly Putty. Half hungry and half nauseous, he was damn near ready to scream.

Kron was trying to read. Reading usually steadied his nerves. Besides, as a writer he could justify it as either keeping up with the competition or trying to pick up some new approaches. *Leonardo's Bicycle*, by Paco Ignacio Taibo II, was propped up against the sugar bowl on the far side of his dead eggs. He was on page twenty-six and stuck like a scratched vinyl record on a sentence that strove for a connection between Leonardo da Vinci and Sigmund Freud. Coming off a sangria night while undergoing a sunshine sodomy, it was too bizarre a concept for Kron to handle.

Paco Ignacio Taibo II—what a wonderful name. It grabbed you by the gonads and shook. The second he had seen it poking out of a slanting, lopsided pyramid in a remainder bin outside the front door of Joseph-Beth's in Lexington, Kentucky, he knew he had to own it. Actually, you never really owned a book, you only held it for a while. If the writing was good enough, it possessed you. Hemingway's best novels and stories were the possessing kind, as were some volumes by Steinbeck, Frost, and Bukowski. Other books were good reads, but never would they possess you, not in a hundred years. Kron hadn't decided about the Taibo book. Early pages hadn't been stimulating. But sometimes it paid to persevere. If it was good enough somewhere along the line, even for a single glorious sentence, it was worth it.

The sentence had to be superb, though. Merely good was never good enough. The words had to possess a radiance that burned into your mind like a blue flame. Kron longed to write such sentences. He had come close once, and the taste of it had lingered on his tongue for a week. Now all that was there was the afterbirth of bad coffee and malevolent eggs. Closing his left eye, Kron held his dancing leg down with a hand that felt detached from his body.

Staccato chatter assaulted his ears and he looked away from the dog and around the room. The words were coming from the American family; now what was their name? Kron was poor with names, and this morning his brain was blended yogurt. Still, he had been riding on the bus-from-hell with these people for the better part of a week, sitting directly behind them for the last two days. He should know their name.

He lifted his coffee cup and the rising steam seemed to lubricate his brain and the name came to him like a vision from an Old Testament prophet. Samuels; it even had an Old Testament derivation. In many ways Kron preferred the Old Testament to the New. Granted, there was a great deal less love and kindness and forgiveness, but there were absolutely splendid tales of rape, murder, and fratricide, not to mention kings and queens intermingled with insects and incest, bulrushes and golden bulls, talents and tablets, and Beelzebub and blood. If it was nothing more, the Old Testament was literature.

A shadow fell like a dark plague across *Leonardo's Bicycle* and Kron looked up into the eyes of the girl who poured the coffee. He couldn't quite recall her name – that blocking thing again – although he was relatively confident it started with either an M or an N.

Her eyes were the color of a deep Vermont pond at dusk and her teeth shyly poked out between thick lips. Kron smiled up into the eyes, nodding when she glanced down at the cup in his hands. He placed it on the table and watched her pour with concentration. Her arms were smooth and round and brown, and, though her hand trembled faintly, she poured well. Kron resisted the urge to kiss her hand, assuring himself that he was a romantic son-of-a-bitch. He told the girl, "*Gracias.*"

"*De nada,*" she whispered and then she was gone before he could recall any more sophomore Spanish.

Curling his neck, he watched her glide across the floor, her feet moving like locomotive pistons beneath the swell of her white peasant's skirt. Her ankles were surprisingly slender for someone who tended toward a genteel plumpness. She paused at a table in one corner of the room the sunlight hadn't reached, where she poured coffee into the cup that sat before a man who looked like he needed a caffeine transfusion. Kron studied the man's face briefly before he realized it belonged to the tour leader. Now what was that man's name? Lifting his coffee cup, Kron sipped absentmindedly. Coffee scalded his upper lip and he said three unholy words before the name of the tour leader came to him.

~ * ~

In the kitchen it was crowded and hot. There were two stoves; one contained six burners, while the other had two, plus a griddle that was used for pancakes in the morning and hamburgers for lunch. There were also two refrigerators and a freezer along one wall. Six or seven people bustled about. All the machines and all the people were putting out heat, especially the stoves, where all the burners and the griddle were going. Sweat rolled down the faces of the people, painting their clothing under their arms, slashing a dark strip down the center of their backs.

On top of the taller refrigerator an ancient black radio blared mariachi music, interrupted now and then when the announcer came on and babbled excitedly for a minute. Occasionally, a commercial blasted. Everyone in the kitchen had to shout to be heard above the radio. When the conversation at the tables ebbed, the people in the restaurant could hear the songs.

Once a serious voice broke in over the music to make an announcement concerning a military action taking place in the north. In the kitchen, the people were quiet while the serious voice spoke. People in the restaurant hushed their voices for a few seconds, then resumed their conversations. Most could understand very little of the language, usually words or phrases they had heard in movies, or perhaps they knew a few numerals. Those who understood more grew silent, finding their appetites significantly diminished.

From his table by the window, Bartlett Samuels looked at the people in the dining room and shuddered inside. Spicy eggs, yellow rice, and tortillas were not his idea of breakfast, even with half a grapefruit on the side. He missed his café latte and Danish, not to mention his computer, the stock market reports, and his office. He actually missed the hard-to-get cabs and the surly cabdrivers he usually despised. Certainly, they were better than that stupid yellow bus he had been held captive in for the past week that felt like a month. Bartlett Samuels jabbed his spoon into his grapefruit half. Juice squirted. Seconds later, his brains splattered a Rorschach across the window.

In the aftermath there was only silence. Then a tinkle of falling glass razored a narrow slit in the silence. Maria let the coffeepot slip from her fingers and it shattered against the wooden floor. A woman shrieked, and suddenly the room was full of screams and shouts and the discordant sounds of chair legs dragging on the wooden floor and breaking glass.

As though the wall of sound had broken whatever invisible barrier held the people entranced, they began to run as quickly as they could, staying as low as they could, praying as hard as they could. Gunfire broke out in a spontaneous benediction to the morning.

Twelve

Jesus, a.k.a. El Puerco – the Pig, crawled through the dust beneath the porch of what had once been a small grocery store. Little light penetrated the cracks and the deeper beneath the porch Jesus the Pig crawled the darker it became.

Jesus the Pig was not afraid of the dark. He had never been afraid of much. Yet he recognized danger and didn't court it. Too many women and too much whiskey for him to ever do that.

Better to stay in the shadows while the fighting was going on. Let the others charge, be heroes, dodge those fucking bullets. He had been there, done that. Discretion was much better. Discretion, ah, he liked that word. He had learned it from the college professor who had been with the men of Carlos for only a few weeks before dying from dysentery.

Shit himself to death. What a damn lousy way to go, even for a schoolteacher. Actually, the guy had not been so bad; the professor had tried hard and he had hated Gutierrez. Oh, how that schoolteacher had hated that bastard Gutierrez. Such hatred was worth much.

Jesus the Pig crawled as far as he could, then maneuvered his bulk until he was facing the street. By jamming the stock of his weapon into the ground and angling it up, he could get a shot at the hotel across the street. At this angle all he could hope to do was hit someone in the ankle, and the odds of that were somewhere between slim and none. He wasn't concerned, however. Much of the real fighting was taking place at the barracks down the street. Reinforcements hadn't arrived and Carlos had been forced to spread the men thinly. Jesus had volunteered for the attack on the hotel. Surely there would be no more than a few *turistas* and a frightened maid or two. Still, no use taking any unnecessary chances.

Sporadic gunfire broke out down the street. Earlier, there had been an initial barrage, followed by a passage of silence. Now the firing had resumed. All that could only mean that the first attack had not succeeded in overwhelming the garrison. Carlos had been counting on surprise.

Perhaps he should have waited, Jesus thought, knowing as the thought flickered across his mind that Carlos was not a patient man, not when his blood was up. Surprise would work, he had told them; always he had a plausible story.

Only new recruits believed Carlos. New recruits believed everything. Jesus wondered how many of them were lying in the street now with their guts in their hands.

Jesus believed nothing he heard and no more than half of what he saw. Unless he was drunk. When he was drunk he tended to believe almost anything. In Lucanzo last year he had believed a dark-haired woman who had told him at two o'clock in the morning that he was handsome. Basking in the glow of her words he had given her all his money. She had then loaned him a small part of her body for a few minutes. The following morning, with a head that felt like it was being split open by a dull axe, he had tiptoed his way down the curving dark stairs, feeling his way with the palms of his hands against the ancient wallpaper and extending his feet carefully, one at a time. He could not remember how much he had drunk, or even what he had drunk. Vague recollections of small blue pills floated across his fractured mind. Perhaps he had even smoked something stronger than tobacco. *Mi Dios*, what a head he had carried that morning.

Voices had come up the stairs to him. Happy, giggly voices that rasped like sandpaper against his raw nerves. If he had not needed his hands for stability he would have held them over his ears.

At first the voices were only sound, like water moving across stones. Then the water formed words and he heard a voice he recognized talking about a fat, ugly man who had given her all his money for five minutes of her mouth. Jesus knew he had been a fool. Wine and women always made him do stupid things. He knew he should avoid them, but he could only prolong the agony of their denial for a short time.

By the time he had reached the bottom of the stairs, the women were all laughing at him. He could see them in a little clutch, their heads bobbing up and down, laughing – laughing at him. He remembered the smooth, cool feel of the knife handle and the way the blood had spurted when he had sliced the nose of the woman from the night before – like he was cutting a salami. Jesus the Pig felt his dick hardening. Smiling, he started pulling the trigger as though he were granting ballistic absolution to a multitude of sinners.

After the burst he lay still, breathing dust, letting the echoes die. There was no answering volley. Restlessness crept through his body like bacteria on the prowl. Nerves rippled in his legs and his left eye developed spasms. He crawled to his right, then slithered forward until the barrel of his gun glinted in the sunlight.

Now he could see the hotel windows. Sunlight reflected off glass, blinding him. Anger at the glare surged through him.

Aggravating inanimate objects always pissed him off. He squeezed the trigger. Glass shattered across the street and women screamed.

A lusty river of power surged through him and he squeezed the trigger again, aiming at the two large windows that fronted the lobby. Glass shards piled up on the wooden porch like clear snow. Screams lingered for a moment in the clear hot air, then dissolved into nothingness.

Satiated for the moment, Jesus the Pig rolled over onto his back and closed his eyes. There was a growing discomfort in his chest and he realized he had been holding his breath. *El Stupido*, he thought as he opened his mouth, sucking in great quantities of air. As his lungs refilled, he wondered how the attack was going up the road. Only silence drifted in from that direction. Was it all over? A sudden burst from an AK-47 destroyed that notion.

A long siege was developing, he could sense it. Sieges never turned out well. He had been involved in several and all had ended badly – men lost, little booty, territory gained at an untenable price. Still, he was not surprised. Though their spies had told them the garrison at Yuscarana had been weakened by transfers, Carlos's group was not strong enough take the town alone. Reinforcements were essential for success, and they had not come. Who knew when they would come? Perhaps the weather had stopped them, or they might have been ambushed by roving government troops; they could even have decided to go with another faction of the revolution. That was the trouble with the revolution. After all these bloody months he could see it as clearly as he could see a full moon rising – too many factions, too many leaders, too many trails leading only deeper into the jungle.

There should be one man who led all the rest. For the common good, for the good of the revolution, everyone should serve under this man. Jesus recognized the concept was only a dream. Never would it happen in Morazon. Too many men wanted to seize power for themselves, not for the good of the people.

Carlos Geraldo was a good man, a strong fighter who fought for the little people: the peasants and shopkeepers and plantation workers of Yuscarana. But he was only one man, and there were not many like him. That was unfortunate, and Jesus wished with a surprising fervor that he had known of this reality before he had joined the revolution. But he had not, and the revolution had seemed glorious and honorable, almost sacred. In those early days, such ideals had still mattered to Jesus. Now, they were no more than empty perfume bottles sitting high on a shelf. A faint scent of flowers still clung to their lips, but they collected only dust and occasionally the carcass of a dead fly.

Jesus the Pig thought of these things without coming to any conclusion. School had been a long time ago for him and thinking about something besides supper and women and how to kill a man came with difficulty.

All the reflecting was giving him a headache. Shutting down his brain, he rolled over onto his fat gut and started firing.... short bursts.... aimed at specific windows.... hoping for a lucky kill.... not particularly caring.

No bullets came flying back at him. Only two of them were keeping whoever was in the hotel pinned down. His partner was a new recruit, as slim as a sapling. Jesus thought his last name was Torrez. From time to time, he could hear Torrez firing. The man had a single-shot rifle that had been old when Jesus had been a boy. Jesus wondered where Torrez found ammunition.

They could have rushed the place. With the lack of return fire, the odds were good that few, if any, government troops were inside. If Carlos had been there, he would have ordered an attack. He wasn't there, however; he was directing the attack on the barracks, and the reports brought in by their spies had consistently noted that officers, especially Captain Morales, often spent time at the hotel. Jesus had heard of Morales. He had two reputations; one of being a bastard, the other of being a fighter. Jesus wanted no part of either one. He liked better odds than good; dead certainty was better than dead. Let Carlos Geraldo be the hero. Waiting was not a problem for Jesus. He would be there when there was killing to be done. He would be there when there were women to be enjoyed. If two years of fighting against Gutierrez had taught him nothing else, it had taught him the value of waiting.

Jesus the Pig spent the morning alternately firing at moving shadows and recalling women he had abused. For a mental change of pace, he wondered what sort of women might be in the hotel.

Around noon, he began to grow hungry and his thoughts turned to food. Breakfast had been an overripe banana and a slice of dry bread. Jesus promised himself a feast, washed down with massive quantities of wine, when the killing at Yuscarana was over. Thinking of fresh meat, warm bread, and red wine caused saliva to flow inside his mouth. He made the sign, swallowed, licked his lips, and rolled out from under the porch, firing as he came to his feet. He zigzagged down the street and around the corner of the building, continuing to fire as he ran, praying perfunctorily to an unknown God.

He got his back up against smooth adobe and thought about what to do. After rejecting several ideas which seemed like too much effort, or were too dangerous, or both, he decided to sit in the cool, shaded alleyway and wait for Carlos or dark, whichever happened along first.

Thirteen

Face buried in her dress so she could not see, hands over her head so that glass, or the world, wouldn't fall on her, Maria Gomez curled around herself in the middle of the restaurant floor. She could feel the wetness of the spilled coffee against her legs and the pricking of the shattered glass coffeepot. They were nothing, less than mosquitoes. It was the voices that bothered her.

She could hear them talking. Talking of revolution and attack and death – words she hated, words that terrified her. From the first day, she had hated Yuscarana. Never had she wanted to come. She had been happy in her small village, waking early when the sun was only a golden promise on the far side of the plantation and the birds fluttered their wings, calling to each other. Then the world seemed to be new, innocent. Maria had helped her mother keep their house clean and watched her baby brother play on the floor. During most late afternoons she had taken herself walking in the cool shade of the banana trees, while a fragrant breeze lifted her long black hair, then strolled home with evening falling all around her like dark stardust. She had helped her mother cook supper, then sat at the table holding her brother and watching her father eat his supper. His black hair had fallen like tired feathers across his forehead, while his jaws worked deliberately and powerfully, putting her in mind of the machines he drove all day on the plantation for Señor Perez. After supper, they would all sit outside the hut on the wooden benches her father had built from plantation scraps, and, if he was not too tired, he would play a few of the old songs on his guitar. Leaning against the still warm adobe, she would tilt her head back, stare at the pinpricks of starlight and dream of the perfect life she would live when she left home.

Only the dreams had proven false prophesies. A blight had struck the plantation, and then her mother had grown sick, and her little brother had the foot that needed an operation. So many bad things had come all at once that there had been no choice, no choice at all.

Before he was married, her father had known a man who now ran a hotel. Together, they had ridden trains and seen the ocean and worked side by side on tall buildings in towns so large that Maria could not even picture them. Once they had even been in love with the same woman. However, she had married a stranger who wore pinstriped suits and pointy-toed shoes. Now her father's friend ran a hotel and her father worked on a banana plantation to support a sickly wife and a son who needed an operation.

There was no choice. Maria had to work to earn money to send home. She kept only enough for essentials. Food and lodging were part of the arrangement, so always there was a little money to send home. Each week she sent it without fail, feeling proud every time she handed the carefully sealed envelope to the sleepy-eyed man behind the barred window. And now...

And now she was going to die. Die in the hotel where she had been so lonely, even when surrounded by many people. She could feel death crawling within her bones.

Plus, she had broken a coffeepot and Señor Herrera would be angry. She was sure he would take the cost of a new one out of her wages, leaving almost nothing to send home. She felt ashamed. Then Maria remembered she was going to die; there would be no more wages sent, ever. She wanted to cry. Instead, she buried her face deeper in her dress and waited for the end.

Without warning, more gunfire rang out and window glass smashed like brittle seashells. Women screamed until Maria shivered deep inside herself as though the ague were upon her. A warm wetness ran down her legs.

Hands tugged at her arms. She fought back, but they were strong hands and they pulled her arms away from her head. She turned her face up to see her killer.

It was not a rebel; it was one of the tourists. Stunned, Maria sat staring into the pale eyes of a hard-faced man with cropped gray hair. He was pulling her arms, trying to get her to rise, telling her to hurry, hurry, hurry. The words came too fast for her to understand, but she caught the urgency in his voice, punctuated by the sound of falling glass and screams that trailed after women running, women who had not run in a long time. They moved like stiff fat bugs. Another blast of gunfire and she quit resisting. The man pulled her to her feet and together they ran from the guns and the falling glass.

She ran not knowing where she was going, or caring – as long as it was away from the guns. Once she stumbled, but righted herself and ran on. In the lobby she caught a glimpse of Captain Morales as she ran by. Immediately, she felt a strengthening of her resolve. Her heartbeat slowed and she pulled away from the hands and worked her way through the crowd into an open space in the middle of the lobby. Quite alone, she lifted her eyes to the ceiling. It looked like an alabaster sky and she wished she could fly.

Some of the *turistas* pounded up the stairs, while others ran toward the back of the lobby. A small Oriental woman swayed across the lobby floor, moving like a poorly animated statue, arms flailing in slow motion like underpowered windmills. The woman's red mouth worked open, revealing white teeth and a tongue that curled and uncurled like a snake. A man who resembled her reached out and tried to ensnare her. With tears streaming down her face, the woman eluded him. Her red mouth formed words that were never voiced.

Maria stared at the woman until she felt her own mouth start to work. She made herself look away. Remembering Captain Morales, she looked for him.

He was leaning against one of the polished pillars. An unlit cigar dangled from his lips as he stared toward the street. One hand was on the pistol butt protruding from his holster, while the other curled and uncurled. Only one side of his face was visible. It was as smooth and polished as the statues that the men in her village had carved and sold in the marketplace of the capital on fiesta days.

Her legs were trembling and Maria sank to her knees, crawling away from the woman of the silent screams. Moving toward the captain, she could feel the hard wooden floor pressing against her knees and the smoothness of the polished planks beneath her palms. She was glad for both the pain and the smoothness, because if she could feel them it meant she was alive, and she did not want to be dead, not before she had begun to live.

Maria crawled behind the huge, cracked, leather sofa where the men sat in the evenings smoking their cigars. She could smell stale smoke and the lingering scent of their cologne. The guns sounded closer. There seemed to be more of them. Her heart throbbed and she pressed against the couch, closing her eyes, waiting until the gunfire stopped. Then she eased her head around the corner, looking again for the captain.

He was speaking to the young lieutenant. Maria felt her throat tighten. Since the first time her eyes beheld him, tall, slim, straight as a tree in his uniform, a strange, helpless feeling had invaded her body. She had told herself that she was a fool, a poor, uneducated girl from a village so small it was not listed on the official maps of Morazon – while he was an officer, a man educated and trained in the ways of soldiering. He would have nothing to do with her. Still, she could not stop herself from dreaming.

His hair peeked out from under his cap in black curls. His eyes were restless, sweeping across the room, resting for a few seconds on the face of Captain Morales, only to sweep the room again. In the diffused morning light, his face looked thin, cheekbones poking against the skin, his jawline hard and firm.

Beyond his high shoulders, she could see people paused in their flight, halfway up the stairs, peering through the railings. All were strangers, *turistas* off the old autobus, their faces hazy from across the room, as though she were looking at them through smoky glass.

She could make out a woman and two children, a boy and a girl. All three looked like they were crying. Two steps above them, a man leaned over the rail. Maria recognized his face. He was the leader of the *turistas*. Poncho had said the man was a sort of priest. His lips moved as though he were praying. Maria fingered her prayer beads as she began to say Hail Marys.

The guns started up again. Soon, she could hear the ping of bullets against the massive wooden doors and the thunk as they sank into the thick masonry. The captain's voice was louder now, rising over the barrage, and she heard him say something about the radio and the men who were housed back of the hotel. A deep metallic coughing sound came from outside, followed by a huge explosion that rocked one end of the old hotel. Plaster, glass, and wood fell like hailstones. Then the captain and the lieutenant were running for the front windows, pulling their guns out as they ran.

Peering through the gaps between her fingers, she could see them dart in front of the windows, fire their pistols, then retreat to the safety of the thick walls. The sound of gunfire was so loud. Never had she been so close to death. She was so afraid. She wanted to run. Her legs would not move. She bent her head, pressing it into her hands as she felt the hot tears on her cheeks.

Fourteen

Damn, but that one had come close. The bullet had buzzed by his ear like a wasp. If he had sneezed, he might be dead. Tony the Demented dropped to his knees and scooted around the corner of a dilapidated building, his gun before him. He expected to die sometime. He saw too much fighting not to. However, that did not mean he was ready to die now. Around the campfires of the revolutionaries, he had heard the former college professors and newspaper reporters and confession-hearing priests call dying the ultimate sacrifice. All had been full of lofty ideals and fine words. Most were dead now, or run off to some imagined safety in the jungle that was far greater than all of them, greater even than the revolution.

Now he could see the peeling paint and weathered boards and sunlight spilling like hot metal on the brown earth. If he could see around the building, then anyone on the other side could see him. Tony slid to the ground and crawled on his belly through the dust, propelling himself with his elbows, knees, and the strange spasmodic motion of his thin torso. Small brown clouds of dust fell against his sweaty face. He ignored the dust.

All that truly mattered to Tony were the bodies of his wife and little son and daughter, their brains spilling out of their skulls, mingling with blood so bright it was beyond red. He never forgot those monstrous visions, not when he was eating frijoles and bananas, not when reading from one of the books the professors had left behind, not even when taking a shit behind a jujube tree. Not when he studied the changing light as day dawned, not when he lay on his back beside the dying campfire and listened to the snores, farts, and whispered intimacies of his companions, not while he gazed at stars floating on the surface of an enormous blue sea of sky. Never did he forget.

He was seeing their faces now, smiling at him through the dust that rose and betrayed him. He smiled back as he wiggled faster across the open ground. A low adobe wall rose a few meters off to his right, flat and smooth like a low-slung mesa, and he changed direction, headed now for that wall.

Beyond the wall was a stretch of open ground, then a plot of tomatoes and beans, and finally the rear of the barracks. Inside the barracks were several government soldiers. He had heard their rifle fire as Carlos and most of the guerillas attacked the front. Tony and three other men were supposed to capture the barracks from the rear while Carlos and the others kept the soldiers distracted. Four men were not enough, but they would have to do. Reinforcements had not come and Carlos had his orders and would not wait.

Carlos was a good soldier of the revolution; loyal to the last, but Tony did not really believe he was a great commander. Not that he cared. It did not matter to Tony whether he died under a great leader of the revolution, or one who was merely brave. Back pressed against the wall, he checked his weapon and counted slowly to thirty to give the others time to get in place.

Once he got to thirty, he was going whether they were ready or not. Yuscarana was as good a place to die as any.

Thirty sounded strange in his ears, as if it had come from far off, from another person. So he said it again, took a deep breath, and pushed with all the muscles in his legs, twisting his torso and coming semi-upright, moving forward in a crouch. Putting the palm of his left hand on top of the wall, he swung himself over, keeping his eyes on the barracks and his rifle.

The wall was thicker than he expected and Tony caught his trailing heel on it and stumbled as he landed, putting his free hand out to break his fall. As he came back to his crouch, he heard the singing of bullets as they whizzed by his ears and the whine as they ricocheted off the wall behind him. His luck was holding. He fired off a wild shot as he sprinted across the open ground, before slipping behind a massive tree trunk, grateful for its bulk.

Whipping his head out from behind the trunk, he snapped off a shot in the general direction of a silhouette behind the glass of one of the rear windows. The bottom half of the window had been pushed up, and when he heard the smash of glass, he knew he had shot high.

A barrage of bullets hammered against the tree and plowed furrows in the dust. Tony the Demented made himself skinny while he looked around for his men. He could hear his breath rasping in his throat.

At first, he could see nothing more than the wall and the road behind it curving white toward the heart of Yuscarana. Then he heard a shout and shifted his line of sight in time to see Borros running through the old graveyard, bobbing and weaving, using tombstones for cover. Seconds later, he caught sight of Manuel the Carpenter coming in from the north, using a shallow ditch to cover his advance. Tony waited for the third man to show. He was new and Tony knew only that the man came from the capital and wore his hair long and a great silver cross on a chain around his buzzard's neck.

Tony waited, listening to his slowing breathing, watching shadows move across the barren ground. He could not see the new man. Bending at the waist to change the image, he twisted around the trunk of the tree, took a rapid sighting, then squeezed the trigger to keep the soldiers in the barracks honest. Whipping his head back behind the tree, he looked again for the third man.

At the southern corner of his vision there was a dark movement. Tony angled his head and watched the man with the long hair run across an alley and up a steep bank. He ran herky-jerky like a puppet on a tight string, his hair floating out behind him like a tattered flag, the cross swinging back and forth like a silver bell.

The guerilla crested the rise and started across the open ground that surrounded the barracks. Forty yards before him was a truck the army used to transport the men. The truck was old, the body rusted, the tires bald, but it was cover and the puppet man ran hard for the cab. The cross glinted in the sunlight.

Firing was coming again from the barracks. Tony could hear the popping and he knelt and fired to cover his man's advance, yelling at Borros and Manuel the Carpenter to do the same. He was taking more time now, aiming carefully, making his shots count.

Herky-jerky, the man ran on, his odd motion coming to his aid. He was halfway there. Suddenly he threw his arms up. His gun flew from his hands and his fingers clawed at the air. The man sank to his knees, sliding down in stages like a collapsible ladder. For a moment he knelt, swaying like a penitent, the cross swinging in counter-rhythm. Turning his head, he looked at Tony. He opened his mouth, but only blood came out. Then he fell forward. Blood began to crawl through the dust like a thin, red snake.

Tony felt his throat tighten as his eyes started stinging. Cursing, he began pulling the trigger. A stream of bullets slapped into the barracks. In their wake, he sucked up his courage and made another dash, trying to reach a small brick building that had once been a smokehouse, diving the last ten feet.

The impact drove the air from his lungs and he rolled over on his back, tasting dust and blood from where he had bit his lip, smiling, glad to be alive. The high blue sky was decorated with a flock of dark birds winging toward the mountains. Tony wondered why men were so stupid as to kill each other. Instead, they should be looking at birds.

Still, he knew that killing had brought him pleasure in the past. He was a spiller of blood – no denying that. Though it sickened him, he would continue to kill. He acknowledged the fact.

More firing now from the front of the barracks. Carlos must finally be getting his men shifted into gear. They had been slow that morning. Many were new men; they didn't know the routines, hadn't faced fire before, hadn't seen death up close and personal. Such men had no idea how difficult death was on a hot sunny morning with the blood seeping out of the chest of a man you had been chatting with seconds before, or the stench the man became when his bowels opened, or the humming bottle flies made as they circled the body flopped in the dust. The movies never got it right.

He waited until he was sure the men in the barracks were engaged, then raised his head. His eyes caught flickering images of moving men, the glint of sunlight on their gun barrels. He closed his left eye, even though he knew he was not supposed to, and forced himself to breathe smooth, slow, shallow. Now that he was this close, he could afford to wait, especially when one of his men was dead. Tony realized he had not seen or heard from Borros or Manuel the Carpenter in several minutes. However, he didn't take his eye off the window. Doing so might cost him a target, and what difference would it make anyway? In his mind, he could hear the sleepy-eyed man who had assassinated General de Le Hoya saying you never took your eye off the target. If you had to sneeze, you let the snot run down your lip, if you had to shit, you filled your pants, if your mother died, you said a prayer and kept your eyes dry and on the target. Later, there would be ample time for wiping and crying.

The long shot was a waiting game and you didn't often get second chances. So you waited, and when the opportunity finally came you took it without hesitation. You simply expelled air, then gently curled one finger. If you were good, or lucky, the world your eye was watching turned crimson. Crimson was a beautiful color at the end of a long shot. Crimson, the same color as the blood of his wife, and his son, and his daughter. Beneath the stock of his rifle, the lips of Tony the Demented curled, but he kept his open eye on the window, fixed on a single pane of glass. Sweat slid down along the side of his nose, but he ignored the tickling. In the distance, a bell tolled. Seconds dripped inside his mind like water from a leaky tap. His guts growled.

Then a shadow floated on the far side of the broken glass. Tony let the air seep out of his lungs. Then it was more than a shadow, but still less than a man. Then it was a man.

He squeezed the trigger.

All the world at the far end of his tunnel of vision went crimson.

Tony grinned as he pulled his head back around the smokehouse bricks.

For some time, he sat with his back against the warming bricks, staring up at a lone bird riding the thermals, making ever wider loops in a sky so blue it belonged in a painting in the Museo de Arte Nacional.

Tony hadn't been to church or confession in a long time. He had served so long in the revolution he was no longer sure he believed in God, at least not in the God offered to him when he was a child.

Sitting quietly, breathing shallowly, Tony's fingers caressed the grenades fastened to his belt as though they were prayer beads. The wall was smooth and warm against his back. The sky was a hard-boiled blue.

Fifteen

Funny what a woman remembers in the frozen hours immediately after her husband's brains have been blown out of his skull as he was eating a grapefruit.

Sharon Samuels couldn't get her mind unstuck. She kept remembering when she was in college and had to study so hard and do her laundry. She could recall being in the old library on campus, her stomach growling as ten o'clock rolled around, the single slice of pepperoni pizza eaten at five-thirty long gone and her Shakespeare book open to *Hamlet*. She had been so young and inexperienced that trying to do two things at once had seemed like cruel and excessively rigorous activity. Now, she handled dozens of projects every day as though they were no more than blowing her nose. Yet here she was in this godforsaken place with her head hanging like a broken bell between her legs and tears streaming down her face.

This was not a normal day. That much she had grasped. Somewhere in one of the furrows of gray matter she knew

Bartlett was gone forever. Still, she couldn't bring herself to even think the word dead. Her psyche would not wrap around the concept. That was the way her mind worked. When the pressure grew too great, the system simply shut down. Always happened along those lines when the world intruded too much, and today was a damn sight too much. She wanted to scream, but the kids were probably watching her through tears of their own. She owed them a modicum of self-control; Sharon Samuels bit her lip as she tried to focus on dirty laundry. What she thought about didn't matter so long as it wasn't seeing Bartlett's brains splattered all over his breakfast.

A hand touched her shoulder and she jerked, swallowing a scream as she lifted her head.

A man with a hard-edged jaw and close-cropped gray hair stood staring down at her. He projected an aura of quiet strength that made her feel young.

"Mrs. Samuels?"

She tried to speak but her vocal cords were out of synch. She swallowed twice and tried again. "Yes." The syllable sounded high and quivering in her ears.

The man smiled with his eyes. "I'm Joe Moby, from the bus." He let his head incline slowly toward a solidly built woman with short brown hair streaked with gray. Her eyes were large and brown. "This is my wife, Amy."

Sharon Samuels tried to smile.

"It's not safe out here on the stairs. Can we help you to your room?"

Sharon looked around, surprised. She hadn't realized where she was. She had run from the gunfire until her legs quit working. Then she had sat down. She hadn't realized she was on the next to last step before the second-floor landing. Without quite knowing why, she had somehow got it fixed in her mind that she was in her room and the children were in theirs.

The children, where were they? Her heart pounded as her eyes swept up the stairs. She couldn't lose them. Not after this morning. Another scream rose in her throat and she tried to pull herself upright, using the railing and Joe Moby for support.

She found the kids standing together in a pocket of shadow at the edge of the stairs where the main corridor intersected with the hallway wings. Both were staring at her, their eyes reddened and wet. Sharon tried to smile, but her mouth was short-circuiting and her legs had stopped working. She sat down abruptly.

The man kept a hand on her arm; she could feel the pressure, gentle but steady. "That's all right. Rest for a moment. Legs always go after a shock. Get your breath and we'll help you to your room."

He eased his head closer. "Need to get you off these steps. We get hit just right with a mortar and they'll be the first thing to go. Not sure how safe any of our rooms will be, but you're not so exposed there, and if the floor goes, it will be a whole lot better to be on top of your bed than falling down with who knows what coming down on top of you." The man nodded at his wife and Sharon felt a smooth hand against the bare flesh of her other arm. "Come on now, Mrs. Samuels, Amy and I will help you."

Sharon felt herself rise, without any noticeable strength in her legs – it was as though they were hollow. Her brain felt hollow, too, and her chest. She wobbled down the hallway like a punch-drunk fighter being escorted back to his corner after a round gone on too long.

~ * ~

The world was hazy, golden, as if a forest of golden rain trees had released all their blossoms at the same time. Swaying gently to inner rhythms as ancient as time itself, she looked down at all the people running like they were on fire. Inside her head a slow, smooth melody played softly, cool and full of strings and reeds, gentle and sweet, yet somehow sad. Only she could hear it. She could tell that by the look on the faces of the people down below. No one was paying any attention to the music; they were all yelling, or screaming, or crying too loudly to hear anything.

Deep inside her brain, Kristin Samuels could feel a shift taking place. Voices were beginning to penetrate her skull, whining like jet aircraft engines. Soon the echoes would begin and she would have to search for more antidote. The shit she had smoked last night had been wonderful, out of this world, and the next one. It had been as though the earth were a ship drifting through a great space ocean, rising and falling on unseen tides.

Her parents had been watching her. Closer than they had ever watched before. Totally because of one son-of-a-bitching cop that she hadn't been able to sweet talk or blowjob into turning his head. God, but she hated that prick. If her dad hadn't known the people you really need to know, and called in a few favors or spread a few bucks around, or whatever the hell he did, she would have had to spend time in jail.

Still, from what her friends had told her, and some of them could testify personally, jail wasn't so bad. You could usually score something: weed, pills, acid, in there. Even without money it was possible. "All you had to do was be friendly," they said, winking. From an early age Kristin had understood about being friendly. Being a good girl was fine, but nothing like being a friendly girl. All her friends understood. Inside the circle word traveled quickly.

Her brother was talking to her, his words striking her face like raindrops. She blinked and the haze parted for a second and she could see his anxious face swarming in on her, his lips throwing out words that buzzed like angry wasps. His eyes were wide and wet and his hands were spidering the air. She smiled at him with her serene, I-am-the-queen smile.

Trevor was an excitable boy, too full of ideas, concepts, theories, and plots for his own good. That was what came of reading dorks with names like Hemingway, Faulkner,

Steinbeck, Sherwood Anderson, and Dos Passos. Dos Passos, for God's sake, what sort of name was that? Sounded like it came from the other side of the world.

Oh, foreign countries were all right, within reason. France and Spain and England were okay, and Brazil during Carnival, and parts of Mexico during spring break, and Hawaii. But then maybe Hawaii wasn't a country. Could an island be a country? Maybe it was a state? Were islands states? Surely not, islands sounded so small. But then there was Rhode Island. She knew that little piece of shit was a state and it sure as hell sounded like an island. Damn, she was so confused.

Thinking was hard anytime, but especially in the morning. And on a morning like this, when she was still half-fried to a deep crackly crunch, with the music lilting inside her head and that beautiful golden curtain swaying in the breeze, and all the people running around like ants and screaming like idiots, well forget it.

There was her brother again. In her face and shouting at her like some mad Captain Ahab; she recalled that name from the movie. She'd scored some good dope that night.

Damn, how could he even be her brother? Surely to God, anyone who read all those stupid books and poems and shit couldn't be any kin to her, let alone her brother. Books were nothing but pages and pages of lies. When she had been a little girl, she had believed all those sweet lies. Now she knew better. Life taught you that all the old words were lies. No, Trevor could not be her brother. Maybe her mother had had an affair. Oh God, what did that boy want? Why the fuck wouldn't he stop screaming?

Kristin Samuels closed her eyes, inhaled all the air she could hold, and started screaming herself. She went on screaming until the walls of her mind reverberated. Soon Kristin could not even remember why she was screaming. Her eyes were shut so tightly that no light was seeping in. She swung her head wildly, so that her hair drummed against her face. Slowly, dimly, she became aware of another rhythm impacting her body. She allowed her eyes to drift slowly open, keeping them slightly unfocused, so that no one could see inside.

She was surprised to find she had been crying. One tear still clung to the curved surface of her right eye. Kristin stared out through the drop; it reminded her of looking up at the surface from the bottom of their swimming pool. She loved to take a deep breath and sink slowly to the bottom as though she were a diver descending, settle slowly on the bottom of the pool, stare up at the sunlight sparkling on the water that rippled when the wind blew, watch slanting shafts of light descending, diffusing until the light was in the water and the water encapsulated the light so that they seemed the same essence. As long as she could hold her breath and remain at the bottom of the pool, she was one with them.

The bottom of the pool was always quiet, cool, and dim. It was peaceful on the bottom, below the world, away from all adults who lived to tell her what to do, how to do it, when to do it, and where to do it. She wished they could all leave her the hell alone and take a flying leap off the top floor of the Chrysler Building. Who the hell was shaking her?

She swam to the surface, blinking away tears, staring into the eyes of a man from the tour. She had seen him lounging across the aisle on that nasty old yellow bus, his nose stuck in a book. His name was beyond her.

Kristin shook her head, clearing away a few of the cobwebs. She tried to focus on the man's face. It was an ordinary face, with an oversized nose topped by dark-framed glasses, wrinkles at the corners of the eyes, and thin lips that were moving. Sounds came from his open mouth, distorted by the time they reached her ears. Vision was ahead of hearing at this moment and she watched his lips closely, trying to make out words. The man seemed disturbed and she smiled to let him know she was trying to be cooperative.

His lips were slowing down now. He put a hand on her left shoulder. She could feel it trembling like a frightened bird. Some of his fear transmitted its way into her brain and more of the spider webs dissolved. Stray words began to penetrate.

"We.... have.... to get off landing.... bullets very... and dangerous your.... your mother... brother... going...."

"What did you say?"

"I said..."

"Something about my mother?'

"Yes...

"Where is my mother?"

She is.... with... brother.... and..."

"What about my father? Where is my father?" Aware for the first time that morning of his absence, Kristin turned slowly, as though she were on a revolving pedestal. Her eyes swept the lobby of the hotel below. What were those strange popping sounds? Chairs were overturned and a large picture of an old man on a burro carrying firewood had fallen off the wall. From the floor, the old man and the burro stared at her with wet brown eyes.

"What is going on here?" She used the impervious tone she reserved for adults lower down the social ladder who needed to grasp the realities of the situation.

The man stared at her with eyes that were brown and moist looking, like the man's and the burro's in the painting.

He stared at her long enough for her to hear the clock ticking inside her head. Kristin didn't like the way he looked at her. Strange lights were running in his eyes. Fear swept through her brain.

His lips moved again. He spoke more slowly now and though the syllables reached her brain in slow motion she could understand most of what he said.

"Your.... father...." he shook his head; "I'm sorry." He paused as if waiting for a response, but Kristin didn't feel like talking. What she felt like was some crack. His words were only words. She needed something more potent than words. Words wafted around her head each day like smoke from a dying campfire, smoke that irritated your eyes and made your nose run. The kind of smoke she had in mind had more pleasurable side effects.

"The revolution has started, you know?" He smiled as though that would somehow make things better. "We have to get away from these stairs now. Let's go with your mother." Using his head as a baton, he pointed down the hallway.

Kristin stared at her mother's back. A woman Kristin didn't know appeared to be holding her mother upright. She was so confused. Nothing about this day made any sense. She needed to score in the worst way.

Kristin nodded at the man and let him see her little-girl-lost smile. She allowed him to take her by an elbow and guide her down the hall behind her mother. Kristin had a sensation that she was a princess following the queen in a tragedy by that English guy, the old one, whose name she had heard a hundred times but never could remember.

She was out of dope, but her dad always kept a fifth of good Kentucky bourbon in his suitcase. Bourbon wasn't her favorite, but it beat the hell out of a cold shower or television.

Her legs were wobbly. Exactly like my mother, she thought; I'm walking exactly like my mother. Will I grow up and look like her? Kristin shuddered. Growing old was for someone else, for the sort of kids who worked at McDonalds and the Cineplex after school and on weekends. Then she thought again about the bourbon her dad always packed. Good old dad, she thought. He might be a pain, but he was okay in certain ways. Some of her friends had worse. She stumbled down the hall on rubber legs. Her head was a minor earthquake and a craving was growing geometrically inside her brain.

~ * ~

This day was straight out of Hemingway, his horrific, chaotic retreat from Caporetto. On second thought, maybe it was more like Faulkner with all his overheated rural incestuous violence. No, wait, it was more Kafka, this morning had progressed beyond the abnormal. Watching your father's brains frost your oatmeal definitely propelled it into the realm of the absurd.

Tears pooled in his eyes and Trevor blinked them away. He never wanted strangers to see him crying. I'm in shock now, he told himself; the admission reflecting a melting effect, as though shock were a covering of snow and as time beat down relentlessly it was starting to melt.

While he could not honestly claim an intimate relationship with his father, they had enjoyed their moments. Time was, no, had been a precious commodity to his father and Trevor had recognized that early. Stress, hard work, and long hours at the mysterious office had left his father ill-equipped for fun and games. Still, there had been an annual outing to a Red Sox-Yankees game, a movie or two during the holidays, happy Christmas mornings, rare long weekends at the beach house, a never repeated skiing trip near Vail – snapshots that glittered like polished glass in Trevor's mind.

Not all the snapshots were of momentous events. There were also odd capsulations of seeing his father peering over the top of his book to watch him toddle off to bed, his dad sleeping in his beach chair with his toes buried in tan sand and the sun baking his flesh, laughing with his head thrown back at some family picnic, mopping at the sweat trickling down his face after a rare Saturday morning golf game. There were other moments, sad ones, like when they got the phone call about Granddad. Plus, a mélange of inconsequential moments. Moments that in themself were not momentous, yet were critical in any attempt to comprehensively define a relationship – those odd little vignettes of life that illustrate that precise point in the compendium of time and space where two lives intersect.

An explosion, deeper and louder than any that had occurred before, rattled the panes in the windows and Trevor blinked and came back into the moment. The landing shook under him and he put a palm flat against the wall to steady himself, easing back from the stairs. The staircase swayed and he wondered if Yuscarana was being struck by an earthquake. Another explosion, louder and closer, caused plaster to rain down. Gunfire followed, short hard blasts, and Trevor heard more glass break and knew the attack had resumed.

Leaning against the wall, his legs gone soft like moistened noodles, he glanced down the hallway where his mother and sister stumbled like refugees supported by United Nations' officials. Society would expect him to turn and hurry down the hallway after them. A man screamed, far enough away so that the cry was faint, close enough so the pain was discernible. Sweat soaked his chest. To hell with society, Trevor Samuels thought. Below, his father lay face down in his huervos rancheros and grapefruit, and men were screaming and bleeding and dying. Life was exploding while a shell-shocked woman and a spaced-out teen queen did the zombie drag down a shadowy hallway.

Trevor licked his lips as he made his decision. Stairs swayed beneath him and his legs felt as if they had been drained of blood. Ignoring everything, Trevor forced his body down the stairs, moving deliberately toward the smashing glass, the gunfire, the cries from men who were terrified, or in pain, or dying in the sunlit morning.

~ * ~

Like a video stuck in repeat mode, the scene kept flowing across her mind. She was a little girl in a frilly pink dress and white hat with a lace veil pinned back. White, shiny shoes encased her feet and white gloves covered her hands. The day was sunny and warm, and she could hear bees humming in the flower beds that bordered the sidewalk. Now and then, white, puffy clouds would pass across the sun and shadows would chase each other across the street. She was pushing a stroller down a long hill. Balloons, red and yellow, were tied to the handle of the stroller and they blew in the breeze, tugging at the stroller as if they wanted to ascend with it to the clouds.

As she moved down the sidewalk, white and hot under the sun, the stroller began to go faster. With each roll of the wheels, it went faster until she was running as hard as she could, barely hanging on to the handle. Her veil had come loose and was flapping about her face. Ruffles from her dress swished against her legs. Her tight white shoes hurt her feet and her hands were hot beneath her gloves.

Above her head, the red and yellow balloons banged angrily together. Before her loomed the dark mouth of a train tunnel, tracks exiting and entering like shiny steel tongues. High screams of a train pierced the air. She was headed straight for the tunnel and could not stop. The wheels of the buggy rolled off the sidewalk, crossed a narrow, paved road, bounced over the curb and landed on the railroad tracks. A train engine roared ever closer, its headlights piercing the darkness of the tunnel. The balloons whipped wildly in a rising wind. Far behind her, a woman screamed her name. The train whistle squalled. Tears rolled down her checks like hot rain. There was a great roaring and a blackness covered the earth. Then the film rolled again, from the top.

Tears streamed down the chiseled cheekbones of Sharon Samuels as she sat on a swaybacked bed in a doddering old hotel on what passed for the main street of a small town that nobody really cared about. Death was thick and hot in Yuscarana that morning, but all Sharon Samuels could think about was the home movie footage that kept rolling, herky-jerky across her mind. The train was coming again. She cried harder.

~ * ~

Feeling the weight of the book in his lap, he glanced down. Pages, filled with black words, stared back at him. The book had been open for hours. What had he tried to read? Honestly, he couldn't recall. Maybe he had flipped a few pages. Probably he had read the same paragraph a dozen times. Since breakfast he could not name one thing that had taken place. Smoke filled his brain. Seeing your father's brains splattered atop your pancakes will do that to you, Trevor thought.

Vague images of standing at the top of the stairs and hearing his mother's crying mingling with the disembodied voices of men, drifted through his mind like windswept fragments. The memory seemed true, but Trevor Samuels no longer felt he could trust anything, or anyone.

He tried to focus on the words on the page, but they were so many microscopic organisms squiggling on the surface of a Petrie dish. Trevor pressed the two sections of the book together. He could not read now and did not mark his place.

He let his eyes swing around the room. His mother was lying on the bed, while his sister sat on the floor beside it, her head flopped back as if her neck had been broken. Closed tightly, his mother's eyes were leaking. Glassy as marbles, his sister's eyes were wide open. He should have stayed downstairs; his mother and sister were in another world – a world he could not enter, a world he could not even imagine.

Trevor pushed himself off the chair and placed his book on the cushion. Katherine Anne Porter peered up at him from the railing of a ship. Trevor stared back at her. Something about the lights in her eyes instilled a vague sense of unease within him. It was as though she could see something in him he had never noticed. Shivering like a kid on a dark and windy Halloween night, he walked quietly to the window.

Sunlight poured over him and he stood blinking and gasping as though the light had sucked the air out of his lungs.

As the sensations passed, he leaned forward and peered out into the world.

Sounds drifted to him from the west, the direction from which the bus had come the day before. The window was open and the wind lifted the curtains. Trevor stuck his head between them.

Figures were moving across the landscape. Distant and small, they grew larger as he watched, until they became men running, soldiers, in full uniform and carrying their weapons, moving awkwardly as if they were tired robots, their batteries running down. From his perch, the soldiers' legs seemed to have a dramatic up and down motion; herky-jerky, his dad would have called it. Damn, damn, damn, how could his dad be dead?

By now the soldiers had faces, and he watched them achieve definition. Strain showed as their legs and arms pumped up and down. Behind them, moving across the middle ground, were other men, bunched in an elastic herd. They were also running hard and carried guns, but were not wearing uniforms. Now and then, one of the second herd stopped and pointed his rifle. Seconds later the report reached Trevor's ears.

As he watched, one of the men in the first herd suddenly threw his arms up. His fingers pointed at the sky. His rifle flew through the air, somersaulting in slow motion. The soldier stumbled on for two steps, three. Then he pitched forward, face against the earth, robot legs twitching. Then he was very still.

No one stopped to help him. Some soldiers ran around him; others leaped over his body. All of the soldiers were running. They didn't slow to turn and shoot. They only ran.

The leaders of the first group were now pounding down the main street of Yuscarana. Buildings rose on both sides of them and dust caked their faces. Sweat was running through that dust, creating an impression that they were crying dirty tears.

They were headed for the hotel; though he was no military genius, he could see that much. The soldiers were going to join forces and make a stand. Trevor felt like a battlefield correspondent. He wondered what Hemingway would have done.

Hemingway would have swigged whiskey, but then he would have grabbed a gun and joined the fight. Trevor Samuels wasn't a drinker. The few times he'd tried beer he hadn't liked the taste, and a single glass of wine during family dinners made him drowsy. Whiskey, he'd left alone. He'd read enough to know that more than alcohol lurked in whiskey bottles. Still, he wasn't going to sit in the room with two dilapidated women and go crazy. He swung back into the room, glanced once at his mother and sister, then headed for the door.

~ * ~

Kron gently closed the door behind him. The snick as the metal latch shot home sounded loud in the hallway. His legs felt suddenly weak and he leaned against the wall. While he had been helping the girl down the hall, he had felt only a desire to get her reunited with her mother and make sure they were as safe as the morning allowed. Now, her brother was moving down the hallway.

Safe seemed a strange word at the moment, as though some linguistics professor had made the word up, or borrowed it from Lewis Carroll. Safe had no more meaning than a puff of wind. Merely sound filling space in an empty universe.

When the trembling in his legs ceased, Kron pushed off the wall. His first steps were toward his room, but then, for reasons he didn't allow himself to explore, he turned and retraced his steps toward the lobby. Cognizant of the danger, he was intensely aware that his behavior was out of the ordinary for him.

Kron kept reminding himself he'd come on the tour seeking adventure, and no one could argue that a revolution was not adventure. Certainly, he harbored no desire to die, and never had he considered himself a brave man. Yet he called himself a writer, and it seemed to him that any writer half worthy of the term would at least have to observe some of the action. Granted, a stray bullet might get him, but, for the present, the stairway landing seemed a moderately safe observation point. To live up to his own image he would have to go there. For a few minutes, anyway.

Living up to the images others held for you could be done, he'd discovered, if you did it only when you were in their presence. Living with the image of yourself you had conjured up was a different matter altogether. A man had to live with himself every hour of every day for his allotted span. Good, bad, or somewhere in the shadowy center, a man had to live with his actions. For more years than he wanted to count, Kron had been living with a man he didn't like. For a moment, he wondered about the life the dead man had lived, then he wondered how his wife and children would live going forward.

Sixteen

He knew in an instant. He had heard the sound before. It was one a man did not forget. The captain willed his mind to go blank, then recalled an ancient dream, one he had experienced many times, of a great black bird with a crimson head circling high above him. Part of him wished he were riding the thermals with the bird. The bird always made him think of death. Perhaps he and the lieutenant would die this day. Captain Morales hoped the lieutenant would not die on this sun-soaked morning. The lieutenant was young. The captain shot a final glance across the courtyard at the rear of the hotel. Flowers bloomed around a statue of a saint whose name he could not recall.

Not a man of great formal religion, the captain said a short prayer for the safety of the lieutenant to whatever spirit guided and guarded the universe. Never had the captain been able to clearly picture the great deity; all that was too much. Yet he was certain beyond any doubt that something far greater than any man, or any consortium of men, had created and still governed the universe. On this lonely planet man was paramount, but in the grander scheme of things, the captain was sure mankind was less than the dark-winged wedge floating in the enamel sky of his dream.

Sounds of firing drifted to him again, louder and sharper, with an urgency that reverberated in his temples. The captain dropped his cigar and ground it out with his heel.

"They are attacking the garrison. Go, Lieutenant, and get a call through to the men. Tell them to try and break out and join us here. If they are surrounded, the rebels will cut their water and surrender will be inevitable. Here at the hotel, we have more supplies and can man the upper floors, thereby occupying the high ground. Besides, there are the *turistas* to protect, and the townspeople. Many who live close by will come here for protection."

The captain looked once more to the sky, then down and across the flat brown ground. He shook his head. "I hope they are not misled." He massaged the back of his neck. "Also, radio to the sergeant at the communications shack. Tell him to get a message through to headquarters. We must let them know that Yuscarana is under attack."

Gunfire rose on the far side of the hotel and the captain slid his pistol out of its holster, trying to recall the last time it had been fired. Louder sounds now – explosive coughs. Grenades, the captain thought – the rebels have hand grenades; I wonder if they have mortars?

"I will go inside and do what I can. The people, especially the *turistas*, will be frightened." He nodded toward the small adobe building beside the barn where two soldiers were billeted. For protection of the interest of the town of Yuscarana, the orders stated. Both men had run out of the building and were standing in the bright sunlight of a Morazon morning. The unit's spare communications equipment was kept there, stored under the men's bunks. In their current state they would never think to use it. "Go now and get the spare radio going and send those messages. Go, Lieutenant, go!"

~ * ~

Panting as he ran through the long narrow hallway, Captain Morales marveled at the way his heart pounded in his chest and his lungs stretched as they sucked in air. Already his breathing was labored. He could hear the faint wheezing. Old age, he thought. In school I could run for miles. Memories of his days as a track star raced across his mind and left him wondering where all his younger days had gone.

I have grown old, he told himself, old before my time, old before realizing it. Perhaps today will be the day I die. That would not be so bad. Not that he particularly desired to die; it was more that he didn't have anything so wonderful to live for.

Light spilled onto the floor of the hallway before him and echoes of gunfire reached him over the panting. Captain Morales felt his mind shift. One way or another, today was going to be different. Excitement surged through him. Today he might die, but it would not be from boredom.

~ * ~

Halfway to the barn, Lieutenant Escobar remembered that when taking evasive action a man was supposed to run in a zigzag fashion. All he was doing was running in a straight line as though hell itself was after him. Immediately he ducked his head and began twisting his shoulders and taking odd spaced steps. He wondered if the two men who had gone back in the shack were staring at him out the window.

Shadows thrown by the barn covered him as he ran along its edge. He heard Gitano nicker at him, but kept pounding toward the shack, expecting with every step a bullet to smash into his body. Gunfire was closer now, sporadic bursts that sounded malevolent. Sweat was running down his face and he wondered if it might soon be blood. His mouth was dry and rawness was ravaging his throat. Nauseous, he prayed he would not vomit.

While he could admit to himself that he was afraid to die, he could not let the men see that. My first action, he thought, and I am not ready. For years I have dreamed of a battle, and now here one has come and I am no more ready than my first day in uniform. The lieutenant reached the corner of the old barn and stopped, getting his back against the roughened wood, gasping for air, dragging an arm across his face as he listened.

All he could hear was his own ragged breathing. He eased his head around the corner of the old barn.

Splinters poked at his cheek and sweat ran down into his eyes, stinging, blurring his vision. Blinking, he peered left, then right. Only smooth brown ground, an old wheelbarrow, and, leaning against that, a broken-handled pitchfork. Were there rebels hiding in the grass, waiting for him to run the gauntlet between the two buildings?

In his imagination, Lieutenant Escobar could feel the bullet strike him, see the warm spurt of the blood and the fluidity of his final pirouette before he pitched face down in the dust. Then, before he realized he was doing it, he was sprinting across the last open ground, slowing only in the final stride.

As he reached for the door it swung open and he stumbled inside, almost falling, but a private, one of the Lopez brothers, caught him. When he had breath, the lieutenant began shouting to get the spare radio out from under their bunks. What were they thinking, simply standing around? Didn't they comprehend they were under attack? He strode to the small table jammed against one wall and sat on the wooden chair just as his legs gave way.

Inside the shack, the air was quieter, thick adobe walls muffling the gunfire. Time seemed to have accelerated as the men fumbling under the bunks behind him moved in slow motion. What in hell was taking them so long? Forcing himself to take a deep breath, the lieutenant stared out the window, hoping his face was calm. All the instructors at the academy had stressed how important it was to show leadership, not fear.

Lieutenant Escobar wished that all those slack-jawed, heavy-flanked, paunchy old men were here with him. Let them show some leadership under fire.

"Hurry up," he shouted, and, hearing the break in his voice, wished that he hadn't. Turning in his chair, he looked into faces of the soldiers. All he saw was sweat and fear.

As the men assembled the radio, he felt his pulse slowing and his breathing returning to normal. He dabbed at the sweat that had eased to a trio of slow trickles. Gunfire was faint now, with long pauses between bursts, and the lieutenant felt confidence seeping back into his body.

Lopez fumbled with the knobs and the lieutenant pushed his hands away. "Get your rifle, you and Hermosa, and keep an eye out there. They may attack again at any time."

"Are there many, Lieutenant?"

"How should I know? Now get to your post."

Lopez studied the face of his lieutenant for a moment, then turned and walked to the other window at the far side of the shack where Hermosa stood with his back to the room. Escobar turned his attention to the radio. It took time, seconds trickling away like precious drops of sweet blood, but at last it crackled as it came to life. It was an old set and the lieutenant had used it only on a training exercise. Twisting a knob, he keyed the set.

The voice of Sergeant Gomez sounded so distant it could almost have come from another planet.

"Sergeant?"

"*Sí.*"

"This is Lieutenant Escobar."

"Oh, *sí*. What is going on...

"Shut up, Sergeant. This is an important military matter. The rebels have attacked."

"Where?"

"Here."

"Yuscarana?"

"Yes, Yuscarana. Do you *comprende*, Sergeant? Can you grasp what I am saying?" The lieutenant could hear the anger rising in his voice, but he couldn't stop it and didn't care. Anger was a stronger sound than fear.

"Yes, yes, Lieutenant, I understand. How many rebels are attacking Yuscarana?"

"Everybody keeps asking me that same damn stupid question and it does not fucking matter. Just shut up, Sergeant, and listen to me. Captain Morales ordered me to tell you to contact headquarters. Use the special line. Do it quickly. Tell them we are under attack and reinforcements are needed, immediately. Have them send a helicopter if they can. Understand?"

"*Sí, sí*, but..."

"But what, Sergeant?"

"What am I supposed to do after that?"

"Just get through to headquarters, Sergeant. Then grab a gun and bring your men to Yuscarana. Sneak up on the bastards. Kill as many as you can. Then come to the hotel. Think you can handle that?"

"Yes, sir," the sergeant said.

Lieutenant Manuel Escobar sighed. He did not have great confidence in Sergeant Gomez.

~ * ~

The chair fell as he pushed away from the radio, clattering against the floor, causing his nerves to twitch.

Lieutenant Escobar shouted at the two men standing by the door. "Where is the telephone? They do not have a radio at the barracks, only a telephone."

Lopez smiled an embarrassed sort of smile. "But Lieutenant, have you forgotten? The telephone is on the wall, there on the other side of my bunk. See..."

"All right, all right. Yes, it slipped my mind, for a moment only."

"Of course. Truly it has been a stressful morning."

"Never mind. Keep an eye on the hotel. If you see any rebels, shoot at once. I have to get through to the garrison. The captain wants them to join us here." The lieutenant stepped quickly across the room, pleased only a faint tremor ran up and down his legs.

"We will make our stand at the hotel?"

"Yes." The lieutenant jerked the receiver up. He punched the button with the label Barracks 1 posted beside it. Only silence answered. Again he pressed the button.

"Damn, they must have cut the lines."

"Lieutenant?"

Escobar swung around. "Yes, Lopez, what is it? And it had better be important. Can't you see that I am thinking?"

"Well, sir, it is true they do not have a real army radio at the barracks, but they do have a two-way radio."

Damn, the lieutenant thought, he looks like a cowering dog. I have to quit overreacting. This is no way to lead men.

"Ah, then the question becomes, do we also have one?"

"*Sí*, in the desk."

"Can you use it?"

"Yes."

"Excellent." He nodded at Lopez. "Get them on the line. Find out if they are under attack. Tell them Captain Morales orders them to the hotel. Understand?"

"Yes, sir."

"Then make the call." The lieutenant watched Lopez cross the room. Then he unholstered his weapon and took the position the private had vacated.

~ * ~

Only sunlight fell on the flat ground between the hotel and the barn, baking it slowly as it had done for eons. Lieutenant Escobar maintained his primary line of sight on the ground, swinging his eyes now and then to capture an image of the front of the barn or the back of the hotel, keeping his eyes slightly out of focus, not honing in on objects, but trying to pick up slashes of movement, or out-of-place shadows.

At the same time, he listened to one side of Lopez's conversation with the men in the barracks. It was taking an irritatingly long time. The gunfire had died and the resulting quiet seemed sinister. Escobar struggled to keep his face smooth and his mind focused. Finally, Lopez placed the two-way on the desk. It clattered loudly in the hollow quiet.

"Did you get through?"

"Yes, sir."

"Who did you speak with?"

"First with de la Hoya, then with Corporal Fuentes."

"Did they understand the message? Are they coming?"

Gomez nodded. The bill of his cap bobbing up and down made the lieutenant think of a woodpecker. "*Sí*, they understood, but they have been under attack all morning, so they will have to fight their way out. Fortunately, the attack seems light. Corporal Fuentes does not think the rebels have many men. He believes they can make it to the hotel without significant casualties."

"Let's hope he's right." The lieutenant turned and gazed across the open ground. Still no movement. He took several deep breaths. Captain Morales was waiting for him and the two privates. The shack seemed quiet and safe. A tide of reluctance to leave rose in his throat. He shook his head like an angry bull.

"All right, the captain wants us in the hotel. Let's go."

The eyes of Lopez and Hermosa were large and dark and seemed to reflect all the light in the room back to him. They did not speak. The lieutenant did not speak again, either. Instead, he turned, jerked the door open, and began to zigzag his way to the hotel. Sunlight struck his face and for a few seconds he was running blind. Then the world swam back into focus. He could hear Lopez and Hermosa pounding hard behind him. He flicked a glance left, then right, but could not see any rebels.

Nonetheless, the lieutenant felt a brief surge of pride for having taken the looks. He was becoming a soldier.

~ * ~

Long before he could see the chaos, he could hear it. People shouting and screaming, footsteps pounding in all directions across the floors. Civilians in a panic, thought Captain Morales, although, to be fair, he had seen his share of panics by army troops, even certain officers. Tides of sound drowned out the sound of his own panting and he no longer thought about whether this was a good day to die.

Reaching the end of the long hallway, he cut through what had been a coatroom in more prosperous times. The lobby opened up before him, looking like the basement of an abandoned museum. Chairs were overturned and shattered glass drifted beneath the windows. Abandoned jackets and hats lay where they had fallen, looking like so many small, dead animals.

An Oriental woman sat on the floor against one of the large columns, her head buried in her hands, shoulders heaving. A man, perhaps her husband, squatted beside her, his hands fluttering around her head like distracted butterflies. He rocked on his heels, swaying rhythmically like a baseball catcher in the seventh inning of a dull game.

Voices drifted from the top of the stairs and Morales glanced up. He could see a knot of people with ashen faces, moving like robots.

The blast of a shotgun ripped his attention from the first-floor landing. He jerked his neck toward the front of the lobby in time to see Poncho Herrera turn from a window with an ancient double-barrel shotgun in his arms. The innkeeper smiled thin-lipped below his Poncho Villa mustache.

"*Revolución*, Captain!" he shouted.

Morales nodded and began to trot toward the window, trying to take the situation in. "Casualties?"

The innkeeper's mouth turned down and his mustache sagged. "One dead, an American *turista*. Shot in the head while eating breakfast. In my restaurant," he added sadly.

Close to the windows now, Morales ducked and slid his body against the wall between what had been the two largest windows. Jagged glass hung from the frames, like broken teeth in the mouth of an old woman.

Captain Morales eased his head around the edge of the wall and took a quick sighting. The street was empty and he could detect only the glitter of sunlight on metal at the corner of the feed store across the street. Making certain his head was out of the line of fire, Morales rested against the plaster wall and stared at the wreck of a lobby while he thought about what to do.

For a moment, there was only the movement of darkness in his mind, as though a strong wind was blowing the night about. Then a blast of automatic weapons fire from across the street brought him back into the hotel and he turned, jammed his pistol through a hole in the broken glass, and fired, aiming in the general direction of the sound, letting the rebels know there were more men with guns inside the hotel, hoping to forestall their assault. It was only a matter of time – he realized that.

However, time was what he was trying to buy, enough time to get the men down from the barracks and Lieutenant Escobar and the two men up from the shack. As for Sergeant Gomez and the men at the communications post outside of town, the captain would count himself as lucky if they sent a transmission to headquarters. If they did and if, for once, headquarters responded promptly, and if he could hold the hotel long enough, they might survive, some of them anyway. Captain Morales was making no bets.

~ * ~

Breathing harder than he preferred, Lieutenant Escobar hurried across the lobby floor, urged on by gunfire emanating from the street.

The lobby resembled a great hollow shell, cast up from an angry sea and deserted by the organism that had been living within. Chairs, couches, and the eclectic assortment of tables had been pushed to the front of the room, forming a barricade that appeared to have been made with rejects from a secondhand furniture store. Captain Morales and Poncho Herrera leaned against the wall next to one of the windows. Only a few panes of glass were left in the windows. Broken shards rose and dangled like crystal stalactites and stalagmites. A pistol hung from the right hand of the captain, while the innkeeper cradled his shotgun. Escobar jogged the last few steps, halted abruptly in front of the captain and saluted.

Morales casually saluted in return. "Did you get through?"

"Yes, to both places."

"Good. And the men who were at the shack?"

"Both came with me. They stopped in the kitchen for water. They had not yet had breakfast when I arrived."

Glass smashed somewhere on the other side of the lobby and Morales rolled his neck and studied the street for a few seconds. Apparently satisfied, he turned and nodded at the lieutenant. "Okay. Now go and tell them to grab some fruit and bread, then take positions. There are two of them, right?"

The lieutenant nodded.

"Tell one of them to go to the back patio, where we were chatting after breakfast."

"Yes, sir."

"Have him operate from there. Tell him to stay behind the wall and to keep his fool head down."

"Have the other man take his rifle and food and go up to the second floor. Señor Herrera says there is a small window across the hall from the staircase that would make an ideal sharpshooter's location. Tell the man you send there to keep a damn close watch on the street and shoot anything that even looks like a rebel."

"Will do." The lieutenant turned to go. The voice of Captain Morales halted him. He turned to face the captain.

"Oh, Lieutenant, also tell that man to keep an eye out for the men coming down from the barracks. Tell him not to shoot them. Unless I miss my guess, we are going to need every man we have." A smile wormed its way across the lips of Captain Morales. "He can sing out though when he sees them. Comprende?"

Lieutenant Escobar saluted, turned on his heel. and started jogging across the lobby floor. Sounds of distant gunfire and the muffled crying of a woman accompanied him.

Seventeen

The president was having a bad morning, to put it mildly. At the state dinner honoring the Ecuadorian ambassador the night before, he had drunk far too much wine. The ambassador was an old friend and a marvelous storyteller and they had swapped reminiscences and told lies until almost three in the morning.

Now it was barely daylight. Except for a glow along the window line, his bedroom was still dark. Someone was pounding on his door like an orangutan. Who was that idiot? As President Gutierrez struggled to sit up in bed and hold his throbbing head still at the same time, he made an executive decision to have whomever it was sentenced to a year of hard labor, starting immediately. Then the president's stomach began to churn and he decided to have the bastard shot, even if it was his brother-in-law. Especially if it was his brother-in-law.

"Enter," he croaked.

I sound like a frog, he thought. As he fought back the nausea, the president decided he was a dying frog.

Light spilled into the room and Gutierrez blinked and groaned. It was disgraceful for the President of Morazon to be treated in such a manner. Through bleary eyes, he peered at the long-faced alarm clock that stood on the mahogany nightstand. The clock had been his father's, procured during a long-ago trip to America, taken before Gutierrez had been born. Until the day he died, the clock had held a place of honor on his father's dresser. It was the only memento of his father the president had kept.

So early, the hour was so early. Surely there was nothing so important that he had to be disturbed at such an hour. Then several thoughts collided in his mind and he wondered if indeed there might be such news. Under his silk sheets, the seventh president of Morazon shivered.

Eighteen

"God, can't you lay off the stuff, even for a few minutes?"

"What? Oh, er, ah, this?" Lord Threlkeld glanced down at the reddish liquid sloshing gently in the glass in his right hand. "No sense in wasting a perfectly good Bloody Mary."

"On a morning like this? My god, Donald, a man just had his brains blown out two tables away from where you were sitting and you go right on drinking as if nothing had happened?"

"Sipping, actually, Di, not drinking. One sips if one is a gentleman, all day, preferably. Certainly in the morning."

"When the town is under siege? When a revolution is starting? Do you drink, oh, excuse me, sip, then?"

"Certainly."

"You are truly a lost cause, Donald."

"My dear, we are all lost causes."

"Was that more gunfire?"

"Afraid so."

"It must really be a revolution, exactly as the man who runs the hotel was saying."

Lord Threlkeld sipped. "Certainly seems like it."

"Certainly seems like it. Is that all you have to say? Donald, darling, are you already so sloshed that you don't realize a revolution has actually started in this godforsaken patch of jungle? Well, are you?"

"No, my dear, not yet. But I do intend to work on it."

Lady Threlkeld rolled her eyes and caught a glimpse of an army officer running toward the front windows. It was the older one, the captain, and not the younger one. Was the younger officer a lieutenant? Or a captain? Whichever, he was slim and darkly handsome, a worthy conquest. She wondered where he was. Dianna Threlkeld realized that she was horny, make that extremely horny. By God, she wasn't ready to die. One great huge hell of a lot of her life was yet to be lived.

"Is that all you intend to do, work on that damn Bloody Mary?"

"Seems to be the thing to do at the moment, as this appears to be one of those, oh what did that fellow call it? You know, that American singer, what was his name?" Lord Threlkeld smoothed down the hair on the back of his head with his left hand. It seemed thinner than he remembered. "Oh yes, Nelson, Willie Nelson. What was it that Nelson chap called it in that song we heard on the radio? A Bloody Mary morning? Yes, that was the phrase and this is certainly a Bloody Mary morning." He bent his neck and lifted his glass.

"Well, I don't intend to stand under this damn stairwell and watch you drink that damn Bloody Mary you are so enamored with while a revolution rages."

"I am not enamored with my drink. Simply don't see the point in wasting it, revolution or no revolution. Besides, what do you plan to do, my dear? Go for a morning stroll?"

"Of course not. I'm going to the room and pack my bags. Then I will be ready should an opportunity arise to get the hell out of this bunghole of civilization. Coming?"

Licking his lips, Lord Threlkeld gazed across the lobby. "Not at the moment. You go on up, though."

"And what are you going to do, stand here and drink?"

"Actually, think I'll wander over and have a peek out what is left of one of the windows. See how the revolution is progressing."

"You'll only get yourself shot, probably die in this middle of nowhere."

"At least I won't die of boredom, my dear."

~ * ~

Standing quietly in a shadowy corner of the lobby, half hidden by a large potted plant, El Cartero watched the people stampeding across the lobby floor as he tried to decide what to do. Seconds earlier he had been quietly smoking his first cigarette of the day, getting ready to stroll down to his old yellow bus and start the motor for a trip to the shrine of Our Lady of the Holy Waters. The *turistas* were supposed to tour the shrine and return to Yuscarana in time for the evening meal. According to the tour book, they were supposed to retire soon after their meal, as they had an early departure time the next day in order to reach Lake Elegante before dark. Now it appeared the tour might linger longer in Yuscarana than scheduled.

Remembering his cigarette, he took a final draw and stubbed it out in the dirt of the planter. He had heard the shot and knew in the moment of hearing what it meant. Now he had to decide what to do. More shots rang out. It had become clear that many people might die in Yuscarana. El Cartero did not intend to be one of them. But what to do?

After a few disorganized attempts, his thoughts began to coalesce. The shooting had been sporadic and there had been no general assault. That indicated the rebels had not yet arrived in sufficient numbers to overwhelm the garrison at Yuscarana. Often, rebel bands in this area of Morazon were small and disorganized. Perhaps the hotel was not yet a trap. Escape seemed a better alternative than waiting. The question became how to escape.

The quickest and quietest way would be if he went alone, El Cartero decided. However, there were the turistas to consider. *Turistas* were very important. All life was important, of course, but to the company the lives of the people on their tours were very important. El Cartero would be a great hero if he helped all the *turistas* escape. Undoubtedly he would receive a great reward. The thought of a reward made him feel much better.

Then he considered how slow, clumsy, noisy the *turistas* would be. Several of them had shown no ability to remain silent for even a few minutes. El Cartero could see his chances for successful escape fading if he took them along. The smile on his face also faded.

Then there was his bus to consider. He owned the bus; at least he was partners with the *banco* in his hometown. El Cartero had been paying on his note for seven years. Three years of payments remained. He must save the bus. It might be old and not in perfect repair, but it ran, and by running helped him provide for all his family. And his family needed him, more than the *turistas* did. After all, they had a tour director and the tour company would surely send out the soldiers. Better if he slipped away alone and saved the bus. His family would be grateful, and so would the tour company, at least when they needed a bus for the next group of *turistas*.

Moving as unobtrusively as possible, El Cartero worked his way along the lobby wall. He kept glancing around to see if anyone was watching, but no one appeared to take any notice of one nondescript bus driver.

At the far end of the lobby, a quartet of windows opened onto a gravel path. The path curved beneath a grape arbor. Benches were scattered beside the path, and trees and shrubs grew along the edges. He walked there in the evenings after supper whenever he brought tour groups to Yuscarana. During these strolls, El Cartero had noticed the ground gave way beyond the hotel property, forming a shallow ditch that curved toward the road, then ran alongside the pavement for many meters. As he slung one leg over the window sill, El Cartero grinned. His sweet, precious, old, yellow bus was parked less than one hundred meters away by the side of the road, only a stone's throw beyond the ditch.

Nineteen

A quiet had settled over the morning hovering around the barracks. The very movement of time seemed to slow in the quiet, leaving Tony with the sense he had been huddled against the old smokehouse for hours. For some time there had been no firing, not from inside the barracks, nor from his companions who were supposed to be attacking. Even the sporadic bursts of gunfire from the hotel had died off. The rebel known as Tony the Demented could not imagine what Carlos was up to. Never had he known the leader to be a coward; had never even imagined it. Now he considered it.

Sweat formed in his hair, then eased down his face, worming its way into his eyes and making them burn. With the burning came anger, and, without thinking, Tony rose and blasted away at the barracks, screaming like a howler monkey.

Immediately, as though they had been waiting, guns blazed from several barrack's windows. Tony fell to the ground and crawled behind the smokehouse, screaming, cursing, shouting for the others to shoot.

Only two shots came from where his companions were supposed to be and he eased his head around the corner of the smokehouse to see what was going on inside the barracks. Then he screamed again.

Uniformed men were running out of the barracks like bees from a disturbed hive, swarming down a narrow lane of dull-yellow dirt. For a second, he was incredulous that none of the rebels seemed to be firing. Then it occurred to him that he might be alone. After a moment of what came as close to shock as his mind permitted, Tony the Demented decided he liked that situation. Alone wasn't all bad. At least he didn't have to depend on anyone else. Others had let him down in past battles, put him in danger, almost cost him his life. Better to be alone. No one to worry about. No one to criticize. No one to place him in jeopardy.

Crouching low, he began to run forward, feeling like he was one of the lions he had seen in a film on life in the Serengeti Plain. Before him, soldiers ran like a herd of wildebeests. They were running hard and fast, but not as fast as a bullet could fly. Tony stopped, curled the rifle to his shoulder, focusing it on one soldier, heavier than the rest, who wobbled as he ran. The man's back looked as broad as a door. Tony aimed, took a deep breath, held it for a second, then released it. At the end of the release he squeezed the trigger, as gently as if he were tugging on the cheek of a child. The soldier jerked once, as though a massive jolt of electricity was coursing through his body, stumbled on for a step, then pitched forward, face down in the road. Yellow dust rose, then settled down like falling ashes.

Tony swiveled the rifle around and began to aim at a tall soldier who ran with a strange stiff-legged gait that made him look like a poorly-designed robot. Before he could pull the trigger, Tony began to laugh. The more he laughed the harder he laughed. As the soldiers pounded down the road, Tony continued laughing. He laughed until they disappeared around the long slow curve. Even after they had disappeared, he was still laughing.

The fat soldier sprawled where he had fallen, absolutely still in the middle of the lane. A slender stream of red grew steadily longer in the yellow dust, spreading slowly, widening until it formed a crimson pool.

~ * ~

Grenade in hand, the man known only as Tony the Demented ran across a patch of grass and down an embankment and onto the yellow dirt road. Before him, he could see the retreating soldiers of Gutierrez. They were running hard, growing smaller by the stride until they were no more than midgets.

Seeing them thus reduced put him in mind of the midget wrestlers he had seen years ago when a traveling wrestling exhibition had toured the country. He had loved all the wrestlers, but especially the midgets with their acrobatic maneuvers, flips off the top ropes, and the way they hid behind the referee when they wanted to surprise their opponents. He had loved watching the midgets so much that he had followed the wrestlers for several weeks, living off what odd day jobs he could pick up and the charity of the villagers whose town was sponsoring the exhibition. He had gotten to know several of the wrestlers quite well, especially a young man who wrestled under the name of Bushman the Warrior.

Bushman had been a sweet kid, dumber than dirt and full of vainglorious boasts and pretensions. Why, the boy had even believed he spoke directly with God. Often God told him to do certain things, such as steal money from the wrestling patrons or eggs from the villagers. Once, God had even told him to attack a man named Juan the Huge with a steel baton Bushman had liberated from a policeman in the capital.

Outside the ring, Juan the Huge was normally a gentle, bumbling giant who carried grocery sacks for little old ladies, played games with small children, and always had a friendly word, a loving pat, and a tasty treat for any stray dog that wandered across his path.

Inside the ring, Juan the Huge was a one-man demolition squad. Over the course of his ring career, he had broken the arm of The Masked Invader, both legs of Tito the Magnificent, three ribs and the clavicle of Pedro the Destroyer, and the jawbone and neck of King Raoul. Raoul had lived, after three months in the hospital, but the only wrestling he did now was with a tequila bottle from the safety of his wheelchair.

One extraordinarily dark night when the caravan was camping on the outskirts of Orija, acting solely on instructions he believed had been delivered personally from the lips of God, Bushman had crept through the inky night, baton in hand, and slipped inside the tent of Juan the Huge. For such a large man, Juan was an extremely light sleeper. He heard the faint shuffle of the Bushman as he moved across the inside of the surplus army tent. Careful to make no noise, Juan cracked open one eye and watched, with amusement that he found most difficult to conceal, the Bushman creep across the floor like an avenging angel.

Allowing the Bushman every opportunity to retreat, Juan had stayed his mighty hand until the Bushman's baton reached the zenith of its first swing. Then, enhanced by years of training in the ring, Juan's right hand slashed through the night and smote the Bushman around his neck before the baton could fall.

With a roar mightier than any jungle beast, Juan the Huge had flung his legs out of the bed and stood erect with the Bushman dangling from his right hand like a live pig. Eyes bulging, veins pushing purple to the surface, and squealing in an even higher voice than normal, the Bushman dropped the baton and begged for mercy.

Juan had glared at the Bushman for a moment that seemed to the wriggling midget to last beyond forever. Then, baring his teeth, he had swung his monstrous head closer to the Bushman, growling and opening his massive jaws as he did so. When the teeth were only two inches away and the fetid breath of Juan the Huge warm against his cheek, the Bushman had shit his pants full and fainted dead away.

Wrinkling his nose at the sudden astringent odor, Juan had carried the Bushman by the throat across the floor of the tent and out into the night. There, he had swung him around and around and around before slinging him into the awaiting darkness. For several minutes thereafter, Juan the Huge had laughed like a hyena. Then he had taken a piss where he stood, turned, strolled back into his tent, and crawled under the sheet, where he promptly fell back asleep.

For the rest of his career, Juan had carried the baton into the ring where he used it with great devastation. Tony had abandoned the tour after that night. He had been out of food and money anyway, and without the Bushman much of the excitement had vanished from the wrestling circuit. As for the Bushman, he vanished that night from the wrestling circuit, from Morazon, seemingly from the face of the earth.

Strictly in honor of the Bushman, Tony the Demented let the midget soldiers run on down the yellow dirt road to Yuscarana. Instead of following them, he angled off the road, cut through a broken line of trees, then jogged across a field of melons, homing in on Yuscarana's blind side.

Twenty

"Turn out the lights."

"Akko, what good will that do? It is daylight."

"Turn out the lights and pull the curtains. Please, husband, do what I say. I do not want to die."

Iwakura Tyshimoda gave his wife a long look. Her dark eyes were wide open and wet. She was trembling, reminding him that this vacation had been undertaken for her nerves. Since the baby, Akko had not been the same. He smiled, trying to provide a modicum of reassurance, then walked quickly across the small room. Before he pulled the curtains he looked out onto the street. All he could see was sunlight blanketing the road in yellow.

After he had pulled the curtains and turned off the light, the room was noticeably darker, although Iwakura could read the dial on his wristwatch. He sat on the bed beside his wife. Her body was quivering as he wrapped an arm around her shoulders and pulled her to him.

"Here now, Akko. Things are going to be all right."

She pulled away from him as though he were diseased. "No, they are not. Things are not going to be all right, Iwakura. They are going to kill us. We are going to die."

"Why would they kill us, Akko? We are not their enemies. We are not even from this country."

"It does not matter. Soldiers are here in this hotel. The rebels want to kill all the soldiers, and they will also kill anyone who is with them."

"Foolishness. Where did you hear that?"

"From the innkeeper. I heard him talking to one of the waitresses last night."

"Idle babble from a gossip."

Akko jumped to her feet, her hair swinging around her head like an empty fish net. Her lips were pale. "Do you call this gunfire idle babble? Do you call a man's brains being blown out gossip? Do you? If you do, you are a fool. A fool. One who will be killed because of his own foolishness and take others down to death with him."

Mr. Tyshimoda waved his hands as though they were warding off mosquitoes. "No, no, of course not. All this violence is horrible, this bloodshed, awful. Certainly far more than idle gossip. I was referring only to the talk that the rebels wanted to kill us all. Surely, they would not deliberately murder innocent people who have done them no harm, who are merely strangers passing through. Surely."

"Surely yes, husband. Surely, even you can see that the rebels do not care who they kill. Perhaps they are even more anxious to kill the tourists than the soldiers for the publicity it would bring."

Mr. Tyshimoda shook his head. The movement made him look like a stubborn child. "Killing tourists would only bring the condemnation of the world down on them. That they would not want."

"Fool, they would not care. No, I am wrong. Our deaths are exactly what they would want. Last night the man who runs this hotel talked about how the rebels already had the support of many of the peasants. I was standing in the hallway in the dark trying to decide if I wanted to ask for a cup of tea and I overheard him talking to one of the waitresses, the young one with the long dark hair. Remember her?"

Iwakura nodded.

"He was telling her the rebels were growing stronger every day. The government has said many times the rebels are not strong, that they are no more than the buzzing of a few bees. However, if they kill some tourists that would show the people of Morazon how powerful they are and many more peasants would rally to their side. Then indeed they would be strong."

Her husband eased back on the bed and cautiously eyed his wife. Her fingers trembled and her chest heaved. Whispers of distant gunfire flicked at his ears. The need to speak with care was obvious.

"What you heard makes sense. We must be cautious." Moving his head slowly, he looked around the small room, evaluating. More sounds of gunfire drifted into the room, faintly, as though they came from some distance. Iwakura turned in time to see worms of fear wriggle across his wife's face. He spoke quickly, using words against the worms, trying to turn them out, drive them away.

"We can lock the doors and hide in here until this is all over."

"There is no use. We are going to die."

"Under the bed, we can hide under the bed. They will not know we are even here."

"The bullets will find us."

"The mattress will protect us." He spoke slowly, but steadily, looking directly into his wife's eyes, trying to convince her.

She turned from him, her eyes focusing somewhere he could not see. She was far away and yet at the same time still very much in the room. "They have mortars and missiles. Missiles powerful enough to shoot down helicopters and planes. Mattresses will not matter against mortars and missiles. Face it, husband, we are going to die, just as our child died."

Akko swung back into the room, her eyes settling on her husband's face, playing across it like a searchlight. It was as impassive as the sheer stone face of a cliff.

His lips were moving, but the words that escaped were no more than murmuring from an unrepentant sea, a soliloquy from stones. A weight was pressing against her, massive and unwavering, forcing her down deep inside herself. Staggering across the darkened room, she eased down onto the bed as gently as descending ash. Her husband was still talking, words slipping across his lips like shallow water flowing across smooth stones.

She understood nothing, cared less. A great weight was bearing down on her chest, crushing her breasts, forcing the air from her lungs. Akko could sense death closing in, coming at her from all sides, edging closer, emitting a dank odor. An almost overwhelming pressure to force herself from the bed and run across the room and down the hall and down the stairs and into the sunlight rose in her. She let it slosh around in her mouth, tasting the strange, exotic flavor before she tried to swallow.

She could not swallow the pressure, however, and wondered how long she could hold out. A page turned inside her mind and she could clearly see it was only a matter of time. Her husband reached through the dim light and touched her. His touch was no more than a puff of hollow wind.

"We are going to die, Iwakura; we are going to die." Tears streamed steadily down the woman's face. She was crying as though an underground spring that had bubbled inside her for years, hidden from her knowing, had suddenly thrust its way to the surface and was now running out her eyes.

"Akko, do not worry. There are soldiers here and more to come."

"How do you know?"

"I heard the officers talking."

"Perhaps they were lying."

She was going to die. She could feel it in her bones, spreading like a cancer of ice. Premonitions, her mother had called them. Visions which came like a chilling night wind, foretelling death and warning of imminent disaster. Iwakura could put on his brave face; she knew it was merely a performance staged for her.

Memories of her mother's visions rolled through her mind. Often, her mother had seen the faces of those for whom death was coming. She had told Akko of the deaths that the day would reveal, naming names and places, telling events that would unfold. Invariably, she had been correct in every detail. As a child, it seemed to Akko as though her mother had been able, in some inexplicable way, to read of these deaths in a newspaper only grownups could see. Now, in her own mind, Akko could see a face now that was marked for death. The eyes were stone; the lips formed the smiling rictus of a death mask. It was like staring into a mirror.

Twenty-one

Sweat trickled in his eyes and he blinked it away, keying the radio, trying to get it work. All morning he had been trying to contact Pena and Marichal. They were hours overdue and he saw no signs of their coming. Without them, taking Yuscarana would be a long, bloody, and difficult process. Holding it would prove impossible.

Only static spoke to him and for the tenth time that morning Carlos Geraldo cursed the penury of the revolution, at least for her soldiers of the line. He had heard that at the headquarters of the Revolución they had meat for the evening meal each night. For weeks, his men lived on weevil inhabited bread and overripe bananas. He had no vehicles, not even a decrepit jeep left over from some almost forgotten war on another continent. And now the fucking radio would not work.

No use to complain. The officious bastards who were running this clusterfuck would only tell him he had not kept it covered and the rain had gotten in. As usual, there would be a modicum of truth to their arguments. Jungle living was, by its very nature, a damp, miserable existence, certainly if you lived in the open and were constantly on the move.

Bursts of gunfire came to his ears, short, sporadic sounds that died as suddenly as they had arisen. Throughout the morning the paucity of gunfire had worried him. With so few men at his command, he had not expected to take Yuscarana quickly. Having to split his band had only exacerbated his problem. Reconnaissance patrols had informed him there were three main positions in Yuscarana to control: the hotel, where the *turistas* stayed and the officers visited when they were not on duty, the barracks, where the bulk of the soldiers were garrisoned, and the communications shack a few miles out of town. Carlos could recall when it had been a relay station for Telefonica Morazon. Shoving the radio into a tall bush shaped like a spider monkey, he rose and started running toward town. Judging from the lack of gunfire, the assault was going poorly. He cursed steadily under his breath as he jogged down the dirt road, sparing no one, including himself.

Twenty-two

He was all right now. Until the first shot he had been trembling, trying not to piss all over his own legs. The sound of gunfire had dispelled that crippling sensation, his legs had steadied, and he had been able to breathe again.

They were advancing now, working their way down the slope toward the communications shack. Made of corrugated metal, the shack shimmered in the sunlight. Glancing at it for more than a second caused a thousand black specks to dance before his eyes.

Others were moving down the slope with him, three men, no four. He could see them, creeping slowly, using whatever was growing as cover. Now and then, one paused to fire. They were not particularly good shots, especially when their arms trembled, but sometimes their bullets struck the shack with a satisfying ping. Surely, Felix thought, those bullets would penetrate the metal sheeting. Perhaps all the soldiers in the shack would be dead by the time he reached the base of the slope.

He had not yet fired his gun that morning. To tell the truth, he had fired it only a few times at the practice range outside their jungle camp. He did not like the loud bang or the kick of the gun, and he had never yet hit his target.

He was not creeping down the slope like the others, for he did not trust his legs. Instead, he was crawling as rapidly as he could, trying to use the bushes and second-growth trees for cover. Thorn bushes grew on the slope and they tore at his clothing and his flesh. Worms of blood trickled to a slow death on his face.

Maybe it was his imagination, but he sensed the man next to him giving him odd looks. Perhaps he had better fire his gun. He did not want them to think he was a coward, that he did not hate the soldiers of Gutierrez. Easing from behind a bush speckled with small, intensely yellow flowers, Felix dropped his chin and lifted the barrel of his gun. The sight at the end of the gun looked very far away. The metal shack seemed to have shrunk. Peering through the sight with his open right eye, he took a deep breath, willing his hands to be still. He squeezed the trigger. In the noise of the firing, he could not be certain if he hit the building or not, but the throbbing in his shoulder where flesh met the stock of the rifle was strangely satisfying.

Felix shot a quick glance at the man on his right. Surely, he must have seen the man around the camp, but could not recall his face. The man was fat; an inner tube of flesh bulged from under his shirt, drooped over his belt. Sunlight glittered on the balding crown of his head. The man smiled, revealing a mouthful of broken, blackened teeth. A warm feeling of camaraderie flowed through Felix. Now, for the first time, he truly felt like one of the rebels. It was as though now he actually belonged to the Revolución, to the universe of men. Euphoria mixed with blood in his veins and he felt invincible. He waved at the fat man with the bad teeth.

The man waved back, then scurried to another bush farther down the slope, wind-milling for Felix to come with him. Felix glanced at the shack. Sunlight glittered off the metal walls. It occurred to Felix that it must be incredibly hot inside. Nothing showed at either of the two small windows. No gunfire had come from the shack for some time. The fat man called to Felix to hurry. Felix recalled how Carlos had stressed that they must take the communications shack quickly, before the soldiers inside could make a call for reinforcements. The face of Carlos swam before him, pleading for every man to be brave for the revolution.

Again, the fat man called. The sunlight was so intense Felix felt that his brain was beginning to bake. He couldn't think. Breathing was difficult. Voices began to echo in his head, running together in a virulent cacophony of sound.

Voices of Carlos and the fat man, his mother and the priest in his village, and his boyhood friend Vincente, all blended together until he could no longer tell them apart. All of the voices were screaming, screaming at him to dash forward. Felix put his hands over his ears, but he could not silence the voices.

He scrambled to his feet. He felt quite tall and his legs seemed strangely distant. The ground seemed a long way off. He tried to look for the building, but all he could see was glittering light. Voices screamed at him. Felix screamed in return and began running down the hill. Wind was cool against his face and his blood sloshed against the inner walls of his skull. Screaming in the sunlight, he waved his rifle above his head like a trophy. The world spun wildly before him as the moment seemed to elongate almost to forever in his mind.

Felix could hear voices moaning in the night. A monstrous demon had wedged its head in his chest. Pain radiated from the insertion, spreading across his body like a tsunami. Darkness engulfed him.

~ * ~

The moaning voice was his; he realized that now. And the demon in his chest was a steel-tipped bullet. Night had not come, only the darkness of pain. He could feel sunlight burning

154

his face and wanted to roll over and crawl out of it. All he asked was to make it to the shade of a tree. Even a large bush would do. The pain was too great, however, too heavy for him to carry. So Felix lay on his back with his dark eyes closed, with sunlight baptizing his face, with only the jungle wind to lip cool kisses on his fever-hot face.

~ * ~

When the sun had been directly overhead, the fat man with the bad teeth had come back, towering over Felix like a giant tree. For a moment, Felix had been sure it was God standing over him, throwing blessed cool shadows across his burning face. Then the man had knelt beside him and brought his face so close that Felix could see his blackened and broken teeth and smell his fetid breath. His vision of God had merely been a joke.

The fat man had wanted to help Felix get to his feet so they could go to a medico, but Felix could feel he was all broken up inside, held together only by his skin, and moving would only hasten death. So he shook his head and cried no, no, no, no, no until the fat man nodded and stuffed a handkerchief into the hole on the left side of Felix's abdomen. Then, despite Felix's cries and protests, he had manhandled the boy to a crescent of shade thrown by old trees. After a little while, he had told Felix he had to leave him. The communications shack was too well-manned for him to take with only two men, especially when one of them, Diego, had a hand smashed by a bullet. He was going for more men while Diego and the other, whose name he had not heard, would keep the men in the shack pinned down. He would try to bring a medico, or at least some real bandages and antiseptic. Felix tried to smile, and they both pretended to believe.

Since then, Felix had been lying in the shade, drifting in and out of consciousness, listening for rifle shots that never came, watching shadows change shape – when he could open his eyes, waiting for darkness, waiting to die.

~ * ~

Thirst gripped him around the throat like an anaconda. He licked at his lips with a reluctant tongue. They were dry and cracked and reminded him of watering holes that dried up during the times when the rains did not come. In the south, where he came from, that did not happen often. Only twice could he recall seeing the shrinking, brown mud with the little remaining water slowly funneling into the sunbaked earth or evaporating into the high clear skies. Water hole remnants always made him think of cattle anuses. Felix tried to lift his head to look through a gap in the branches so he could see the sky. Pain coursed through his body. Groaning, he let his head fall back, wondering if he would ever again see either the curving blue of the sky, or the brown remnant of a dying water hole.

Twenty-three

Joe Moby stood at the doorway, looking back at the women, hesitant to leave. Mother and daughter sat beside each other on the bed, both faces turned toward the light drifting in through the window glass, as though it carried some element their bodies needed. The women appeared lost, as if they were the only two survivors of some monumental calamity, drifting through empty space toward an uncertain eternity.

As the gunfire had faded, screams and sobs had given way to silence. His wife was standing beside him and he could hear her soft breathing. Angling his neck, he covertly studied her face. Gray was more prominent in her hair than he had remembered and the crow's feet were etched deeper in the skin around her eyes. Yet those eyes were still that warm brown color he loved. Funny, Joe thought, how you could look at a person a thousand times a day for over thirty years and never see them truly.

Bowing his head, he whispered in her left ear. "Hate to leave them like this." His lips were so close to her ear that the words were as much caresses as syllables.

Scents of lilac, roses, soap, and sweet sweat coalesced in his nostrils and he pressed his lips to the soft spot on the back of her neck where her blouse gaped open. Kissing her always seemed to him like kissing spring.

"I know," she whispered, nodding at Trevor Samuels who sat in the only chair with a book spread open on his lap. Words on the visible pages of the book were arranged in the shape of poems. "I'm glad he came back, but I don't expect him to be much help."

"I agree," said Joe Moby. "I'd stay, but they may need me more downstairs. If this thing gets uglier, it may be every man on the ramparts." He looked down at his hands as if they were separate creatures. "Don't reckon I've forgotten everything I learned in Nam."

"I understand. You'd better go." She nodded at the two lost travelers. "I'll stay for a while, until they come back to us."

"You be careful."

"I will, and the boy may be more help than we think. I'm sure he's still in shock."

"I know that feeling," Joe said as his mind shifted to a different jungle, a different day of death.

Amy lifted her face to her husband and pressed her lips against his. "Go on now, Joe. The captain didn't seem to have many men. He may need you."

"Many? Hell, one good strong push and Yuscarana goes over like a domino, maybe the first of many, if the rest of Morazon is as poorly defended as this place appears to be. Remember the domino theory?" he asked, not really expecting an answer.

"Surely the man has more troops than what we've seen. I saw a couple patrolling on the way in and then there was the lieutenant last night. With two officers, there almost has to be at least a small garrison close by. If he can get them here..."

"Better go, honey. It's been quiet for a while."

"Yes, that worries me, too."

Joe let his fingers trickle down Amy's check. Like water over smooth stone, he thought. "Love you, baby," he said, and turned quickly, glancing at her face as he began moving.

"Love you, too," she whispered.

Joe Moby strode down the hallway, a hint of a smile tugging at the corners of his mouth. He felt young and vigorous and strong. Acting like a damn kid again, he thought, as he felt his smile broaden.

Twenty-four

Fried plantains and still warm bread and soft butter and sweet syrup and freshly squeezed orange juice and baked potatoes as big as a man's hand and juicy steaks two inches thick and bottles of cool red wine and Kentucky bourbon, plus coffee so hot that steam rose from the lip of the cup like it was coming out of the mouth of a volcano. Jesus the Pig licked his lips. Father above, but he was hungry. Nothing since supper last night except a pone of dry bread and a handful of pistachios scraped from the bottom of his pack.

Hunger was one thing, but thirst was another. Hours now in the broiling sun and not a drop to drink; he was going to die of thirst in this hellhole of a town. That was as plain as the hotel across the street. No telling how many of the soldiers of Gutierrez were in there. And he, Jesus, was out in the open with only a couple of men up the street and three or four more swinging wide to come at the hotel from the back. Alone for hours in the hot sun of Yuscarana. He moaned in masochistic self-misery. Everyone knew how damn hot the sun could be in Yuscarana. And him with no food or water; not even a good place to get out of the sun. Where was Carlos?

Blinking against the light, Jesus asked himself a question he knew he could answer. Was this any way to treat a loyal son of the *Revolución*? A veteran of many battles? A true friend of the peasants? Of course not! Where was Carlos? He had many things to tell that man.

As his anger grew, the temperature seemed to rise in response. First, he had been going to die of hunger. Then thirst. Now he was going to melt. Jesus ordered himself to think of something besides the injustices being done to him. However, the only thing on his mind besides food and water at that moment was women. Women of any age, shape, color – such factors didn't matter – not after so damn long.

Jesus shut his eyes and tried to think cool thoughts. Unable to unearth any, he instead focused on what he needed to do next. He remembered he had not fired his gun for some time. In fact, he had heard no firing for a long time. Where was Carlos? When did that sunbaked lizard plan on showing up? The attack was going nowhere.

Well, he mumbled to himself, never let it be said that Jesus let the *Revolución* down. Moaning, grumbling, cursing steadily under his breath, he crawled cautiously forward and eased his nose around the corner of the building. The hotel stared back at him with broken eyes. Jesus drew a bead on one of the few remaining panes of glass. Then he squeezed the trigger and watched the glass explode. Now I, Jesus, have again done my duty for the *Revolución*. Bring on the wine, and the beefsteaks, and the fat, bare-naked screaming women. Where the hell was Carlos?

Twenty-five

"Who through faith are shielded by God's power..." the words from Chapter 1 of 1 Peter kept bubbling up in his mind like gases rising from the bottom of the pool of a hot sulfur spring. He had seen one when he had once taken a busload of church youth on a trip to the American west. Where had that spring been? Yellowstone? That trip had been a long time ago and his mind wasn't what it had been in those days, even under the best of circumstances, and no one, not even a Unitarian, could argue with any degree of veracity that these were the best of times.

Reverend Thomas Malloy smoothed his hair with both hands, pushing it into a loosely formed duck tail. Always, he had been proud of his hair. A little vain, he would admit that, acknowledging that it was a sin, but, he would argue, as sins go, a rather small one. Anyway, there was the passage that said, "Let he who is without sin cast the first stone." And Reverend

Malloy had no desire to be a caster of stones. During his long ministry he found it was much more pleasant, not to mention rewarding, to be a breaker of bread.

As he turned to leave his small room, a flash of light caught his eye. He stopped and stared at the face staring back at him from the mirror. Perhaps there were a few more wrinkles than when he had left his home in Owl Creek on the eastern edge of Louisville to board the plane at Standiford Field. Certainly more gray and silver among the brown, not that he minded. More mature colors, as he referred to them when discussing such matters with his colleagues, lent him a distinguished air, one that tended to inspire confidence among parishioners and aided in loosening their checkbooks. Reverend Malloy always recommended the distinguished look to the younger members of the calling.

Sharp, staccato blasts of gunfire reached his room. These sounds seemed to come from the front of the hotel. He turned toward the gunfire. It was a sound he had been dreading since that awful incident in the dining room that morning. He had been holding out a faint hope that the shooting had been the act of a lone gunman, a peasant driven crazy by debt or death or disaster so personal that only he and God knew why. With the crackle of gunfire, he felt that hope fade.

They would be wanting him now. No, expecting him. In his mind he could see them, returning from their rooms where they had retreated earlier, to congregate in the lobby, seeking to draw support from the presence of other living souls, for, after all, if others lived it was possible for them to go on breathing, too. That was the way the human mind worked; he had studied it at seminary and read about it a hundred times since. Once or twice, he had even seen it in the flesh. Terrified people were not a pretty sight. Reverend Malloy could not fathom how they could be a thing of beauty and a joy forever to the Lord.

They could be demanding, too. The group, at least most of them, would be gathering in the lobby and looking to him for spiritual guidance in their times of tribulations, expecting him to produce divine intervention by direct prayer to their Heavenly Father, demanding he be at their call around the clock, whenever and wherever they needed him, until the crisis was over. Then, after a few effusive, yet hurried thanks, some hugs sandwiched around manly handshakes, a rare tearful "thank God," he would go back to being merely another tour guide, the one who happened to be there on the trip of all trips, the one who happened to be a retired man of the Lord.

Sighing loudly, Reverend Malloy slipped a hand inside the top drawer of his dresser and rummaged beneath his clean underwear, smiling as his fingers closed on smooth rounded glass. A sip would do the trick.

Paul had once written, "take a little wine for thy stomach's sake." Granted, the contents of the bottle were not wine and he was taking it more for his nerves than his stomach, but the principle was the same. Good old Saul of Tarsus would surely understand.

The reverend lifted the bottle, unscrewed the cap, raised the bottle to his lips, and took a medicinal sip. Whiskey ran cool and smooth down his throat, generating pleasant warmth in his stomach. After eyeing the amber liquid for a moment, he screwed the cap back on and slid the bottle back beneath his boxer shorts. Then he knelt and prayed to God for the right words to say and the strength for the ordeal that awaited. He prayed for several minutes.

When his mind was more at peace, he rose, undertook a final review in the mirror, picked up his black leather Holy Bible with the words of Jesus in red and the pages trimmed in gold, squared his shoulders, and started marching for God. Halfway to the staircase he found himself humming, "Onward Christian Soldiers."

Twenty-six

Liquid splashed against the side of a glass, the sound blatant in the late morning quiet, especially to ears straining to hear the next volley of gunfire. Lady Dianna Threlkeld wheeled around and glared at her husband.

Peering around the glass, Lord Threlkeld studied his wife's face, realizing after a couple of seconds that he hadn't truly looked at her in some time. Damn, but her face looked hard. Her bones seemed to protrude more prominently; the jaw line appeared more rigid than he remembered. Lifting the glass higher, he nodded at her in a mock toast, curled his arm, and brought the glass to his lips.

He allowed no more than a splash of the liquid against his mouth. A few drops slipped through the narrow gap between his lips and he savored their flavor on his tongue. He had no intention of getting a buzz this early; merely enjoy a sip or two to help the morning slide by. It promised to be an interesting day. God, but he was glad of that. Boredom, the great crippler of most adults, was killing him. Boredom was worse than cancer. At least with cancer he could undergo chemotherapy, or radiation, or take the latest miracle drug. Plus, he might receive a bit of sympathy.

As he swallowed, the thought occurred to him that his wife was beginning to resemble a statue. Perhaps she was turning to stone. The concept intrigued him and he played with it inside his mind for a time. Farfetched, but he appreciated the hypothesis. And there was evidence to support it; her heart had already solidified into granite. He chuckled at his own humor.

"What's so damn funny? Bullets flying everywhere, people getting their brains splattered all over their breakfast, armed rebels attacking, and you are laughing your fool head off. You must be drunk."

Donald Threlkeld, Sixteenth Lord of North Malverton, raised his glass to his lips and took a healthier sip. "No, my dear, I am not drunk. Yet."

Dianna Threlkeld stared at her husband, her eyes glittering like blue lake-ice. Time seemed to stretch like a rubber band. Quiet crept into the room and captured it.

We are frozen here in Yuscarana, frozen in time, Donald thought. We have become the statues of my mind. I have slipped a cog, he whispered to himself, not minding in the least.

Dust motes drifted in the light that shafted between him and his wife. Faint breathing was the only sound in the room. Time became an element of weight, a component of the universe that pressed down upon the linings of the mind. Pulses and heartbeats were actively discernible. A bird flew between the sun and their window, its shadow flashing across the floor.

"Bastard," Dianna Threlkeld said coldly.

Donald sipped again, mutely toasting the broken quiescence of the morning.

Lady Threlkeld brushed past him as she crossed the room, her high heels clicking. The door slammed behind her.

Lord Threlkeld felt his mind drifting and he settled in an easy chair, holding his glass carefully, studying the sunlight, and the shadows shifting in the wind.

Twenty-seven

Sucking air, Carlos Geraldo slowed his pace and tried to massage the stitch out of his side. His calves ached and his hamstrings were tight. Getting too old for this shit, he thought. Immediately, he castigated himself for his negativism, his acceptance of decline, his lack of loyalty to himself, and to the revolution. Carlos cursed with the little breath he had left and ordered his aching legs to move faster.

He was inside Yuscarana now, following a path made by animals. It was rough and uneven and he stepped on a stone that gave way, thrusting him forward. Wind-milling his arms, he stumbled on, gradually coming erect. Houses, low-slung, with crumbling edges and cracks in the adobe, rose before him. Stopping in the shade of the first one, Carlos leaned against the wall, luxuriating in the cooler darkness, wiping the sweat of his forehead with the back of a hand.

Gradually, his breathing returned to normal. He could hear gunfire in the distance. Not nearly enough shots for the attack to be going well. This day was not proceeding as he had planned. No reinforcements and no way of contacting them. Carlos Geraldo was tempted to curse again, but it seemed wiser to reserve his energy. It was beginning to look like a long day.

Carlos pushed himself off the wall and broke into a trot. Coming around the corner he could see the main street of Yuscarana flowing before him like the dry bed of an ancient river.

He could see the front of the hotel now, and most of one side. Almost all the windows in the front appeared to be shot out and the openings stared back at him like tunnels into another realm. Wondering how many guns awaited on the other side of the portholes, Carlos crouched low and curled into the street. Fronting the building to his left was a porch where a corner support post provided a slim column of safety. He could feel the involuntary contractions as his muscles flinched in anticipation of the impact of the bullet with his name on it.

Never had Carlos been a superstitious man, but all morning he had been sensing a strange presence. Quiet, too heavy for the street, ribboned with a sweet, damp heaviness, hung in the air. The taste of death was bitter on his tongue. Having tasted it many times, it was taste he knew well. The taste for death was a sure thing; once you had its flavor, it was yours forever. Carlos wondered why he had been cursed with the taste; then he wondered if he was tasting his own death.

Up the street, a gun blasted. He jerked his head in time to see Jesus pull back around the corner of a building. Carlos pointed his pistol at the window closest to him and squeezed the trigger, merely trying to draw fire. There was no response from either his shot or that of Jesus the Pig. Carlos backpedaled to the shelter of the building and listened. All he could hear was his own pulse in his ears. After counting to sixty, he began heading for a rendezvous with Jesus.

~ * ~

Carlos prayed as he covered the ground behind the buildings that separated him from Jesus, running hard enough to get where he was going expeditiously, but not so hard he had to gasp for breath.

It was cooler in the shallow shadows thrown by the buildings. A light breeze wafted across his face and played in his damp hair. For a few seconds it was as though he were a young boy in another world.

Then he rounded the corner and could hear the sound of men running and the hot violent Yuscarana morning rose up and smacked him between the eyes.

"Jesus," he called, "it's me, Carlos," letting the man know he was coming. As wild as Jesus was, he was as likely to shoot him.

Jesus turned his head and grinned at Carlos, exposing yellow teeth and a fat pink worm of a tongue. "Where have you been, Carlos? You've been missing all the excitement."

"Trying to call for reinforcements," Carlos panted.

"And they are coming when?"

Carlos shrugged as he sucked air into his lungs. It tasted warm, stale, and faintly metallic, as though the essence of gunfire had leached into the atmosphere. "I could not get through."

Now it was the turn of Jesus the Pig to shrug. He did so, accompanying the gesture with a meaningless extension of his smile. The bastards in charge of this revolution were total fuck-ups. Jesus doubted if they knew how to wipe their dirty assholes.

"*Bueno*, there will be more women and whiskey for us."

He was going to make a comment on the ancestry of the leaders of the revolution, but before he could launch into his speech, the sounds of men's feet and voices reached the two rebels. Moving as one, they leaned around the corner, eyes widening at the sight of the running soldiers.

Carlos groaned. "Damn, Tony and his men did not take the barracks, or even hold them in place."

Jesus spit in the dust and swung his rifle up. "Not the time for words, Carlos. It is the time for killing." He squeezed the trigger. All the soldiers kept running. There were at least ten of them, maybe twelve. Jesus cursed and took more careful aim. Before he could squeeze the trigger again, a bullet smashed into the building an inch from his head. Adobe snow showered down on his head.

Jerking his head back, he rolled his eyes at Carlos. His heart was doing somersaults in his chest. His elastic grin had stretched too thin. It felt like an embarrassing memory.

"My God, that bullet almost had my name on it," Jesus the Pig screamed. His eyes, which normally appeared half closed and small in the fleshy folds of his face, were now open wide, pulsating and throbbing as though preparing to lift off from his face.

Carlos gave Jesus a smarmy grin. "Only the good die young, you pig. You should float by two hundred years like you were a sailboat pushed by a strong sea breeze."

"Asshole."

"Save the words, we have no time to waste. Get your fat ass around to the other side of this building and see how many soldiers of Gutierrez you can pick off. I'll blast at them from here. Now go." For inspiration, Carlos Geraldo prodded Jesus the Pig with the toe of one of his boots.

Mumbling words about the mother of Carlos, Jesus started running in his splay-legged style, leading with his gut. Carlos watched the broad backside of the man who thought like an animal until it rounded the corner of the building. Then he whirled and stuck his pistol around the corner, where he snapped off a blind shot at the hotel.

With his back against the warm wall, he counted to five. No return fire. Carlos eased away from the building, staying as deeply as possible in its shadows. He peered down the street. Soldiers were still running. Some were very close. One was curving onto the narrow dirt alleyway that ran next to the hotel.

Carlos raised his pistol and took careful aim at a tall solider who seemed to sway as he ran, as though he had recently disembarked from a deep-water ship and was still plagued with sea legs. Carlos squeezed the trigger. Momentarily deafened, he stared at the running man. He was still running, so close now that Carlos could see dirt streaks on his face. Carlos squeezed the trigger again and again and again. The man kept running toward Carlos for a few strides, then veered right and pounded down the alley. Cursing, Carlos swung the end of his pistol until it pointed at a fattish soldier and pulled the trigger. The plump soldier's hat went flying off. Without his hat the soldier looked enough like the man who had once taught science to Carlos to be that man's brother. Carlos fixed the round black hole of his pistol squarely in the middle of the fat man's forehead. He let his breath out slowly and squeezed the trigger as gently as if it had been the forefinger of a baby.

The hammer clicked. Damn, Carlos thought, out of bullets. He dug in the left front pocket of his pants for bullets, feeling the sweat on his face, waiting for a bullet to smash into his body.

By the time he reloaded, only three soldiers were still running. One soldier lay face down in the street, a pool of dark liquid spreading out from his face, his cap still atop his head. Carlos swept his eyes across the three remaining runners. A young face, replete with pimples and the start of a shoe brush mustache swam into focus. He aimed carefully, watching the face bob like a fishing cork. He fired.

The boy screamed and fell down. He rolled over twice, then he rolled up into a sitting position. A look of great surprise crinkled his face. He looked down at his left arm. Blood poured from his bicep and dripped onto the asphalt.

The boy lifted his eyes and stared at the face of Carlos Geraldo. The brown eyes of the soldier seemed to have a hypnotic effect. As Carlos watched, the young soldier pushed himself off the road with his good arm. He rose slowly, an old man ascending. For at least ten seconds the soldier stood swaying. To Carlos, he looked like a tree swaying before a rising wind.

Then, almost as though he had run out of other options, the soldier began to walk down the alleyway. He walked quite slowly, a hand across the wound – blood seeping between the fingers. Carlos did not fire again, although he could not say, even to himself, why. After the soldier was gone, the street was empty except for the young soldier's hat and the man lying face down in the dark shimmering pool.

Suddenly there was shouting down the street and the sounds reminded Carlos of the exposed nature of his position. He stepped back behind the building on trembling legs. Cold sweat poured down his face as though an icicle was melting on his forehead. Dull anger pounded at his temple.

Twenty-eight

She stood in the smoke-colored shadows at the top of the stairwell, keeping well back from the edge, leaning forward only when a sound from the lobby floor attracted her attention. Nosey? That, she would admit. However, she didn't want to die, certainly not this morning.

Voices now, curving up from below like auditory smoke. Lady Dianna stepped from the deepest of the shadows and leaned cautiously against the banister. When temptation grew too strong, she inclined her head over the smooth wooden railing. Her hair fell forward across her face like a curtain of strands of dark beads. Pulling it back with one hand, she peered at the two men standing near the front of the lobby.

Light from the gap-toothed windows highlighted their faces, and in that moment they looked like saints in an El Greco painting. Then they turned their heads and illusion became reality, or at least a different illusion, and she could see they were the two army officers she had noticed in the hotel the night before. The older one glanced up and she shrank back, half convinced he had seen her; although why that should bother her was not clear. For the moment she wanted to remain the observer.

The officer looked away and she expelled her breath, realizing for the first time she had been holding it. The men stepped away from the window into a different light. It softly caressed their faces, as though this morning were the first ever on Earth. The young officer looked up and Lady Threlkeld noticed again how beautiful he was. His hair glistened and the line of his lean jaw might have been sculpted by Michelangelo. His body looked hard, and when he turned his head, lights glittered in his eyes. Leaning further into space, she could feel the railing pressing against her breasts. She was moist; she wanted him.

Twenty-nine

In the distance there was the sound of gunfire, heavier than it had been for some time. Captain Morales carefully tapped the ash off his cigar and positioned it in the ashtray. The ashtray was formed from thick green glass and Poncho always kept it on the check-in counter. It had been there for so long that neither Poncho nor his wife, Juanita, could recall where or when they had purchased it. The ashtray had assumed a smooth, glassy permanence in the life of the old hotel. Cigar smoke rose in a gray-blue plume above it.

Morales listened as he walked across the lobby floor. Gunfire seemed to be coming from the west. Both the barracks and the communications shack lay in that direction. Standing before a window, Morales forced his face against one of the few remaining sections of glass.

He could see nothing except the empty street and the blank-eyed buildings on the other side. No rebel faces sneered back at him and no rebel bullets hummed in the sunlight.

Morales edged right, curving his neck, looking west, feeling the hair on the back of his neck bristle.

He could make out only the curving snake of the road running to the end of Yuscarana and beyond, slicing between two green masses of encroaching jungle until it blended into the hills and disappeared as if the black and cracking asphalt had been swallowed whole. He couldn't see either the barracks or the communications shack, but he knew where they were and he looked first toward the communications shack. Seeing no movement, he looked a few degrees to the south toward the barracks.

Ants, a small army of them, swarmed over a low hillock, heading toward him. In seconds they had grown from ants to grasshoppers, then they grew larger, becoming men, his men, running hard, running for their lives. As he watched, one of them flung his arms skyward, stumbled, then pitched forward. He did not get up. Morales let out the breath he had been holding and became instantly conscious of the fingers on his right hand opening and closing on the handle of his pistol. Staring at the fallen man, he cursed, then said three Hail Marys.

Now he could see men's faces, and their fear. "They're coming, Lieutenant, the men from the barracks are coming," he shouted without turning his head. He waited for more shots, but none came. Morales turned his head, his fingers closing firmly on his gun, dragging it out of his holster.

His eyes swept the buildings across the street, not lingering or focusing, but taking the panoramic view, picking up shapes, lights, textures, and movements; a thousand elements cascading against the synapses. Images blurred as though he were driving by in a fast car. Captain Morales was searching only for something that seemed unusual, out of place. Something glittered suddenly, glittered where there was no glass, and Morales stilled his head and swung the gun up.

It was no more than sunlight striking metal where there shouldn't be any metal. Morales peered across the street. The metal protruded from deep shadow. All he could see was what appeared to be a few inches of blue-gray polished steel. The captain took careful aim and squeezed the trigger. In the echo of the discharge, he eyeballed the shadows where the polished metal had been. It was no longer there.

He could sense the presence of someone standing beside him. He turned his head ninety degrees.

"Lieutenant, they are coming."

The lieutenant was peering over the captain's head. "I see them. They are the men from the barracks. Did you shoot at a rebel?"

"I shot at something. I could only see metal and thought it might be the end of a rifle. Worth wasting a bullet on, anyway." Morales grinned at the junior officer. "I'm not a great shot, certainly not with a pistol at such a distance, but perhaps I might get lucky."

The captain straightened and eased the pistol back into the holster. "Go, and make sure that our lookouts don't shoot our own men. Before this is over, we will need every man."

Thirty

Was he still alive, or had he died? Felix was no longer sure. A great warmth had encompassed his body and he seemed to be floating in an ocean darker and thicker than water. Waves of pain rose in his body, or his corpse, crested, then passed, only to rise again. Perhaps he was dead, the rebel, who was really no more than a boy, thought. Perhaps pain still existed after the final crossing and it was only his soulless corpse that lay in the grove of trees.

The sun had moved fractionally across the sky. He could tell because at one time his entire body had been shaded and now sunlight highlighted the toes of his boots. Suddenly it seemed important to the boy to know if he was alive or dead. His brain sent a message to his toes and they wiggled feebly in response. Alive then, the boy thought, uncertain whether to be glad or disappointed. He supposed that he should be grateful, but then the pain rose higher and he moaned, all thought obliterated. Then there was only darkness.

From a flat brown rock two feet away from the inert body, a green lizard with bulging amber eyes watched the boy. The boy and the lizard were both very still.

~ * ~

Thirsty, oh merciful God but he was thirsty. Desire for water had been slowly consuming him, moving through his body like quicksand, inching out from his throat, creeping across and up and down and around his body until it seemed that even the linings of his bones screamed for water. Surely, he could withstand even the awful grinding pain if only he could slake his monstrous thirst.

At last, the day had begun to die. He had begun to believe it never would, that this day had evolved into eternity, the day the world decided not to end.

Only now, the world had changed its mind. In those interludes when the pain spasms paused, he could see the angle of the sun was sharper now, slanting viciously against his scorched face as it slid slowly toward the horizon he could no longer see. A great weakness had overcome him and he was no longer able to raise his head. Not that it mattered. No longer had he any desire to see the horizon, or anything else. All that was of even the most infinitesimal importance was that he be pardoned from his pain and that water flow over his parched lips. With swollen tongue, he licked at the cracked flesh; it felt as though sandpaper were rubbing against his flesh.

Now and then, the boy could hear sporadic bursts of gunfire. When these coincided with his rare moments of lucidity, he realized his companions were attacking the soldiers in the town. He wondered if any of them would make the effort to come for him. The fat man had promised, but by now he might be dead. A fly buzzed at the boy's face, then settled down on one cheek and began a slow walk toward an open, fearful eye. The fly did not bother the boy any more than the thought that his companions might never come for him. He only wanted water, water and relief from the pain.

Flies and rebels were now merely abstractions in an uncaring universe.

Thirty-one

The sound of a man running broke his train of thought and the Reverend Thomas Malloy paused in the middle of his prayer and eased one eye open.

Beyond the small flock huddled before him in a corner of the hotel lobby, he could see the young officer headed toward the back of the building. Reverend Malloy wondered what had happened, what new disaster had befallen them. It was all getting to be too much, far more than he could cope with.

Whiskey would help, he opined to himself. First, however, he needed to finish the prayer. He could hear the shuffling of the people before him as they grew restless, confused by the length of his pause. He took a deep breath. Help me, God, he prayed silently.

Aloud he said, "We began our prayer service by reading from the Bible the Twenty-third Psalm, that passage that has given mankind succor and comfort for generations. Now, with our heads bowed before the Almighty and our eyes closed so we can see Him as He comes to each of us in the way we need Him most, let us join together and recite in unison that great prayer His Son, the blessed Redeemer, the great Comforter, taught us."

A lump was forming inside his throat and the reverend choked it down. Then he licked his lips and began. "Our Father, Who art in heaven, Hallowed be thy name." One at a time, in a ragged chant, the others joined in. Some asked to be forgiven for their sins, others their trespasses. All prayed with eyes squeezed tightly shut, sweat beading their brows, and legs that trembled.

Thirty-two

Jerking back the covers, the seventh and current president of Morazon sat up straighter in bed. A figure, backlit by the hall light, stepped into the room. For a moment it was merely a body outlined by light, without face or features, advancing on him like an apparition. President Gutierrez, not unfamiliar with voodoo, considered the possibility that Queen Maria had sent him a messenger from the dark side. Then the apparition spoke and Gutierrez recognized his aide, Colonel Francisco.

"I regret disturbing you so early. However, there is trouble, Señor Presidente."

"Trouble," the president croaked, "trouble where?"

Colonel Francisco took off his cap and tucked it under his arm with a noticeable degree of formality. "We are receiving scattered reports from all over the country. Several attacks appear to have been initiated at roughly the same time. Most have been beaten back, but one area has called for reinforcements. They report they are under attack from all sides."

President Gutierrez could feel his stomach churning. In fact, he could hear it. He hoped the colonel could not. "Who is calling for reinforcements?" he asked in a loud voice, trying to cover the rumbling emanating from his gut.

"Captain Morales, from Yuscarana."

"Morales, that name is familiar., Yes, I remember him. A good man. And Yuscarana is vital. Morales must hold Yuscarana. Get him on the phone, Colonel. I will direct this operation myself."

Thirty-three

Between the pantry shelves the air was dark. The pantry was adjacent to the kitchen, under the back stairs that the maids used to reach the second floor. Shaped like a wedge of cheese, it was wider at the opening, gradually narrowing and growing darker as it burrowed beneath the stairs until it ended abruptly in a flat darkness. Only a single sixty-watt bulb hanging naked from the ceiling provided light beyond that spilling in from the kitchen. Holding a jar of pickles she had put up last summer, Juanita Herrera leaned against a shelf lined with canned goods as she peered through the dimness at her husband. In the poor light he does not look so old, she thought. In fact, if I squint and pretend a little, he looks almost like a boy. Aloud she said, "The Revolución has come to Yuscarana after all, husband. You said it would not come. I can hear the shooting in the streets this very moment. Are we going to die, Poncho? Are we going to die today?"

Poncho Herrera rubbed his luxuriant mustache as he stared at his wife. In the semi-darkness her face was a pale moon rising. Worry, fear, and doubt trembled in her voice. For months he had been assuring her that Yuscarana was too small, unimportant, and out of the way to warrant more than a cursory glance from the rebels. Not that he had believed his own words. What he believed was not important. What counted was that Juanita not be alarmed. Since the death of their child several years ago, she had been given to moods and tears and collapses.

He had not wanted to upset her, yet he had not lied to her. Yuscarana was small and not near any important road, military installation, or source of water, oil, or critical food supply. Poncho, however, was no longer young and naïve. Plus, he kept his eyes and ears open. He knew that none of what he had told his wife in an effort to comfort precluded an attack by the rebels. They were bastards, bastards who had killed his cousin, Manolito, and carried his niece off into the jungle. Never had she been seen again.

He counted in his head—that had been over seven months ago. His blood pressure was rising; the pulse in his temple had begun to pound. Poncho Herrera had it from more than one unimpeachable eyewitness that his niece had screamed and kicked and begged to be let go. Tirina had been fifteen years old, a beautiful child with eyes like her mother's, large and dark and full of dancing lights. He struggled to choke down his rage.

"No, Juanita, we will not die today. Are there not many soldiers here? Is not Captain Morales a good leader?"

"And how many revolutionaries are there, husband? Can you say?" Her fingers rubbed against the smooth glass of the jar as though it were a container of magic.

"You already know I cannot say how many rebels there are in Yuscarana. So why do you ask the question? Do you derive pleasure from pointing out my weaknesses? No, I do not know how many rebels are here today, but I do have it on good authority that deep down most of the rebels are cowards. Time and time again, the papers have noted how they fled in the face of fire from the brave soldiers of Morazon."

"Poncho, why do you always believe what you read in those papers of yours?"

In the near darkness he shrugged. "They must contain truth or the government would shut them down."

"The government runs them. Why should they shut them down?"

"I will not argue. I must get back to the lobby. Captain Morales may need my help until his men arrive."

One hand lifted away from the jar and traced the worn smooth paths down one side of her husband's face. She could feel the roughness of the day's whiskers, and she wondered if he would live to shave them off again, or if she would be alive to feel his face another day.

"Will you be able to pull the trigger of your shotgun, husband? Will you be able to kill a man? I know you say you can do what you have to do, but can you really, truly?"

There were many words Poncho wanted to say, words of love, reassurance, and comfort, words of truth, and words that were lies disguised as promises, guarantees. He took a deep breath, only to find he could not speak. Instead, he kissed his wife's cheeks as he ran the fingers of his free hand through hair that hung well below her shoulders and had once been black. A lump filled his throat until it was difficult for him to breathe. When the lump would not go down, he gave his wife a final kiss, turned, and walked out of the darkness into the hot light. The shotgun seemed inordinately heavy.

Thirty-four

Beneath her left breast her heart was pounding, beating rapidly, skipping a beat when a door slammed or the cook clanged one metal pan against another. In the subdued light of the alcove, she could see her white blouse rise and fall. Weakness ran down her legs as though she had lost control of her bladder and the muscles in her thighs felt as though they were turning to strands of cooked spaghetti. A disconcerting lightness filled her head as she leaned against the plaster wall for support, listening to the sounds of men running and shouting, praying for an ocean of silence.

Shouts and the footsteps pulsed closer. More shots were being fired now: across the street, in the street, from the alleyway, within the courtyard. Gunfire buzzed at her from all angles like a hive of angry wasps. Uncontrollable trembling seized the muscles of her legs and they gave way beneath her. She sat down, a quivering clump in a dark corner where dust collected and house spiders spun their webs.

Angry steps pounded closer. A man shouted. Words banged against her ears like waves from a violent sea. She threw her hands against her ears and shut her eyes until she could see stars in the blackness. Her body shivered as though jungle fever had taken possession.

A shadow she never saw fell across her. As her shivering faded, she became aware of another's breathing, counterpoint to her own. She eased one eye open, then the other.

A man towered above her, his face dark under his cap, nose and lips protruding from the shadows. She blinked and knew the face; it was the young lieutenant. Maria could not recall his name. He stretched out a hand and she grasped it, smiling in relief as he pulled her up. On her feet, the top of her head reached the bottom of his chin. Her eyes stared at his chest.

"What are you doing here?"

"I do not know. There was gunfire and that *turista Notre Americano* was killed right before me at the breakfast table. May God have mercy. I was so frightened I ran without thinking. Then I was in here and it was darker and quieter, as though I were out of all the fighting and killing. But just now there was more shooting, very close, just beyond the walls."

Maria could hear her words coming faster and faster, spinning and whirling inside her head until she no longer knew what she was saying. She made her lips quit moving and stared down at the floor. It looked far away.

The lieutenant was standing very close to her. Maria could hear him breathing. His fingers brushed against her bare arm.

"Yes, there was more shooting. Our men were coming in from the barracks and some of the rebels started shooting at them."

"Were any killed?" She spoke before she thought and instantly wished she could call back the words. She had asked on impulse. Maria realized that she truly did not want to know. If someone else did not speak the death words, then they would not be reality.

The lieutenant was silent. She glanced at his face. He was looking straight ahead, staring at the red and white curtains covering the one small window. His eyes had a faraway look, as though he were looking over a great stretch of distance, or peering into the past. Cheekbones pressed outwards against his flesh and the line of his jaw was hard. A pure heat seemed to burn within his dark eyes. Maria thought he looked handsome, and said a quick prayer that his blood would never stain his uniform.

The lieutenant swallowed. His tongue licked at the center of his thin top lip. "Most of the men made it to the hotel in safety. However, I saw at least one man go down. Others may have fallen. I'm on my way now to check on them and get them to their positions."

He adjusted his cap as though he were leaving. Maria did not want him to go. Within his presence she felt safe. She tugged at his shirt, shocked at her own boldness. "Will the rebels attack again?"

"Almost certainly, unless our reinforcements arrive before they are ready."

"More soldiers are coming?" She felt her heart pulsate with hope.

"Captain Morales has made the request."

The lieutenant did not say any more. He knew how hopeful his words must sound, and how hollow they might prove. To deny the girl hope would be cruel, he thought. If the reinforcements came, he would have saved her a great deal of worry. If the message had not made it through to headquarters, or if headquarters had no men to send, or if the reinforcements were ambushed on their way to Yuscarana, it might not matter anyway.

Gunfire dragged Lieutenant Escobar back to the reality of the morning. Gently he pulled his sleeve from the girl's fingers. "I must go now," he said, looking into the girl's face. She is quite pretty, he thought. There were words he wanted to say, but he did not say them. Instead, he pressed the tips of four fingers against one of her cheeks. Her skin was warm and soft.

A gun sounded in the courtyard and a man shouted in the alleyway. Abruptly the lieutenant pulled his fingers away, turned, and ran out of the alcove and down the narrow dark back hallway.

Thirty-five

Breaking off from the herd of men moving before him like frightened wildebeests, Tony cut across a small pasture and over a mound of earth that rose from the flatness like a loaf of baking bread. On the other side of the rise, he picked his way through a patch of rocky ground until he was running between two lines of sutra nut trees, their canopy full and green above him, the nuts thick. Deep shade covered the dirt path paved with the cracked shells of nuts that had fallen in prior years and never been collected. The footing was unsteady, but it was cool in the dimness, and quiet. He could hear himself think.

Tony knew men referred to him as the demented one. He didn't mind the term, viewing it as giving him not only a certain status, a label of respect, but also an advantage when doing battle with men who knew him. Thinking he was crazy, they could never with confidence rely on any logical progression of thought to plan a defense or launch a counterattack.

He freely admitted that in the heat of battle there was nothing he would not do. Some of this behavior might indeed be temporary insanity, a term the doctor from the medical center had once used, but the majority of the bizarre action was precipitated by the fact that he no longer cared. When a man no longer cares whether he lives or dies, and actually longs for death in a way so secret and subtle that he can glimpse it himself only as though from a great distance through a clinging fog, his actions are of no consequence. He can run headlong into machine gunfire, hold a grenade with the pin pulled to the nine count, walk boldly in the night camp of the enemy with his head up and his eyes and ears open.

Being demented had its place, but Tony could still think and act in a manner many would view as logical and all would acknowledge was effective. He was thinking now as he ran, his mind moving in rhythm to his footsteps, planning when and where and how he would attack next. Carlos knew he was a good, seasoned fighter, and that he did his best work in a solitary fashion. Therefore, Carlos often left him alone in battle. Tony viewed this freedom as a mark of respect and, consequently, reflected his own style of honor back to his chieftain. He did his best for Carlos, and for the cause, although he liked to think he would have done so under any circumstances.

Half lost in the workings of his mind, Tony was startled by the sudden blast of sunlight that struck his face. He hadn't noticed the parallel lines of trees were coming to an abrupt end and he was startled to find himself running across open ground. I will have to maintain better focus, he told himself as he sprinted for a small concrete block building. I could easily be killed here on this stupid patch of overgrown grass, he thought. Would I care, truly? I do not honestly know, he admitted as he covered the final yards of open space.

Thirty-six

Sounds reached her, strange, distorted, exceedingly distant, transmitted from another planet, passing through radiation belts, meteor showers, and the tails of comets. Once, she thought she heard the sound of her own name. She had rolled over then, burying her face in her pillow.

She seemed to have lost the ability to keep track of time, so she turned over and looked at her watch. It was a small, round, white-faced watch on a gold band with diamond chips marking the hours. Her husband had given it to her.

But for what? For a moment, Sharon couldn't remember and a scream began to rise in her throat. Then the memory of the restaurant with the dark wooden floors and the metal fish swimming across smooth seawalls the color of warm butterscotch floated across her mind and the nascent panic died.

It had been their anniversary; which one she could not recall. Candlelight had flickered on their corner table and from the far end of the shell-shaped room a trio had poured forth a cool jazz concoction.

He had liked the arrangements, the mellow rhythms, and the sudden atypical notes that changed the flow and shifted your mind. She had loved the tall blue vases, the chattering parrot, even the angel fish that swam in the aquarium shaped like a sunken ship.

They went only on occasions special enough to warrant the pureness of the pleasure. After every meal they had gone to the Bentley Hotel, having earlier procured the presidential suite, and made love until they collapsed in each other's arms, exhausted, satiated, in love with each other and life... if only for a few hours.

Sunlight and the sounds of the city had been their wakeup call on those special days that followed those special nights, and the thought that they would never again hear them together hit her with the force of a brick falling from a great height. Rolling over, she stared at the ancient watermarks on the ceiling while tears rolled down her face like tropical rain and her body convulsed.

Thirty-seven

"You were in the armed forces of the United States?"

"Served a tour in 'Nam."

"Then you are familiar with firearms? You know how to use them?"

Joe Moby smiled, no more than a slight upturning of the lips. "I can take care of myself."

Gunfire blasted from across the street and both men ducked and turned their heads. Joe Moby peered out the window, trying to catch a glimpse of sunlight flashing off metal, or the telltale movement of a shadow that should not have moved. The intensity of the sunlight was too much, however. Though mid-afternoon had come and gone, the street remained saturated with a blinding light. Blinking, he glanced at the man who stood beside him. Stubble had begun to show along the line of the man's jaw and in the hollows of his cheeks. His face was placid, but tiny stress fissures spread from the corners of his eyes.

The American cleared his throat. "This day is beginning to stretch a touch long, Captain. Thought I might lend a hand, maybe give one of your men a break. That is if you want me, and if you have a spare weapon."

Captain Morales stared at the face of the *turista* before him. His first inclination was to thank the man, but reject his offer. Not one to trust men he had not personally trained, the captain was doubly suspicious of a foreigner and a civilian. Still, the man was right about one thing – the day had begun to assume the characteristics of chewing gum, stretching until it seemed that it surely must snap.

It was the imagination coupled with the waiting that made it seem everlasting. Plus, he had lost three men already, one killed and one wounded on their way from the barracks, with the third man being shot just above his right ear an hour ago when he had gotten careless and a sniper had been alert. Furthermore, there had not been even a message from the men at the communications shack on the hill. Perhaps they were under attack. They might be circling around to attack the rebels from the rear. Prone to assume the worst, Morales figured those men were either dead or running away. He wasn't counting on reinforcements any time soon.

The man before him was an enigma. Middle-aged, with that certain softness age brings to every man, he was far too old for a soldier. Plus, he was not a man of Yuscarana, or even Morazon, so his heart surely held no passion for the forces of Gutierrez.

Still, this *norteamericano* standing calmly before him seemed a sane man, little disturbed by the violence of the day. Surely, Morales thought, this man undoubtedly wished to see the sun set that evening and desired to watch it rise in the morning. Yes, this man must want to live to hunt again, or fish, or read Hemingway, or watch Bogart, or smoke a Cubano, or make love to his wife.

Morales sensed these things. He almost always trusted his intuitions, his gut feelings, as General Urbana so indelicately expressed them. This knack for seeing through the skin and muscle to the heart and soul of a man had played a vital part in his rise to captain. Beyond all those things was the simple truth that every man had the right to defend himself and those he held dear. Captain Morales would deny no man that right.

Smiling faintly, he nodded at the *Americano*. "Very well, Señor ..."

"Moby."

"*Sí*, Señor Moby, the official army of Morazon, which is still loyal to President Gutierrez, will accept your generous offer. Volunteers are rare these days. We shall certainly find a place for you. I spoke a moment ago of a wounded man. He is in room number four. His rifle should be with him. Go and tell him I said for him to give it to you. Then come back to the lobby. You can stand in the center with me."

Captain Morales turned and looked into the main street of Yuscarana. Jagged shadows had begun to infiltrate the sunlight.

"Unless I have misread the situation, we will soon need every man at the barricade."

The captain continued to stare into the street as if a message lay there waiting for the proper moment to open its secret. He did not speak again. Joe Moby turned and walked toward the main hallway and Room 4.

Thirty-eight

She sat quietly in a high-backed chair on the landing, the lobby spread out before her. Again and again, she slid one palm across the smooth wood as though it were a talisman she was rubbing for luck.

Fingers of the hand not stroking the wood caressed the cool smoothness of a cut-glass tumbler. Lady Threlkeld had begun her vigil with the tumbler so full of whiskey that when she sat down a few drops sloshed out of the glass, falling like amber raindrops against the curving flesh of her hand. For a moment she had stared at them. Then she had licked them off.

Now, as the shadows fell like benevolent gargoyles on the living and the dead of Yuscarana, and those who were somewhere between, only a small thin pool of whiskey remained.

Lifting her eyes from the lobby floor, she peered at the remnants. She considered refilling her glass, but that would have required her to leave her chair and the action below. Even with its padded seat cushion covered in red Chinese velvet, the chair was not comfortable. Still, she had grown accustomed to it and felt a great reluctance to leave. Dianna Threlkeld did not want to miss anything, most of all that delicious young lieutenant.

Thirty-nine

Jesus crawled along the shadow line. Here, in the darkness cast by an old store that had once sold mining hats, picks and shovels, and promises of gold, he felt safe, imaging himself one with the thickening shadows and the gathering darkness.

He was glad to be moving after a long afternoon huddled against the side of a building with Carlos, the sun pressing down on them like iron. At intervals, he had crept to the edge of the building, flung himself around the corner and snapped off a quick shot. He had no illusions that his bullets had done more than keep the soldiers in the hotel honest, and afraid. That was enough. Experience had shown him fear worked on men like a purgative, leaving them weakened, dowsing their desire for battle.

For several minutes now there had been no shooting. In the cone of silence that had descended on the side street where he crawled through the dust, he could hear a growling in his gut. Since noon, all he had eaten had been a handful of raisins and a narrow strip of dried beef. The last of the warm water that tasted faintly of metal had been gone from his canteen for over an hour. A man who needed his creature comforts, Jesus crawled faster.

At the end of the side street he could see a final patch of daylight. Thirty yards beyond that daylight the hotel stood silently waiting. Within its walls he was certain were sides of beef hanging in the pantry, bottles of wine racked in the cellar, and women of all ages and sizes and shapes. Jesus the Pig felt his penis grow hard. He licked his dusty lips as he crawled toward daylight. The gurgling in his gut grew louder.

~ * ~

Scents of horses and cattle, oiled leather, grain and hay, old wood and dust, and manure filled his nostrils as he climbed. The barn looked old, but the ladder that led to the loft was solid beneath his feet and nailed tightly to wooden cross beams.

As he climbed, Tony the Demented felt the strange sensation of being onboard a ship of sail, rising and falling on a great sweep of blue-green ocean. It seemed to him that he had climbed the tall masts of ships a thousand times before, and he wondered if in another life he had been a sailor.

Glancing upwards where the beams ran like ebony fingerprints across the V of the ceiling, he could not see the loft floor and was tantalized by the impression he was climbing a ladder to heaven. A dimly lit heaven, one smelling smelled of oats and aged horse sweat. One where dust floated in sallow light shaped like eternal apostrophes.

Then he ran out of rungs and his head popped over the loft floor like an ejaculated champagne cork. Swinging his legs over the top, Tony crawled through hay that still smelled faintly of clover, his rifle banging against his back and the hotel swimming in and out of focus like a mirage through the open ventilator window.

Rough straw poked his bare arms, rustling like a dry wind rising. Then there was a sudden sharp piercing cry and a black wedge whirled furiously out of the darkness and went shrieking across the loft. Turning his head, he followed the swooping dives of the barn swallow until it disappeared in the shadows at the far end of the barn.

The heat of the day had settled among the rafters of the old barn and by the time Tony had traversed the loft floor his face was slick with sweat and a wet streak ran down the middle of his back. Sweat dripped under his arms, slid down his ribs, and pooled between his legs. Though the wind had paused, by the window it was a few degrees cooler. There, he lay on his belly in the hay and pushed his nose out the window.

The air had gone suddenly very hot and still as it does before a storm and he could hear the rustle of mice in the hay and the cries of the barn swallows as they dove from the eaves. Below, off to his right, horses snorted or stamped their feet. Gunfire from the far side of the hotel sounded like little boys' firecrackers.

Unstrapping his rifle, Tony swung it in front of him. Wiping the sweat off his face with the palm of one hand, he jammed the butt of the rifle against his right shoulder. Squeezing his left eye shut, he sighted down the barrel of the gun, swinging it in slow motion from window to window. The instructor Carlos had brought to camp a few months ago had told him to keep both eyes open when he fired, but Tony had learned to shoot with his left eye closed; he had always shot with his left eye closed, and he didn't see any point in changing. A man was surely as dead when you shot him with one of your eyes open as with two. Besides, he had not liked the instructor. Something about the man had been faintly holier than thou. Tony's finger tightened on the trigger as he imagined the sight at the end of his rifle squaring up in the center of the man's bony face.

~ * ~

There was a thickness and a stillness to the air as if the particles had begun to coalesce into a new form. Pale light

203

drifted in through grimy windows as though the journey had worn out the vibrancy of the color. Hundreds of dust particles floated aimless through the air as he passed down the hall.

There was a quiescent quality to the old hallway, as though it had been through a tremendous upheaval and now was lying fallow before the next invasion of turmoil. Echoes of his footsteps reverberated off the walls, loud in the aged silence.

Why was he walking down the hall? His intention had been to join the captain and the other soldiers in the lobby, but at the top of the stairs, for reasons he couldn't comprehend, he had turned and walked down the hallway to the end. There he had gone through an archway and climbed the stairs to the fourth floor, arriving sweating, with his breath coming in short hard huffs.

Since then, he had been walking up and down the hall. Now he turned and entered a room at random. Through the windows he could see the rear of the hotel. Crossing the wooden floor, he flung himself face down on the bed. Dust rose, hung quivering in the air, then fell like brown snow across the back and head of Trevor Samuels.

An underground river of hurt rose within him and he buried his face in the musty green comforter. He kept seeing his father's face shatter like exploding glass, and remembrances of all their good times flooded his mind. Tears flowed: hot, bitter, unbidden.

Gradually, he began to cry himself out and he could hear his own racking sobs. Rolling over, Trevor stared through the last tears at the watermarks on the ceiling. After some time, they began to look like Venezuela and he felt silly and vaguely ashamed to be thinking about geography when his father lay dead four floors below. Lifting his head, Trevor peered out the dusty window.

He could see the edge of the small patio that formed the tail of the hotel and the empty open ground beyond where the last sunlight of this day lay like drying mustard. At the edge of the tired yellow light was a corral. In the corral were a number of horses. One magnificent white animal stood out like a new moon rising. The boy studied the handsome head for a moment, half-wishing he could ride the creature. His gaze drifted to the old barn. Its straight lines and flat façade covered in faded red paint made him think of the Edward Hopper that hung in the Dorchester Museum on Forty-third. As he began to turn his head a flash of light caught his eye.

He let his vision float across the face of the barn and caught it again, a flicker of light in a flat red sea. Moving his line of vision in ever smaller orbits, he finally pinpointed the flicker. It was emanating from a crack in the loft door. Looking carefully, he could see the narrow black line of the opening of the loft door and the glitter of sunlight off metal.

Forty

Poncho closed the door softly. Twisting the knob, he listened to the deadbolt click home. Then he turned and took a long careful look around the room. No one was supposed to be in the room, but Poncho Herrera was not a man to take chances, especially where his money was concerned. That aspect of his life was his own business. Private, not the business of anyone else – not even his wife.

He covered the room in half a dozen strides, moving quietly for a large man. Poncho eased open the middle drawer of a five-drawer dresser that had once been his mother's. He soaped the metal runners regularly and the drawer slid open quietly. He pushed a hand through a pile of soft cotton shirts. Reaching the bottom of the drawer, he slid his hand to the back right corner where his fingers closed around a flat wooden box. Once it had held six fine Cubano cigars. Now it held his get-away money. Never had Poncho told anyone about it; except for that bug-eyed whore in the capital. Damn, but he had been drunk that night.

He pulled the box out, slid the lid back, and stared at the most money he had ever possessed at one time. He planned to hold on to it. At the first opportunity, he intended to blow out of Yuscarana like a dust storm. Life was too short, way too damn short. Poncho Herrera hoped he had not waited too late.

Tugging his shirt a few inches away from his chest, he slid the slim box beneath the cotton. No rebel would get his hard-earned money, not if he had anything to say about the matter. Poncho knew many hiding places better than the drawer of his mother's dresser. The box felt cool against his chest. Smiling to himself, he crossed the floor, clicked the lock, and pulled the door open. For a moment he stood still, listening. Then he stepped into the hall, looked both ways, turned left, moving on the balls of his feet like a big jungle cat, or perhaps a gorilla.

Forty-one

Mind games, that is all we are playing. So what? Games were better than that great awful nothingness that consumed the mind like a sticky fog which clung to the brain walls and clogged the synapses, slowing the flow of thought to a thick ooze. No, Iwakura Tyshimoda thought, better to make a game of it, set a goal, issue a challenge to oneself. Not like Akko. At the first sign of strangeness, she panicked. Merely perceiving there might be a threat and she was screaming, crying, begging for mercy. Not for him – he had a code to follow.

It wasn't one of the more famous ones, like Bushido. Instead, it was a code with a small, although devout following, scarcely more than a poorly defined cult. He had learned of it through an uncle, dead now for twenty years, who had come across it during seafaring days. The name of the code was not important; in fact, it was known by several names. This code stressed honor, bravery, and self-sacrifice for the good of the larger community. For over thirty years, Iwakura had studied the code, but never had the chance to use it presented itself. Finally, his moment had come. How brave would he be?

When he had been a young man, he had known with a boisterous certainty he would feel no fear, regardless of the enemy. The intensity of that certainty came rushing through him now, cresting before flowing away like a rogue wave.

Straightening his back, he walked briskly down the hall. Stairs loomed in front of him. At the bottom of the stairs, men in uniforms were running across the lobby. He could hear the irregular rattle of gunfire. Without hesitation he started down the stairs.

~ * ~

"You there, get your back against that wall and keep away from the window. Use the proper angle of vision and you can see out. No, no." Lieutenant Escobar sighed in frustration and jammed his hands against the man's chest, shoving him against the wall. The man looked up with hot dark eyes. He had lost his cap during the run from the barracks and his hair stood up like wild grasses. Beneath the lieutenant's palm, the man's shirt was damp. He must have run hard. Escobar decided that under the circumstances he, too, would have run hard.

"All right, Tiant, stay there until I change the orders." He smiled faintly at the man, pleased the name had come to him at such a moment. Tiant was a new man, having arrived from the south only last month. "Understand?"

"*Sí*."

"*Bueno*." The lieutenant inclined his head toward the window. "From here, you can see all the way to the corral, as well as one corner of the barn. You can even see my beautiful horse. Do you know my horse's name, Private?"

"No." Tiant spoke softly, as if he did not trust his voice. His legs were weak beneath him and he eased against the wall.

"His name is Gitano – the gypsy. When I got him he was wild and free and beautiful like gypsies in the movies. There are days when he still longs to be free, but he is always beautiful. Do you not agree?"

"*Sí.*"

"He must be kept that way, soldier. Keep your eyes and ears open and do not let any rebels near him or the other horses. Those are very valuable animals and it would not do for them to fall in the hands of the rebels. Agree?"

Forgetting himself, Private Tiant nodded.

The lieutenant did not notice. He was a young officer and not a great stickler for detail, unless there was a senior officer present.

"Excellent. Now watch closely, because those rebels may slip in from the rear. Tricky bastards. We must be ready. If you see them, call for me, then begin firing." He turned to go.

"Lieutenant?"

Escobar pivoted. "Yes?"

"When do you think they will come? The rebels, I mean. When do you think they will attack?"

"I would not be surprised if they came before dark."

"Not after dark? When we can't see them."

"Perhaps. However, you must understand that if we cannot see them then they cannot see us." The lieutenant shook his head at Tiant, heading off the next question. "I must go now and see to the others. You are not alone on this back wall. Corporal Alou and Private de la Hoya are in the next room. Hold your place and keep a sharp eye out. I will send your relief later."

Escobar turned without saluting and walked toward the door. At the edge of the hallway, he turned. "Keep away from the window, Private. We don't want to lose you, now do we?"

The lieutenant disappeared before Private Luis Tiant could respond. The soldier peered out the window. All he could see were a few horses at the north edge of the barn and deepening shadows. He wished someone were in the room with him. It was a lonely room. He wondered when the lieutenant would send his relief. Probably not until after supper, he guessed, his stomach gurgling at the thought of food.

Luis Tiant could not understand how he could think of food when he might be dead in the next moment. What good would food do him if one of those rebel bastards fired a bullet with his name on it? He felt like a condemned man. He wondered if he would get a last meal. Inside his uniform, the private felt a chill move across his body. Only my sweat drying, he told himself, shivering.

~ * ~

"Lieutenant, what is going to happen to us? Are we all going to die?" Lady Dianna Threlkeld leaned over the banister, smiling in what she hoped was a waif-like manner, exposing two of her more formidable attributes.

Lieutenant Manuel Escobar paused, an act he performed with great reluctance. Captain Morales would be waiting on his report on the men from the barracks, their condition, and how he had arranged them along the back. The lieutenant was anxious to make his report, shift some of the responsibility back up the chain of command. In the sharing of responsibilities there was comfort.

The lieutenant looked up at the woman leaning over the railing, smiling at him. She had a mouthful of very white teeth, and she was showing a considerable amount of flesh. For a *turista*, she was rather attractive. Most of the female tourists were, to put it politely, matronly.

"The men from the barracks are here now. I have just arranged them along the back and sides of the hotel. Captain Morales and I, along with more of our men, will be at the front. Other men should be here soon from the communications post outside of town and reinforcements have been requested from headquarters. Our position is very strong here, *Señora*."

"How many rebels are there, Lieutenant?"

He shrugged. "Who can say? There do not seem to be so many. Otherwise, I think they would have assaulted us before now. Now, they have waited too late. Our forces are consolidated and we have a strong defensive position." He offered up a faint smile; one that felt phony on his face.

"This old hotel makes a good fort. Windows in the upstairs rooms give us a strong vantage point and excellent lines of fire. We can see them as they attack and shoot them down in the street."

Lady Threlkeld straightened. Keeping her eyes fixed on the lieutenant, she walked down the stairs in her most regal manner. She kept walking until she was inches away from Lieutenant Escobar. She could smell his cologne and see the bluish-black tinge along his jawline. Gently, she placed a hand on his upper arm.

"I am scared, Lieutenant. Already today one man has been killed – an American. And the firing has continued all afternoon. I think you are only trying to make me feel better so I will not cry on your shoulder."

"But, no..."

"But yes." She massaged his bicep. It was quite firm. "I am sure Morazon trains all their officers to be diplomatic, especially with female *turistas*. You want us to feel safe and secure, and spend our money and leave you alone to do your manly, army things."

Dianna Threlkeld allowed the fingers of her left hand to stroke the bare flesh of the lieutenant's forearm. His skin was smoother than she had anticipated and the dark hairs that grew there in profusion were surprisingly soft. With her right hand, she adjusted the bill of his cap. Her face was now very close to his. His breath was soft against her cheek. "And I am a female, you know." Her voice was little more than a whisper.

"Yes, I know," the lieutenant said, leaning back.

"And I have a good deal of money."

Lieutenant Escobar nodded, regretting it instantly as the movement brought his face dangerously close to the woman's. He stepped back.

Lady Threlkeld laughed. "Do I make you nervous, Lieutenant?"

"No, no. It is only that I need to report to Captain Morales. You will excuse me?"

"Certainly. Never let it be said that Lady Dianna Threlkeld kept any man from his duty." She patted him on one cheek, fingers lingering longer than etiquette would have advised.

Blushing faintly, the lieutenant executed a half bow and a rapid retreat.

Lady Threlkeld stood leaning against the base of the stairs, staring at his back until he turned the corner. Then she sighed, smiled, and started climbing the stairs. Time for a drink, she told herself.

~ * ~

Bullets peppered against the walls of the hotel like hard rain. Faces turned toward the sounds. Captain Morales did not turn his head toward the wall. Instead, he closed his eyes. That sound he knew too well.

Damn, he muttered, here they come, for real this time. All day he had known this moment was coming. He had been dreading it, yet, in the next thought, anxious for it to happen. It was like waiting for a dose of medicine or the first blow of a beating. Even in his youth he had always preferred to get the worst over with. Delay was pointless, anticipation more torturous than reality. He opened his eyes.

People were rushing away from the windows and the walls, screaming, waving their arms like windmills gone berserk – their faces creased with fear, their eyes stretched wide.

A woman stood in the kitchen doorway. Her face was passive, frozen in its serenity. Morales paused for a moment in his sweep of the room to study the woman. He had seen a face like hers only a very few times. Each time it had been a face awaiting a certain death. As he studied the woman's features, he realized that the woman was one of the tourists. Something akin to fear crawled across the flesh of his forearms.

Captain Morales was not a man given to ordinary fears, but the lines imbedded in the woman's face were not natural. It was a face possessed. He recalled various voodoo spells he had heard about over the years. Some of them made death seem a blessing. Shouting for Lieutenant Escobar, Morales started walking toward the kitchen.

Halfway to the kitchen, he heard a man scream in pain from the rear of the building. Bullets pounded against the walls. The screams went on and on. Morales kept walking, shouting again for the lieutenant. If the lieutenant answered, Captain Morales could not hear him.

The woman was close now. The captain glanced at her face. It was oriental in structure. Chinese, Thai, Korean, he couldn't tell. Strange, astringent odors emanated from her. He glanced down at her feet. A pool of yellowish liquid shimmered on the floor. More of the liquid was still running down one leg. Morales held his breath as he squeezed by the woman, taking care to step over the puddle.

~ * ~

He could see only a small patch of grass and a few banana plants growing in the shade of an adobe wall. The green leaves made him think of 'Nam. *At least I'm not out in the fucking jungle surrounded by God knows what or who. Somebody has my back here and I've got protection, food, and water,* he told himself. *Plus, the commanding officer seems like he knows what he is doing.*

It was one fine mess to be in, but Joe Moby had been in a hell of a lot worse. He kept telling himself that as he sighted down the barrel of the rifle they had given him. He had given it a quick inspection, enough to know it was loaded and there was no obstruction in the barrel. As to the accuracy of its firing, well, he'd know when he pulled the trigger. He peered into the afternoon.

Daylight was giving way to an early darkness. Moby glanced at his watch. Far too early for dusk, but darkness was definitely spreading like a dirty blanket across the grass.

Thunder began rolling in the hills and he lifted his head and gazed out into the unnatural twilight. Leaves rose and fell in the rising wind, putting him in mind of small green sails.

Metal glinted in a late shaft of sunlight and something dark and bulky moved behind the elephant ears next to the building. Joe Moby dropped his head, sighted, and squeezed the trigger. The butt recoiled heavily against his shoulder as the bullet chipped adobe off a wall. He sighted again, tensing for the return shot. It did not come. He took careful aim at the biggest leaf. Then he squeezed the trigger again.

Screams reverberated in his ears. Then they were drowned out by thunder rolling. Tightness seized his throat and he sucked air though his nose. Glass shattered to his left, but he did not turn his head.

Firing was heavy now from the street. Over the roar of gunfire, he could hear the captain shouting for the lieutenant. This had to be the main attack. Thunder rolled, closer now. At the edge of his vision were streaks of lightning. Joe Moby did not take his eye off the narrow slice of courtyard before him.

He did allow a portion of his mind to wander, a trick he had picked up one long afternoon as he lay in the tall grass above Khe Sung beside Corporal Herndon, who was gut shot and going in and out of consciousness, with enough Cong around them to fill Marble Collegiate. Forced to stay awake the night before, his exhausted mind kept compartmentalizing, thinking about Thanksgiving, and the Stone family, and his cousin Mike all at the same time. And, of course, he had to keep eyes out for Cong. He had simply done what he had to do. Now, he watched the huge leaves quiver and the lightning flash and thought about Amy, wondering if he would ever see her again. Then something bulkier than leaves moved and he squeezed the trigger.

~ * ~

Standing precisely where the second-floor hallway merged with the landing, Kron could see the old hotel open up like a

215

hibiscus. Behind him was only the late afternoon darkness of a windowless hallway. Below, people moved across the lobby floor like gigantic ants, hurrying frantically on their hind legs, crossing the room rapidly, only to cross it again a few minutes later, heading back the way they had come.

Leaning against the plaster wall, he had a sensation of being an observer of a trial run of a dramatic play when the cast was still locating their proper spots on the stage, learning their lines while searching for their characters' motivations. It seemed this cast had a great deal of work to do before the play was ready to open on Broadway. Still, there was something in the frantic ant movements that caught his eye and imprinted themselves on the surface of his brain. Already, he could imagine using such movements in a story.

A stray thought nagged him to push himself off the wall and keep moving until he made the lobby. From boyhood, something in him had longed to be a soldier. Adult fears of death had proven stronger, however. Kron pushed the stray thought aside and listened to rising shouts from running men.

No matter how hard he tried to ignore it, the promise he had made himself kept pricking his conscience. He reminded himself he should move, that he needed to go down the stairs, needed to go, for his own sake.

He didn't want to go. Merely thinking about going down to the lobby made him sweat. He stood with his back against the smooth wall, arguing with himself. After some time, it seemed to him the floor of the hallway was vibrating beneath him and he wondered if an earthquake was rumbling through Morazon. Gradually, it dawned on him it was not the floor that was moving. Tremors were simply running through his body. Cursing against his trepidations, Kron pushed himself off the wall and started walking. His legs were unsteady and at the top of the stairs he paused and put one hand on the railing. Then he started down stairs that appeared a quarter mile long.

~ * ~

Kristin Samuels ran her hands along the wooden floor. Then she pressed her face against it, feeling its hard smoothness against her cheek. A gurgling had begun in her stomach and that certain buzzing, like a distant hive of honey bees, was rising again in her brain. Kristin recognized the signs; she had felt them swirling within her a thousand times. Question was, what she was going to do about them?

Lifting her head a few inches, she could see her mother's face. It was turned toward her and Kristin could see the blue eyes open and staring straight ahead at the closed door. Her mother wasn't really seeing the door, though. Kristin knew because she had seen the same look on her own face countless times in mirrored sunglasses that hid soulless eyes. Her mother was seeing something beyond the small hotel room; she was looking across uncountable time and space to a different universe, seeing people and events that had gone before or were yet to come. Kristin knew because she had seen them herself and the visions always blossomed when that look of the endless sky rose in her eyes. Sending her mother a blessing, Kristin slowly sat up. She could hear people moving on the stairs.

Her head was spinning as though her equilibrium had shifted off center. Hunger crawled through her gut like a moving line of red ants. She couldn't remember when she'd last eaten. She knew she should eat, but there was a stronger urge rising. Damn, but she needed a fix. Figuring that out wasn't a problem; she was an old hand at reading the signs. Problem was, at the moment she was out of the entire holy trinity: dope, booze, and money.

The room seemed to be moving, gyrating like a faltering top. Kristin closed her eyes and watched curling circles of light swirl in looping elliptical orbits in the dark regions of her mind. Like the rings of Saturn, she thought.

Kristin giggled softly as the lights revolved. Sure, it was wrong to giggle when her father lay face down in his breakfast one floor below, his brains splattered across tables, chairs, windows, and the floor. She knew it was wrong, and she didn't think any of it was funny; she simply couldn't help the giggles. They came unbidden and, until they had run their course, they were unstoppable.

It wasn't that she lacked respect for her father. In her own way, she had respected him. And, in a way that she could only hazily define, she had loved him. He had been good to her, generous with his money, green bills with such nice large numbers. Involuntarily, her fingers closed around empty air, opened, then closed again.

Urged on by the revolving lights and a growing desire, Kristin crawled to the door, reached up a trembling hand and grasped the door knob. Taking a deep breath, she pulled herself erect. For perhaps a minute she stood swaying, getting her legs under her, calling on reserve strength, driven by a desire she could no longer control. Kristin Samuels tugged the door open and stepped into the hall.

The day had moved on and the hallway was darker than she had expected. The day was dying, fading light falling feebly through the trio of tall narrow windows at the end of the hall, throwing slim ingots of light down the hallway. Light splashed around her ankles like fading starlight and threw a pale ethereal glow into the telescoping recesses of the hall. Kristin swiveled on unrepentant hips and stumbled off toward the far end of the universe cleverly disguised as a darkening hallway in a decrepit hotel in a country whose name she couldn't remember.

Her legs weren't working properly. They seemed distant, so far away from her torso that it was almost as if they belonged to someone else. She looked at them distrustfully, placing each foot with care and precision. One step, two. Then the walls started to buckle and the floors undulated and she stumbled forward, catching herself with a hand against a wall.

Slowly the walls firmed up and the floors grew still. Kristin started forward again, moving with exaggerated care, keeping one palm flush against the smooth plaster. Ahead, doors lined both sides of the hall, and beyond the doors were rooms where people stayed. People who might have booze or drugs or money. The first room was close and she stopped. The door was closed and Kristin advanced cautiously, sliding her face along the wall until one ear was pressed against the wooden door.

No sounds came from the room, but she could hear a faint popping sound reaching her from a greater distance. It sounded the way a brown paper bag sounds when it is filled with air and the neck of the bag is closed tightly and then someone smashes it between their hands. She placed one hand on the doorknob. It was an old one made of grooved glass. She twisted the cylindrical knob. With a faint squeaking, the door swung open.

Kristin stepped inside. The bed was neatly made and suitcases were arranged in a straight row against the wall. Clothes hung in managed rows on wire hangers in the single closet. Kristin walked unsteadily to the closet and thrust her hands deep into pockets. All she encountered was lint and a few loose Morazonian coins in one pocket of a tan pair of slacks. She stuffed the coins into the left front pocket of her jeans.

Forty-two

The heat of the day seemed to press in on itself and mound up. The breeze faltered and the air grew as still as yesterday. Leaves of the trees, bushes, and the gigantic ferns hung limp. In the tops of certain trees, monkeys leaned against smooth-barked trunks with their mouths open, idly picking fleas off each other. Black snakes, brown snakes, and snakes with stripes of blue or silver or gold lay indolently on lower branches. Under the canopy, the big cats dozed in the deep shade. Only certain insects and a handful of red soldier ants showed any signs of animation. A few insects hopped from leaf to leaf or droned incessantly at flower blossoms. Only the ants marched on relentlessly in the heat, up and down logs, over and under leaves, a vermillion army marching to their own drummer.

High above the canopy a few clouds began to darken and coalesce in a birdless sky. They hung like ripening purple plums above the peaks, throwing dusky, restless shadows that slid down the mountain before collapsing into shards which painted hieroglyphics on the jungle floor.

~ * ~

Carlos looked at his watch. It had come from Cuba and a blurry but recognizable face of Fidel Castro stared back at him. Carlos was not a fan of the aging Castro. However, he still held respect for the young Fidel. The way he had led the guerillas down from the mountains to overthrow Batista and then repel the unprovoked invasion from the United States was inspiration to him. Still, Castro was old now and seemed only to make speeches that rambled on forever.

Cuba, in myriad ways, had regressed under Fidel's leadership. Carlos had often wondered if the people of Cuba would not be better off if Fidel were to step down, giving way to some younger man, one with more energy and fewer of the old hatreds that consumed the revolutionaries of the fifties, sixties, and seventies who still lived.

They were dying now, or growing so old and feeble that they were virtually impotent. In his imagination, Carlos had dreamed of leading the revolt that toppled Gutierrez and becoming the man who would shepherd Morazon into the current century. A man of the people who would return the land to the peasants, provide transportation for the poor in the cities, and redistribute the wealth that a few had accumulated and kept unto themselves at all costs.

He was sure he would be a just and honest president, keeping little for himself and his family – only enough to meet their needs, and that the people of Morazon would be grateful, and, in turn, refrain from greed and bloodshed and the worship of money and power. It caused Carlos great perplexity as to why the poor and oppressed did not rise in unison to throw off the oppressive regime of the puppet Gutierrez and the wealthy bastards who pulled his strings.

Carlos sighed and glanced again at Fidel's face. The big hand was still stuck up Castro's nose, while the little hand pointed to a jaundiced left eye. That was exactly where they had been the last time he looked. Carlos lifted the watch closer to his face and inspected it carefully. The second hand was not moving; it appeared to be hung up in Fidel's beard. This was not the first time the watch had stopped. He stared at the watch in disgust. Then he shook it vigorously and inspected it again. None of the hands had moved. Fidel appeared weary. Perhaps having your face on a thousand watches was exhausting. Fidel might have been a great revolutionary, Carlos thought, but his country made damn poor watches.

Carlos looked down the dark battered snake of a road that wound itself out of Yuscarana. Shadows fell across the cracked asphalt. Without warning, the afternoon had grown old. By now the men who had attacked the communications station should have come down that road.

Carlos shrugged. He could not make men appear by magic, any more than he could make the peasants rise en masse against Gutierrez. Words might move certain men, deeds others. Nothing would make all men act in accordance with truth. That he had learned during his life, if nothing more.

His cousin, Manuel, had argued this was because no two men viewed the truth in the same way. Carlos could not agree with this. To him, truth was truth. Truth was without adulteration or shading. Anger always accompanied this argument and he could feel the burning start. Cursing the men who would not come, he took one last look at the great green jungle that surrounded him, turned quickly and began jogging down the dark snake road toward the heart of Yuscarana.

Echoes of gunfire reached him. They were few, with significant spaces of time between them. He cursed himself for leaving Jesus and the others to wage the battle. Coming back to check on the missing men had been an exercise in futility, a daydream he should never have indulged. Carlos ran harder.

~ * ~

Buildings floated by him in a blur. The old hotel bobbed before him like a ship on an ocean of earth. Thirty yards away, he slowed, swinging his automatic pistol out in front of him and squeezing the trigger, cursing and running with anger rising like lava in his throat and sweat rolling down his face like hot rain, burning his eyes until the entire world was a blur.

He could hear the shouts of his men now and all of their rifles seemed to fire at once until the sound of their firings became a single great roar that rattled in his brain and merged with his own screams until there was only sweat and sound.

Forty-three

Now there was only pain. He lay as still as stone and tried to focus on something other than death. Anything else would be a blessing. He tried to remember when he was young and his mother and father had loved him. However, whenever an image of those happy times flashed in his mind, it lingered for only an instant before the next wave of pain erased it. Sometimes the image was there so briefly the boy was sure he had only imagined it.

A great rumbling sound filled his ears and his world grew instantly dark. Shivering inside the pain, the boy wondered if he had heard the footsteps and seen the shadow of God.

~ * ~

Cool blessings fell on him and he was grateful. In some strange way, Felix could not explain the rainstorm's easing his suffering. He welcomed the falling drops and the wind shafts that were cool against his fevered flesh. He could feel them both and he was grateful. There was no more he could feel – only pain, nothing more. No thoughts or feelings of anything except pain, and now the cool relief of rain. The boy lay immobile on the hillside, immobile and immaculate in his pain.

Forty-four

All the ice had melted and he stared at the amber liquid with distaste. Warm whiskey wasn't a proper drink. Still, it was certainly a preferable alternative to no drink. With a sense of resignation, Lord Threlkeld lifted the glass to his lips.

Holding the liquid in his mouth, he savored the taste, wondering vaguely where his wife had gone. Not that he particularly cared, but the bottle standing on the table beside his chair was empty and he wasn't enamored of having to push himself up out of his chair to go and rummage through his suitcase.

What if he was out of the elixirs of life? The thought popped sweat on his forehead and caused his left leg to begin pistoning up and down.

Then his mind shifted and he remembered he still had one full bottle of good Kentucky bourbon, a half-full bottle of Absolut vodka he had picked up at one of the duty-free stores they had visited on this tour from hell, and a couple of swallows swirling around the bottom of a bottle of cheap Jamaican rum. And, surely to God, the innkeeper had a bottle or two stashed away for emergencies. Any sane man would.

For a moment, he savored the smooth warm richness, allowing his mind to wander. A long summer's afternoon at Stonehenge drifted softly across his mind. He could distinctly recall lying there on the carpet of grass after the last tour bus full of loud-mouth Americans, their bellies pushing the fronts of their noxious tangerine golf shirts, had departed for their overpriced hotel. "God save us all from American tourists," he had said to Roger, who had laughed and rolled his hard-boiled blue eyes and pointed his long, thin nose at the great monoliths. "Yes, indeed, Donald," he had replied. "Only a few more meals for some of those chaps and they will be able to form their own Stonehenge."

Lord Threlkeld took a cautious sip of bourbon; his glass was getting dangerously low. Who else had been there that afternoon? He sipped again. Oh yes, Bert Westphell, with his twitchy lips, and George Arbershire, already going bald, and that chap who was so good at sports. What was his name? Griffiths? Yes, Griffiths, like the gamekeeper who had delighted Lady Chatterley. Whether Griffiths had been the chap's first or the last name was no longer clear. Those fellows for certain, oh, and Teddy Henly, whose eyes had been a truly remarkable shade of blue.

He raised the glass to his lips, saw there was only a swallow left, then lowered it. For some time, he simply sat in the chair, his glass at half-mast, recalling that elongated late summer afternoon when the air had gone deadly still and a single bird made great wide black orbits in a high, hollow sky that seemed to take forever to grow dark. He recalled the banal chatter and the harsh, fine burn of the cheap whiskey Griffiths had procured, the pleasant, distant aroma of freshly mown hay, the way the white clover heads sprouted up through the verdant grass, and that good empty feeling in his stomach. Especially he retained a vision of that afternoon light, going from gold to rose to purple to smoke to almost ebony, with a fine faint rim of scarlet lining the horizon. It had seemed to him then that such light must surely go on forever.

His mind filled with sad wonderment, Lord Threlkeld lifted the glass and toasted his companions from that long gone day, wondering idly where they were now. Teddy, he knew, was married and living somewhere on the south coast. Hadn't heard from him for years. He had run into Griffiths once at Harrods, must have been ten years ago now. Griffiths had grown a rather disreputable looking mustache and put on at least twenty right around the old belt line. As for the others, well he couldn't say. Someone, damned if he could remember who, had told him old Twitchy-Lips had died in a car crash outside Bristol, and rumor had it that Roger had become a barrister. Arbershire might just as well fallen off the face of the earth.

He let the bourbon slide down his throat and licked the last reluctant drops from his upper lip. Gunfire rattled against the hotel walls like annoying hail.

Damn foolishness this revolution; all this shooting was absurd. Grown men should know better – all those bullets flying around were going to kill somebody. He seemed to recall Dianna telling him that one of the tourists had actually been shot at breakfast.

Another hailstorm of bullets rattled the walls as Lord Threlkeld rose, then made his way across the room on unsteady legs. Damn fools, he thought as he began digging for the bottom of the suitcase. Must have been fellows who played a lot of rough sports in their youth. As his fingers slid across smooth glass, Lord Threlkeld felt his lips begin to curl upward.

Forty-five

He was amazed at the rapidity with which the landscape was growing dark. Shadows streaked the treetops, the old barn, the corral and the horses, and all the ground that lay between the corral and the hotel. Massive clouds, purplish turning black, smeared themselves across the sky until the sun was no more than a pinprick of light in the west. Dusk had arrived in the middle of the afternoon. Out in the corral, horses tossed their wild-eyed heads and stamped their feet, calling to each other in loud, strident voices. Kneeling on the floor, Iwakura Tyshimoda pushed his face into the gap between the windowsill and the bottom of the raised window, sweeping the landscape with his eyes, looking for revolutionists.

His trousers were thin and the wooden floor boards pressed painfully against his knees. Warm, humid air puffed at his face. With one hand he gripped the barrel of the rifle he had been given. Iwakura was unaccustomed to guns and the weapon felt heavy and strange. He noticed a faint tremor working its way through his left arm.

Lightning flashed, great sheets of it above the jungle, each flash streaking closer to the green canopy. Thunder rolled again and again in the distance, coming closer with each roll. The sun was only a faint orange pinpoint. Soon, it would be no more than a memory.

Movement caught his eye and he jerked his head in time to see men running across a stretch of open ground beyond the barn. They were running from a small grove of trees some twenty yards in front of the main jungle line. They were running hard. Two of them wore blue jeans and work shirts. One wore the white, wide-legged pants and loose shirt of a peasant. The final man wore dark trousers and a white shirt, as though he were dressed for the office. Iwakura swung the rifle up and tried to focus on the running men. Uncertain because the men were not in uniform, Iwakura hesitated. Then he saw that they were all carrying rifles and he tried to draw a bead on one.

By now the two men in jeans had reached the shelter of the barn. The man in the peasant shirt paused to fire. Iwakura pulled the trigger. He could see a puff of dust rise two feet in front of the man. The man turned and sprinted for the barn.

The last man, the man in the city clothes, ran slower than the rest. He ran as if his feet hurt him. Iwakura took careful aim. Beneath his right index finger the trigger retracted.

The man in the dark trousers fell down. One of his legs simply collapsed and he sat down. Even from the second floor of the old hotel, Iwakura could see a look of great surprise on the man's face. Then the man hugged his uncooperative leg and pain replaced surprise. The man's mouth flew open. Whatever sound he made was drowned out by a drum roll of thunder.

Lowering his rifle, Iwakura watched the man try to stand. The man rose only a few inches before he collapsed again. He started to crawl. Not until he was almost to the barn did Iwakura remember that he was trying to kill the man. By the time he had raised the rifle to a firing position, the man had been dragged into the shelter of the old barn by the two men wearing jeans.

Iwakura lowered the rifle once more and stared across the empty ground, gone gray in the dusk that gathered before the storm. Tree branches in the front ranks of the great jungle swayed before the wind.

Thunder rolled as though the sky had turned over and lightning flashed against the angry purple and black sky. The sun had disappeared, covered by massed clouds, dark, heavy, somber with rain; gone as surely as if it had been permanently erased from the sky.

~ * ~

Wind was hammering against the old barn. Boards squeaked as the wind smashed against them. One of the shutters had swung loose and banged against the side of the barn like a drum beating out of rhythm. Tony eased closer to the edge of the planking and peered across the yard. Loose leaves were swirling on the open ground; then the wind shifted and they were flung up against the stone wall of the patio where they fluttered and burrowed like small wild animals. Tree limbs swayed in the rising wind. Above the hills, lightning flashed and thunder rolled in counterpoint to the banging shutter.

Staring at the coming storm, Tony could feel something rising within him. He couldn't put it into words, but he recognized the great upswell of desire, so strong that it was uncontrollable. It was the hideous, glorious, irrepressible orgasm of death welling up inside him.

Something scurried in the loose hay behind him, something small and alive – afraid or hungry. Tony didn't care. His attention remained focused on the old hotel. Nothing except the swirling leaves moved before it. All the soldiers who were coming were surely inside the hotel by now. Wiping a bead of sweat off the end of his nose with the back of a dirty hand, he began to eye the windows, going down them slowly, peering carefully into each one, staring at them straight on, then turning his head fractionally, glancing back obliquely, hoping to catch a flash of metal or the lightness of flesh. He started with the bottom floor, working from his right to his left, going slowly and carefully. The urge to kill was still rising.

He could hear the horses now, their shrill whinnying rising above the wind. Since he had been five years old, when he had seen a glorious palomino in a parade, he had wanted a horse of his own. Even though he had never ridden a horse, for a second he thought about climbing down and throwing a rope around the neck of one and swinging up his back. He had no idea where he would ride, or what he would do when he arrived, but he toyed with the thought until the wind smashed the shutter against the barn again, blowing the daydream away. Tony turned his focus back to the windows.

On the first pass he missed it; on the second it was a sound, the sound of a rifle that caught his attention. At first, Tony thought it was one of his compadres firing. Then he glanced down and saw four of them running out of the trees, coming straight toward him. They were running hard. Even from the loft it was easy to see the fear on their faces. When one stopped and snapped off a quick shot, Tony swiveled his head and followed the line of the rifle.

A flash of metal, that was all he saw before the movement of his head transformed the line of sight into distorted glass and reflected light. He swung his head back with deliberate slowness. Nothing. Then another flash of metal.

Tony inched left, keeping his eyes fixed on the window; a face swam into focus, distorted like a fish on the far side of cloudy aquarium glass.

Something was wrong with the face. He was too far away to tell exactly what the unnoticed feature was. Now if he had binoculars, but no, there were none in the revolución, at least not for him. Why, if he only had field glasses, he would be the greatest scout in the whole entire history of the revolución. But no, Carlos and the other officers had denied him, exactly as they had denied him a hundred times on other requests. He hated the officers, hated them and their denials. Hated them nearly as much as he hated the men of Gutierrez. Tony spat into the wind.

Rats were gnawing on grain; he could hear kernels cracking open. They had to be close or storm sounds would have drowned them out. Thunder hammered against the mountains as though determined to crack them. Echoes rattled in the streets.

Tony the Demented closed one eye as he tried to shut down his ears. Even with all the noise and the lightning flashes, he could sense the urge singing in his veins. Jamming his left elbow against the loft floor, he steadied the barrel of the gun with his left hand. Gusts of wind buffeted the old barn. Thunder rolled. A blast of wind ripped the banging shutter from its hinges and flung it halfway to the hotel. Tony let out his breath very slowly. He squeezed the trigger.

Glass shattered. He squeezed the trigger again. If the man screamed, the wind and the thunder drowned out his cry. Tony squeezed the trigger again. The rats kept chewing on the kernels of last year's corn.

~ * ~

He could hear his own screams. The entire left side of his body was on fire. Something had smashed into him with incredible force, driving him back from the window and flinging his body across the bed. In strange ways, the body no longer seemed his own; it felt distant, violated in some sacrosanct manner. Pain burned through this disassociated body.

The concept of one's self seemed as foreign to him now as life on Uranus. He had no body, only scattered white-hot fragments of a mind. His entire being seemed to focus solely on pain. Pain, not as a concept, but as a life force creating its own universe. Iwakura Tyshimoda writhed on the old bed that sagged beneath him, biting his upper lip, trying to stifle the moans that were not an acceptable part of the code. He forced his eyes open. A blurry ceiling swung above him, an undulating, cracked sky. He tried to sit up, but a wave of pain pressed him back down against the worn beige comforter.

In a moment of half-clarity, he wondered who had slept under the old comforter, who had made love under its reassuring weight, who had died under its unyielding heaviness. Without warning, another wave of pain swept through him and all wondering ceased.

When the wave had subsided, Iwakura pressed a hand against the center of the pain. A warm wetness spread across his palm. Lifting his hand, he watched dark liquid drip away. Unable to stop himself, he drew his hand closer to his face. The warm animal smell of his own blood filled his nostrils. Blood dripped against his face.

His heart was hammering now, working against the pain, and he bit off a moan that escaped his mouth without warning. He tried to think of anything except the pain. But there was only the pain.

Iwakura felt the blood soaking his chest and crawling down his torso. Iwakura Tyshimoda could smell his own death. The realization that if he did not get up off the bed and find help, he would die swept over him and he struggled against the pain. His head rose slowly. Never had he known it so heavy. A great weakness had invaded his body. His heart seemed to pump more slowly. Iwakura struggled to a sitting position. His head whirled and lights spun as if all the lights in the world were contained in a single kaleidoscope, and that kaleidoscope was turning without mercy inside his mind.

It all seemed too much trouble. Blood gurgled up from the wound. His eyes fluttered. Pain coursed through his body. Iwakura Tyshimoda fell back on the old bed. Dying no longer seemed a noble art.

Forty-six

Darkness covered Yuscarana. In the sky, light no longer existed except for occasional lightning flashes exploding like random artillery fire. Wind pushed massive limbs of tall trees around like cardboard. Thunder hammered the clouds. Rain pelted Yuscarana – drops striking every animal and bird, every building, every tree and bush and plant and rock, every square inch of earth.

Carlos and his men heard the rain moving down from the same hills they had so recently abandoned. Water smashed against leaves and branches. The noise was that of a thousand jungle drums. Rain ran down the trunks of the trees, pooling against their roots until the earth could absorb no more. The water began to work its way down the hillsides, settling into the natural depressions, gathering more running water until it filled the paths and bubbled up in the gullies. Unstoppable, the storm rolled across the peaks, down the slopes, through the jungle and into the valley that cradled Yuscarana.

The insurgents heard the rain coming a long way off and as it rolled closer, they sought shelter, but there was none. Rain pounded against them. In an instant they were soaked to the skin, their clothes plastered to their hides, their hair matted. They could only hunker down, bow their necks, surrender. They let the storm wash over them in waves, biding their time, thinking about their wives or girlfriends or mothers, or when they would ever be dry again, or where their next meal might come from, or if they would be alive to eat it.

Carlos knelt beneath the low-hanging leaves of a banana tree, water trickling down the back of his neck, splashing against his face when the wind shifted. He had not factored the storm into his equations. The rainy season had come early. Still, it did not upset him. If he could not attack, Morales undoubtedly could not escape. He had lost men today, but so had the army of Gutierrez lost soldiers. Not a trade he would have chosen to make, but there was nothing he could do about it.

Fatalism rose within him and he struggled to force it back down. When a man began to believe only in fate he was doomed. It was like accepting a self-inflicted death sentence. Experience had taught him that lesson. He must not give in. A death sentence for Carlos the Guerrilla was not something the Revolución could afford. At least that is what he believed. Many of the generals of the popular force were old, if not in years, then in their thinking. Their timidity had led to defeats and setbacks that, in his eyes, were indefensible. Indefensible and inexcusable. Unacceptable to the glorious Revolución.

Now the rain was slacking and thunder rolled only against the far mountains. A shard of lightning lit up the sky. Carlos knew the darkness was not due solely to the storm. In less than an hour there would be no light except that cast by the lights of Yuscarana. If the clouds broke apart, there might be shafts of moonlight and the glittering pinpricks of light cast by the stars he had studied as a young man.

Listening to the rain drip off the massive leaves onto the sodden earth, it was almost impossible to believe that he had once dreamed of becoming an astronomer. Studying stars now seemed only a dream from another life, hazy, flickering in sepia tones, an ancient movie too long exposed to air and light. Carlos stared through the rain as he counted the lights in Yuscarana. Tomorrow, he promised himself, those lights would come on for the *Revolución*.

Forty-seven

In the poor light the walls appeared dingy, as though they needed a fresh coat of paint. A single bulb of dubious wattage hanging naked from a twisted black cord cast a thin yellow light. Beyond that, the only light was faint seepage from cracks and one windows set high in the wall like the eye of a Cyclops. Lieutenant Escobar hurried down the hallway, stepping around chairs and tables, hearing floorboards creak as though they were urging him on. It was an urging the lieutenant didn't need.

Captain Morales had seen to that. His words still burned in the lieutenant's ears. No vulgarity, no direct criticisms, merely the implication that he should have checked on those men at the rear of the hotel some time ago. The words had been few, delivered *sotto voce*, yet carrying with them a stinging implication.

Dodging furniture in the dingy hallway, he hurried, anger coloring his mind. He was angry at the captain for the indirect accusation, angry at himself for not thinking of the rear guard sooner – being busy was no real excuse, angry at the rebels for attacking, angry at the storm for coming when Gitano was not in the barn, and angry at God for letting all this happen.

All his life he had heard from the priests about the love of God, the love God gave to mankind, the love mankind was supposed to share one with another. He had joined the army to serve his country, not to kill his countrymen. The lieutenant did not understand at all. Never had he been able to explain it, even to himself. Frustration rising, he broke into a trot.

Cursing, he rounded a corner and bumped hard into something soft. The something bumped back against the wall.

"Well, Lieutenant, you are in a hurry."

"Yes, I am. Sorry." He wanted to say more, but his mind was hurrying on. He couldn't even think of the woman's name, though she seemed to suddenly be appearing with a studied regularity in his life.

"What's the big rush? There hasn't been an attack for some time. All I can hear is rain." The woman stepped away from the wall.

"Captain Morales ordered me to check on defenses at the rear of the hotel." The lieutenant studied the woman. Her eyes were moving up and down, looking him over. Her gaze felt hot.

Lady Threlkeld smiled. Her teeth were remarkably white. "Can't you stay here for just a minute and talk to me?"

"Orders."

"Don't I need defending?" She took another step. The hallway was not exceptionally wide.

"Of course, but I have orders from Captain Morales. He would not be happy if I disobeyed."

"And what about me? Don't I count?" She put one hand on the lieutenant's left arm. She had large hands with smooth palms and long fingers. "Besides, you won't really be disobeying, merely taking a few minutes longer to check on those men. They are doing fine. No rebels have made it into the hotel."

"I must make sure the line is holding. Our defenses must not be breeched." The lieutenant stood quite still. The sense of being on parade filtered across his mind.

Dianna Threlkeld stroked the lieutenant's arm. She could feel the muscles bunched beneath the skin, thick and rigid, like coiled rope. Widening her smile, she allowed the tip of her tongue to protrude. Only the tip, no more; she was careful about that. It paid to be careful in certain ways, especially when one was taking action that encapsulated danger. "Well, I won't keep you this time, Lieutenant. But do hurry back. I'll be waiting."

He knew he should go. One leg trembled. Words formed inside his mouth. He told his mouth not to open, not to let them spill out. It disobeyed orders. "Where will you be?"

She nodded at a closed door behind him. "Behind that door. It's a small room, with only a couple of chairs, a couch, and a three-legged table. A layer of dust covers everything in there. They must never use the room, except for storage."

She pushed her face closer. She could see the stubble on his chin. It was thick and black. She could smell his sweat and cologne mingling with an indescribable, yet certain, maleness. "Hurry back, Lieutenant." She let her hand fall from his arm as though a great weakness had invaded her body.

For a moment, he stared at her face, then turned and trotted down the hall without looking back, still smelling her perfume, asking himself how crazy he truly was. Faintly, like sticks striking an old drumhead, he could hear the rain peppering against the walls of the old hotel.

Forty-eight

She pressed her face harder against the floor. The storm was smashing against the walls, the wind wailing through the cracks. Somehow this all seemed right and proper, vaguely familiar, as though the attack and the storm had been foretold in a vision. She screamed against the floor, the wood hard and painful against her lips.

Where was Iwakura? Why did he not come? She had waited for so long and then she had gone looking for him. But he had disappeared, and now she had another vision of her husband. Blood seeped around the edges of the vision. Closing her eyes, she focused on the vision. She could see his face now, dimly, yet clearly enough to register the pain etched there. Blood darkened his face and death clouded his eyes.

Screaming, she struggled to her feet. Akko ran blindly, bumping into furniture and walls. The door held fast for a moment, the wood swollen with moisture, but she tugged once more, harder, and it swung open.

As she was running down the hallway, her hair billowed out behind her. With every stride she could feel it falling against her neck. She had not felt that sensation since childhood. The taps from her hair only served to make her run faster. She could hear people shouting, calling for her to stop. Her legs swung faster. A man in a soldier's uniform tried to grab her. Fingers clung to her arm, but she jerked hard and swung free, running even faster.

A door loomed in front of her, dark and hard, standing between her and the storm. A compulsion to merge with the darkness, the thunder and lightning and the rain, filled her soul.

She twisted the knob and pulled, but it was locked. Her fingers fumbled with the deadbolt. A young girl, the maid, screamed at her in a tongue she could not comprehend. The girl grabbed for her, but Akko screamed and clawed at the girl's face. The girl fell back with her long brown hair swinging like a windswept curtain. One more push and the deadbolt moved. Jerking the door open, Akko ran screaming into the storm.

~ * ~

He could hear screams rising above the storm. At first, he thought it was only the wind curling around some jagged corner, but when the sound rose again, he recognized it. It was a sound Jesus the Pig had heard before – the sound of a woman screaming.

When the storm first struck, he had crawled under a porch that fronted one of the vacant stores, working his way to the base of the building. Now, he laboriously turned around and began to wriggle his way back toward the street. In his mind, he looked like a gigantic mole burrowing in the darkness.

The rain had begun to slacken and he could see lights burning in the hotel. The screams seemed to come from that direction. Easing his head around one of the support pillars, he peered through the feeble light that belonged more to the night than to the day.

At first the figure was only a blur, an enigma rather than a reality. As Jesus watched, the blurriness began to dissolve, as though he were twisting the settings on binoculars. Now he could see a small woman running down the main street of Yuscarana. Every few steps she would scream. Her hair strung out behind her, whipping in the wind. She was running toward him.

Something akin to passion rose inside of him, and, thanking God for answering at least one of his prayers, he rolled out from under the porch and scrambled to his feet. Rain still fell, but no longer in sheets. Rain did not bother Jesus the Pig. To him, it simply meant he would not have to bathe for a few days.

The woman was still running toward him. Blind with fear, he figured. Trotting a few steps out into the street, he began to cut the angle on the running woman. She was still running hard, arms flailing, stumbling now and then, but coming on. He could see her face now, wet with the rain, eyes wide open, mouth open as she gasped for breath. Ten yards away she saw him and tried to turn, but her momentum carried her forward and Jesus stepped to meet her.

As they merged, the force of her movement sent them reeling into the darkness. Falling, they separated, but Jesus began his roll even before his body hit the street and he got one arm around the woman and kept rolling, pulling her tighter against him with each roll. He had slung his rifle across his back and, amazingly, the old strap held. Wood and metal dug into his flesh, but, with a woman within his grasp, he ignored the pain and began struggling to his feet, pulling the woman along. He had felt the softness of her body beneath him as they rolled and now a great urge was rising in him. Soon, he would be unable to control it.

Jesus jerked the woman's arm, pulling her toward the darkness and safety of the porch. There was the possibility that one of the soldiers inside the hotel might be an excellent shot with a long-range rifle. A sniper was always dangerous. In the near darkness and the rain and the distance the odds were poor, but, despite his urge, it was a chance Jesus simply did not want to take.

Her screams angered him and he struck her open-handed across the face. Her knees buckled as the screams died. Jesus the Pig got one arm around her waist and, pressing her body against his for leverage, half-drug, half-carried her across the street. As he knelt to begin the crawl under the porch, she began to fight back, slapping with open palms and hitting with small hard fists. Grunting, half in anger, half in pain, Jesus drove an elbow against her jaw. The woman moaned and went limp, not unconscious, but no longer fighting back. Jerking her to the wet ground, he began to crawl under the porch, pulling her behind him by the hair. She came now, unwilling to resist, digging her heels into the ground and pushing off, propelling herself into the cavernous darkness.

He rooted like a peccary against her neck, smelling her woman scent, feeling the great hardness within him; then he ripped at her clothes, sensing a sweet satisfaction as fabric ripped and soft skin met his fingers. The woman was silent, except for a moaning that was like that of a dirge. Her face was smooth and wet against his and she was all softness beneath him. He did not kiss her or caress her; he only smelled her woman-essence as he grasped and molded her flesh, half-crushing her body beneath him as he entered her.

~ * ~

His smell was that of a wild animal, furtive, foul, fecund. Beneath the protective layer of blubber, his muscles felt like iron. His hair was long and wet and hung down in her eyes. His stubble was sandpaper against her skin. She tried to fight back, but she could sense there was no use. Her hands and teeth were like toys of a small child against this creature. Taking a deep breath, she held it for a few seconds, letting it out slowly as her body grew soft. As he entered her, she closed her eyes, wincing and moaning softly.

She could feel him in her, fat and hard and pounding at her soft walls. She could smell his animal funk and hear his running dog panting, but all she could see inside the corridors of her mind was a vision. The vision was the same one she had seen before – her husband lying across a bed with blood on his hands and face and body. He was dying. She was certain, as certain as the knowing that she would soon be joining him.

Akko lay quietly, surrendering everything to the animal who crushed her breasts beneath his body, who violated her most private sanctity. He was hurting her and she tried to choke back her crying. She heard him give a great grunt and felt the hot spurt of his ejaculation. Gradually, his breathing slowed and his weight became only a final burden. Akko lay still, silently thinking of her husband as she listened to the rain, slow and steady now, beating a death march against the old boards of the porch that hung above her like prison bars.

Forty-nine

Poncho Herrera moved quietly down the back hallway. It was the dark of twilight there and he placed his feet carefully. The single light bulb had burned out a week ago and he had not found the time to replace it. Now, he was grateful for the darkness.

The package of money felt heavy inside his shirt. Never had he had so much money at one time. The tour had been a godsend, dramatically increasing the meager savings he had accumulated over his lifetime. Of course, there were bills and the help to pay, but the attack changed everything. People were dying. A bullet with his name on it might come at any minute.

Captain Morales and his men had held off the rebels so far, but who could say how long they would prevail. Perhaps they could hold out. Perhaps the rebels would tire of the fight and move on to easier pickings. Perhaps the generals of Gutierrez would send reinforcements. Who could say? Hell, perhaps he would die of a heart attack tomorrow.

No, Poncho told himself, all his life he had waited for a moment such as this. Teachers had told him and he had read in books that great opportunities came along only rarely in a man's life, and when they came a man must seize them. That was what he was doing now as he walked softly down the dark back hall few knew existed. He could hear the rain beginning to slacken and began to walk faster. The storm must be his shield. No one would venture out in this. But what was a little dampness? He had been wet before; he would be wet again. Gladly would he exchange the soaking of his life for the riches of his life. He would dry out; the money would dry out. Poncho Herrera walked faster.

Turning the corner, he thought of his wife. Juanita was a good woman and she had been a good wife. Maybe she nagged too much, but at least she had been willing to work. So many women today simply refused to do much more than read magazines, watch television, smoke their long thin cigarettes, paint their fingernails, and complain. Juanita had not done those things.

What she had done was to settle slowly, over the years, into a comfortable middle-aged plumpness. Juanita was a good cook; he would give her that. She had served up many fine meals for the guests of the hotel, and for their own table. Unfortunately, or fortunately – depending on how you wished to view it – she also greatly enjoyed her own cooking, most especially her banana pie topped with the ice cream they could get only once a week when the truck came from the capital. Now she moved slowly, and he had great need for rapidity.

Sad in a way to leave her, certainly, but it would surely turn out for the best. After all, there were many women in the world, some very beautiful women indeed. Poncho did not deceive himself; he understood that the money he carried inside his shirt, while it was a great amount to him, would not buy the affections of a truly beautiful woman for long. Truly beautiful women had truly expensive tastes. At least that is what he had heard. He had no experience with such women.

Juanita had always had a certain beauty, more of the subtle kind. Poncho sighed in regret, but only once. He forced his legs to move more rapidly, fast enough to make his breathing labored and audible. Daylight was spilling in around the crack of the door at the end of the hall that was always locked. It led only to a small cellar where, in the days before the road was finished and the trucks came, he had stored eggs, vegetables, and fruits canned in jars. Only to there, and to his freedom.

~ * ~

He had been out of action a long time. Sweat slicked the palms of his hands and he wiped them against his shirt, telling himself it was only the tropical humidity, knowing he was lying. Sweaty palms had always plagued him when he was on patrol in enemy territory, sweaty palms and trembling knees.

Bracing one leg against the wall, he stretched the other one out so that the muscles were forced to hold their tautness, and peered through the jagged edges of the glass still clinging to the wooden frame. Damn window had been stuck fast, nailed or painted shut. He hadn't taken the time to look; he had simply smashed out the glass with the butt of his rifle and got down to business. Not that it was much of a rifle, but it was reasonably clean and all the parts seemed to work.

Waiting had always been the hardest part. During firefights there hadn't been time to breathe, let alone think. It had always been kill before you got killed. See the enemy, or feel them in some instinctive way before they sensed you. Memories of rice paddies tinged with blood rose in sudden mists across his mind, and he bit his lip and made himself peer out into the thickening darkness.

He wondered if the rebels were night fighters, or if the storm had knocked them back and they would wait for morning. He simply didn't know. Hell, he hadn't realized there was even a revolution brewing down here. Damn newspapers were nearly worthless these days. All they seemed to print were stories about drug arrests, or what Hollywood lamebrain was marrying what Hollywood dumbass, or some self-centered politician's latest lie.

God, politicians made him sick. Not a goddamn one of them could tell anything straight. They had to embellish or waltz around the facts, or slather so damn much salad dressing on them that no one could really understand the truth. Not to mention they were all negative as hell and could only see their own point of view. What had happened to saying what was good about America and working together? If he had his way, he would throw all the bums out and start over. Only he wouldn't allow any lawyers, preachers, or rap singers to serve.

Ah shit, I'm simply a bitchin' old man, too set in my ways, he told himself as he strained to see into the darkness that covered the earth. At least I'm inside this time and not in the middle of some fuckin' booby-trapped jungle surrounded by men who want to kill me, he thought, grinning. No, this time I'm inside a freakin' old hotel half-ready to fall down by itself surrounded by men who want to kill me. Joe Moby shook his head, unsure whether to laugh or curse.

~ * ~

"Want a gun, señor?"

Kron glanced down at his hands. They looked small and weak. He did not feel at all confident. He hoped his voice wouldn't betray him. "I guess so."

The uniformed man nodded, bent over, and picked up a weapon from a small pile with each hand. The man had a pistol in his left hand, a rifle in his right. He rolled his eyes to the left, then to the right. He had a thin mustache, very black, and it moved like a small snake whenever he rolled his eyes.

Kron stared at the guns. The only gun he had ever shot was his grandfather's twelve-gauge shotgun. The recoil had knocked him on his butt in the dirt and left his right shoulder sore for three days. The pistol was smaller, less powerful, but there would be a degree of comfort in the bulk of the rifle. "That one," he said, pointing.

The man nodded and handed him the rifle, replacing the pistol on top of the small stack that reminded Kron of a woodpile. "Know how to use it?"

"I think so," Kron said. He had seen a lot of movies and he had watched his grandfather and his uncles some. "Is it loaded?"

"*Sí.*"

"All right. Thanks." He nodded at the soldier with the mustache. The soldier looked a few years older than Kron and was a good two inches shorter. Kron took comfort in that. Today, he had to take his comfort where he could find it. He smiled at the man to show he was not afraid.

The soldier smiled back. Beneath his mustache he had most of his teeth. "*Bueno.*"

Kron started to ask the man where he should go, but the man was already turning around and Kron did not want to bother him, or appear stupid. Instead of asking, he looked around the room.

Seven or eight men were scattered around the lobby. Most were leaning against a wall, staring out into the night.

One man sat with his back against the wall with his right hand wrapped around his left bicep. His face was drawn and his eyes were closed. Blood seeped from under the man's hand and wormed its way down his arm. He was the only soldier not at a window, except for a man who sat on the floor directly across the room from Kron. That man was eating what looked like beans out of a can. As he ate, he stared at Kron across the top of his can.

Uncomfortable under the man's stare, Kron glanced around for an unoccupied window. There were three at the far end. A bulb or two had blown out or been shot out, and that section of the lobby was rather dark. Kron didn't really want to go down there, but he also didn't want to stay here where the man could stare at him.

Kron tried to step quietly, but the floorboards seemed abnormally full of squeaks. No one else seemed to notice. His face felt flushed and he was glad to reach the darkness.

Selecting the middle unoccupied window, he stood in front of it. Before he looked out of the window, he glanced over his shoulder. No one was looking at him. A man in uniform was coming out of the hallway that led to the kitchen. His face was lined and he appeared very tired. He looked older than the other men. The tired man paused and said a few words to one of the soldiers. Kron wondered if the tired man was the commanding officer. He recalled glimpsing some officers at the get-together the night before, a time that now seemed a lifetime ago.

Turning, Kron peered out the window. As his eyes began to adjust, objects began to come into focus.

Problem was that there were very few lights burning in Yuscarana. Kron bent his neck and looked as far as he could to the left, then to the right. He could see only three lights. One of them, at the edge of his vision to his left, looked like a streetlight. The other two were lower and dimmer and Kron guessed they were lights left burning in stores for security purposes. Rain still fell, harder than a mist, but not as hard as the flow from his showerhead back in Oak Park.

Outlines of buildings formed and the road began to shimmer faintly, still more mirage than reality. Yet, it gave him a sense of space and dimension, and, in a way he could not explain, made him feel better. Once, a dark wedge flew through the rain between him and the light and he guessed it was a night bird.

What other creatures were moving about in the dark? He wasn't certain if the rain would drive them to shelter or if they would brave the damp. A line from some song he had heard a long time ago kept running through his head – something about snakes crawling at night. He wondered if that was true. Then he wondered if the guerillas were crawling about in the rainy darkness, slithering closer every minute. Kron squeezed the rifle tighter.

Memories of nearly forgotten dreams were gathering in the shadowy corner of the room. He could sense their presence in the half-light. Kron had never been a fan of the dark. When he had been a child, he had been frightened of the night. Oh, he would go out of the house at night and catch lightning bugs or play tag under the streetlights with the other kids, but he had no interest in spending the night in the woods, or sneaking around neighbors' back yards in the dark, or crossing the railroad trestle bridge on a midnight dare.

Kron began to recall one night when his family had traveled to his aunt's house in northwest Missouri for a family reunion, only to find out that Uncle Larry had shown up unexpectedly so that there was a bed shortage. Being the oldest, Kron had been elected to spend the night at the next-door neighbor's house. Despite protests, his father had grasped him firmly by the hand, and led him out the front door, down the steps, and across the driveway to the strange house. The old lady who lived there had been nice, but her spare bedroom had been upstairs at the end of a long dark hallway, and he had cried when his father left.

The old lady had heard his cries and showed him mercy. She fed him apple pie with ice cream and put a horse-head lamp in his room. He could remember lying awake for what had seemed like hours, staring at the light, gazing at the shadows fingerpainting the wall.

Kron poked his nose against the glass. All he could see was darkness and the faint sheen of rain on the pavement directly beneath the streetlight.

~ * ~

Maria crawled beneath the thin spread that lay across her bed. Her lamp was turned off and the door to the hallway was bolted. There were no windows in the small room and the only light was a thin trickle around the base of the door. Maria had lived with the dark for years in her village. She was not afraid of the dark. However, she was afraid of the guerrillas. Stories she had been told about their atrocities made her cry; she tried never to think about them. She had believed Yuscarana would be safe, safer than the countryside, anyway. Now, she knew that was not true. She worked deeper under the spread, pulling it over her head until even her long black hair was covered.

If only that strong, handsome lieutenant was here; she would feel safe then. She would slip inside his arms and squeeze him so tight his ribs would ache. She would pull him down and kiss his face and lick his chest and make love with him until daylight. He was so handsome and fearless that she wished he was with her all the time. But he wasn't, so Maria closed her eyes and prayed.

She prayed the guerrillas would go away, and that if they did attack, they would be beaten back, and if they got inside the hotel that they would never find her small, dark room, and if they did, all would be over quickly. Then she prayed for her mother and father and all her sisters and brothers, and for all the people of her village. Next, she prayed for her church, especially for the priests. Finally, she prayed for all the soldiers at Yuscarana, but most absolutely especially for the lieutenant.

~ * ~

Pain flowed from his chest like current from a severed electrical wire. He could feel it arcing down his body. He struggled to rise from the bed, but no strength remained in his legs or his arms. Life seemed to be draining from him. The room was gently spinning. His body felt very hot, then it was ice.

His brain no longer seemed to function. For a moment, the face of a woman flickered before his eyes. His wife? Her name would not form in his brain. He tried to recall the code under which he had fought. Not a single word or technique came to his mind. No longer could he see Yaku, his instructor. Not even his face. The spinning became more pronounced. He no longer knew where he was, or even who he was. The pain was more than he could bear. Then it was gone, fading into a great roaring darkness. Iwakura struggled against death's unrelenting onslaught. His final thought was that the code had been of no value.

Fifty

This night was so dark that he could no longer see the end of his pistol. Rain dripped from the tip of his nose. He shuffled his feet and felt the mud cling tenaciously to his boots. The only sound he could hear was water dripping off tree leaves and plopping to the ground at the edge of the jungle.

Carlos peered into the jungle. Yes, the trail they had followed flowed out of the jungle here. He had come to search for some of his men. None of those he had sent to attack the communications building had come on to Yuscarana. Earlier in the day he had heard gunfire from the direction of the communications post. By now the attack should have succeeded, or failed. In either case he would have expected at least some of the men to return. None had, however, and that worried him. He had no men to spare – not if he were going to successfully attack Yuscarana.

His eyes had grown more accustomed to the dark and he pushed on down the trail, each step taking him deeper into the jungle. Wet leaves brushed against his face. He could hear animals moving in the underbrush and he wondered about snakes. Not much scared Carlos, but snakes made his skin crawl.

As he pushed deeper into the jungle, trees blocked out the distant lights of Yuscarana and only a very faint glow from above splashed tentatively along the trail. The rain was easing at last. Nodding his head in satisfaction, Carlos called out the names of the men he had sent to attack the outpost.

He called all of the names he knew. Men came and went, and he made no real effort to learn the names of new recruits. They were far too likely to soon be dead to make it worth the time and effort. Most fighters for the Revolución did not last six months. Six weeks was average. By then they were dead, from gunfire or disease, or they had run away, whether to home or another sanctuary, he could not say.

Nor did he care. There was no future in caring. Some men lasted only six days. Carlos could recall one man who had lasted perhaps six hours. During his first night, the man had been bitten by a Peruvian viper. The snake had undoubtedly sought the man's blanket – for warmth or shelter. Carlos could not recall the man's name, if he had ever known it, or even recall what the man looked like. The single point he could recall with certainty about the man was that he had been a barber.

The trail bent down a slope, curling through a gully that was stones in the dry season. Now it was filled with water flowing half-a-foot deep. Beyond the gully, the trail, barely more than a vine-infested path, wound uphill. The incline was steep and Carlos was panting by the time he reached the crest.

Here the land flattened out in a plateau and spread with only gentle undulations for perhaps fifty yards. A dozen years ago, one of the foreign timber companies had denuded the plateau. None of the trees had been especially valuable, but there had been a great many of them and the company had made a fair amount of money. They had not replanted with trees of potential value, instead allowing the jungle to grow up naturally. Many trees had taken root and grown rapidly in the tropical climate and now the flattish land was nearly overgrown with thin-trunked trees. In places, they grew so tightly even vines had trouble working their way between them. The path, however, was still reasonably clear of vines, and Carlos walked on, scouring the landscape for moving shadows, the flicker of light from a campfire.

Above the plateau, clouds were coming apart at the seams and moonlight splashed on the ground before him. Glancing up, he was rewarded with the sight of a single star staring brightly back at him through a hole in a cloud.

At the base of the next rise, Carlos paused to peer into the darkness. The incline was steep here and there had been no timbering. Trees towered above him, thrusting at the clouds with limbs as large as small boats. The leaf canopy was thick, virtually impenetrable in the night. For a moment he stood silently, uncertain as to whether to go on or reverse his course. They had come this way from their base camp, pausing among the trees before him to drink from a small stream. In the absence of the rain, he could hear the stream murmuring, accompanying the percussion-like drips of water falling from the leaves of the trees.

Here they had split, Carlos and the main force heading south for Yuscarana, the smaller band, now missing in action, curling north to attack the communications post. When those men had not come on to Yuscarana, he had wondered if they might return here. Guerrillas were not particularly adept at following orders. For several minutes, he stood listening for the sound of men, peering into the weighty darkness, trying to discern moving forms.

Broken moonlight fell softly against his face. All he could hear was the stream talking to itself as it flowed through the night, and the plop, plop, plop of water dripping from the canopy and splashing against the floor, the nervous twitter of birds, or staccato chattering of monkeys disturbed by his presence.

The night was slipping away from him, but he did not hurry. His forces were too few, scattered, and undisciplined to launch a night attack. Morning would bring time enough to die.

A soft, almost subtle, peacefulness settled across the plateau, and it seemed to Carlos the guerrilla that it was a night boomeranging from the times when he had been Carlos the boy. A sudden pressure against his shoulders made him jerk his head, his timeless mind expecting to see his long-dead father, but only the wind caressed his face.

Time drifted on in the quivering moonlight, a forever moving presence in the universe. Carlos felt its flow and called out to his men. Only a monkey screamed in response. Shrugging, Carlos turned and started back down the path. A few hours' sleep before daylight could not hurt.

~ * ~

They had allowed the room to grow dark. Two women sat quietly, not speaking, thinking their own thoughts. Throughout the afternoon there had been the sporadic sounds of gunfire, punctuated by shouts and curses of men. Then wind-driven rain had pounded against the window glass. Now, the gunfire had died and only a faint mist fell without sound.

A coolness had come down from the mountains with the storm, but they had not reopened the window and the air in the room had grown warm and stuffy with their expelled breath and the heat from their bodies. They were silent, unconscious of time. Before midnight even the drizzle stopped and the clouds began to separate. Moonlight spilled into the room in the unexpected moments.

I wonder what she is thinking, Amy Moby mused. Can she even think? Shock renders the brain numb. She knew that from reading, watching terrorists blow up babies on television, and listening to Joe talk about combat in a halting voice.

Perhaps the woman is simply temporarily out of her mind. Seeing your husband's brain blown out of his skull would do that to anyone. It might be a long time before the woman came back, Amy told herself, if she ever does.

Thinking about the dead man ricocheted into a wondering where Joe was. Normally, they were both busy during the day. She had her volunteer hours at the hospital and her watercolors; Joe had his flowers and his Louis L'Amour books. It was in the evening, after supper and the dishes, when they enjoyed their together time. Their time, that was the way she always thought of it. Their time simply to sit together in the den with the television off and only the twin cat-lamps glowing. Their time to sit and talk.

Such talks were never forced. Silences frequently grew long between the words, comfortably, casually, as if they were simply part of the day's natural ebb and flow. They would be remembering their day, or planning for another. At least that is what she did. She assumed Joe did the same; in fact, she could sense it. They had been together so long now, ever since he returned from Vietnam, and had shared so many experiences, hopes, dreams, successes, and failures that they had begun to think alike. They finished each other's sentences with an almost humorous regularity. At times, only an exchange of looks was necessary.

Amy treasured that sense of connection. She was a capable woman – she could honestly admit that, proud and independent in a hundred ways. Yet, whenever she and Joe experienced a moment of connection, a certain sense of well-being flowed through her. No, she was wrong; it was more than well-being. The luxuriant comfort that surged through her like warm caramel was a transitory moment of perfection in a blemished-saturated universe. She stirred in her chair, sitting up straighter, massaging the aching in her hands. She could certainly use one of those moments now.

She gazed through the poor light at the woman sitting on the side of the bed, sitting extraordinarily still. Her arms dangled limply, as though all the motor connections had burnt out. It was a high bed and her feet did not quite touch the floor, even though she did not have particularly short legs. Her clothes hung poorly on her and her hair needed brushing. The only things that moved in her face were her eyes, and they were unfocused. Her chest rose and fell slightly as she breathed, and, except for a tiny glittering when her eyes and the moonlight moved in converging angles, that movement was the only way Amy could be certain the woman was alive.

Alive was perhaps not the most accurate word, but Amy knew what she meant. A great sorrow for this other human being filled her, and the woman's loss made her think again of Joe, sending her wandering down the back roads of her mind.

~ * ~

She kept asking herself why.

Bartlett had not been a perfect man. He had always been too preoccupied with work and sluggish on most weekends, except for golf, but no one was without imperfections.

Still, he had not been a murderer. He had never abused her or the children or small animals. Never had he embezzled money, or even knowingly ran a stop sign. Usually, he drove only five miles per hour over the speed limit and stayed in the right-hand lane except to pass. He hadn't told her big lies, only stretched the truth on occasion, perhaps forgot a fact or two somewhere along the way.

As far as she knew, he had been faithful. And what if he hadn't? He still didn't deserve to die. Not like he had; not with his brains blown out as he ate grapefruit. No, never like that. Not in this hellhole.

Sharon Samuels felt a shiver course through her body, a body that seemed quite far away, as though it belonged to someone else. Although the air in the room felt warm and moist against her skin, she felt cold and dry inside. Even her mind seemed frozen. She couldn't think – at least not a rational thought. Every time she tried to decide what she needed to do next, a barrage of gibberish assaulted her. Every sound was in his voice and the cacophony made her want to scream.

She forced herself to sit very still on the edge of the bed, feeling like she was perched on the edge of the world, and if she made the slightest movement she would fall off into the great black nothingness looming before her. She tried to be as still as a rock, as though by transforming herself into stone the waves of emotion that rose and fell and rose again would wash around her and press on toward distant shores.

She was trying so very hard, but she could feel her body rocking, vibrating to an unknown energy. Her mind was even more restless, filled with red and black images spinning in a vortex. Spinning faster and faster, until they were hurled like plaster saints to smash at the stony walls of her mind.

Sharon Samuels wanted to scream. A Bartlett montage was moving on a shimmering silver screen in the center of her mind: his face the first time they'd met, lean and tanned, framed by the white shirt and the knotted tie, the smooth hardness of his body the first time they had made love on the couch that was always six inches too short, no matter which way they positioned themselves, walking through that Connecticut snowstorm with the wind-driven flakes wetting their faces like icy tears, Trevor throwing a baseball to him – over and over and over and over – in the shady backyard of that corner lot on Farmington. Images flickered across her mind like a movie shown through a projector set at a too high speed. Years swept by – no more than a handful of dry leaves flung into the air by an excited child and carried along by a late November gale.

She ran the palms of her hands along her inner thighs as if to assure herself that she had a body. A faint smoothness, a soft subtleness, was all she could feel, nothing else. Yet, in her mind she could also feel the sandpaper that grew on his jaw line when the moon rose and they crawled between silk sheets, smell the unique aroma of cigar smoke, coffee beans, cologne, shampoo, ink, and Preparation H that was Bartlett Samuels. She could hear the way he snorted over some article in the newspaper that aggravated his sensibilities and scratched his head when numbers puzzled him. She could see him, feel him, hear him, taste him, and smell him a thousand ways.

She wanted to scream, but there was no use. If anyone heard her it wouldn't matter to them. Screaming would relieve the crushing pressure for only a few seconds. Then it would come back, rejuvenated.

Other pictures flickered on the screen. Bartlett drunk, Bartlett angry, red in the face and shouting at her over some misdeed now forgotten a dozen years, Bartlett disappointed like a little boy over a poorly chosen Christmas present, Bartlett turning and walking out of the room with long furious strides and a board-stiff back after she had voiced her accusations. There were a hundred more such images, but Sharon Samuels did not want to remember any of them, so she gnawed on her lower lip, trying to remember only the good times.

~ * ~

Seven minutes after midnight. Later than she had thought. Better get back and check on her mother. At the end of the long corridor, Kristin Samuels paused and looked back over her shoulder, peering into the dimness. Seeing no one, she lifted the bottle to her lips. There was less than an inch of amber liquid sloshing around the bottom. She let her lips come apart. Whiskey slid into her mouth and she captured it there; holding it, allowing it to submerge her tongue. Sloshing the whiskey around gently, she decided it would make a fine mouthwash.

She loved whiskey, absolutely loved it. Loved the smell of it, the taste of it, the texture of it, the way it floated atop her tongue, the way it burned on the downward passage.

Lowering the bottle, she studied it regretfully. Empty. For a moment longer she held it, relishing its cool smoothness. Then she bent and slid it behind the large urn that stood at the junction of the two hallways. It was nearly full of dirt, so she figured it was supposed to be serving as a flower pot. All that was growing in the urn, however, was a modest collection of cigarette butts.

Running her fingers through her hair, Kristin started down the hall toward her mother's room. She strolled at a modest pace, pleased her legs moved steadily beneath her and the walls seemed to be holding firm at the correct angles.

She had drunk most of a half-pint of good Kentucky bourbon and taken one of those little round blue pills that were supposed to ease nerves and promote sleep. The combination had merely given her a pleasantly mellow buzz. She could never recall the name of those pills, so she always referred to them as blue drowsies. She had found them in the reverend's room.

As she neared her mother's room, the hallway floor seemed to slope gently upward, then bent down and slightly left. She didn't feel that high. Probably all the stress was affecting her. After all, it had been one hell of a day.

Her hair seemed thicker than usual and slightly matted, as if someone had begun to weave strands together, only to give it up for a bad job. She bet she looked a fucking mess. Kristin glanced around for a purse she wasn't carrying. Damn; she could have used a mirror. She despised looking like shit. Not that her mother would notice; she never did, at least if she did, she didn't say anything.

Her dad, however, would have noticed. He always noticed, when he was home. Kristin wished he'd been home more. She had overheard other men call him a bastard and a son-of-a-bitch, but he'd always been sweet to her. Not only with money, either, although he had given her generous amounts of cash. He'd also given her what she felt were the two most important things one person could give another: attention and affection.

Kristin didn't believe in love; that was for fairy tales and Democrats. Republicans, her daddy had said, don't love anything, not even money. They merely worshipped that.

Pausing outside the door, Kristin reflected that even worshipping was worthless. In her own way, she had worshipped her daddy, and now he was dead. The word dead sat in the middle of her brain like a freshly dropped dog turd, the steam still rising.

A sudden rawness invaded her throat and moisture pooled in her eyes. Blinking, she wiped her nose with the back of her hand. She wasn't going to think anymore. She was simply going to get high and stay there until all this emotional crap passed. Now that she had copped a few pills and had another half-pint wedged into the back pocket of her jeans, she was set, at least for the next several hours. Planning ahead, she'd also liberated enough cash so she could make a decent buy, that is if she could ever find some dope.

Out here in the middle of this fucking nowhere God-forsaken jungle you would have thought you could have scored at least once a day. But hell no; she'd finished all the reefers she'd brought from home, and, except for one small bag she'd been able to buy at some village whose name she couldn't begin to pronounce, that had been it. Even that bag had been crap. Definitely not quality stuff.

Damn, but she was dying. Fucking withdrawal symptoms in the middle of the fucking jungle, talk about your trip from hell.

Smoothing her hair, she wet a fingertip and wiped at the mascara she knew had run. Then, for some reason she had never been able to figure out, she smoothed her eyebrows out with the dampness. Some psycho psychologist would have a fine time with that quirk, she thought as she twisted the doorknob.

~ * ~

Sharon Samuels did not stir as the door squeaked open, remaining still and silent on the bed, as though she were a papier-mâché image of herself. Random moonlight had broken through the clouds and in the fallen light her face glittered like pale sandstone.

At the first sound, Amy Moby came alert like a cat. Unmoving in her chair in the dark corner, only her eyes were alive, narrowing, watching.

She had no clue who might be coming through the door and suddenly longed for a weapon, a weapon of any kind. A pistol would be nice, but a knife would do. For that matter, so would a hand grenade. There had been no firing since the storm hit, but the rain had stopped now and the wind fallen away. Fear surged though her. Making a conscious effort to rise above the fear, she got her mind under control, then sat watching with guarded eyes.

Kristin slipped quietly into the room and slowly pushed the door shut, holding on at the end so the click was muted. She began to work her way across the room, setting her feet down as lightly as she could, heading toward the window. Easing across the floor, she studied her mother's face, wondering at its rigidity. There was a cushioned ledge attached to the wall below the bottom of the window and she pulled the bottle out of her hip pocket and eased down into a puddle of moonlight shaped like Lake Huron.

Splinters of moonlight stabbed the glass, making it sparkle. Raising the bottle to her lips, she sipped delicately. A fine lady was how she expressed it to herself.

Amy Moby sighed as the moonlight splashed against the ascending bottle. The sound was too faint for anyone even a foot away to hear. She and Joe had wondered about the girl. From day one of the tour, they had talked about their concerns.

A couple of times she'd been almost sure the girl was high or hung-over, but she'd never been certain. Sad to see it in one so young, but under the circumstances, it was hard to be overly critical. Heck, she could stand a drink herself. The day had been hell and the night was stretching out like a highway that ran to the end of the map.

Amy cleared her throat. The girl's shoulders jumped like she had been stung.

"I was just sitting with your mom for a while."

"Oh."

"I'm so sorry about your father."

Kristin tucked her chin against her chest. Her eyes analyzed moonlight Rorschachs on the wooden floorboards. "Thank you."

"Anything I can do for you?"

"There's nothing anyone can do."

Silence settled into the small room. The only sounds came when one of the women breathed deeply. Clouds drifted across the moon, causing a deeper darkness infiltrated the room. There was only the silence, darkness, and the faint breathing of sad, lonely women. Finally, deep in the distant jungle, there was a final roll of thunder.

Amy Moby positioned her hands on the arms of her chair. "If you're sure you don't need me, and if you're going to be here a while, I'll go and check on my husband." In the dark, the girl's face was nothing more than a splash of alabaster.

Seconds ticked.

A rogue wind rattled the window glass.

"I'll be here."

The older woman rose. Her muscles were stiff and one of her knee joints popped. Wonder how long I sat there, she asked herself. Aloud, she said, "I'll be back in a little while and check on you. Just stick your head out the door and call if you need help."

The girl nodded – the movement barely discernible in the poor light. Amy Moby tiptoed across the room and slipped into the hallway.

The door clicked gently shut behind her.

Wind pushed the clouds apart and moonlight streamed again through the glass, splattering like poured cream on the girl's hair.

Fifty-one

"We hear that you are a priest." The boy was remarkably thin. His arms looked like slender limbs from young trees. He had a thin black mustache that quivered when he talked, as though he were afraid. He might have been seventeen.

"Well, not really a priest. Not a priest as you know them. However, I am a minister of the gospel." Reverend Thomas Malloy looked around him. He had been trapped in the kitchen by a number of the hotel staff. They were all shorter than he was and he found himself looking down on a sea of dark heads. He turned slowly, smiling as he rotated his body. Truly, he was surrounded. He felt a little like he was Jesus, surrounded by his disciples.

The boy nodded as he looked up from under a shock of black hair, gesturing with his thin arms. "We have been talking. This attack by the guerrillas is a very bad business. We do not want any more people to die. We are ignorant people, peasants only. We know nothing of politics. To us, the Revolución is

267

nothing. To us, Gutierrez is only a name. We are nothing. Dust only. But we want the fighting to stop."

He paused and shrugged his narrow shoulders. "We thought that since you were a man of God you must also be a man of peace. Therefore, we decided to talk to you, to tell you how we feel." Again, the boy shrugged. "Perhaps you could carry our words to the soldiers of Gutierrez, and to the guerrillas."

The boy made expansive movements with both arms. He looked like a dark bird flapping his wings. "The others, they chose me to be their spokesman. But I am no orator, my words are poor."

Reverend Malloy looked again at the circle of people. Except for one old man, the young man who had spoken, and another boy who could not have been more than nine or ten years old, the rest were women. Easy to see why the boy had been elected spokesman.

Reverend Malloy was not sure what he should say. Guerrillas made him very uncomfortable. So did the hotel staff. They were all staring at him as if he were an important man, waiting for him to speak, as though his words would bring succor. Nerves jumped in his cheeks. To paraphrase the Apostle Paul, he thought, it would be good to take a little wine for the sake of his nerves. He tried to smile at the women and the old man and the two boys. His lips felt heavy and tired.

"My words carry no weight in Morazon. I would not be a good spokesman for you. Naturally, as a man of God, I am willing to listen and help where I can."

"Are you not a priest?"

"I'm like a priest, only not exactly a priest."

"But you can hear our confessions?"

Reverend Malloy shook his aching head. He was quite tired, in need of a little pick-me-up. "You need to make your confessions directly to God. I can counsel with you, but only God can truly hear your confessions and grant you forgiveness. I am a man of God, but only a man."

A man in growing need of a drink, he added to himself as he nodded at the people crowded around him in what he hoped they perceived as a benign dismissal. Never before had Thomas Malloy identified personally with Jesus; he had only worshipped him. Now, however, he could honestly state that he felt he understood how Jesus must have felt at times when he longed to escape the throngs.

Granted, Jesus probably wanted to commune with his Heavenly Father, while he was more interested in a spiritual encounter of a different sort, but the desire to get away was almost overwhelming.

The boy stepped back, licked his lips and looked around at his companions. They stared back at him, but gave no sign of surrender. He tried again. "But, Father…"

"Reverend."

The boy made a truncated bow. "Reverend Father…"

"Really, my boy it is just, oh, never mind." He clapped a hand on the boy's left shoulder in what he hoped would be construed as a friendly manner. He could feel bone under the skin, hard and thin, like a petrified stick. "I am not a priest, but I can pray with you." He lifted his eyes and, with the ease gained by much practice, let them wander across the small circle of brown faces. My little congregation of the southern hemisphere, he said to himself. Aloud, he said: "Would you like for me to pray?"

The boy turned and spoke a few words in Spanish. The reverend could speak a little Spanish, and read it quite well, but the boy spoke far too quickly for him to follow, except for the word *padre*, which the boy said twice.

There were murmurs of what sounded to the reverend like assent, and the boy turned, smiled broadly, and said: "*Sí, Padre. Sí.*"

Reverend Malloy nodded and said: "Let us pray." A great rustling sound filled the air, and he eased his eyes open a crack. All the people had knelt on the hard tile floor and bowed their heads. What simple people, the reverend said to himself, thinking at the same time on some more intrinsic level that their kneeling was, in some way far too subtle for him to fully understand, a humbling experience.

A thin film of sweat had formed on his forehead. Tiny tremors, no more than faint neural vibrations, rippled deep inside his body. The urge to drink was rising like a new sun. It was a very powerful force. He could feel his resolve melting like a thin April snow.

"Let us pray," he said, his voice cracking. Pausing, he cleared his throat. Then he closed his eyes tightly. "Let us pray," said Reverend Thomas Malloy, and all the people listened of one accord.

~ * ~

Lord Threlkeld opened his eyes slowly. He had not realized he'd gone to sleep. He could vaguely recall pouring a drink and sitting down in the chair. Seemed to him that Lady Threlkeld had been there.

He looked around the room, swiveling his neck slowly so as to not upset the equilibrium, half expecting to see her, sitting with her legs crossed, a drink in one hand, a cigarette in the other, smiling that thin, knowing smile. Oh, but he knew that smile. At one time he had found it utterly captivating. Now... he shivered as he pushed his way gingerly out of the chair.

Damn, but his head ached. Squaring his body, he took a careful sighting on the far side of the room. From years of enforced study, Donald Threlkeld knew the only cure for what ailed him was, as his Uncle Arthur, Lord Farrington, had been fond of saying, a touch of the hair of the dog that bit you. Taking a deep breath, he set sail.

The floor seemed to sway beneath him. Walls undulated as if they were being squeezed and released by some gigantic, unseen hand. He stopped, closed his eyes, and counted backwards from thirty in Mandarin. Languages had been his only significant accomplishment in school and he liked to stay in practice.

When he opened his eyes, the room seemed to have recovered its balance. However, it was remarkably quiet. Hadn't it been quite noisy earlier? He puzzled it out as he fixed his drink. Lord Threlkeld was pleased at the steadiness of his hands.

He poured the drink, then sipped daintily while the glass was still on the dresser. He picked up the glass and began his journey back across the room. Absolutely noisy it had been, nearly as bad as riding that damn bus full of tourists chattering like magpies. Lord Threlkeld shuddered. Oh, how the mighty had fallen. Not that he expected things to be as they had been in his grandfather's time, but...

He stopped and sipped. Better. He resumed his migration. Selling the ancestral home had been one thing, distasteful, yet necessary. However, riding around in an ancient bus through some godforsaken country on deplorable roads with common people who never ceased chattering, and, to be frank about it, often stank, well, that was simply common.

And to think that he, Donald, had sunk to such a state. Why, it was completely disgusting – precisely like this country. Full of nasty peasants, snakes, monkeys, and mosquitoes nearly as big as small birds. Revolting. Certainly not civilized.

He eased himself into the chair, spilling a few drops. One fell on his hand and he licked it up. Smiling, he lifted his glass in a toast to civilization. Then he took a drink and eased his aching head against the padded back of the chair, gazing up at the ceiling. It needed a fresh coat of paint.

Closing his eyes, he listened to the quiet. Storm must have passed, he decided. Wonder what happened to those damn guerrillas? Really, he should go check. Wonder what happened to Dianna? Definitely should go check. Maybe he would wait a few, finish this drink. Surely the wench would turn up soon. Lord Threlkeld sipped his drink, and wondered idly – between sips – where his own life had wandered off to.

~ * ~

The needle pricked her finger and she looked up from her sewing and sucked at the pain. Her tongue touched a drop of blood and she made a face at the coppery taste. She had been sewing for some time and she realized in that moment her shoulder muscles were trying to cramp.

Juanita Herrera glanced at the clock on the small table she used to house her sewing kit and whatever book she might be reading. The clock and table had been her mother's. The clock was very old for a clock, as her mother had been dead for over ten years, and as far back as Juanita could remember it had stood on her mother's bedside table. Only twice had it needed repairing. Granted, it had to be wound every day, which she did the first thing each morning, but it kept accurate time. She studied the clock again. No, her eyes had not been deceiving her. The day and half the night were gone. The men would be wanting hot food. Rising quickly, she thrust her sewing onto the chair, then hurried from her room still wearing her thimble.

The hallway was dimly lighted, but she knew it well and walked rapidly toward the kitchen. No aromas of food cooking greeted her and she guessed the cook was hiding in her room, probably under the bed. The woman was always looking for excuses. Usually, Juanita kept watch on her, but today the guerrillas and the storm had conspired to throw her off. Juanita could not hear the storm now and she wondered if the guerrillas would attack again. She would ask Poncho. Where was Poncho? She tried to recall when she had last seen him.

Events of the day tumbled through her head like a bag of marbles emptying onto a glass plate. Marbles and shattered glass tumbled in a noisy kaleidoscope. She could not recall her last Poncho sighting. For a second she even forgot the cook's name. Then she remembered it and shouted for Pillar. She called three times before the woman answered in a timid voice. By the time she had finished chastising the woman and rounding up all the maids she could find, thoughts of Poncho had vanished. Little food had been prepared and Juanita Herrera was very busy.

~ * ~

The storm had passed. Only a light wind still pushed through the cracks of the old barn. Water dripped slowly, rhythmically from the eaves. Tony lay on the hay peering into the darkness. The lightning had moved on and the moonlight was thin and erratic. A few faint lights glowed behind curtains at certain windows of the old hotel, but the people inside were careful not to cast shadows. There was light in the room where the man he had shot had been. Idly, Tony wondered if the man was still there. A few shadows did flutter about the grounds, but he knew those were only thrown by trees.

He listened for sounds of men moving in the dark. There might be a relief column of soldiers sent by Gutierrez, or Carlos might risk one more attack under cover of darkness. He did not think Carlos would make such an attempt, but he was not certain. Carlos could be a surprising man.

All he could hear was the wind, the gnawing of the rats in the barn, and, now and then, the restless movements of one of the horses in the corral. Then he could hear the empty gurgling of his own stomach. My god, but he was hungry. Breakfast had been a pitiful affair and almost an entire day ago. It was bad business to ask a man to fight on an empty stomach. Many men would not do it, not for long, anyway. Tony sighed as he shifted position; hunger he did not mind so much. Yes, of course, he would like to eat, but he could go days without eating. Water, however, was another matter.

Scooting closer to the edge of the platform, he stuck his hand out. Seconds later a drop of water struck it, then another. Turning onto his back, he eased his head out of the barn. Closing his eyes, he opened his mouth. He could not say how long he lay there with the water dripping into his open mouth, but he collected several swallows of water before he turned and worked his way fully back into the barn loft.

The hay was much softer and smelled better than the jungle where he usually slept. Closing his eyes, he listened to the wind and the dripping water and the comforting sounds of the horses in the night, thinking about Carlos, Jesus, Felix, and the rest, wondering if they still lived. Then he thought about when he was young and his mother would tell him stories of the gauchos she had known as a girl. Never had Tony seen a gaucho, but he liked horses. He listened to the horses for a moment longer, then he was dreaming, dreaming he was floating high in the sky, holding on to the tail of a kite. Below him, shadows of clouds moved across a vast flat landscape where horses ran freely across a grassy plain.

~ * ~

The lieutenant rapped softly at the door with two knuckles. It was not completely shut. He knocked anyway. He rapped twice, quickly, then paused, waiting for a response.

"Come in." The words were scarcely more than a whisper.

He glanced quickly up and down the hall, then, feeling foolish, eased the door open. It squeaked as it swung in and he stepped inside under cover of the squeak. No lights burned in the room, and he stood for a moment, waiting for his eyes to adjust.

"Why don't you close the door, Lieutenant?"

Leaning against the door, he twisted the knob with his hands behind his back, hearing the click with satisfaction. His fingers moved over the wood but found no deadbolt.

It was so quiet in the room that he could hear her breathing. He first knew where she was by the smell of her cigarette. Then, as his eyes grew accustomed to the dimness, he could see a pale outline of a human figure in the chair that stood in front of the room's only window. Heavy, dark curtains hung in front of the glass, but the two panels did not meet. A gap of three or four inches allowed a thin soupcon of milky light to float into the room. Uncomfortable in the quiescent murkiness, Lieutenant Escobar shifted his weight from one foot to the other as he ran a hand along the planes of his face. The rustling of his stubble was audible.

"Not afraid to come closer are you, Lieutenant?"

He walked cautiously across the floor, his boots squeaking, the floorboards moaning as a nail moved inside the wood. It was a modest-sized room and his long strides traversed it quickly. Closer, he could see the narrow line of light striping her face. His eyes drifted southward. Lady Dianna Threlkeld was as naked as if she had just stepped from her bath. Lieutenant Manuel Escobar felt a warmth on his cheeks, and was grateful for the poor quality of the light.

"So nice of you to come calling, Lieutenant."

"You asked me to stop by."

"So I did." Lady Threlkeld rose slowly from her chair, the mixture of moonlight and starlight highlighting her slimness. In the velvety light, her skin looked soft, smooth, unlined. She was a tall woman, almost as tall as the lieutenant. Lustrous eyes moved like pools of disturbed water as she worked her gaze across the young officer's face. "You took a long time to get here. Was beginning to wonder if you would come."

"I had much to do. See to the men, make sure they were fed, provided with ammunition, and in proper position."

Lady Threlkeld took one step forward. Half her face was now in the light. "Are our defenses holding?"

"So far our losses have been light and our line of defense is unbroken."

"Excellent. And are our soldiers brave?"

"Of course," he said, though as he said it doubts formed in his mind.

"Very good. Reinforcements?"

"If," he shrugged, "if the call got through, and if headquarters responds quickly, and if the trucks are ready, and

if the rains do not come again, and if the roads are not closed –
if all that happens, then reinforcements could be here by
morning."

She laughed, tinkling glass wind-chimes in the falling
starshine. "You, Lieutenant, are a pessimist."

"And you, señora?"

"Me?" She took another step, lifted her right hand and ran
her index finger down his cheek. "Why, I'm a sensualist."

He could smell her perfume, and the scent triggered the
realization that he had not been with a woman in a long time.
He tried to remember exactly how long, but the woman with the
strange accent took another step closer, and then her hair was
tickling his face. Her body came up against his in the quiet
darkness and he could feel her slimness was not all skin and
bones. Her fingers fumbled with the buttons of his shirt. He did
not resist.

Fingertips traced ancient patterns across his chest. Those
fingertips felt hot to him and he felt himself grow hard against
her softness. The fingertips moved lower, unbuttoning as they
moved. As they fumbled with his belt he thought of the men,
and Captain Morales, and the guerrillas, and where his duty lay,
but then the fingers encircled his rigid penis and as hair
brushed across his chest and fell against his stomach, he forgot
about all of Yuscarana except for the small, quiet, dark room
and the woman with her head between his legs and moonlight
branding her back argent.

Fifty-two

At the reception for the Norwegian Ambassador, President Gutierrez distinguished himself solely by the quantity of whiskey he consumed. Since he was the President of Morazon, at least for now, and since the ambassador was a polished diplomat desirous of finalizing a complex trade agreement – involving computers, bananas, electrical turbines, and a certain wood, scarce and known for its unusual, distinctive coloring and durability – nothing was said. In fact, the ambassador did not once raise his formidable eyebrows, eyebrows which were quite famous within diplomatic circles.

Due to the rapidly deteriorating condition of the president of Morazon, the reception was diplomatically truncated. Finance Minister Allende made certain each guest received a gracious sendoff. The president's press secretary, a man who wore wire-framed glasses and was known as La Lengua (The Tongue), made certain Jorge Ruiz was able to report the following morning on Solovision that the reception had been a

277

great success. Colonel Munuoz, the president's personal aide, made certain President Gutierrez successfully perambulated the twisting corridors of the palace. Only once did they have to stop. The pause allowed the president to be sick in a large flower pot containing a species of fern native to Morazon. Fortunately, the hallway was empty of all personnel except for Private Hernandez who, while not overly bright, knew enough to avert his eyes.

After the episode, President Gutierrez felt sufficiently improved to want to talk about the most recent crisis created by the Revolución.

"I tell you, Colonel, the bastardos are driving me crazy. That is why I drank so many whiskies tonight. It was not that the ambassador was so awful, although I do think that he is, perhaps, homosexual. But that is not the point, Colonel," Gutierrez said, catching the toe of a shoe on an edge of the carpet and stumbling against Colonel Munuoz.

"No," the president said, after he had recovered his balance, "no, it is not. These rebels are the point, you see. Rather, they are the problem." Pausing, he tilted his head to one side, looking remarkably like one of the Morazonian buzzards who nested high in cliffs and lived off carrion. "Did you hear, Colonel, that the bastardos attacked Yuscarana this morning?"

Colonel Munuoz carefully surveyed the corridor that led directly to the president's private quarters. They were alone.

"I was the one who informed you of the attack," was all he said. However, if one had listened carefully, certain implications were contained in the enunciation of the words. Not all the implications were flattering to the president.

Gutierrez did not seem to notice, although certain movements of his eyes indicated that perhaps he was not as drunk as he had been earlier in the evening. "Well, that is the third rebel attack this month. Such attacks cannot continue. Our army is stretched thin and the country is tired of blood. My generals and their men have killed many guerillas, but more always take the place of the dead." He weaved slightly, as though the floor had begun to undulate. Moisture formed in his eyes.

"What are we to do, Colonel?"

Colonel Munuoz studied the face of the president of Morazon with care. He had certain ideas about what to do. However, the moment was not right. In a few more days, a week perhaps. After the next defeat for certain. It had been decided by the very generals to whom the president had just referred.

Colonel Munuoz smiled to himself. Aloud, he said: "What we are going to do is get you to bed."

"To bed? But I could not sleep, not with Yuscarana hanging over my head like a gigantic stone, ready to fall." He waved his arms. "I need another drink to help me sleep." President Gutierrez leaned toward the colonel. "You know," said the president, "I have not truly slept for weeks now. Not deep, refreshing sleep."

The colonel stepped back. The breath of the president would paralyze an anaconda. You need another drink, he thought, like Captain Morales needs more guerrillas to attack Yuscarana.

"I will get you another drink," was all he said.

Smiling, the president let his chin drop to his chest.

Colonel Munuoz sighed as he draped an arm across the shoulders of the president of Morazon. They walked through the open door into the bedroom of the president like brothers.

Looking through the shock of hair that had fallen across his face, the president studied the colonel with alert eyes.

Fifty-three

He was very tired. Exhaustion had invaded his bloodstream. Throughout the afternoon he had wandered the hallways of the old hotel, pausing, as the urge struck, to sneak quick peeks out windows. At odd, quiet moments he thought of his father.

Trevor could recall his father reading to him. He had been quite young and his father had seemed very large sitting in the big red chair at the foot of his bed. The deep huskiness of his father's voice and the way he crossed his legs and swung one dangling foot remained vivid in the boy's memory. His father's shoes had always been highly polished, the leather glistening when the light struck it. His father had not worn reading glasses in those days and his hair had been dark and thick.

Trevor could not remember how long each of the nightly reading sessions had lasted, but he could still smell the aftershave his father wore and the way his daily stubble had sandpapered his cheek during their goodnight kiss. He tried to recall when the sessions had stopped.

A sudden desire to be with his father swept over him and he decided to go and sit by the body. He realized his father was dead, but Trevor still wanted the sense of being in the same room with him, sharing a final meeting of souls.

He walked quickly down the hallway. Now that he had made up his mind, he was in a hurry.

The hallway had grown dark as night fell. Paintings and photographs of men in out-of-date clothes stared down at him from frames peeling gilt, and floorboards moaned beneath his steps as the wind worried the loose glass in rotting frames.

Damn, this is an old hotel, the boy thought. Why didn't the rebels simply wait a few years; the place would simply fall down around itself. "Reminds me of the house in *Psycho*," he murmured, not realizing he had spoken.

Pausing at the top of the stairs, Trevor leaned against the banister and studied the lobby below, relishing the sensation of being a king staring down at his subjects.

Only a few lamps were burning, casting barely enough light for him to see shadowy soldiers. A few were talking in voices pitched low and soft. Faint murmurs, like the rumbling of cars rolling in the distance, reached him.

As quietly as he could, he walked down the stairs. One man looked up, but Trevor merely glanced at the man and kept moving. At the bottom of the stairs, he turned left.

Twice he had experienced a strong sensation that someone was actively watching him, but when he turned, all he could see were tired men leaning against tired walls, shadows falling away from columns, ratty couches, and potted plants in need of care and attention.

At the edge of the dining room, Trevor paused. Dirty dishes and half-filled glasses surrounded by used silverware still lay atop soiled tablecloths. A faint buzzing filled the air. He held his breath and listened. Flies. Huge, green, bottle flies were doing barrel rolls around the room, dive-bombing dry bread, marching across plates of congealing eggs and meat going gray and hard. Chairs, overturned in the madness of the morning, lay where they had fallen. With their legs sticking up in the air they made Trevor think of dead horses.

Stepping into the room, he made himself look toward the table where they had been in the morning that seemed another lifetime ago. Then he made himself walk across the litter-strewn floor toward the tablecloth-covered bundle. The white tablecloth was streaked with red. As he drew closer, he could see a dark stain spreading out from beneath the tablecloth. In the dim light the streak looked wet. Three feet away, Trevor could smell the blood.

Nausea swept over him and he stopped, closed his eyes, and took a deep breath. He let it go slowly and when it was gone the nausea had passed. Another step and he knelt. Trevor stretched out a hand. His fingers were trembling.

They were still trembling when they touched the bundle. Thoughts and memories rolled across his mind, tumbling so rapidly they were no more than a glittering kaleidoscope of blurry images forming and reforming. The tablecloth felt as smooth as marble. He pulled it back slowly, not wanting to look, unable to stop.

Lifting the cloth with one hand, he reluctantly slid the other hand under the white shroud. He was trembling so hard he worried he wouldn't be able to keep from falling. Then his fingers touched flesh and he cried out. He closed his eyes and his body shook. He wanted to cry. Opening his eyes, Trevor saw an arm more familiar than his own. He began to sob.

He cried for a long time. He had never imagined that anyone could hold so many tears. When the tears finally slowed, he bowed his head and placed his cheek against his father's arm. The flesh was cool, as smooth as stone.

~ * ~

Pulling the bill of his cap lower, Captain Morales let his eyes wander across the lobby. There was very little lighting, which was good. There were very few men, which was bad. Another strong push by the rebels and the line would not hold. He had a good position, not fortified, but still providing substantial cover; they had a fair amount of ammunition, and his men were warm and fed, now that the señora of the hotel had taken charge.

None of that would matter if the rebels had enough men. That was his big problem at the moment. He had no idea how many rebels there were, or if there were more coming, or even if the generals of Gutierrez had authorized a relief column. Without intelligence, he was fighting blind.

Morales was glad to get most of the men from the barracks, but none of the men from the communications shack had come. They would not come now, he thought, not even if they could. They would see he was surrounded and retreat toward the capitol. He could not blame them – Yuscarana was beginning to take on the appearance of a death trap.

Thinking of Señora Herrera made him wonder where Señor Herrera was. Perhaps he was in the back with the lieutenant. Or dead. Captain Morales tried to count the number of men he had. He counted three times. Each count proved unsatisfactory.

Someone had touched a match to a drunken line of candles on the registration counter and the flames flickered in an unseen breeze. Shadows danced on the plaster walls, reminding the captain of earlier days when he had lounged around a campfire in the great alive jungle with his men, watching shadows dance at the edge of light, taunting the beasts of the jungle in the night. He had been younger then, oh so much younger.

He tried to recall the names of the men around those campfires. Their faces were a blur, vague outlines of jaws and single eyes staring at him like surrealist paintings coming to life.

Morales shook his head. That had been another time. He had been another man.

How many of those comrades were still alive? Most had been his age, or younger. Only a few, like the sergeant with the Poncho Villa mustache, who loved tequila and tacos, had been older. The sergeant, who had had gray streaks in his hair and a pot gut that looked like he had swallowed a small melon whole, had seemed old then to Morales. And now I am even older than that sergeant, Morales thought. No wonder I am tired.

The captain let his vision drift around the lobby. A few men were stirring, wandering over to get a drink of water from the pitcher on the counter, or chatting in subdued voices. A wounded man, blood seeping through the bandage on his arm, sat in the shadows. His face was turned toward Morales, but the captain did not think the man was seeing him.

The lieutenant was not in the lobby. He should have been back, Morales thought. A moment later, he dismissed the thought. No use worrying, the lieutenant was probably with the men in the back.

A sound caught his attention and he lifted his head in time to see a young boy coming down the stairs. Morales recognized the boy. He was the boy whose father had been shot at the breakfast table that morning – the morning which seemed so long ago. He started to call out to the boy. Instead, he silently watched him enter the dining room. Captain Morales wished him well.

Closing his eyes, he considered whether or not he wanted to get up and go and grab a sandwich, or a bowl of the *sopa* Señora Herrera had simmering on the stove. It was *sopa de polloup*, with chicken, vegetables, and arroz floating in a steadily thickening broth, *arroz con polo sopa*. He preferred *sopa de legumbres*, but then he was a captain and not a cook. He had not tried the *sopa*, but he had overheard some of the men talking about it. Apparently, it was very spicy.

Normally, he liked spicy foods. Tonight, however, his usually calm stomach was sour. Full of acid, the way it always got in battle. Earlier, he had lifted an orange from a blue and yellow bowl in the kitchen. Now, he pulled it from his pocket. It was one of the smaller varieties, easy to peel. His fingers were still nimble. Seconds later, he was sucking on juice.

As he sucked, he let his mind ramble indiscriminately over memories that lay like great, fertile fields between the mountains of his mind. That was how he always thought of his memories, as being contained in fields, like crops, fenced and framed neatly, so he could return to them without searching. There was a field for childhood, one for his school years, one for his mother and father, and one for his early army days as a young lieutenant – green and hard as an unripe banana.

Tonight, his mind drifted to the field of the women: women he had known intimately, women he had only glimpsed in passing, women he wished he had made love to, women he regretted ever taking in his arms, women he had seen only in his dreams, and women who still gave him nightmares after twenty years. He often thought of women after a battle, perhaps due to the push and pull of life and death. However, Morales could not say exactly why he thought then of women.

Sitting quietly on the smooth floor of the hotel that was even older than he was, Captain Morales thought about a particular girl. She had not crossed his mind in years and he could think of nothing that had made her rise up out of the mists. He could no longer recall her name, if he had ever known it.

Yet, he could see her as clearly as in that first moment, when she had leaped from a crowd of gitanos and began to dance around their campfire. She had been a wild woman, animalistic in her movements, with a montage of emotions rippling across her face. Throwing her long dark hair back and lifting her arms toward the night sky, her body pulsating and throbbing to the rhythm of the firelight, her lips parting to let soft moans escape, she had danced like a heathen possessed.

He had been a young man then, out of the academy for only a few months, not yet experienced enough to take advantage of her dark savage beauty and the wild passion of that moment.

The moment of the dance had occurred on his first southern posting when he had been assigned to build a fortress twenty-four miles outside Zapata, a stronghold of the rebels at that time. "Young, I was so young," he murmured. If I had only known then what I know now, what I wouldn't have done. Or would I, he wondered.

Life was a great teacher, that he comprehended. Perhaps certain lessons were required. Perhaps a man simply had to undergo certain trials. Even if he was told indisputable facts by an acknowledged expert, maybe he still had to learn them for himself. But why did the learning always have to be the hard way?

Under the brim of his cap, Captain Morales smiled, to no one and to everyone. Sometime after midnight, Morales began to wonder what lessons Yuscarana had to teach him.

~ * ~

The jungle is never quiet at night. Even on the rare nights when the wind blows so low that man cannot discern its presence, it is there, breathing among the leaves at the very top of tall trees, sixty, seventy, eighty feet in the air, rustling them in a nocturnal lullaby. Always there are birds, fluttering their wings and crying out in the night. Their shrill cries mingling with the howls of the monkeys and the deeper, rougher growls of the big cats. All the while, beneath the more overt sounds, there were the slitherings of snakes over branches, through leaves, and down tree trunks. Finally, in the background – always – was the sound of water: dripping, flowing, falling, forever present... the blood of the earth, and its music.

~ * ~

Layers of clouds, as fine as silk, lined the horizon. The sun was an unripe papaya, pale, flattened, burning faintly beyond the clouds. Above the clouds, the sky was a blue so pale it might have been imagination.

It was so early in the morning that the animals of the earth still slept. No more than a few birds twittered tentatively in the easternmost branches of the tallest trees in the great green jungle. The night prowlers had already returned to their dens, thickets, and caverns. The wind, however, was waking, rustling a thousand leaves at once. But the men and women of Yuscarana were all asleep. Even those soldiers of Gutierrez who were on sentry duty nodded at their posts.

In all of Yuscarana and the narrow ring of fields of grain and hay that surrounded it, in the banana plantations that lay beyond the fields, in the great green jungle that rose like a separate world on the far side of the plantations, even in the mountains that poked their stony promontories into the blue-sky sea, only one human was awake. On the flank of a hill indistinguishable from a hundred others a boy named Felix opened one eye and stared at the strange, innocent glow in the eastern sky. He had not expected to live out the night and for a few moments he wondered if the glow was God. Then, for the space of a half dozen heartbeats, he was granted a reprieve from the pain that had been consuming his body in the dark and he could see it was simply the sun rising on a day he had not expected to see.

His lips were as dry as the bleached bones of a long dead cow. The boy wanted to lick them, but all his strength had gone into the opening of a single eye. He stared into the ascending glow until he was blind. Then, there was only the pain, a great horrible ripping burning pain. Yet it was one that he had now known for so long that within its cocoon he found a certain masochistic comfort. Inside the shroud of pain, he felt one more morning being born against his face.

~ * ~

He was dreaming of an ocean he'd never seen. Then a bird screamed and he came awake, startled, gasping for breath, feeling he had overslept and missed something important. Carlos sat up and surveyed the morning.

He was in a clearing at the edge of the jungle. Twenty yards away, a dirt road ran red and crooked. Down the red road a quarter mile, a huge piece of earth moving equipment sat abandoned, rusting by the side of the road. Already, jungle vines thicker than a man's forearm were growing up between the sections of the machine, claiming the metallic monster for the jungle.

Carlos wondered why the machine had been abandoned. It must have broken down and the crew had left it, planning to return with parts and a mechanic, he decided. They had better hurry, he thought, or the jungle will swallow it whole.

He stretched, rolling his head on his neck, glancing around. Sunlight had not yet penetrated the clearing. There was merely a faint yellowing of the texture of the grass and the leaves – the way old movie film looked when it had been exposed to weak light for a fraction of a second. In the thicker jungle beyond, night still held.

Seven of his men slept nearby on the damp ground. Three of them were wrapped up in the blue and gray blankets they had liberated from Tuscarolla a few weeks ago, while the others simply lay curled in on themselves. Carlos wondered where the rest of his men were.

Since the Revolución began, Carlos had never liked to sleep inside walls. They made him feel trapped. Not trapped like prison. More like he was a wild animal being held in a pen on some game preserve, waiting for his turn to be shot. No, the walls of buildings offered false protection, precisely like the government of Gutierrez. They merely kept you sedated with a fallacious sense of security, so that you relaxed your guard and became easy prey for your enemy. Carlos preferred the jungle with its rustling leaves, restless monkeys, and rebuking birds.

As though he had read the mind of Carlos, the bird screamed again. Carlos lifted his eyes and nodded at the blue macaw swinging from a dead branch of a nearby tree. Shifting his gaze to the fine gold rim of the eastern horizon, Carlos took a deep breath, and stretched.

Spitting the last of the sleep out of his mouth, Carlos stood, growling and cursing at the sleeping men, ordering them to get up. He was hungry, wondering what the hell he would eat.

As he rummaged in his pockets, he remembered the stores in Yuscarana. Carlos grinned. They were fighting for the people of Yuscarana – let the people of Yuscarana feed them. The blood urge was rising as he kicked a man who looked like his cousin, Tolar, only without the beard. The man shouted and rolled on the ground, wrapping his arms around his ribs. He scrambled to his feet and Carlos watched the man's right hand go for the machete hanging from his belt. Recognition grew in the man's eyes, and he settled for a dirty look before he bent and picked up his hat.

"Get up, you lazy pack of dogs. There is work yet to be done in Yuscarana, and I want to get to it before the sun becomes too hot, or the sorry ass-licking generals of Gutierrez actually do something for once and send more soldiers to Yuscarana. Come on, you baboons, you *bastardos*, there are soldiers to be killed in Yuscarana and the day is growing old. Get up, you sons-of-whores. Now is the time to go to Yuscarana. Now is the killing time."

Carlos felt the warmth of sunlight on his face and turned to welcome it. The sun was a ball of reddish gold cresting the hills that sprawled like dead men's fingers. Without speaking again, he turned again and started walking toward Yuscarana. He did not look back. He could hear the men shuffling into line behind him. Much blood would flow in Yuscarana today.

All his instincts were telling him that now was the time for the all-out attack. Tomorrow would be too late. No rebel troops were coming to help him, but in his mind, he could hear the diesel motors of the big army trucks turning over as the soldiers of Gutierrez hauled their carcasses into the back. Gutierrez could not afford another defeat. Reinforcements would surely be sent. All the troops in his army would not help him hold the palace if the forces of the Revolución could encircle the capital city and cut off the supply lines. Let the bastardos starve to death would be the rebels' motto.

Today was the day. Today was his day. Carlos could feel the certainty growing inside him.

Sunlight splashed hot against his face. Except for a few shadows that remained in the deepest part of the great jungle, all darkness was gone. Yuscarana lay before him, burnished by the sun, his citadel of glory.

~ * ~

First light of morning fingered his face and he came awake as sweetly as a baby. He did not open his eyes; rather he sensed that the day had begun. He had sat up too late drinking, thinking about what it did no good to think about, and as a result his head felt like the inside of an overturned washtub being pounded with pneumatic hammers.

Groaning at the aching going on inside his head, Lord Threlkeld straightened in the chair and massaged his temples. My god, how much had he drunk last night? He tried to recall his intake. Next, he tried to remember yesterday. For a moment, he could only see a blank slate and he felt a surge of panic. Then a rumbling from downstairs worked its way through the floor and he remembered the storm, then the rebels, and everything was all right; at least it was normal, if normal was the operative word, that is.

Lord Threlkeld moaned at the drumming going on inside his head and lethargically cursed his sensitive eyes. Another hour of sleep and he might have been ready to face the world. Turning his head, he tried to drift back to the land of dreams, but sunlight pressed unpleasantly warm against his skin. Placing his palms against the chair arms, he pushed himself upright.

He opened his eyes, and wished he hadn't. Dirty clothes and empty bottles lay where they had fallen. Dianna was not there, although he could smell faint traces of her passing, a lingering concoction of her perfume, the stale aroma of her cigarettes, her woman scent.

Tugging a feather pillow over his head, he shut his eyes as tightly as he could. While the room stopped spinning, he wondered where his wife was. Gradually, he felt sleep returning and smiled beneath the pillow.

~ * ~

A strenuous tugging dragged him out of that deep sleep that often comes in the moment before waking. He blinked at the strange banded light above him. It took a moment for him to realize he was lying on his back in the damp earth, staring up at the underside of a splintering porch. Remembering the woman, he rolled his head toward her.

He had never truly seen her face or body. Only glimpses in the flashes of lightning had been possible the night before. Not wanting to lose his booty after a single interlude, Jesus had tied her hands together behind her back with a coil of rope he always carried looped to his belt. Then he had tied the rope off again around one of his thick ankles.

The woman was turned away from him and he ordered her to roll over. Either she did not understand his language or she was ignoring him, because she only scrunched her knees in tighter against her chest. Aggravated at having to make the effort, Jesus stretched out an arm and burrowed his fingers in the long black hair. He gave a hard jerk and the woman moaned, but came willingly.

Damn, he thought as her face became visible. She was certainly not young, nor would she ever win a beauty prize at the fiesta. Her sallow face was plain and wrinkles lined her mouth and spread heavily from the corners of her eyes. Foreign, too – Asian. Dirt smudged one of her cheeks and he reached over and tried to wipe it away, but merely managed to smear it.

He could see the fear in her eyes and smell it emanating from her body. The sight of her face had elicited no arousal in him, but now he felt himself starting to grow hard. Grinning, he slapped her face. She yelped at the stinging and he crawled over and climbed atop of her, his fingers ripping the already shredded clothes from her body.

As she struggled beneath him, he felt the urge rise. Her flesh was smooth and he raked dirty fingernails down her breasts, pausing to grab a nipple, twisting it until she screamed. His lips were covering hers and the scream echoed in his mouth. His hands roamed across her body, pinching, gouging, squeezing. Remnants of her clothes fell to the damp earth. When she was naked, he unzipped and entered her without further preliminaries.

She was soft, wide, and deep. No virgin; but what the hell? Besides, he had not had a woman for two months and now he was gouging one twice in less than eight hours. Jesus the Pig grunted with pleasure as the sunlight worried its way through the cracks in the porch floor, painting haphazard stripes of light across his bare ass.

~*~

Akko Tyshimoda lay still beneath the man. Under his weight she was helpless.

She tried to turn off all her senses and turn her mind into a blank slate, but his animal stench was pervasive and she could hear him grunting like a wild pig. Rough hands savaged the most sensitive parts of her body. Worms of blood were slowly working down her breasts and her nipples hurt so badly from his twisting she wondered if they were going to fall off.

He was inside her now, plunging deeper with each thrust. He was bigger than Iwakura, longer and thicker, and more powerful in his thrusting. Still sore from the nocturnal rape, she felt as if her vaginal linings were being scraped raw.

Thoughts of her husband made her wonder where he was. Why didn't he come for her? She suddenly recalled that when they had first been married they had tried to send each other messages without speaking. Mental telepathy, Iwakura had called it. There had been times when it actually seemed to work. Perhaps if she sent him a message he would come for her. He was a brave man and a proud one. Fear would not deter him.

Why didn't he come? She whispered his name as she strained to send him the message that would save her. For several seconds, the intensity of the message did not waver. Then her brain grew fatigued and her body became steadily more conscious of the thrusting and she thought of Iwakura only in the interludes.

Words poured from the man atop her in a language she did not understand. His voice grew louder and spittle flew from his lips and splattered against her face. Long, dark, greasy, smelling of sweat, his hair hung down in her face. Lowering his head, he bit her savagely on a bare shoulder, worrying the flesh between his teeth until she wondered if he was rabid.

The angle of his body was painful to her and with much effort she worked her hips lower and spread her thighs and wrapped her legs around his broad back. It was as though he were a horse and she the rider, only their coupling was surreally inverted.

Her hands were bound tightly and wedged beneath her, rendering her helpless to resist. All she could do was to try and survive as painlessly as possible. So she wrapped her legs more tightly around the man as he mashed his face against her neck and tried to accommodate his rhythm. Above her, she could see daylight slanting through the raised porch and she ignored the spit, and the stench, and the salty sweat dripping off the animal upon her, focusing instead on the light as she prayed for the end to come quickly.

~ * ~

Eyes burning, Lieutenant Manuel Escobar peered out the window at the coming dawn, wondering when the rebels would attack. Fervently, he hoped they would have the decency to wait until he had a cup of coffee. He rubbed at his eyes. Sweet Jesus, but he was sleepy.

He had slept for only a few minutes after making love to the foreign woman. She must have left him soon after his eyes had closed, and, while he did not hear her leaving, the absence of her body woke him. He had reached for her soft warmth and, when it had not been there, he had come instantly awake. After dressing, he had meandered back to where he had positioned the men at the rear of the hotel and relieved Corporal Jimenez. The lieutenant knew he should have reported back to Captain Morales, but it had been late and he figured the captain was probably asleep and surely needed his rest. At least that is what Lieutenant Escobar had told himself, knowing he was actually simply reluctant to face the captain because the man had an uncanny way of discerning the truth.

He should have awakened Private Henrique at least two hours ago to relieve him, but thoughts of the strange woman and her surprising body, and Gitano, and the guerillas, and what Captain Morales was thinking had been working in his mind like so many industrious ants. So, he had stoically held his position, peering into the darkness, watching intently, waiting for the attack that had not come.

Energized by his brief siesta and the energy of his thoughts, stimulated by the vibrating of his nerves, he had not been even remotely sleepy. Now, his eyes were hot and heavy, feeling as if they were full of sand. Rubbing at them, he peered across the flat ground. Nothing moved all the way to the edge of the jungle. Altering the angle of his line of sight, he looked up. The pale blue sky was clear except for a handful of clouds that appeared to him as shreds of white gauze.

He would have liked to have seen Gitano, but the corral was on the far side of the barn and from this angle he could not even see the fence. His horse must be getting hungry and thirsty. Anger at the rebels for their interfering surged within him. He was strangely grateful for the anger; at least it was helping keep his eyes open.

His throat was dry and his stomach growled at him. Wondering what the captain was doing, he tried to formulate a satisfactory explanation for the night before. Lack of sleep, however, had dulled his brain until he could think only of coffee, breakfast, and bed. Except when he thought of bed, he thought of the strange English lady, and that path led only to trouble.

Coffee aromas reached him now and he surmised that Señora Herrera must have Maria and the others working in the kitchen scraping together some sort of breakfast. Escobar felt a flicker of guilt when he thought of Maria.

Not that they had ever done more than talk and steal a kiss or a quick embrace in the dark, but he was cognizant of the fact that she was kindly disposed toward him. Plus, he thought of her as attractive. In the deeper recesses of his thoughts, the lieutenant had always pictured them together some day. He had made no commitment. Marriage was not an option he was ready to consider at this stage of his career. But when the summer evenings were sultry and the perfume of the flowers strong, and when the moon was right, one never knew what might happen.

Now, though, he needed coffee, food, and sleep – even an hour would help – before the guerrillas came. Daylight was painful to his eyes and the aroma of brewing coffee was torture. Lieutenant Escobar was exceedingly glad to see the overweight figure of the sergeant come stumbling down the hall with his rifle in his left hand and a mug of coffee in his right. In the pale light of morning, steam rose above the lip of the white porcelain mug like a holy blessing.

~ * ~

He woke with the smell of hay strong in his nostrils and a horse's whinnying high in his ears. For a heartbeat he was a boy again. Then he opened his eyes, and in the blanched light saw the old hotel framed by the dark wood that surrounded the opening in the barn loft, he knew. For a second longer he wished he were a boy again. Then the shifting began inside his brain and he was back in Yuscarana with all the old wounds raw and open, bleeding inside his mind.

Stomach growling, he turned onto his right side in the hay and dug in his pockets. His fingers closed on a few nuts along with a pair of dried figs wrapped in cellophane he had overlooked before. Not a breakfast for most warriors. But food was merely fuel to Tony. He chewed slowly, eyeing the hotel windows, watching for movement, waiting for targets.

The storm had passed and the morning sprawled clear and open before him. Sunlight glittered off the glass in the hotel windows. The wind shifted and he could smell horse manure in the corral below him. A rodent rustled in a corner of the loft. Dust motes quivered in the shafts of light. Tony swallowed the nuts and figs he had been chewing. His throat was dry and he wished he had water in his canteen, or a bottle of whiskey. He licked a trace of salt from his lips. Wind wafted cool against his face. Taking a deep breath, he squeezed the trigger. Glass exploded. He squeezed again.

~ * ~

She came slowly out of a dreamless sleep, warm and cozy as if she were waking in the old Connecticut farmhouse on a cold winter's morning, with a trio of her grandmother's quilts pulled up to her nose and the Warm Morning in the kitchen blazing away.

Why had she awakened thinking about the old home place? She had not lived there in forty years, nor spent the night there in twenty-five. In fact, she's rarely thought about it since her mom had died a dozen years ago.

Amy Moby tried to recall the last time she had spent the night in her little room in the old white frame house that mirrored the New England farmhouses you saw in the magazines, with the stone fence along the road and a narrow, curving drive leading up to the house. Twin maples flanked the entrance to the drive and Highlander rosebushes grew close along the house. Out back, there was a garden, with a small grove of cherry trees just beyond. Hills rose behind the place, all shades of green in the spring and summer, going crimson, untarnished gold, and butter yellow in autumn, turning brown-limbed and black-trunked against the snows of winter.

She had loved all the seasons, but she had loved spring best. Early spring, when the first blades of grass sprung from the earth, so green you could never quite believe it, and the leaves started to unfold on the maples like mouse ears, was her favorite season. Those first days of spring you could smell the promise of what was to come. Why in the world had she thought about a farmhouse in Connecticut here in the middle of a tropical jungle?

Rolling over, she blinked at the morning light pushing into her room. Maybe it was because of Joe. She had gone to sleep thinking about him, the way she had every night for two years when he was gone overseas, wondering in each darkness if he was still alive. And if he was, did he still love her? And if he did, would he come home with a complete body or a sane mind?

After he shipped out, she had gone back home. Too lonely otherwise. Maybe if she'd had a baby to watch after, she would have stayed on at the base. But some things were simply meant to be a certain way. God's will. She had accepted that in those long nights at the old farmhouse when she laid with eyes wide open in the dark, asking God why, then praying for Joe before crying herself to sleep. Amy had not cried once since the day he came swinging up the lane with his duffel bag slung over his shoulder, his cap pushed back, whistling "When Johnny Comes Marching Home."

She still prayed, however. Had prayed for a lot of people last night. Not for herself. But for that Samuels woman who had lost her husband, and her kids, and the other passengers, and the soldiers who were fighting to protect them. Especially, she had prayed for Joe, who was too old to be on the front line with a gun, and way too proud not to be.

Amy hadn't planned on going to sleep – simply lie down to rest for a few minutes. Close her eyes and say a few prayers. It had been an awful day and she could certainly stand to pray. There was a lot of comfort in a good prayer.

No matter how hard she prayed, though, she kept seeing that man's face blowing apart. So she had stopped praying and started worrying about Joe. He would be mad at her if he knew she was worrying, but that was simply too bad. She had every right to worry. She loved him. He knew that, and, if he thought about it, he would know she would worry, and, if he thought long enough, he would decide that worry was okay, actually the way it should be.

Joe Moby had his faults all right, every man and woman did. But he was a fair man, and an honest one. If not overly affectionate, he was faithful. And that was enough for any woman to ask for. At least Amy Moby saw it that way. Their love might not be romantic enough for some, but it was a good, decent, workable love, and it suited. Thoughts of Joe brought a smile to her lips.

Pans rattled in the kitchen below and the smell of coffee drifted to her, along with the unmistakable scent of meat frying, and the aromas transported her once more to that white frame farmhouse on the western Connecticut border. And in that moment Amy was sixteen again. Morning light lay as softly on her face as any springtime caressed New England.

She lay there listening to the subdued kitchen clatter, smelling coffee brewing and meat frying, thinking about the one man in the whole world she truly loved until a restlessness began working through her. Wide awake then, she began thinking all at once of a dozen things that needed doing. And she was a woman who did what needed doing. But before she swung her legs out of the bed, she whispered another short prayer, one straight from the heart.

Fifty-four

Startled by the smashing glass, Maria dropped the pan she had been carrying. The pan was full of water and clattered against the tile floor with a damp thud. Water splattered in all directions and she moaned as she knelt to clean up the mess.

She could hear Señora Herrera screeching at her. The señora had been in a querulous mood all morning, and Maria had overheard her asking different people if they had seen the señor this morning. Now that she thought about it, she realized she had not seen the señor for some time, which was most unusual. Often, he hovered around her asking silly questions, patting one of her arms, breathing warmly on the back of her neck. His breath usually smelled of stale cigar smoke, stale beer, and Brillar, which was a cheap mouthwash sold in the small store directly across the street.

Though the señor had never done more than touch her arm or stroke her hair, Maria knew from the way the señora looked at her that she suspected her husband had done far more.

The señora had never liked her, not from the first day. Maria was scared of the señora and did her best to stay out of her way. Now, as she swiped a kitchen towel across the damp tile, she could hear the señora calling her stupid and clumsy and wasteful and uncaring. Maria wanted to cry.

It had been a long night, one during which Maria had slept in fitful snatches filled with disturbing dreams of big, dark, dirty men with long knives and guns. All these men seemed to want to kill her or rape her, or both. She had lain fully dressed in her small bed for hours, staring wide-eyed into the darkened room, listening for guerilla sounds in the night. She kept seeing blood gushing out of the skull of the dead *Notre Americano* and running down his face like *rojo* cake icing melting in summer sunlight.

Just before dawn, the shrill song of an unseen bird had brought her out of a shallow sleep. Now, she was thick headed, her fingers felt stiff, and her legs were heavy as stone. Maria thought of her mother and father and wished she were with them again in the small, sheltering village where she had grown up.

A shadow fell across her arms and she looked up into the angry face of Señora Herrera. The señora was screeching at her like a mynah bird and Maria nodded as she bent her neck and started mopping even more quickly. Tired, sleepy, and afraid, the girl longed for even a few stray strands of kindness. Affection to her seemed to be a product of another country.

~ * ~

Voices murmured in the distance, like the gurgling of a stream he'd often fished. They formed a pleasant sound and he listened, lingering just below the surface of sleep, until the aroma of fresh coffee penetrated and he came awake wondering if it had all been a nightmare. Cracking his eyes open, he saw the young soldier next to him and Joe Moby knew it had not been a dream.

Yawning, he rubbed at the sleep in his eyes and nodded at the man beside him. Actually, he was hardly more than a kid. But that was the way society had always been – ripping the young men from their families, molding their bodies into soldiers, rearranging their minds into a willingness to die that ranged somewhere between sacrificial ardor and fearful tepidness, placing them in the front lines, ordering them forward, knowing death sat waiting, then eulogizing their bravery after they were on the wrong side of the ground.

Eulogies were easy. Dead men don't complain. That was a fact of life, a sad fact, but a fact nonetheless. Once upon a time, he had been one of those fine young men, ready to kill and ready to die in Vietnam.

Joe Moby always swore his tour had been the best education any man could have. The first night he spent alone in the rice paddies he learned more about life, and himself, than he had in twelve years of the standard compulsive education offered by the state of Minnesota. Seeing your best buddy's guts hanging out and crapping in your pants you always remembered. The worst of it now seemed to him that he never really knew why he was over there or exactly what he was fighting for. Truth, justice, and the American way now struck him as about as phony as artificial tits. Pushing his ass off the floor, he eased his eyes above the window ledge.

Daylight spread like fresh butter across the open ground. Beyond the town, the jungle looked freshly washed – the leaves green and shining in the new light. A flock of small dark birds was feeding on the ground – the scene looked like a photo from a travel magazine. He could almost taste the quiet. In that instant he distrusted it completely. Experience had long ago shown him that when a scene looked too peaceful and quiet and beautiful to be real, it was.

The smell of coffee brewing was stronger now and he wished for a cup. Additional aromas joined the coffee. Joe could smell meat and onions frying, along with a scent of citrus. His stomach gurgled. His last meal was fuzzy in his mind.

The windowsill was smooth against his fingers. A match clicked nearby and the smell of burning tobacco drifted across the morning. His stomach gurgled again. Damn, he hoped somebody would bring some grub soon. Joe Moby sighed. A cup of coffee would taste fine right about now.

Thinking of coffee reminded him of his breakfast ritual with Amy. He wondered where she was now, and how she was holding up. Thoughts of her started a smile and he let it grow as he stared out into the opening morning.

Shooting now, somewhere around the corner to his left, and he felt his abdominal muscles tense and the sphincter grow tight. His eyes wanted to go off in a dozen different directions, but he took a deep breath and made them conduct a steady panning of the ground in front of him, looking for something that didn't belong, movement, the flash of sunlight off metal.

A careful scan revealed nothing more than open ground, a few buildings that appeared to be unoccupied, and green leaves sparkling in morning sunlight. The gunfire had spooked the feeding birds and they were swirling uncertainly in the sky, moving black question marks.

There was a pause in the shooting and the soldier beside him coughed into the sudden quiet. Joe turned to look at him. The soldier's face was half turned away, leaving Joe to study the profile, a short, cut-off jaw and flat cheekbones, with a forehead that sloped back slightly into black hair spilling out below an army cap. One dark eye protruded slightly and the soldier wore a thin mustache that looked like a smudged line drawing. The soldier coughed again and as the man turned his head, Joe saw how truly young the soldier was. No more than a boy.

Joe nodded at the soldier. "Looks like daylight has arrived."

The boy nodded and said, "*Sí.*" Turning his head, the boy stared across the sun-splashed ground. "We have survived the night."

"Were you worried?"

The soldier shrugged, his mustache wiggling. "One never knows, especially in the dark. I do not like the dark. Who knows what is going on out there?" He shivered as though a chill, or a snake, had wriggled through his body.

"Well, it's good daylight now. Think they will attack again?"

"Who can say? Guerrillas, they are very strange. They do not act as normal men." The soldier shook his head sadly, as if disappointed in all guerrillas in general and the ones attacking Yuscarana in particular.

~ * ~

Steam rose from his coffee cup like the mists that rose from the small, yet deep mountain lakes above Andular. Leaning against a plaster wall, Captain Morales watched the changing light in the street. The plaster was still cool against his skin, the light soft, diffused. Shadows still lounged in the doorways and corners of the buildings. A thin ribbon of saffron ran down the middle of the black asphalt.

Morales took a sip of coffee, holding the warm liquid in his mouth for a moment before he swallowed. Setting his cup on the window ledge, he reached in his shirt pocket and pulled out the stub of a cigar he had been smoking the night before and stuck it between his lips. He dug his old lighter out of his pocket, flipped the top back and spun the wheel. The flame flickered yellow and he stared into it for a second before he bent his head.

Smoke filled his lungs and he savored its harsh heat. Newspapers and radios these days were full of reports of the dangers of smoking to one's health. Captain Morales was not particularly worried. Never had he planned on an exceptionally long life. Pleasures in the moment were his preference. Seeing the sun come up for him was a blessing, not a guarantee.

Peering through the undulating blue-gray smoke, he tried to slip inside the mind of the leader of the guerrillas. Unless this was a renegade band from the north, he could narrow the choice down to three men: Manuel, who preferred to attack at night, Esteban, who preferred bazookas and grenade launchers, and Carlos, who could only be trusted to do something different. For some time, he deliberated on the matter.

It must be Carlos, he decided. Manuel had been seen two hundred miles away late the week before and rumor had it that Esteban had contracted a bad fever. Settling on Carlos made it easier and harder at the same time. Easier, because the number of men Carlos led was small; harder, because you could never figure out his tactics in advance. One could guess, but then one had better be very lucky. Or one could wait and see, then counterpunch. Never had the captain been a lucky man.

The captain took a long draw on his cigar. He held the smoke for a few seconds. Making an O with his lips, he blew out three smoke rings, all perfectly round. As they rose, they gradually spread and lost their roundness, becoming thinner, more elliptical. Ultimately, they broke apart and disappeared. Stubbing out his cigar against his heel, he spat on the burnt end. Then he tucked the butt back in his shirt pocket. Only three whole cigars left and he had no idea when he would be able to buy another.

He finished his coffee, leaving the cup on the window ledge, and began to stroll along the wall, nodding and speaking a few words to each man. Caffeine and nicotine still clung to his tongue, while sunlight had spread across the main street of Yuscarana. Despite the heaviness of his eyes and the aches in his joints, he felt dangerously good.

~ * ~

Beneath the palm of his left hand, the leather felt pebbly. Against his right palm was the cool smoothness of glass. Less than an inch of liquid remained in the bottom of the bottle. The reverend's eyes were closed, but he was not asleep. Still dressed, except for his shoes, he was lying flat on his back in the middle of his bed. Light pressed against his eyelids. He had not dozed off, not even deep in the night. All night long, while moonlight was throwing shadows around his room, he had sipped whiskey, read his Bible, and prayed.

He decided to open his right eye a crack. Squeezing his left shut even more tightly, he eased the right orb open. Daylight was falling unencumbered against his face. Damn, he thought, I am as blind as Saul on the road to Tarsus.

After a few seconds, his eye began to adjust to the brightness and he opened the other one. Soon, the only pain he suffered was where his skull was cracking. Reverend Tom Malloy moaned and buried his face in the sheets.

The crackle of gunfire reached his ears and he felt a weakness in his bowels. He squeezed both the Bible and the bottle tighter.

~ * ~

As the door swung open, Dianna Threlkeld stood in the hallway watching the room open up. She was sleepy, but nothing that a couple of cigarettes and a red pill wouldn't cure. When she could see the bald spot on the top of her husband's head, she stepped into the room.

She did not try to walk quietly and the floorboards squeaked vigorously beneath her feet. As she began to unbutton her blouse, she felt her eyes grow heavy and her fingers thick. A nap would be nice. She glanced at the bed. Her husband's eyes were closed, but his mouth hung open. In the quiet room she could hear his gentle breathing. In sleep, he looked innocent, almost young. Then he caught his breath, snorted, and turned his head to one side. Smiling, she unbuttoned the final button.

Water left from the afternoon before still stood in the ceramic basin on top of a wooden dresser. Lady Threlkeld picked up a clean washcloth from the dresser and dipped it into the water. The damp cloth felt soft and cool against her skin. Watching herself in the swiveled mirror atop the dresser, she washed her face and arms and torso, paying special attention to her breasts, allowing the washcloth to linger against her nipples, finally giving them a damp tweak before moving on.

Opening her case, she selected her long comb and began to run it through her tangled hair. Her comb caught in a tangle tougher than the rest and she grimaced.

"You know, my dear, you look rather a mess."

Dianna jerked at the sound of his voice. Before turning toward the bed, she paused, still working the comb through her hair. After a decent pause, she turned and stared at the man lying in the bed. There were times when she found it remarkably difficult to conceive of him as her husband. Which of them had changed so dramatically, she wondered. Perhaps, she decided, they both had.

"With your clothes still on from the day before, you hardly look resplendent yourself." She pulled the comb through the tangle and wrinkled her lips. "My god, Donald, your trousers are soiled."

"Care to show me your panties."

"In your dreams."

Lord Threlkeld rolled onto his side and propped himself up on one elbow. "Ah, my dear, did anyone ever tell you how lovely you are when you are angry?"

"Fuck you, Donald."

"Don't you wish."

Lady Threlkeld threw her comb at Lord Threlkeld. It struck him on his nose. He laughed, a high-pitched boy's laugh.

"Bastard," she said.

She crossed the room and opened her suitcase. Inside, clean and dirty clothes tangled together amid slick-covered magazines, half-empty packs of cigarettes, traveler's checks, blank postcards, crumpled tissues autographed with lipstick lips, along with a Spanish-English dictionary with a broken spine. One of her makeup jars had popped open and a fine powder covered the contents like beige snow. She dug to the bottom of the suitcase and tugged out an unstained white blouse that was only slightly wrinkled. She slipped it on and buttoned up. Leaning close to the mirror, she painted her lips. Then, Lady Threlkeld whirled and walked out of the room, without speaking or looking back.

As soon as the door clicked shut, Lord Threlkeld rolled over and slung his legs out of the bed. They were only slightly unsteady as he walked across the floor. A tiny man with a large hammer seemed to be pounding an anvil inside his skull. That, however, Lord Threlkeld viewed as only a minor inconvenience. He was well traveled in such circles. Once, in a moment of extreme weakness, he had taken the cure – painful memories still lingered: long, miserable days, followed by even longer, lonelier nights. Hours of misery followed by a shot of a certain drug prescribed for him by a doctor of dubious reputation from Vienna. He had zero intentions of walking that path again.

Lord Threlkeld slid the bottle of good Kentucky bourbon from between shirts. Holding it up to the light, he examined it with squinted eyes. Between pain waves, he could see that he had half a bottle left. He decided he would save this good stuff for emergencies.

This being one, he unscrewed the cap and lifted the bottle to his lips. To hell with glasses. Desperate men take desperate measures, he said to himself.

Tasting faintly of smoke and charcoal and sin, the bourbon slid smoothly down his throat. Closing his eyes tightly, he watched tiny stars shoot across the deep space of his mind.

The afterglow of the bourbon made him feel warm all over. After a moment, the anvil pounding in his brain began to recede into the distance.

Opening his eyes, Lord Threlkeld eyed himself in the mirror. The face that stared back at him was wrinkled and unshaven. There was a hollowness to the eyes and a sardonic slant to the lips.

You are a rather dilapidated bastard, he told himself. Taking his bottle, he walked slowly over to the chair he liked and sat down. He lifted the bottle and let the bourbon splash against his lips. Then he eased his head back against the chair and opened his eyes as wide as he could, letting the sunlight drift into the room as it chose and the world whirl on as it would.

~ * ~

His chin bounced off his chest and he came awake with a start in a strange room, his mind not engaged. Then he saw uniforms and Kron knew he was in the lobby of the old hotel in Yuscarana.

He was surprised to be there. He had been dreaming of Colorado, with snow falling on ponderosa pine growing on mountains that pressed against the clouds. In his dream, he had been a boy skiing with other boys, and he was reluctant to leave.

Rearranging his back more comfortably against the wall, he quietly watched the soldiers moving about the room. One or two were checking their weapons; the others were eating from brown bowls and drinking coffee from white mugs. Coffee would be good, Kron thought. Remnants of his dream clung to the walls of his mind.

His rifle lay beside him on the floor, the round black hole of the barrel pointed toward the reception desk. Kron recalled the soldier with the mustache telling him it was loaded. He could also recall staring out into the darkness where the rain was falling and the road had been no more than a shimmer of black where stray streetlight burnished the asphalt. Strange, but he couldn't remember turning from the window, or placing his rifle on the floor, or closing his eyes. Gradually, he came to the realization he was surprised to be alive.

He had survived the night. He wondered if he would survive the day.

~ * ~

Daylight warmed the small, reddish-brown monkey. He had spent the night on a wide tree limb growing below the primary forest canopy. He had not foraged well the afternoon before and now he was hungry. He yawned, showing the rest of the troop his set of yellowish monkey teeth. Then he stretched and began to swing down the tree. Halfway down, a large, dark object lying out in the open caught his eye. Curiosity began to grow inside his monkey brain and, as he traversed the bottom limbs, he decided to investigate.

Grass on the slope grew high, but the shrubs were sparse and the monkey approached the object with caution. Its outline was not that of any predator he was familiar with, but strangeness often equaled danger in the jungle and, besides, it was in his nature to be cautious.

Whatever it was grew larger as he drew closer. When he was less than twenty meters away, he could see its face looked like that of a creature he had seen before. However, those creatures had always been upright and moving. This one was lying down and moving less than the grass which bent before the morning breeze.

Slowing, the monkey circled the creature in ever tightening spirals, moving with caution, going slowly and quietly, always leaning back fractionally, so that if the creature moved, he could jump away without having to shift all his weight. No longer did he think of the object as a possible breakfast. For the moment, his curiosity was stronger than his hunger.

The monkey crept closer. The creature did not move. Its eyes were closed. The monkey's shadow fell across the creature's face. The monkey stretched out one hairy, leathery paw. The paw touched the creature's face. The eyes of the creature fluttered open and a primal moan escaped its lips.

Startled, the monkey jumped, turned, and ran on all fours as hard as he could go back to the tall trees, chattering in a high loud voice. He did not stop moving or chattering until he was near the top of a large mahogany tree.

For over an hour he stayed rigid and silent in the shadows. Finally, hunger got the upper hand and he cautiously swung across a series of trees before descending to the jungle floor. The monkey made sure that he traveled away from the creature lying in the grass on the slope. As he ate fallen fruit, he kept glancing over his shoulder.

~ * ~

He had been so near death that the taste of its foulness coated his tongue like rancid honey. He had not planned on opening his eyes again. It was far more comfortable not to make the effort. Then he felt a strange, small, rough hand touch his face and Felix wondered if it was the hand of God. After considering the idea for a few seconds, with the fragment of his mind not consumed by pain, he willed himself to open his eyes. His eyelids were incredibly heavy. Breathing hurt. Opening his eyes was agony.

The boy opened his eyes and saw the face of God. God looks exactly like a monkey, he thought and closed his eyes again. He wanted to laugh, but he hurt too damn much.

Fifty-five

Maria hummed as she hurried down the dim hallway carrying a tray of dirty bowls and coffee mugs, the tray that held them preceding her like the flattened prow of a ship. She was surprised at how fine her mood was. After all, the guerrillas were still out there. She could hear their guns. And Señor Herrera was definitely missing, not to mention the driver of the bus, and, of course, the dead *norteamericano turista.* Furthermore, one of the upstairs maids had told her that two of the soldiers were dead.

Still, the sunlight was warm and reassuring and all of the soldiers had smiled at her when she brought them breakfast. They had chatted and flirted with her when she returned for their dirty dishes. Even Captain Morales had smiled. She did not mind that his smile was somewhat distant. He was a powerful man and she always felt an extra degree safer in his presence.

Rounding the last corner before the kitchen, she nearly collided with a woman in the shadows. Maria shrieked in surprise. For a second, her mind convinced her that the woman was one of the guerrillas. Then Maria could see that the woman was only one of the *turistas*. "*Buenos dias*," she said, laboring to remain calm.

The woman rearranged her thin face and placed a hand on Maria's left arm. Her touch was gentle.

"Good morning. Is there any more coffee?"

"*Sí.*"

"Splendid. I absolutely need a cup."

Maria nodded. She was not certain what to do. Not often was she alone with a *turista*. Waiting on *turistas* in a brightly lighted, crowded dining room was one thing; being alone with one in a poorly illuminated hallway was another.

The woman took a small step forward, bringing her face quite close to Maria's. "Would you mind to bring me a cup? I'm desperate."

Maria instinctively inclined her head slightly away from the turista. The woman smelled of cigarette smoke, stale perfume, and alcohol, plus other scents that Maria did not recognize. Maria kept smiling as she nodded. "*Sí*, I will bring you a cup *immediatamente*. Where do you wish me to bring it, *señora*?"

The woman moved her head and indicated a room behind her. The door was open a few inches. "In there will be fine."

Maria had to look up to see the woman's eyes. "But that is *Señor* Herrera's office."

The woman's smile spread. She inclined her head toward Maria. Strands of the woman's hair brushed softly, like butterfly kisses, across Maria's face. "He's not in there at the moment," she whispered. Her breath was warm against Maria's skin. "I don't think he'll mind if I borrow his couch for a few minutes. Do you?"

Traces of alcohol scented the woman's breath. "No, no, I am certain the señor would not mind," Maria said. "I must go now. Señora Herrera is waiting for these dishes. I will bring your coffee to you." Ducking her head, Maria stepped around the woman.

"I'll be here," the woman said softly.

Maria nodded and kept walking. Mugs and bowls rattled on the tray.

~ * ~

Still clutching his Bible, he rolled out of bed and sank to his knees. The floorboards were hard and cool, the wood pressing firmly against bone and cartilage. Strangely, he didn't mind the pain. Pain took some of his mind off the awful aching of his head. Though he knew better, he was still half convinced his skull was cracking.

He had kept his eyes closed during his descent and did not open them now. Instead, he shifted the Bible until he held it with both hands as though it were an offering to a higher power. He bowed his head.

There was only darkness and pain. Reverend Malloy's mind turned to the bottle he had left on his pillow. There wasn't enough whiskey in it to wash away the pain. He wondered if there was enough whisky anywhere.

Gradually, the pain began to dissipate. Words began to gather.

"Dear Lord, I come to You a sinner, begging for Your forgiveness. I know that because I am supposed to be a leader of Your people, my sins are of far greater magnitude. I feel so black inside, so corrupt. I realize what a problem strong drink is for me, and I sincerely want to quit it. However, I cannot summon the strength on my own. Which is why I am again calling on You for help. Please deliver me from this awful place and take away my urge to drink.

"I am among heathens here, Lord, and I know I should try to bring them to Christ, but these are not ordinary unbelievers. They are violent people, fond of killing and full of the spirit of rebellion. This country is not fit for Your people. Certainly not a gentle, loving person like Your humble servant. Oh God, I am lost here in this wilderness called Yuscarana and I desperately need Your help. Oh Lord, please do not fail me now."

In the inner silence created by the passing of the prayer, he could hear gunfire. Squeezing his eyes even more tightly shut, he rubbed the insides of his thumbs and fingers against the pebbly grain of the leather as though there were a great healing to be uncovered if he rubbed hard enough and long enough. Then he could hear the shattering of glass and the shouts of men. The man of God rubbed harder. His entire body swayed. Shouts grew louder. Tears pooled in Reverend Thomas Malloy's eyes and dribbled down his cheeks like warm, salty raindrops.

"Oh dear Savior, do not forsake me now," he cried aloud.

Down the hall more glass shattered.

~ * ~

Jesus the Pig was crawling out from under a wooden porch. Even from this distance, even while running, Carlos was certain. The man was unmistakable – truly an animal. A fucking animal, Carlos thought. Jesus the Pig, if ever a man was appropriately named, he was the one.

Still, Carlos admitted to himself, he was glad to see the Pig. Call him what you will – filthy, nasty, gross, ugly, stinking – it did not matter; it did not matter because the man could fight. And he needed fighting men, especially today in Yuscarana. The men he had sent out in the countryside to attack the communications shack had not yet returned, and Carlos doubted they would. If they did not, they had better be dead. If they had deserted the Revolución and he ever found any of them alive, by the grace of the good God, he would make them wish they had died at Yuscarana. His breath was loud in his ears now and the blood spirit was rising within him.

Carlos kept running toward the heart of Yuscarana, twisting his neck, trying to count men as he ran. Seven or eight ran beside or behind him. Jesus and another man, one of the new ones, were already in position along the main street. Carlos hoped more were inside the buildings. Ten men would have one hell of a difficult time taking the hotel with Morales defending.

Damn, where were those men who had attacked the communications shack? Surely they could not all be dead.

He was sweating now and he swiped at the perspiration dripping into his eyes with the back of his free hand. Rising temperatures had followed the storm. Humidity was nearly as thick as rain. Gunfire reached his ears and he slowed, listening, trying to place it. It sounded as if it came from the back of the hotel and he felt encouragement bubbling inside. If there were enough men at the back, he could pull this off yet.

Carlos started shouting orders, waving men into position. Jesus waved at him and Carlos caught sight of what looked like a woman with him. My God, where had he found her? And why would any woman stay with such an animal? The woman's face was strange, oddly shaped, vaguely yellow. What if she had the plague? Cringing at the thought, Carlos yelled at Jesus to start firing to give them cover. Nothing could be done about the woman at the moment. And if things did not go well this day, it would no longer be a concern.

Carlos screamed encouragement at the men. Knowing it was a wasted shot, he fired his pistol anyway. The noise was terrific in his ears and he felt the temperature of his blood begin to rise. His heart was pumping like some great machine and his legs were driving pistons from a train.

All the running men were shouting now as they spread out like wild horses across an open range. From the street, Jesus and the other man were firing steadily. Glass shattered, sounding like the high keys on a dozen pianos being struck simultaneously.

~ * ~

Glass stopped shattering. Tony could hear the empty, hollow click of the hammer. His fingers fumbled at his beltline for cartridges. Empty-handed, he rolled over onto his back and stared at the dark ceiling of the old barn. Nests of swallows huddled in the corners and daylight peeked through holes in the roof. After the storm a dampness permeated the air.

Where he lay it was dry and the straw was rough against his skin. Horses were moving restlessly below. Hunger was gnawing inside his body. He tried to recall when he had last eaten. As he fumbled in the straw for his canteen, he realized he was out of ammunition, and food. Only a little water he had captured from the storm still sloshed around the metal bottom. He considered waiting, but his thirst pushed him on and he unscrewed the cap. The water was warm and tasted of metal, but he swallowed every drop.

He lay there listening to the milling horses and the rising wind. His eyes closed. Perhaps he dozed, but if he did it was only a brief, shallow sleep. Gunfire from the far side of the hotel jerked him back into the morning. He lay listening to it, placing it, making up his mind. Finally, he screwed the cap back on his canteen, picked up his rifle, and began crawling toward the ladder.

As he descended, he could hear more gunfire, muffled now by the barn walls. This must be the big attack of Carlos. The one he had been talking of for weeks. With a vague curiosity, he wondered how it was going. Tony had been in so many battles, large and small, that one more did not matter.

Tony had never understood the strategic importance of Yuscarana. Sure, the highway ran through the town, but the same highway ran for hundreds of miles, winding like an anaconda through the bowels of Morazon. Undoubtedly, there were dozens of locations where it would have been child's play to take control of the road and hold it, perhaps for weeks. Never had he understood the need to attack Yuscarana, unless it was to destroy, or at least divert the small garrison of troops stationed there. Killing soldiers of Gutierrez, now that he could understand. However, an ambush would certainly have been safer.

Don't worry, he told himself as he stepped off the ladder and brushed straw from his clothes, Carlos would have his reasons. Carlos might have heard something directly from the central committee of the Revolución that precipitated this attack. He was not crazy about Carlos; the man was too soft on the rest of the guerrillas. However, he could not argue with the man's success. Carlos had led his men to many victories. Granted, there had been a few defeats along the way. "Setbacks," was how Carlos referred to them. Still, even those had been minor, more a loss of position than a pulverizing disaster.

Men had died under the command of Carlos, true. But what else could one expect? Deaths were part of any campaign. Actually, Carlos had lost fewer men than most commanders would have. Clever in his attacks, he made them when and where it was not natural, attacking even at night. Tony slung his empty rifle across his back and began working his way toward the other side of the hotel, staying low, using the horses for cover.

From the far side of the corral, he could see a body lying face down on the flat ground. The man's arms were flung out as though he had been grasping at something as he fell. Tony did not recognize the body; even if he had been able to see the face, he still might not have known the man. Men came to the Revolución, then left so quickly. All he knew was that it was not Carlos or Jesus. He truly knew few of the others. They were no more than a blurry face on the other side of a campfire, seen through a rising curtain of smoke, or a back ahead on the trail, trudging through a fine silver rain, or, like the man with his face in the grass, merely another body, going rigid and swelling in the sunlight.

Sunlight glittering off metal caught his eye and he paused, crouching low behind an old wagon with one broken wheel. Tony looked at the man's gun, debating with himself. The gun was more than likely loaded and more ammunition probably hung around his waist or back. Temptation was strong. Measuring the distance to the dead man with his eyes, he was uncertain. He glanced at the windows at the back of the hotel. Sunlight flashed of the remaining glass, blinding him. He looked away, wondering what was behind the glittering glass, recalling that only yesterday there had been soldiers with guns behind those windows.

He hesitated, unable to make up his mind. Once he started for the gun, but stopped before he had taken a full step. Tony hunkered back down behind the old wagon. The wood smelled faintly of melons. The aroma triggered a hunger in him. The few nuts and dried figs he had consumed in the loft seemed like a meal from another season. His stomach growled.

Tony took a final glance at the rifle and started running, keeping low and zigzagging, moving parallel to the hotel as he began to work his way around to the front side. He still had one grenade, his knife, and a short stick of dynamite taped to the outside of his left leg. Besides, Carlos and Jesus and the rest would surely be around on the other side of the hotel. He could hear gunfire even now. And if they were not, he would simply break into stores until he found ammunition.

Ten yards ahead was a mound of dirt covered with melon rinds, rotting fruit, and disintegrating eggplants, cucumbers, and tomatoes. Broken eggshells glittered. The stench was tremendous and flies buzzed sonorously in the sunlight. Tony crawled around the compost, moving through the grass barely inches away from the rotting fruit and vegetables, his nostrils filled with the smell of decay.

Suddenly, there was a long steady sweeping stream of gunfire and then rotten fruit was raining down on him. Vegetation smacked damp against his face. He spat out a piece of something that tasted black, scrambled to all fours and crawled like a wild animal across a narrow stretch of open ground, diving behind a cinder block building that had once been used as a garage for well-heeled guests. Now, it was full of old tires, used oil, crawling bugs, and spider webs. Such things did not disturb Tony. He did not enter the garage. There was protection all the way to the corner and he rose, put his head down, and ran hard. Around the corner were his compadres.

Coming to the side of the building, Tony slowed and dropped to all fours. Cautiously, he eased his head around the corner.

Quiet still held the main drag of Yuscarana. He scanned the street, then the buildings, looking for a familiar face. Seeing no one, he swung his eyes to the hotel. Glass lay in small pyramids below each window, glittering where the sunlight struck.

Tony watched the windows for several minutes, staying in the darker shadows of the building without moving. Only his eyes shifted now and then. He could see no guns, no faces, not even any moving shadows. He stepped up onto the low wooden sidewalk. Boards squeaked beneath his feet and his body tensed against the expected bullets.

No gunfire rang out. He quickstepped down the sidewalk and leaned against a door. It was locked and he took a step back, then lunged forward and threw his shoulder against it. It groaned on its hinges, but held. He threw himself against it again. Wood cracked, but the door did not open. Taking a step to the right, he smashed the window with the butt of his gun. Glass showered around him like angry rain. He cleaned out a good-sized hole with his rifle and stuck his arm through carefully. Then he unlocked the door and stepped inside.

It was one of those small stores that sold a little of everything and a good deal of nothing. The few dusty shelves were filled with canned goods, paper to write on, and ink pens still in plastic packing. Large sacks of grain, stacks of shingles for roofs, and piles of plastic piping stood on the floor. Hammers, saws, and shovels hung on the walls.

A large wooden counter stood in front of one wall and behind the counter were shelves filled with canned goods, fresh fruit, and boxes of crackers. The fruit was going bad; flies, bees, and wasps hummed steadily. Tony hustled around behind the counter, grabbed a box of crackers off a shelf and ripped open one end. He carried it back to the counter and sat it down on the scarred wood. Leaning his rifle against the counter, he plunged a hand into the box, tore open the plastic sleeve and pulled out a handful of crackers. They were already crumbling as he stuffed them into his mouth. He plunged his hand in the cracker box again.

In a moment, his mouth was so full of crackers that broken pieces tumbled out of the corners like sawdust. He chewed and stuffed and chewed and stuffed and chewed. Slowly he began to get his appetite under control. Thirst assaulted him then and he looked around for something to drink. There was occasional gunfire and someone was shouting, but those sounds seemed to come from the far end of the street and he did not pay much attention. He was more concerned about finding some whiskey or wine.

No wine on the shelves and no whiskey. Of all the places to pick. Well, he supposed there were other stores, but suddenly the gunfire grew more insistent and he didn't want to delay. He needed a good position before the attack, one where he could watch the flow before throwing himself into the fray. Rather than rushing blindly, he had found it advantageous to thrust himself into a critical part of the battle.

He wasn't afraid of bullets, because dying was a certainty whose only variable was time. It was the Revolución that mattered, and he, the man they called Tony the Demented, intended to make a difference. He lived to kill the soldiers of Gutierrez, and prayed every evening before he went to sleep and every morning when he awoke that he would live long enough to see Gutierrez hung by his scrawny neck. Many days he found it of great difficulty to believe in God, but he prayed faithfully anyway, always ending with a promise to believe forever if he could live to see the death of the man who had destroyed his world.

More gunfire now, closer, more persistent. Tony looked around again for something to drink. In one corner was a short pyramid of Coca-Cola bottles, the old-fashioned six-ounce ones, with the bottles standing like prisoners at attention in small wooden cages. Five or six of the boxes were stacked in the corner. Tony crossed the room and pulled out a bottle with each hand. There was an opener screwed into one side of the counter, and he carried the bottles over and opened them with a flip of his wrist. He drank the first one without stopping.

An explosion blasted on the street. A hand grenade. It sounded like it had come from the hotel side of the street. Sipping on the second Coca-Cola, Tony picked up his rifle and started toward the door. Cracker crumbs crunched beneath his feet like tiny seashells.

~ * ~

Maria knocked lightly, timidly, on the door. There was no answer. She knocked again, a few decibels louder.

"Come in." The voice on the other side of the door was firm, but somehow distant, as if a part of the speaker's attention was focused elsewhere. Taken slightly aback, Maria hesitated, staring uncertainly at the door. "Well, come in."

Balancing the tray in one hand, Maria turned the door knob with the other. The door swung open. Tray proceeding, she stepped into the room. Behind her, the door snicked closed.

The room was as dark as early dusk. Heavy, dark drapes had been drawn across the windows and a single, shaded lamp on one corner of a large wooden desk cast a shallow, yellow arc into the room. Light flowed like a low tide cresting against an invisible beach, running thinner and thinner as it flowed toward the walls, collapsing finally in the dark pools of the corners. Lady Dianna Threlkeld lay on the couch, head propped up on one cracked leather arm, left hand shading her eyes. She did not look at Maria. Instead, she stared at a large dark oil painting on the opposite wall. The sound of gunfire came faintly through thick old walls.

"You know, the more I study that picture, the more convinced I am the painter was an alcoholic, or a druggie. Why, look at that horse's head. It's all out of proportion to the body, one of the legs doesn't bend quite right, and the tail positively looks as if moths have been at it." Pursing her lips, she adjusted the angle of her neck. "Yes, an alcoholic, definitely. What do you think?"

She turned her head slowly toward Maria. Actually, it was more as if it moved on its own in response to some unseen vibration of the earth, and she merely allowed it to follow the gravitational pull. "You're trembling, my dear. What's wrong?"

Maria had not realized she was trembling, though she had been vaguely conscious of a rattling sound so faint that she had assumed that it was a distant vibration. She looked down. Her hands were not quite steady and the cup rattled delicately against the saucer. Suddenly the tray seemed heavy. Quickly she stepped to the desk and placed the tray down next to the lamp.

"Nothing, señora." She shrugged and smiled at the English señora. "I am a little tired, perhaps. That is all." She shrugged again. "All those guns and that storm, I did not sleep so much last night, and we have been very busy this morning."

Lady Threlkeld parted her lips. Her teeth were quite white in the darkened room. She swung her legs off the couch and patted the leather. "Here, come sit down beside me."

"Oh, señora, I could not."

"Oh, yes you can."

Maria shook her head with an isolated vengeance, flinging her hair about like a broken, dark wing. "No, no, I must not."

"And why not? If I might ask."

Maria made a monkey face and inclined her head toward the hallway. "The Señora Herrera, she, she..."

"She what?"

"She would not like it."

"Piss on her." Lady Threlkeld let her head fall back against the back of the couch and studied Maria over the bridge of her aristocratic nose. Without shifting her eyes, she patted the dark brown leather beside her.

"Now, you come over here and sit down. That's an order. You are supposed to do what the guests want, aren't you?"

"Well, yes that is so. Still…"

"Oh, come on. Just for a couple of minutes." Her teeth were very white. Her eyes were lost in the shadows. A hand smacked the leather with authority. The sound was loud in the quiet room.

Thoughts rushed through Maria's mind. Already, she could hear the shrieking voice of Señora Herrera. It vibrated against the walls of her mind like hail against a tin roof. If she were caught sitting on a couch with a guest, especially a high-class English *turista*, she would be fired. What would she do then? Where could she go?

She could not go home. More gunfire reached her ears, closer now. Replaced almost instantly by the sound of shattering glass. A scream rose in her throat. Part of it escaped before she could swallow it. Her legs were damp reeds beneath her body. As they started to go, she stumbled across the floor, collapsing onto the couch.

Leather sagged beneath her sudden weight, bowing up around her on both sides and pulling the English woman toward her. The other woman's skin pressed against her bare arms. Maria felt a flush flash up her cheeks. A sudden urge to urinate struck her and she pressed her legs together. A projectile smashed against the outside wall and exploded, the force rocking the walls. Then she could hear the waspish whine of flying bullets and glass shattering like cheap crystal behind the curtain.

Maria screamed and flung her face against the chest of the English woman. It was softer than she had imagined and smelled faintly of soap, lavender, and cigarette smoke. She was so shocked at her own behavior that she could not move. Then her senses returned and she tried to pull her head away.

The English woman had been quicker, however; Maria felt an arm curling smoothly around her, while a hand stroked her long hair. She tried to pull away, but she had no real strength and the slim arm was python strong.

"There, there," the English woman said as she stroked the girl's long, dark, soft hair. "There, there."

Fifty-six

Tremors ran through his arms. Eyelids flickered and sweat trickled down out of his hairline, sliding into his eyes. Keeping one hand on his rifle, he wiped sweat away with the other.

Nerves. He recognized the signs from his days in 'Nam. Jungle visions flashed like sheet lightning across his mind. In that moment of immense clarity he remembered everything. In the end a man remembered everything: the good and the bad and all that lukewarm gray porridge in between. He recalled events he had not thought of since they happened. Actions and reactions so awful he had not been able to share them, not even with himself.

He had told army stories, of course, every soldier did. He had always tried to tell the true of it. People who embellished he slotted directly behind liars. Of course, he told only the stories that made him look good, as close to a hero as he was likely to get. Actually, he reconsidered, every man who lined up in the line of fire was a hero. Unfortunately, many soon became dead heroes.

He had told the good stories, the ones that did not tell of grown men crying, and the guts of his buddies oozing out like blood-soaked snakes, and men taking a shit who suddenly were hammered by a bullet to the brain, and then, even as their brain explodes, they go right on defecating. No, he hadn't told those. No one would want to hear them; few would even believe them. Believing them would be difficult if you hadn't been there. Being there made forgetting them impossible.

More gunfire now, the third round of it this morning, and he could feel the sweat start to trickle faster. He still had not seen any guerrillas, but now he heard glass shatter. The shattering went on for some time. He would not have believed there was that much glass in the hotel. Finally, he realized that some of it had to be coming from the stores across the street. Undoubtedly, some of the rebels had taken up positions inside them. For what had to be the tenth time, he wondered how many rebels there were. Never had he fought an action where he'd been given so little information. Even during the ambushes in 'Nam, word had spread. This was fighting half-blind.

Joe Moby let his line of vision drift out across the open ground. A light breeze had sprung up and the leaves at the edge of the jungle fluttered like green flags, their movement a dramatic contrast to the stillness of the open ground. Not a thing had moved across it all day, not even a stray dog. But then, dogs usually had better sense than to trot across battlefields.

Suddenly, something was different on the backside of the old hotel. It took him a moment to realize what the difference was. It was silence. The world had gone quiet as though it were holding its breath. He realized then he was holding his.

A loud ping hammered at his eardrums and he ducked down below the window. Fucking sniper. Another bullet sang above his head and smashed into the wall on the far side of the hallway. Plaster fell like green snow.

All along the line now there was firing. Cautiously, he raised his head. Still no movement. Then, just where the jungle gave way to grass, he saw a glint of metal, low to the ground and moving, there for a second. Then there were only moving leaves and tangled strands of grass at the line of demarcation. Sunlight glinted off metal again and another bullet whizzed by his head.

Joe let all the air out of his lungs and squeezed the trigger. Two feet above the ground and half a foot right of where he had been aiming a large, fan-shaped leaf fluttered to the ground. Easing the rifle a fraction of an inch to the left, he lowered his aim. He hadn't had an opportunity to sight the gun and he felt better now that he knew what to expect when he squeezed the trigger.

Firing on either side of him now. More shooting from the jungle. The rebels must be making a push. He kept his eye on the quadrant of jungle where he figured the sniper was. A shadow shifted and he fired.

Grass flew into the air. Overadjusted, he told himself. Trying to maintain a smooth level of breathing, he eased the sight on the rifle a few centimeters higher, and a touch left again.

More gunfire along both lines – followed by silence. A bird squawked in the trees, sounding as if it had a seed stuck sideways in its throat. Down the line he could hear one of the soldiers shout for more ammunition. From far back in the hotel he could hear another sound. A soft sound, breaking off, then resuming. It sounded like a woman sobbing.

An unnatural quiet fell. This quiet had a weight to it. He could feel it pressing down on him as though the pressure of the atmosphere had suddenly undergone a transformation. The bird had fallen silent. He could hear his own breathing.

Time ticked inside his head. His life was ticking away one metronomic second at a time. Joe began to count. He had reached seventeen when he saw movement. He squeezed.

A thin shaft of metal flipped into the air at the edge of the jungle.

Then a heavy object fell on him, driving him to the floor and smashing the breath out of him. Gasping for breath, he struggled to get out from under the weight. The air smelled of cigarette smoke and sweat and urine and blood. Pushing the weight away a few inches, he could see a man's hand dangling in front of his face. Blood dripped onto his face like warm rusty water from a loose tap. Adrenaline rushed through his body and he gave a shove and the weight rolled off, thudding onto the floor like a tombstone toppling.

Unable to stop himself, he stared down. The young soldier with the mustache stared back at him with wide-opened eyes as full of life as polished stones. The soldier's face was smooth and unmarked, though his mouth was twisted as if some great force had jammed wires into the corners and jerked. His throat was open and red with the blood that oozed out and pooled on the floor beside his head. The blood looked like a small red lake, shiny bright in the sunlight.

~ * ~

Water spots formed Byzantine patterns on the ceiling that looked as high and far away as a mountaintop. Sharon Samuels lay on her bed, staring at the strange designs, trying to find a meaning hidden in their twistings. Sudden, sharp noises poked at her consciousness. They faded, rose again, then fell to silence. They might have been so many wasps.

The room grew quiet, the absence of sound filling the room like a palpable essence until it seemed as if all the air was being forced out. Her breath came in audible little gasps, her chest rising and falling with the suddenly conscious effort of breathing. Sharon Samuels dragged her eyes from the entrancing patterns and watched her breasts rise like small volcanoes forming, then sink as if the inner walls had collapsed. Her breath was hot in her lungs as she roused herself, propping her weight on her elbows.

Diffused sunlight, filtered by thin curtains, filled the room. She glanced at her watch. It was the middle of the morning. She hadn't realized that morning had arrived. She had never really adjusted to the time change, and she would never adjust to yesterday. Even now, it seemed an unreality. A segment of her mind still expected Bartlett to walk through the door. She glanced at the empty bed beside her, knowing he was not ever going to be there again. Part of her mind accepted that. Yet, she could not make herself say the words, nor whisper them to the empty room.

Heat began to invade her brain. Her skull felt hot, as if all the gray matter was coming to a boil, so much oatmeal cooking. Her face felt flushed and the core temperature of her body seemed to be steadily rising. A thin, fine sheen of sweat glistened on her face and dampened her skin. The small room felt like a sauna.

She gasped for air, sucking in great gulps. Then she started screaming. She screamed for some time, no words, only sounds that vibrated off the hot walls of her skull until there was nothing else in the world.

Finally, the screaming stopped and she turned over on her left side and stared out the window into the sunlight. She could hear gunshots and the shouts of men. After a while she began to cry fat, slow tears. Sharon Samuels cried for a long time. Then she fell into a deep sleep.

When she awoke, the light in the room had grown older and there was a used feel to it. She sat up, letting her feet dangle over the side of the bed as she came fully out of the sleep cycle. Then she put her bare feet on the floor and walked to the dresser, where she poured water from a pitcher into a bowl ringed with painted flowers, washed her face and ran damp fingers through her hair. Smoothing her clothes, she slipped on shoes. Then she went to look for her daughter and son.

~ * ~

All morning, the guns had been starting up and dying off. At first, the firing had been accompanied by the shouts of men and the screaming of women. Fear had threaded through both sounds. All were afraid, the women and the men. They simply expressed their fear in different ways.

He was not afraid. Well, perhaps a little. Actually, he didn't much care what happened to him. In the darkest corner, he sat with his back against the wall, peering across the room. He could see tables with tablecloths jerked to the side, glasses overturned, and plates still smeared with food gone dry and gray.

Beyond the furniture lay his father. If Trevor altered the angle of his head, he could see his father's legs extending from the edge of an overturned table. From where he sat, he could pretend they were only the limbs of a stranger. To look at his father's face was unbearable. During the night, in the shallow, flickering lamp light, he had stared at it until it seemed to be taking on a new identity, a life of its own.

He wasn't ready to give him up. He wanted to remember him always. Trevor had never been sure of his father, never sure if his father loved him, or would make time for him, or would be there when he needed him. In this, his hour of immaculate honesty, he could admit he had never been sure of his own love for his father. Love came hard when he felt he occupied a distant second to mutual funds.

Still, there had been something, an indefinable essence of emotion running deep inside his father, like a subterranean current. In the quiet reflective moments that appeared without warning from the far side of shadows, Trevor could sense it bubbling just below the surface. Often, Trevor had held his breath, waiting for it to burst forth. But it never quite made the big push. Now it never would. But it had been there. For the frightened, lonely boy in the room of the dead, that was enough.

The subterranean image had made him think of Kerouac and The Subterraneans. Trevor liked Kerouac's *Lonesome Traveler* best, but all his books were good. At least they were different, not the same old bland smoothness or calculated shock that filled the pages of so many modern novels. The Beats may have been dirty, crude, drunken, dope-head sex-fiends, but at least they loved literature and were not afraid to try to write out their lives. Trevor wondered if he would ever develop enough courage to write.

In a way, he wanted to read now, but he didn't want to leave the room where his father's body lay. Lying in state, like some famous politician, that was how he thought of it. Only not in any government building, but in the Holy Temple of the Disordered Room in Yuscarana, Morazon.

It didn't seem right to leave his father's body alone. Settling deeper into the corner, Trevor Samuels allowed his heavy, hot eyelids to close. He listened to the sporadic gunfire from the street and the answering salvos from the hotel. During his nocturnal vigil, he had not slept and now he sensed a vast drowsiness he could not resist. *Perhaps I will write of this moment* was his final thought before sleep overwhelmed him.

~ * ~

The woman was getting to be a bother. She seemed to be constantly moving and each movement jerked the rope he had tied to her left wrist and his belt. She was giving him a backache; plus, he couldn't concentrate on his shooting the way he should. Jesus was a pig – that he acknowledged. Yet he maintained pride in his marksmanship. Always he had believed he would have been an excellent sniper in the Morazon army, if they had only treated their men right. Now he would never serve in the army of Gutierrez. Once, however....

He had never mentioned this fantasy to anyone. At least not after the first time when he had told some of the guerrillas at the base camp following an early day of training. When they had finished laughing at him and taunting him and calling him all manner of crazy names, such as Sure Shit, instead of Sure Shot, he had stood up, unbuttoned his trousers, and pissed on the campfire. Then he had spit into the wind and cursed the other men until a mosquito would have feared to light on them. Finally, he had informed them, almost in a whisper, that he would piss on their graves.

He had kept that promise. All those men from that early camp had died in service to the Revolución. Not that many of them had fallen in battle as glorious heroes. In fact, of the six, only two had truly been killed in action. The fat-faced one had caught a bullet with his teeth the very next day when one of Gutierrez's units launched a surprise attack on their camp. And the man who walked with the limp had hobbled too slowly across a road one evening. A bullet from the rifle of a government sniper had severed his spine.

The other four had met unheroic ends. Chaco had died of dysentery in a swamp somewhere south of Jalapa. The one they called Motor-Mouth had been bit by a viper while taking his morning dump; he had not lived to wipe his ass. El Baldo had been stabbed in the back in a bar at some crossroads corner that Jesus could only vaguely recall. Manuel the Midget had fallen out of a stolen jeep one night south of the capitol. He had been dead drunk. Then he had simply been dead.

Jesus grinned at the memories of the deaths. They made him feel justified. He had predicted them. He had pissed on all their graves. Actually, he had pissed on the bodies. There had not been time or energy to dig a grave.

A bullet sang in the morning, smashing into the wall above his head, showering plaster down on his face. Cursing, he twitched his head around the side of the building and snapped off a round, aiming in the general direction of a gap-toothed window, smiling with satisfaction when he heard the tinkle of glass.

The woman moved again and he turned in aggravation and slapped at her. She jerked her head away and all he struck was her dark, swinging hair. He settled for spitting on her face and cursing.

He was frustrated. Frustrated with the woman and with the holding action Carlos had been using after the first rush failed. Why did they not attack? What were they waiting for? Surely, Carlos did not truly expect reinforcements. Oh, he told that line about reinforcements to all the new recruits, and they believed it, the first couple of times. After that, they knew it was only so much campfire smoke.

Why had they spent all morning shooting around corners and hiding behind adobe walls? They should either attack or set fire to the hotel and retreat to the jungle. Jesus sat down with his back against the wall of the building and thought things over. Not a quick thinker, nor a clever one, he was a thorough one. As he thought, he scratched his head and spat. Now and then, he kicked absentmindedly at the woman, as though the action were a byproduct of his thought process.

The more he considered setting fire to the hotel, the more he liked the idea. Throughout the morning, Jesus studied the idea, speculating on ways to do it. Inside his brain the idea grew like a mushroom.

When the sun was directly overhead, he stood and led the woman to a sapodilla tree that threw a ring of shade onto a poorly manicured lot behind the row of buildings. He tied her to the tree with the Ecuadorian half-hitch his Uncle Hector had taught him. Then he tore off the tattered remnants of her clothing and bit both her nipples, hard. Jesus spat into her face, turned, and began jogging toward the main street of Yuscarana, angling his trajectory so he would come out several buildings to the right of the hotel. For at least a block, the screams of the woman tormented him.

~ * ~

Toward the front of the hotel, it had grown strangely quiet. Lieutenant Escobar leaned against a wall, closed his eyes, focusing on the absence of sounds. None came from the other end of the hotel. Opening his eyes, he glanced at his men arrayed along the back, next at the flat ground with the grass cut low, and then beyond, to the line of trees and bushes that formed the perimeter of the jungle. Except for a few leaves of a small cluster of banana plants that fluttered in a light breeze, nothing moved. Turning, he walked down the hall as far as the bend in the corridor.

Full light hadn't reached this interior corridor and the air retained a certain coolness. The lieutenant felt as if he stepped into another stratum of Yuscarana. Escobar took a deep breath of cool, quiet air and closed his eyes.

Very faintly, as though the sounds had traveled a great distance, and lost decibels with each mile, he could hear the rattle of cookware, and, even more faintly, talking voices. All the guns on both sides had fallen silent. He wondered what that silence foretold.

Except for occasional sniper fire, things had been quiet along his line all morning. Earlier, there had been flurries of gunfire along the front, one of which had been so heavy and prolonged that he had expected at any moment to hear a messenger from Captain Morales ordering him to send some of his men to the front. That order had not come, and, for the better part of an hour, only silence had drifted back from the hotel lobby.

Silence worried the lieutenant more than gunfire. Silence had the element of the unknown running through it. Gunfire allowed him to estimate the number and type of weapons, and feel with some degree of certainty he knew the strength of the enemy. Silence told him less than nothing.

He was tempted to jog up the hallway and find the captain. Talking things over would help, even if nothing was decided. Then one of his men coughed and another made a bad joke about a nun, a politician, and a donkey. The lieutenant wandered slowly back down the hall.

Cigarette smoke drifted in the air like a low-hanging cloud gone bad in the heat. The acrid smell reminded him of the cigarette the English lady had smoked the night before after they had made love. He had never made love to an English woman before. She had been astonishingly thin, but above the hard bones her skin had been velvet, and her breasts had been high and firm, especially for a lady who had not been a young girl for some time. Her lips had been soft and yielding, and her tongue had moved like a wild young animal. She had been warm and moist and ready for him, her long slim legs spreading like scissors opening and then closing, clamping around his back like twin coils of smooth wire. He could still taste her whiskey kisses and hear her high hard moan that metamorphosed into a scream as she climaxed. The scream had reminded him of a cat in the night.

~ * ~

Señora Herrera was hot, tired, and frustrated. She could not imagine where her husband had gone. It was not in his nature to be absent whenever there was any excitement going on in Yuscarana. Certainly not if such excitement was at their hotel. No, it was not like Poncho to be somewhere else when so much was going on here.

But this morning – with all the shooting and shouting and screaming – he was not here. Very strange indeed, Señora Herrera thought, as gooseflesh pimpled her forearms. Someone has walked across my *madre's sepultura*, she whispered to herself, making the sign of the cross.

After such a morning, there was a great weariness in her legs. She leaned against the cutting board that stood like an island in the center of the kitchen, thankful the morning rush appeared to be over, although why Maria had to take the English señora a special cup of hot coffee at this hour was beyond her. The hotel was under attack by all those vicious guerrillas and her best servant had to make a special trip to take a cup of coffee to a *turista* who had not even acted friendly when she checked in.

Señora Herrera frowned as she recalled the cold eyes, the unsmiling lips, and the nose pointing in the general direction of the ceiling. No, she did not care much for this *turista*. Imagine worrying about a cup of coffee for herself when the hotel was under attack and there were the soldiers of Gutierrez to be fed. Indignation flushed Señora Herrera's face.

She glanced at the old clock on the wall beside the window. Like most of the other clocks in the hotel, it had been her mother's. The positions of the hands astounded her. Why, the morning was gone. Time to begin lunch. She shouted at the girls to wash faster, wondering at the same time where Maria was.

~ * ~

He was behind the row of buildings that ran along the opposite side of the street from the hotel. The sporadic firing had died off again and in the ensuing silence his footsteps sounded loud. Even his ragged breathing was audible. The sense of something portentous hung in the air. He could feel pressure building and wondered what was about to happen. Whatever energy was affecting him steadily increased until the moment of creation seemed imminent.

Halfway down the line of buildings someone had begun to build a wall, only to abandon it. Piles of sand and tumbled down piles of bricks spread out around a wall that varied in height from two to five feet. Grass and weeds grew around the base of the wall and stubborn plants stuck their heads up through openings in the piles of sand and bricks. A few hardy weeds had found enough dirt to sprout on the top of the wall.

Angling away from the wall, he swept around the end, jumped an overturned wheelbarrow, stumbling as the dirt gave way. A hand on the ground and he regained his balanced. An urgency he could not explain poured through him.

Movement off to his right caught his eye and he slowed. What looked like a human figure was tied to a sapodilla tree. The figure appeared to be naked. Perhaps it was a vision. People saw visions, after all. Of course, those seers were very religious. Tony slowed to a jog and angled toward the sapodilla tree. Now he could see that the vision was a woman. Her breasts were swinging as she moved. They looked like small, unripe fruit.

Tony the Demented stopped running. Dust rose in brown puffballs, decorating his boots. It had been months since he had had a woman. So long he could not clearly recall the last time. Undoubtedly, he had been drunk on that occasion.

The woman had seen him and had started running about madly, going as hard as she could away from him until the rope stretched taut and jerked her to a stop. Sometimes her feet slipped and she fell, screaming. Always, she scrambled back to her feet, but Tony could see that she was tiring. Each time it took her longer to get up and she did not dash about as wildly as when he had first seen her. He began to follow her as she ran around the tree in slowing, diminishing circles, tracking her like she was a wounded animal.

Tony had never seen an Oriental woman in person, let alone naked. Her face looked strange and she shouted at him in jabbering monkey-talk. She could no longer scream as she gasped for breath. She fell against the tree. Tony moved in.

He reached out for her. He could feel his hands trembling. It had been far too long since he had been with a woman.

A flurry of gunfire rose from the far side of the buildings and he paused. The woman looked up at him with dark eyes that seemed to have no bottom. Her mouth hung open like a broken gate, revealing small, sharp teeth. Her lips moved as if she were formulating a silent prayer.

Yuscarana fell silent again. Tony took another step. He could smell the woman. She made low, guttural sounds from the back of her throat.

He was inside the shade ring now and let his fingers slide across the woman's breasts. The nipples were like small rubber tips.

She opened her mouth wider. He felt as though he could have thrust his fist through the opening. She made a small mewling noise. Grabbing her hair, Tony pulled her to him. She tried to raise her hands, but the rope jerked her arms and she would have fallen except for his grip on her arm.

He unzipped and twisted her so that her entire body was inside the curvature of his legs. Her lips were still mutely praying. He mashed them with his own. They were softer than he had expected. From behind the lips came a small moan. It could not be heard above his animal grunts. He was mashing her lips against her teeth and he could tell it hurt. She was trying to scream at him, but he got one hand around her vocal cords and squeezed until her eyes went glassy, then hollow. It seemed as if they might pop off her face any second. She squirmed against him and tried to pull away. Tony felt stronger than he had felt in years. His weight bore them down.

She hammered on his back with her heels, but he curled his fingers into a fist and drove it against her temple. She moaned and quivered, then went slack beneath him. For a second, he thought he had killed her. Then he felt her breath on his cheek.

He kicked his pants down around his ankles, ignoring the rattle of small arms fire. He grinned; let someone else die. He had not had a woman in so long. He moaned as he entered her. She gasped and started to sob.

When he was spent, he lay on top of her softness for some time, satiated for the moment, listening to the sporadic battle for Yuscarana, tasting the salt of her tears.

~ * ~

What were they waiting for? After the one flurry of gunfire, quiet had descended. Morales kept hearing intermittent gunfire from the rear of the hotel, but it seemed to be merely sniper fire. Even if the main enemy thrust was to come from the rear, there should be more activity along his line. The captain was tempted to take a stroll and check on Lieutenant Escobar. He was still concerned, and a touch peeved, that the lieutenant had not reported back during the night. What had intervened? The captain jerked the stub of his cigar out of the shirt pocket of his uniform and stuck it between his lips. There was, of course, the possibility that the lieutenant had been hit by a sniper's bullet and lay in the bowels of the old hotel, bleeding or dead.

Taking another glance out the window, the captain flicked his lighter. If Escobar was dead, he was dead. If he had fallen asleep, he had fallen asleep. Whatever had happened during the night was over now. He had survived the night, and morning had come, flooding Yuscarana with sunlight.

He felt like a father who has waited up all night for his son to come home and now it is morning and he still doesn't know whether the son is dead in the morgue with a sheet over his boyish face, or lying somewhere in a ditch with his life-force bleeding out of him one drop at a time, or in a bed with a beautiful woman, smoking cigars, sipping coffee, getting ready to make love again. And there was nothing he could do about any of it. What had occurred, had occurred.

In his own mind, Morales was always on duty, even when he was on leave. Over the years, when he had taken his few short trips, one could not really call them vacations, he had checked in virtually every day, either with the local post commander or by telephoning headquarters.

The army had been his family, for more years than he liked to recall. Thousands of sons had come into and gone out of his life. From the moment they stumbled down off the buses to the moment they walked or were carried out of camp for the last time, they had all been his sons.

Naturally, he had been closer to some. Hundreds, he had most assuredly known only by faces, or the way they walked, saluted, or wore their hair. Yet, they were his sons, too, as much his sons as those who cursed him when they were drunk on Saturday night, only to beg for his mercy and forgiveness when they woke on Sunday morning with a head like a rotting melon and visions of the stockade dancing like butterflies before them, or those who sat across his cheap, battered desk, bowed their necks, and shed real tears over senoritas who had left them for a richer man, or one with a larger manhood, or even those who had stared up at him with hollow eyes as he held them in his arms and wiped away the crimson bubbles from their pale lips as he listened to their final gurglings.

Yes, they had all been his sons, and they would always be his sons. Forever and ever, Amen.

Captain Morales crossed himself as he peered out between the jagged shards of glass that rose like clear, mutilated cathedrals. The dark asphalt before him was empty. He blew smoke out the gap in the glass and let his line of vision drift along the buildings across the street. The only things that glistened were the glass eyes of the old buildings.

Nothing moved, not even shadows from passing clouds. The world was extraordinarily still this morning, as though it were holding its breath, waiting for an energy lost in the cosmos.

His stomach growled at him, reminding him he had passed on breakfast. The captain was certain the guerrillas would come again. They would not have gone to such trouble for a hit and run. They were still out there. He could sense them. Hell, he had been fighting them for so long he could smell them. One thing was certain, he could not fight at full strength on cigar smoke.

Plucking the cigar stub out of his mouth, Captain Morales shouted for Señora Herrera to bring him some *el café* and *tostada* and *anchoas, venga pronto, por favor*.

Fifty-seven

The hands of the English lady were very soft, yet contained a strength that was palpable. She could feel it flowing through the lady's fingers as they ran down her hair and the slope of her neck before kneading her shoulders. The guns started shooting again and she burrowed deeper into the chest of the English lady. The *turista* looked lean and hard, but Maria could feel the softness of her breasts as they gave way beneath the pressure of her face. She felt herself blushing. No woman except her mother had ever been so close to her. She tried to pull away, but the English lady was strong, and then the guns went off again and she quit struggling and snuggled deeper. Soft, strong hands stroked her hair.

"Afraid of the guns?"

Maria moved her face up and down against the breasts of the English lady. For some reason she could not explain, they made her feel safer. She felt so extraordinarily weak. Never had she felt this way before. It must be the guns, she told herself.

"Well, don't worry. There are many soldiers here. Surely they can protect us from a few rebels."

Maria lifted her head and gazed up at the English lady. She found herself looking up into the woman's nostrils. They were narrow and dark, like a cave.

"I do not know, señora. The rebels are very good fighters. Sometimes they kill many soldiers. They have captured several villages. I am very afraid."

"You mustn't be. Being afraid never helps."

The woman turned her head until Maria could see the lower half of her face. For someone so thin, her lips were surprisingly full. Between them her teeth were large, but very white. Maria decided that she liked the mouth of the English *turista*.

The lips moved. "Tell me your name." The words were only a whisper, so soft they might have been the wind.

"Maria," she whispered back, speaking so softly she could barely hear herself.

"Maria, I like that name." The woman made her eyes widen and smiled. "Do you know," she said in a serious voice, "I do not believe I have ever known anyone by that name."

Maria nodded. She felt like she should say something. She wanted to say many things. However, no words formed on her lips. Her mind seemed to be filled with an ocean, full of sand and foam. All her thoughts floated below the surface of the ocean of her mind.

"Are you truly scared of the rebels?"

"Yes," Maria said, hearing the quiver in her voice. "I am very scared. They are not men with whom you can reason. They are violent, very violent, more violent than animals."

Maria shook her head so that her hair swung in front of her face like a dark curtain. "Truly, señora, they are worse than animals. Animals kill because it is their nature. They kill for food, or to save their own lives or the lives of their babies. But not these men. They kill because they want to kill. Because by killing they can come closer to overthrowing Presidente Gutierrez. That is all they want, all they live for. To overthrow Gutierrez and take over Morazon. Yes, señora, I am very much afraid of them."

"You must call me Dianna."

"Oh, no, I could not do that."

"But you must. I insist." Lady Dianna stroked Maria's cheeks. "After all, I intend to call you Maria. Do you mind?"

"No, no, of course not."

"Well, then you must call me Dianna. Okay?"

Maria hesitated. She did not feel at all comfortable calling the English señora by her first name. Thoughts of calling her anything except señora made sweat pop out across her upper lip and turned the muscles in her legs to jelly. She felt warm all over.

Still, the foreign señora was so nice. She was being so kind and smiling at her. Not like Señora Herrera, who was forever frowning or speaking hatefully to her, and who did not mind at all to shout at her. Sometimes she even screamed like an angry jungle parrot. This English lady was nothing like that.

In an odd way, the English señora made her think of her mother, or an older sister if she had one. No, that wasn't quite right. An aunt perhaps? Yes, her Aunt Isadora. Maria had always liked her Aunt Isadora, her mother's sister. She was a tall, beautiful woman who was always sweet to her, giving her candy and little presents of money or sometimes a bracelet or earrings she no longer wore. Yes, the English señora was very much like her Aunt Isadora. Perhaps, after all, it would be all right to call her Dianna.

"Okay," she said, smiling a little.

"Then say it. Say it now. Say Dianna now."

The face of the English lady had inched quite close to hers. Maria could feel her breath, warm against her flesh, smelling of cigarettes, and more faintly of whiskey and other scents Maria had never smelled.

"Dianna," she said, whispering like a schoolgirl. The name felt strange on her tongue, like some new exotic fruit she had never tasted before.

"Good, very good." Lady Dianna Threlkeld ran the forefinger of her right hand down the left cheek of Maria. When she reached Maria's chin, she pressed a little harder and then flipped her finger away as if she were flicking a drop of sweat.

A loud bang shattered the quiet. The walls of the old hotel shook as though an earthquake had struck Yuscarana. Maria screamed and jumped to her feet, flinging her hands in front of her face. She went on screaming and jumping up and down as though the floor were hot beneath her feet.

Lady Threlkeld reached out and got a hand on each of Maria's shoulder and pressed gently until the movement stopped. Cradling the girl's shoulders with one arm, she guided her to the couch. "Merely a single grenade, Maria. We're not hurt. Let's sit down and have something stronger to drink than that coffee you brought me."

Maria felt the woman guiding her as though she were a small, lost child. That was the way she felt. The explosion had been terribly frightening. The guerrillas seemed to be well armed. The storm had not driven them away. Oh yes, she was very afraid. Her legs were trembling. The English señora, Dianna, seemed strong. Maria was glad. She was so afraid; it was good to be with someone who was strong.

The leather of the couch was cool against her bare legs. The muscles in her legs held no strength. They gave way and she sat down, straddle-legged, on the couch. Her neck couldn't hold up her head and it flopped against the leather. Gunfire broke out from the rear of the hotel and she felt the last of her strength rush from her. The room darkened and began to spin. A thousand black specks pin-wheeled before her.

"Here now, let's get you propped up."

Maria felt herself being tugged into a more comfortable position. Her head was wedged in the corner of the couch and her body sagged in the crevice. No strength remained in her body. She could hear gunfire, and she shivered.

"Now, here is something that will most definitely help. Drink up."

Maria tried to lift her arms, but they were filled with straw. All the dark squiggles kept swirling. She closed her eyes. An arm slid around her and the smell of a woman's perfume filled her nostrils. A force was lifting her head and she tried to help. Glass tinkled against her teeth. Liquid slid across her tongue and down her throat, strong and raw and burning.

So that is whiskey, she thought. I have never tasted anything like it before. She slit her eyes open. The English lady was smiling at her. "There, isn't that better?"

Maria tried to say "*Sí*," but made only the noise of a mouse squeaking.

"Here comes another one. Now take a bigger sip this time. It will make you feel better. There's a girl."

The whiskey was warm in her stomach. She knew she should not drink such strong stuff. Her mother had warned her against drinking such powerful spirts. She tried to protest, but she was so weak, and already the English lady was pressing the glass against her lips. She could hear gunfire again, but muffled, and she wondered if the whiskey was already working. Perhaps it was not such a bad thing after all.

Maria could hear Dianna talking. Her words were so soft and flowing that they were no longer words, but only a soothing sound. Resting against the woman's arms, she squeezed her eyes more tightly shut and opened her mouth – the wetness washed down her throat in a small stream.

Gunfire sounded closer, like a dozen strings of firecrackers all going off at once. Maria wanted to scream. She threw her face into the bosom of the English woman who seemed so much like the aunt she had always adored. Always, she had wanted to be close to her Aunt Isadora, but had never dreamed of closeness like this.

She could feel a fullness in her eyes and her head felt hot and heavy. Then, before she realized they were coming, tears began to flow, wetting her face and the señora's blouse. Maria cried for a long time. As long as she could hear gunfire she cried. She could feel her entire body rising up from and falling back against the softness of the señora. The señora's hands stroked her hair and the small of her back. The touch of another felt foreign to Maria. Since the day she had left home, no one had touched her with such kindness.

After what seemed like hours, the gunfire died and she felt the tension begin to evacuate her body. Sobs began to ease and the tears stopped. Their salty stickiness dotted her cheeks.

The body of the English lady felt soft and warm and safe and comforting. She snuggled in closer. Maria could feel the woman's breasts, soft and full through her thin blouse. This feels very strange, Maria thought, but she was so tired and scared that she did not move. She needed someone to protect her. Always she had wanted someone to take care of her. In the warm closeness of the señora's lushness, she smiled to herself.

"There now, the shooting has stopped. Didn't I tell you it would?"

The señora's fingers tracked figure eights on Maria's back. Maria could feel the fingertips through her blouse. They felt like soft rubber erasers such as children have on their new pencils. She moved her head up and down against the silk of the señora's blouse in acknowledgement.

"Would you like more whiskey?"

Maria did not know what to say. She did not want to make the señora angry by refusing her hospitality, but she could already feel a great warmness in her belly and when she opened her eyes the room seemed to be off center. She had never drunk whiskey before, only a little wine during Fiesta, and its potency was already working on her. Perhaps the señora had added something to her drink. Maria did not know what to say, so she simply shrugged in a way that indicated her indecisiveness, and her malleability.

"Well, I think another shot is in order. Matter of fact, I'll join you this time. Here now, sit up a little so I can pour."

Maria felt herself being gently maneuvered until she lay more than sat in one corner of the couch. She sensed herself sinking deeper in the leather, as though it were smooth quicksand that was slowly swallowing her. A weakness, greater than any that had come before, enveloped her. To lift a hand taxed her energy, and to hold the glass of liquid was almost beyond her powers. She watched the señora pour a glass for herself. It was like watching someone pour a drink in a cinema film.

"Cheers," the English lady said, and touched her glass to Maria's. "Here's to peace in our time, to quote a countryman of mine who is held in rather ill-repute these days." Glass tinkled sharply in the room that had again grown quiet.

Sipping steadily, Maria glanced around the room. Everything seemed new and strange, as though she had never really seen it before, as if she had only glanced in as she passed by. Of course, this was not true. A dozen times she had dusted the books and the tables in this room, polished the wood, and cleaned the window with soap and water. Her brain felt thick and hot. If she held her head quite still, the room seemed to kaleidoscope in and out of focus. Her tongue had suddenly grown too large for her mouth and kept slipping out of a corner and lying across her lower lip like some wide, wet pink ribbon.

A large seven-day clock sat atop the mantle. Maria could hear it ticking. The ticking was faint, as though the clock had been moved to the far side of the room. Squinting, she could make out the face. She knew where to look because she had dusted it many times. Each time Señor Herrera noticed her dusting the clock, he would tell her about how it had come down to him through many generations of his family. His father, who had given it to the señor as a wedding present, had received it from his father, the writer, who had received it in turn from his father, the judge, who... oh, it went on and on and her head was so full she could not keep the Herrera memories straight.

Maria concentrated on the face of the old clock, trying to determine what time it was. The hands were bending as though they were melting, cursed with voodoo. Time ticked on, but time no longer mattered, so she closed her eyes and eased deeper into the soft leather, where she sipped her drink. Her entire body felt warm, her eyes were heavy, and a mellow aura wrapped itself around her like a soft cloak. She could hear the English lady talking, but the words were only impotent buzzing.

Maria wondered if she were drunk. Never had she even been high, not even on fiesta wine. But she had seen drunken men in her village, and here in the hotel many drunken men, along with a few drunken women. Hazily, she could recall some of the silly things such people had done and said, and how stupid they had appeared when they lost control of their tongues and their bodies.

Only a small amount of amber liquid was still pooled in the bottom of her glass. Suddenly, as if she had made up her mind after long reflection, she lifted the glass to her lips and tilted it up until the very last drop of whiskey clung to the rim of the glass. That, she licked up with her fat, pink, drunk tongue.

Now she knew she was definitely a little drunk. She wondered vaguely, as though she were thinking of another person, what she would say or do in such a state. She was afraid of saying or doing something stupid, or dangerous. A small noise made her glance up and she found herself staring at the face of the English señora. The señora was watching her sideways out of the corners of her eyes, the way a leopard watches the small animals of the jungle. A cat-smile spread slowly across the face of the señora and Maria was no longer afraid. The señora would take care of her. She felt very sure of this.

The glass had grown heavy in her hand and she let it fall. It must have fallen forever because she did not hear it strike. Settling even deeper into the leather, she closed her eyes. Golden light flooded her mind and her body felt as though a late afternoon sun were shining on her. Maria scarcely recognized that she had entered into a world she had never visited before.

No longer did she feel as if she were in the office of Señor Herrera in the old hotel in Yuscarana. She could not say with any precision where she was. The world seemed a strange, and perhaps wonderful, place. She had no idea what would happen next. Even so, she felt safe and warm, the way she had when she was a child and she did not have to worry about where her next meal would come from, or where she would sleep at night, or if she would be killed before morning. This was so much nicer.

She wondered if it was the whiskey making her feel this way, and, if that were it, why she had not tried it before. If it had not been for the English señora, what was her name... ah, yes, Dianna, she would not have tried it. Never would she have had the courage to try it on her own. Kind thoughts about her new friend circulated through her mind. Maria was content to lie still and bask in the warm glow of the whiskey, enjoying the pleasure of the comforting moment. She felt sleepy. Then a stray thought about the English señora drifted across her mind and she was suddenly afraid the woman had left her. Maria could no longer sense her presence in the room. Her heart was palpitating wildly and a chill swept through her. She blinked her eyes open.

The English señora had not left the room. Her face was only inches from Maria's. Maria sighed a long sigh of comfort as she gazed lovingly at the English face. She had never noticed before how pretty the señora's face was. Maria had never seen eyes quite like those staring at her, glassy and glittering, seeming to see right through her.

The pretty face was very close. Maria could feel the warmth of the woman's breath against her face. It confused her; her mind could not think at all. Thoughts were in there, but they kept spinning. She tried to say something, but all the words jammed together in her throat, and when she swallowed and tried again, they came out as a cross between a groan and a moan. Maria felt foolish, yet there didn't seem to be anything she could do about it. The strange lassitude that had infiltrated her body continued to grow. English face dipped lower.

What is she doing? Maria could not imagine why the English señora was coming so close. Why didn't her own body move? Had the whiskey paralyzed her? Has she been drugged? Why could she not move? Why did she not want to move?

Very faintly she could hear the pop-pop-pop of the guns. They sounded so far away that Maria wondered if she were imagining them. It was as if all the shooting and killing were going on in another world. She could not understand it, but she knew she felt safe and warm, which was all that mattered to Maria. She snuggled into the corner of the couch, wriggling deeper and deeper until she felt entombed.

Closing her eyes, she watched dark and light whirling inside her head, mixing together like chocolate and vanilla cake batter. She thought of the great layered cakes Señora Herrera made, and smiled. Once, when the señora had been looking the other way, she had run a finger alongside the bottom of one side of the cake, pulling it through the icing that had run down the side and pooled into a chocolate lake. It had been so sweet; she could taste it still.

Then she could feel the icing on her lips. But no, it was not icing. It was soft and molding to her lips, but there was a force behind it. Vaguely, she realized other lips were kissing her lips. Finally, the lieutenant had kissed her; she had dreamed of his kisses for weeks. But the aroma that accompanied the lips did not make her think of the lieutenant. It was a softer, sweeter, more subtle aroma than his. Maria was terribly confused. She was not thinking at all straight. The whiskey, yes, it had to be the whiskey. Slowly she forced her eyelids open, like the heavy velvet curtain rising from the stage before the first act.

The face of the English señora rose before her like a lovely moon. The señora's eyes were open, tracking her in their glittery glassy way, narrowing to slits. What was happening? This had never happened before. This should not be happening. This was not supposed to happen.

Maria opened her mouth to protest, but before she could utter a sound, the señora's tongue slid inside her mouth. She could feel it moving, a thick, wet, alive thing licking her tongue and caressing the inside of her lips. Never had she been kissed like this. One woman should not kiss another like this, never. And yet, it did not feel so terrible. She did not feel the flames of hell scorching her body like the priests and her mother prophesied. Instead, she felt tension seeping out of her body.

No, no, it was all wrong. She should not be doing this. Maria groaned and wriggled, putting her palms up against the señora's chest and pushing. She was so weak; the señora did not go away. Her body only pressed closer. Maria tried to say no, but then the señora's fingers were busy with her blouse and the señora's tongue was alive in her mouth. The weight of the English lady was pressing her deeper into the leather. For a moment, she kicked her legs wildly about, trying to regain leverage, but all they struck was air. She felt a great dizziness, so great it seemed she must fly apart into a hundred pieces. Closing her eyes tightly, she tried to hold herself together.

The señora's hands were very busy. Maria felt her breasts come free and the señora's fingers as soft as flower petals upon them. No one had ever touched her breasts before. She was scared, yet the feelings were more of pleasure than pain.

In her pleasure was an overwhelming helplessness. Maria did not struggle any longer. She could not. The English señora was too strong, and sure, and knew too well how to bring out the pleasure.

Maria felt the pressure come off her lips and the tongue come out of her mouth. Then she felt them moving down her face and neck, smothering them with kisses. She slitted her eyes open and watched the head of the English *turista* descend. In seconds, the woman's tongue was licking her right nipple. The sensation was exquisite. Maria had never felt anything like it. Then the señora's lips were kissing and sucking at both of Maria's breasts, one after another. All resistance left her body and Maria lay limp and open, ready for whatever the señora chose.

The señora's fingers were busy in Maria's special area. Maria knew what was happening was wrong. It was a sin, a great sin against God. Yet she no longer cared. Denial was impossible; the pleasure too much. The señora's head slid lower. She kissed the inside of Maria's thighs. Then her mouth moved to the special place and Maria moaned with pleasure and wrapped her legs around the shoulders of the señora.

Outside the firing of the guerillas intensified.

Inside, Maria heard only the slurping sounds coming from between her legs, interspersed with her own moans of pleasure and tiny, high new cries that her violated lips uttered.

Fifty-eight

"Oh God, oh great and merciful Lord hear my plea." Reverend Thomas Malloy paused and buried his face in the rumpled covers of his narrow bed. He had been praying since the latest round of firing had started. There had been sporadic outbursts throughout the day, and each time he had prayed for God to cause them to cease. Each time the firing had been short-lived and the reverend had begun to wonder if, for a change, the Lord was listening to his entreaties. Though it was one of the basic tenants of his faith, Thomas Malloy had always harbored a sincere, if secret, reservation concerning the answering of prayer.

Oh, he emphatically believed that God could answer prayer. God could do anything He chose to do. Doubt factored more on the 'what-God-would-do' side of the equation. Sometimes God chose to answer prayers and sometimes He didn't. Reverend Malloy had seen it happen both ways, but he had never been able to isolate the precise factor which determined whether the good Lord would choose to answer a prayer or not.

And answer them He certainly did. Reverend Malloy recalled a certain drought in Texas and a lost child in Missouri. The one he remembered most, however, was a woman in California who had been struck blind in an instant, shortly after breaking her two-year-old's arms.

No, the reverend thought as the floorboards pressed painfully against his knees, he was completely convinced the Lord could answer prayer. The question remained would He, and if so, when.

He shifted position in an effort to bring relief to his aching knees. Not that Reverend Malloy minded a modicum of pain. In fact, one of his much-cherished beliefs was that a little pain was good for the soul. Pain, in reasonable degrees, was a modest expression of the penance many of the saints had performed. Plus, it made one appreciate more what one had received. Such philosophies often made their way into Reverend Malloy's sermons.

As he knelt on the hard floor listening to the persistent gunfire, he decided if God answered his prayers and stopped the fighting long enough for him to ride that horrid yellow bus out of this Philistine town, he would write a special letter to President Mitchell at the seminary for use in the curriculum. Perhaps he would be called to serve as guest lecturer, for an appropriate remuneration, of course. After all, as the Bible said, a laborer is worthy of his hire.

Another thought sprang to light within his mind. A candle lighting the darkness, he thought. The reverend tended to think in biblical terminology. He would write a book about this trip to a place called Yuscarana, which he would subtitle *A Second Hell on Earth*.

Such a book was sure to be a bestseller, which would finally answer all those who had doubted him over the years, those who had called him a Doubting Thomas. Well, perhaps he had been one to harbor a few doubts. But he couldn't help that. Doubting was his nature. Since he had been a young boy he had doubted things. He had doubted Santa Claus and the Easter Bunny. As he grew older, he doubted evolution, and man traveling to the moon, and almost anything politicians said.

Never had he doubted God, however, not really, although he found some biblical tales, such as Jonah and the whale, difficult to swallow as absolute truth. He preferred to think of them as allegories. Always he had tried to keep his doubts to himself. True, he had expressed enough in seminary to earn the nickname Doubting Thomas. He could still hear the laughter of his fellow students, especially that wall-eyed George Leforce. That was one man, even to this day, that he found hard to think of in the true spirit of Christian charity. Well, he would show them now. Yes, old Doubting Thomas Malloy would show them.

Sounds of gunfire intruded into his thoughts and he resumed his prayers, saying them more fervently than ever.

"Oh Lord, deliver me from this place of pestilence, from this din of iniquity. I have been a loyal and faithful servant to You all my life, and now I come to You in this moment, in my hour of need, to beg You to extend Your great hand of mercy and pluck me from the clutches of mine enemies. I believe with all my heart this is within Your power, and I pray that You will judge Your servant worthy of release. I know You can perform great miracles, such as parting the Red Sea, and turning water to wine, and raising the dead. Therefore, my request may seem exceedingly insignificant to You. However, I assure You it is of the utmost importance to this humble servant who has labored long in Your vineyards."

The sound of gunfire grew louder, more intense, and Reverend Thomas Malloy surmised the rebels must be attacking again. Thoughts of more armed rebels descending on Yuscarana made him dizzy.

Head swimming, the reverend looked up from his prayers. All the thoughts about water turning to wine and laboring in the vineyards had created a craving for a drink within him.

Sunlight was pouring in through the window above his bed, spraying illuminating light. The glass bottle sparkled, scattering myriad reflections. Thomas Malloy studied the sparkling glass, reflecting on God, struggling with his doubts. When thoughts of doubt became thick as banana pudding, he sat up in the bed and unscrewed the cap.

~ * ~

At last they were coming. Sweat formed on his palms and Kron rubbed his hands on the legs of his trousers. All morning, he had been waiting for the rebels to launch their next attack. Minutes dripping as if they were fat, tired raindrops sliding down a wavy pane of old glass.

Across the lobby floor, the captain was shouting orders in Spanish too quickly for him to do more than catch every fourth or fifth word. Kron was no military man. Hell, he hadn't even done any National Guard training. And he was woefully aware of his shortcomings. It would tax his limits to simply fire his rifle. If he actually hit anything smaller than the side of a building, he would consider it pure luck, like when a blind man stretches out a hand to ascertain what's on the table before him and his fingers close around a twenty-dollar bill.

Kron had absolutely no idea what he was supposed to be doing now and he was nervous. A strong urge to urinate garnered his attention, but he didn't want to be surprised with his manhood in a hand by some rebel squeezing the trigger. Scrunching his legs tighter together, he twisted his body and craned his neck so he could see over the bottom edge of the window sill.

Sunlight filled the street. He could hear the rebels, their guns coughing and their bullets twanging in the clear air, but he couldn't see them. Were they coming, or not?

His eyes swung up and swept the storefronts across the street. Empty windows stared back at him. Turning his head, he watched the soldiers in the lobby. A few were running to the walls, while the captain walked to the hallway, shouting down the dim recess. Most of the men, however, were doing what he was doing, kneeling in front of the windows, rifles in one hand, staring out into the still empty streets.

Sounds of shattering glass jerked his head around. Two windows down one of the final remaining panes of glass had been smashed to glitter. Kron wondered where the bullet had lodged. The soldier at that window, a nondescript man whom Kron did not recognize, quickly raised his rifle to his shoulder and squeezed the trigger. The report seemed obscenely loud to Kron. A barrage of gunfire answered and near the front door a man screamed and fell back, his fingers fluttering at his right breast as if his flesh were on fire.

Kron jerked his eyes away as he tried to swallow the rising nausea. His stomach was a sea of churning acid and sweat was popping out all over his body. His left eye twitched uncontrollably. Kron closed it and raised his rifle to his shoulder. The gun seemed vulgarly heavy as he stared down the barrel. When the first shadow moved, he squeezed the trigger. In that instant he was momentarily deafened by the blast and blinded by the sweat rolling into his open eye. Kron blinked away the sweat in time to see a man running between the back walls of the two buildings directly opposite him. Kron squeezed the trigger again and watched dirt fly at the man's feet.

~ * ~

Never had he been more confused during a battle. Carlos peered through the gaps in the porch railing at the hotel across the street. He was sighting from around the corner of what normally served as the town café of Yuscarana and his angle of vision was poor. In fact, with the sunlight glancing off the shards of glass in the hotel windows, it was difficult to see anything. He turned his head away and blinked, then closed his eyes for a moment to let the black dots dissipate. When he opened his eyes, Carlos began looking for his own men.

After a few seconds of searching, he could see two, no three of his band. Two were huddled together like scared ducks behind the small outbuilding twenty yards to his left. From the expression on their faces, they were about ready to crap in their pants.

Carlos did not know their names. They had joined him only ten days ago, part of the ragged gaggle of misfits old one-eyed Raul had sent down from the north. For the most part, they were virtually useless, barely able to march and carry a gun at the same time. Of the seven or eight who came in that bunch, he doubted if more than two had ever fired a rifle at a target, let alone aimed at a man. And as for shooting at a man who was shooting back at you, and shooting to kill, well, one could forget about that. Such men were virgins when it came to killing.

The third man, whose name was Diego Estrada, knelt in the dirt to his right. At least he seemed to know how to hold his rifle and he had his eyes fixed on the hotel. Carlos knew his name because the man had played football with a couple of Carlos' cousins. While a fervent believer in the Revolución, Diego had proven to be about as fine a soldier as he had performed as a midfielder. He had been a mediocre midfielder.

Carlos peered up and down the street, then to the right and left behind the row of buildings that fronted the street, looking for his men. Although he could hear intermittent gunfire from his side of the street, he could see no more of his troops. Sighing, he duck-walked forward a few short steps. At least his men were firing occasionally.

At the edge of the porch, he risked a quick peek in both directions, looking for some of his old regulars, the good men, the ones he could count on in a firefight.

Hustling back to more substantial protection on the far side of the building, he thought about all the really good men, fine soldiers he had known. Not many of them were left. They had died in swamps and forgotten crossroads and villages that had no name. They had died of gunshot and snakebite and dysentery. At first, he had buried them. Later, he had covered them with their own blankets, then with only a blanket of leaves or fronds. Finally, he had simply abandoned them where they had fallen. Such disrespect for the dead was not right. At first it made him sick, but as the bodies mounted, he became more angry than sick. Lately, it had only made him sad. Soon, he thought, I won't even care. He spat into the dust at his feet. "Then I might as well be dead," he mumbled to himself, not realizing he had spoken aloud.

Thoughts about dying frequented his mind these days. Carlos had not yet decided if they were omens of his future or if he had simply seen so damn many men die that such images were taking over his brain.

Death was not a major concern for Carlos. Every man had to die sometime. Many men believed that their day of death was already written. Carlos was uncertain. He liked to think he might have some say regarding such a significant matter. A man's death was certainly significant; no man could argue that point. And yet, all the dying he had seen had made him realize that a man's death was probably significant only to him.

Oh, if he had a family, then it would matter to his wife and children. Or if he were young, his mother and father would care.

Even then it was often over so quickly – between one breath going out and the next one coming in – that it seemed no more than the closing of a door.

Carlos struck himself on the leg and stood up. He was turning into a campfire philosopher. Soon he might decide to become a university professor.

"Damn," he shouted, trying to vanish the worry demons rising up in his mind. "Where in the hell are my veterans? Where are Tony and Jesus and Felix?" Breaking into a dogtrot, he headed toward the two men hunkered together. Halfway there, he remembered he had sent Felix with the group that was to attack the communications station outside the town. Oh well, he was really merely a boy anyway, Carlos thought. He yelled for Tony and Jesus. The two men behind the outbuilding lifted their heads and stared at him, but no one answered.

Fifty-nine

How much goddamn further could it be? He had been on this trail for hours. Late the afternoon before, he had picked it up, figuring to be across the ridge and down the slope and into Metalazaton by dark. He had made this trek before; of course, that had been years ago, when he had been a much younger man.

That, and he had not foreseen the storm. Poncho was willing to admit a storm such as that one had been would throw even the best planned schedule off by a considerable margin, and his schedule had been a sketchily drawn one, based on a pair of excursions he had taken with some drinking buddies a dozen years ago. At that time, there had been two very fine brothels in Metalazaton.

Stopping to scratch at one particularly irksome mosquito bite, Poncho leaned against a smooth-barked tree that arched above him like a living cathedral.

Glancing at his arms, he was amazed by the number of mosquito and other insect bites. In places, his flesh appeared as if every square inch was punctured. Blood, dried and fresh, stained his light brown skin where he had scratched bites in the madness of itching.

Poncho shuddered to think of all the creatures that had swarmed over him during the night. The shudders sapped the last of his energy and he let his knees bend and settled back against the damp earth.

A sigh of relief escaped his thick lips as the weight came off his leg muscles. He had not realized how tired he was. *Mon Dios*, how his thighs ached, and as for his calves, why they burned as if a tiny flame thrower had been surgically inserted in them during the night. Without his permission or knowledge, his entire body seemed to have transformed into a single ache. Even his eyelids ached, and he let them close as he tried to shift into a more comfortable position.

Finding some position that was in any way comfortable proved difficult. Even under the canopy of leaves, last night's rain had pounded down on him like a mother beating a bad child, soaking him to the bone. Hours later, his clothes were still damp against his skin. Damp fabric had chafed his upper leg. Inside his boots, his socks remained soggy and blisters were forming on the balls of his feet and the bottoms of his toes. Mumbling to himself, he began to unlace his boots.

High above him on one of the lower tree limbs, a trio of spider monkeys chattered. Poncho gazed up at their small, dark forms as they played, swiping at each other in mock combat, then hanging by their tails for a moment, before pulling themselves upright and leaping to another limb. He envied them their agility and energy. For the first time in his life, he was envious of monkeys. Then he remembered the money and smiled. In all his life he had never been so rich, especially as he no longer had to share.

Feeling better, he tugged off his boots and damp socks and carefully examined the bottom of each foot. As he had feared, blisters were forming like mushrooms in the dark dampness of the jungle floor. Already, one had burst. Groaning loudly,

Poncho made a halfhearted attempt at drying his feet with the least damp sections of his shirt. After a few minutes the innkeeper gave the job up as a lost cause and lay back.

Grass grew around the arching tree, green and thick. Poncho jammed the bundle of money under his head. It was the most wonderful pillow ever. Having slept only in wet, fragmented snatches the night before, his bed of grass-covered earth seemed luxurious. It felt safe to lie on the soft sloping bank with the sunshine filtering through the leaves and falling warmly on his upturned face.

Great waves of tiredness from a seemingly inexhaustible ocean swept over him. Sleep hovered around him like a mild, benevolent fog. Poncho Herrera did not resist. His penultimate thought was of the monkeys chattering above him.

He slept the sleep soldiers, mountain climbers, athletes, lumberjacks, and men who fish deep in the ocean with large, heavy nets sleep, a sleep so deep no sound or change of light can disturb. His sleep was so deep it fell below the level of dreams.

For hours, nothing disturbed him. Not the wind waltzing among the leaves, nor the monkeys chattering, nor the sunlight whose changing angles struck his face.

Gradually, the level of his sleep rose and he dreamed. Herrera the innkeeper dreamed he was in a great hall in a palatial building in a large city. The walls of the hall were marble and the great curving ceiling, painted the blue of the Morazon sky and trimmed in gold, was supported by twin rows of massive alabaster columns. The floor was of the finest handmade tiles with flowers and vines and small birds etched artistically, each tile inlaid with diamond chips and strands of silver so thin that they were no thicker than the hairs on his head. Bronze sculptures of beasts were strategically placed throughout the hall; renowned works of art in gilt-edged frames hung on the walls.

In his dream, Poncho Herrera, the innkeeper of the old hotel in Yuscarana, was on his knees. Dressed in his best black suit, he wore his favorite tie, black with an indecipherable pattern of red and gold lines. A hammer was in his hands.

For reasons the innkeeper could not explain, he was crawling methodically across the floor, smashing the hammer against each tile. Raising the hammer high above his head, he drove the hammer down with all his strength. Time and time again, he drove the steel head against the tile with a shattering force. Fragments of tile were thrust into the air like lava spewed from the mouth of a volcano. Occasionally, a tile fragment flew against his face, stinging like a wasp, sending rivulets of blood sliding down his face. He spat flecks of tile from his open mouth and blinked against the rising dust. Always he kept moving across the sea of tiles without end, a living, breathing, hammering machine.

After what seemed like hours, Herrera began to hear voices. At first, they were faint and he ignored them. Slowly, the voices grew louder. Herrera hammered harder. Tile flew into the air like shrapnel during battle. Now he could plainly hear the voices above the smashing tile, shouting at him, ordering him to stop. Herrera hammered like a man possessed. Screaming voices assaulted his ears.

Herrera the innkeeper woke to the sounds of a parrot screaming. The bird was green with a head the color of fresh blood. The tips of the wing feathers were indigo. Daylight lingered, although the quality of the light had changed. The sun slanted below the bottom branches of the tree above him, not as strong as it had been.

Blinking against the light, he reluctantly opened his eyes. The innkeeper did not want to go back to sleep – his dream had been far too intense. Yet his mind was infused with a strange aversion to waking. He shifted his head and the pillow shifted beneath it and he remembered all his money.

He wanted to shout at the parrot to shut up, but his head hurt and his throat felt raw. I have probably caught my death of cold being out in that terrible storm last night, then having to walk through the steaming jungle and sleep on the bare ground, he thought. His throat was indeed aching and he wished fervently for a shot of whiskey. However, he did not have even water to drink, so he sat up, looking around for a rock or stick to throw at the bird.

Halfway to upright, he saw it lying across his legs. As long as a man's arm from his elbow to his wrist and no bigger around than child's pencil, it was as deadly as a bullet to the brain. Its slim green body, banded with narrow, lemon stripes, was unmistakable. Every child of six knew never to go near such a snake. Venom of the Calluses tree viper was so poisonous a single bite would kill a man within three minutes, a horse within five. Although most rapid, such deaths were not painless. As the jungle swayed, Poncho Herrera shuddered. Before he fainted, he said three Hail Marys.

He could not have been out for more than a few seconds. He came to, stomach queasy, head spinning, eyes searching only for the snake. It still lay across both legs, unmoving, except for its forked tongue, which flickered every few seconds. Its eyes glittered in the sunlight like precious stones.

Sick to his stomach, Poncho Herrera felt the urge vomit. However, he dared do no more than breathe as shallowly as was humanly possible. His heart pounded as though he had just run an Olympic marathon. As he watched, the snake swung its head toward his knees and began to slide up his leg.

Even before he was aware of the warmth rolling down his leg, he smelled the astringent odor of the urine. The snake hesitated, lifting its head as though it had picked up the odor. Poncho held his breath.

His mind gradually grew intensely aware of the brightness of the sunlight on the grass between his legs, the screeching of the parrot, the way the shadows were falling across his upper torso, and the scents of wet earth, rotting leaves, and his own urine. The coppery taste of fear coated his tongue.

Poncho wanted to jump to his feet and run away. To hell with the money. He could always come back for that. He wanted to scream. He wanted to cry. He could do neither. Both were invitations to his own death. All he could do was breathe shallowly and pray to God.

The viper crawled past his knee and over his groin. It slithered steadily up his abdomen. Poncho could feel his throat tighten until breathing was scarcely possible. Even the faint rising and falling of his chest seemed to the innkeeper to be challenging the reptile to a duel, a duel whose outcome was preordained.

How much time passed he could not say. Seconds stretched like eons. Gradually, the snake began to change its course, curving left as slowly as clouds drifting. Poncho dared not let himself hope.

With a nerve grinding slowness, the snake slid off his chest and onto the grass. Sweat streamed down Poncho's face as he watched the viper slide slowly through the grass. He did not take his eyes off the snake until the tip of the tail merged into the great green jungle. Then, Poncho Herrera, the innkeeper of Yuscarana, rose on trembling legs from what had promised to be his early grave and, tugging at his belt, squatted. Five seconds later, he emptied his bowels.

Sixty

Velvet red curtains were drawn and a deep indigo twilight filled the room. The president of Morazon sat in an oversized chair in the darkest corner of the room, hands resting on the arms of the chair. The seat of the chair was deep and its arms were set high, so that President Gutierrez appeared to be sitting on a throne. His head was thrown back against the chair, with his feet sprawled out before him. He looked quite relaxed.

Years earlier, Gutierrez had learned it was most often to his advantage not to reveal his true feelings. A word, a gesture, a facial expression, even the manner in which he held his body could divulge what was going on inside his brain. He had trained himself to adopt poses which reflected nothing of what he was thinking; in fact, they often made him appear to be in an entirely different frame of mind than he was truly in.

Such poses were extremely useful. He had practiced his technique for long stretches in front of full-length mirrors until he was able to rapidly transform his face and body. Over the years, he had done it so many times it was no more challenging than turning on his bedside lamp.

Perhaps he was an actor, he thought, one of the greatest of all time. After all, actors had time to prepare, to read a script, to spend hours meditating on precisely how their character should behave. Plus, they got to practice their upcoming performances dozens of times. And, if their performance was for the cinema or television, retakes were possible.

No retakes for Gutierrez, the president of Morazon. All his performances were live. Without fail they had to be good ones. If not, his next performance might well be that of a corpse. That was one role President Gutierrez wanted to avoid as long as possible.

At the moment he was not acting, other than trying to assume the role of a patient man, not a particularly easy role for him. From boyhood he had been impatient to succeed, to get ahead, to make things happen. Ambitious in a country where ambition was not the great national ideal.

Gutierrez had never been able to isolate the moment his ambition had been born, or from where it came. Nonetheless, it was there, and he had been driven by it. Ambition was a powerful driver, Gutierrez admitted. It made one not averse to lying, stealing, raping, or killing. Powerful, yet dangerous.

So far, Gutierrez had always proved stronger than any ambitious opponent. And yet, this Revolución was different. Despite the best efforts of his generals and his spies, he had been unable to find indications of either foreign involvement or traitors among his officers. The revolt seemed to stem directly from the people themselves, the pitiful peasants, *esos bastardos* who did nothing but whine and cry about how difficult their lives were, and how they were overworked, underpaid, sick, and hungry. Oh God, but their litany of complaints seemed to go on forever.

The only action the peasants seemed to take was to form bands of guerrillas in every village throughout Morazon. The

Revolución had happened rather suddenly. One day there was a report of a small insurrection in the southeast. A company of troops was dispatched to put it down. The next day another report came in from a slightly larger village a hundred miles to the west. More troops were dispatched. Two days later, three more acts of rebellion were reported, two in the north and one on the eastern border. Government troops by the hundreds were rolled out to repress the rebellion before it could gather momentum. In some of the more remote areas of Morazon, the roads were badly in need of repair. By the time the soldiers of Gutierrez arrived, fires that had consumed certain government buildings and the homes of Gutierrez loyalists were barely smoldering. Bodies lay where they had fallen. Within two weeks, over one hundred villages were in revolt, with more joining daily. It was as though a thousand blood vessels had burst at once in the body of Morazon.

Gutierrez shifted in his chair as he stretched out a hand to turn on the lamp standing on the teakwood table beside him. Halfway to the switch, he changed his mind and let his fingers close instead around his glass of bourbon. It was fine American bourbon, single barrel, from Kentucky. His drink of choice when he had thinking to do, thinking and waiting. All afternoon he had been doing both. Waiting for the call that would tell him what was truly happening with the latest outbreaks. Thinking how he must respond.

Sipping bourbon, he sighed and settled even more deeply in his chair. All these attacks were discouraging. Even after two years of fighting the rebels, his army was still in reasonably good shape, certainly capable of crushing any single outbreak. It was that there were so many outbreaks, and they occurred all over Morazon. No single disaffected region was rebelling. Instead, the whole country was rising up against him. Every day he received reports of more casualties. Why, only this morning at breakfast his aide had told him about the loss of Major Renardo and thirty-five of his men near Oriciono. Gutierrez had never heard of Oriciono, but he had been fishing many times with the major. Several times they had flown to the ocean for to try for game fish. The major had been especially good with marlin.

The president of Morazon allowed his eyes to stare at the silver phone on his desk, the one that had obstinately refused to ring all afternoon. Gutierrez glanced at his wristwatch. In the dusky room, the luminous hands glowed faintly. The hour was late, but surely not too late for the call. If the call did not come soon, it would be a very long afternoon.

It had grown quiet in the room. Traffic on the boulevard seemed to have died off, along with the wind. He had sent his aides away after lunch and given orders to the guards who always stood with rifles outside his office door not to disturb him. His office was equipped with a radio, a television, and four telephones: one for general calls put through by his secretary, one for only his five closest aides, one solely for army headquarters. The fourth was his private line. Calls put through on this line rang directly into the silver instrument on his desk. This was the one he always listened for. Only seven people in Morazon had the number that would make the private telephone ring. Three of these seven were women. At one time, ten people had been given the number to this private line. Three of them were no longer living. Only one had died of natural causes.

Darkness was overwhelming the room. Gutierrez glanced at his watch again. The angle of the sun would have fallen behind the tree line by now, but in the open spaces a subdued half-light would still prevail. Before he began his journey to the presidency this had been his favorite time of the day. He had enjoyed strolling along the sidewalks, peering into storefront windows displaying merchandise he could not have, watching pretty girls he would never know strut by, sitting on a black wrought-iron chair at a café while he sipped on a café au lait, wandering without purpose through the park on the south side of the central plaza. Gutierrez honestly could not remember the last time he had strolled at dusk.

The room in which he had spent countless hours seemed somehow strange to him. The furniture, the flags in the corner, the plaques hanging on the wall, all looked foreign, as though he were a visitor and they belonged to another man. Out of synch with time and reality, as if the silence and gathering darkness had somehow shifted his mind into another universe, President Gutierrez wondered if he was going crazy. Men unaccustomed to silence often experienced delusions when placed in solitary confinement. For some time, he considered that possibility. Then he looked again at the silver phone. He would give it until midnight; then he would notify his pilot.

He allowed himself another sip. Just as his glass touched his lips, a telephone rang. It was not the silver phone. Each phone had a distinctive ring, and Gutierrez knew instantly which of his four telephones was ringing. This time it was the one that connected directly to army command.

Reluctant to leave the comfort of the chair, the president hesitated. In all likelihood, the message would not be good. Generals rarely called him with positive information. They were too busy espousing their great, heroic triumph to the media. *El Presidente* usually got the call when an attack had gone wrong. He wished he had directed headquarters not to call unless the capital itself was in danger. The phone rang again and he set his glass down and pushed himself out of the chair. He had been sitting so long, one foot had gone to sleep and his legs were stiff. He walked like a marionette across the thick, sky-blue carpet.

His hand hesitated above the instrument. Gutierrez noticed, in a detached, clinical manner, that his fingers were quivering slightly, as if they were vibrating in response to a weak electrical current. The phone rang again, startling him, as though he had expected the other party to have disconnected. He picked up the receiver.

"Yes." He tried to make it sound as if the call were an intrusion, disturbing vital business of the government of Morazon. Long ago, he had learned never to let the general staff think too highly of itself.

"President Gutierrez?"

"Yes." He drew the word out, making three syllables out of it, each one intended to infer something negative to the caller.

"Bueno. This is Colonel Perez. General Gomez said you had asked for an update on the situation in Yuscarana."

"Yes, yes, that is so. Tell me the news. What do you have?"

"Not much, sir. As General Gomez may have told you, communications with Yuscarana were broken yesterday."

"Yes, yes," Gutierrez interrupted, "certainly I know that. Tell me developments. I trust you have not wasted my valuable time with a call concerning old information." The president tried to leave the implication dangling in the air that it would not be good for the colonel's career if this were the case.

"No sir, I would not do that. Just within the past half hour we received a report from someone who was at Yuscarana when the attack started."

"And why did you not call me immediately, since I had personally requested prompt updates?"

"Sir, we were verifying the information. Sometimes the reports we receive are no more substantial than the strands of a spider's web."

Gutierrez took a deep breath, made himself hold it, then let it out slowly. "Such caution is to be commended, Colonel. Proceed with your report."

"Certainly. As I stated, this report came in only minutes ago. One of our patrols happened to overhear a conversation in a village sixty or seventy kilometers north of Yuscarana."

Something in the colonel's voice aroused a suspicion in Gutierrez. He had heard hundreds of such reports over the years and often learned more from the voice inflections than from the questionable information.

"And where was this conversation overheard, Colonel?"

"I believe the name of the town is Limon."

"No, no, not the name of the town. Where in Limon was this conversation overheard?"

"Well, sir, I, er, ah, understand..."

"Just tell me, Colonel. Believe me, I will not be surprised; I have heard it all before."

"Yes sir. I understand that it took place in a café, or perhaps a bar. Both are good..."

"Of course, Colonel Perez; both are indeed good sources of information, and I do understand that soldiers, from time to time, need a little drink and diversion. So do not concern yourself. After all, I am a man and, therefore, understand such things. Now, tell me the information you have." Gutierrez designed his remarks so the colonel might draw the inference that the president had once been a soldier. This was not the case, but the colonel did not need to know that fact.

The colonel coughed, then cleared his throat. "But certainly, President Gutierrez. Yes, now that I look at my notes, I can confirm it was in a bar, a bar that also serves food." He cleared his throat again. "In any case, one of our men, a Lieutenant Cardenas, happened to be returning from answering a call of nature when he overheard two men talking in the dark. Normally, he would not have paid any attention, but he heard the word Yuscarana whispered and of course he had read the reports on the rebel attack there, so, when he had an opportunity the next day, after his maneuvers were completed..."

"Excuse me, Colonel, but do you not mean after he sobered up?"

There was a pause. Then the colonel murmured, "Perhaps."

Gutierrez could hear the shrug in the colonel's voice all the way from army headquarters. He grinned.

"In any case, Lieutenant Cardenas did advise his superior, Captain Vincente, and the captain contacted headquarters."

"And who was this person talking of Yuscarana?"

"That was a part I had trouble getting the straight of, sir. After several calls, my staff has determined that it was a man who calls himself, or is called, El Cartero. As near as we can understand it, this man drives a bus for a company that conducts expeditions for *turistas*, and this El Cartero happened to have just delivered his busload of *turistas* to their hotel when the rebels attacked. Naturally, while he would have liked to have rescued the *turistas*, he could see that because of the ferocity of the attack he would only have been committing suicide, accomplishing nothing. He saw that by acting quickly, he could keep the bus out of rebel hands and save it for his employer. So he started the engine and drove it out of town. I am sure his employer is well pleased, and certainly the army is grateful that a fine bus in good running order is not in the hands of the revolutionaries. Do you not agree, President Gutierrez?"

"Of course, but how many rebels did El whatever his damn name is see?"

"He says there are a great many, and that they are well-armed."

"And, Colonel Perez, how many men do we have stationed in Yuscarana?"

The colonel cleared his throat again. Gutierrez wondered if the man were coming down with a cold.

"Only a small contingent."

"Under whose command?"

Papers rattled. "A Captain Morales, according to my notes."

"Ah, yes. I think I may know Captain Morales, slightly, you understand."

"Certainly."

Colonel Perez could hear the faint hum of the line, and, now and then, the sound of breathing. Uncertain as to what to say next – he did not want to upset the president – he remained silent.

His nerves begin to act up. For a colonel, he was a nervous man. He reread his notes to make sure he had not omitted an important fact. He tried to think of something clever to say. Finally, he could not stand the silence any longer.

"What would you have us do next?"

His question was greeted only by more silence. For a moment, one that stretched beyond its natural boundaries, the colonel thought perhaps the president of Morazon had abandoned the telephone. Then he heard a soft sigh.

"Have we sent troops to relieve the siege at Yuscarana?"

Colonel Perez grimaced. "Yesterday we did order a hundred men under Colonel Aquino south, but before they had been on the road for even an hour, we received reports of a large rebel convoy approaching the oil fields in the north, so they were rerouted."

"Were others sent to replace them?"

"All the other troops are committed, either in the field, or here, defending the capital."

"So there will be no relief for Yuscarana?"

The colonel swallowed. "Not at this time. However, as soon as men are available they will be ordered to Yuscarana."

President Gutierrez carried the telephone to the window and pulled the curtain back. Shadows fell long and black on the palace grounds. They seemed to grow as he watched them.

"Tell me, Colonel," he said finally, "do we have any observation planes available?"

"One moment and I will check."

"All right."

As he waited, President Gutierrez tried to imagine what Captain Morales was going through at Yuscarana. All his thoughts along this line were unpleasant, so he mentally ran through the prospects of the young ladies who were possibilities to become his next mistress. None of them made the earth tremble. Voices babbled down the line, distant and blurry. What were they saying, he wondered. What they were thinking? Gutierrez could only wait.

After a moment, he could hear breathing on the other end of the line. "We do have one observation plane available."

"And a pilot?"

"One will be found."

"*Bueno*. Now, I want you to get that plane in the air as quickly as possible. Have the pilot fly down to Yuscarana and report the situation back to you, personally, over the radio in the plane. Then you, personally, are to call me immediately, no matter the hour. Time, after all, is only a variable in our lives, Colonel. Oh, and Colonel, do not share the information you receive regarding Yuscarana with anyone else. I alone will decide when and how such information is to be released."

"Yes, sir."

"Now, do not worry about security, Colonel. The rebels have no way to listen to our military communication channels. In any case, the need for information is urgent. Yuscarana may be the start of the big offensive of the Revolución. I have this feeling in my gut, and when I feel something there it almost always comes to pass. Do you understand your orders?"

"Yes, sir."

"Then get moving."

After the colonel disconnected, the president of Morazon stood with the receiver in his hand, staring out across the shadowy landscape, seeing nothing, thinking hard. Finally, he hung the receiver up and put the telephone back on his desk. Then he picked up a different telephone receiver and called his most trusted aide. Gutierrez directed him to contact the man who served as the personal pilot of the president and have him ready Gutierrez's personal airplane for an imminent departure, destination to be revealed personally by the president of Morazon.

Gutierrez replaced the second receiver and walked slowly back to his chair of security. He sat down and picked up his drink. El Presidente sipped slowly as he waited for a telephone to ring.

Sixty-one

Even in daylight, the interior hallways were dark and gloomy, with the only illumination provided by bars of light that pressed through grimy glass of windows set in rotting wood. By the time they had traversed the width of small, half-forgotten hotel rooms and breached the hallway, only sad, diffused light remained. Spider webs hung in somber corners and dust particles wandered slowly across the hallway, as if they were marathon dancers struggling to keep rhythm after a long night.

Moving like a somnolent ghost, Sharon Samuels drifted down the hallways, pausing to poke her haggard face into doorways and peer into rooms reflecting an aura of eternal emptiness, as if they had never been occupied and over the years had given up any pretensions of entertaining guests. It felt like walking in everlasting twilight.

She had begun at one end of the top floor, worked her way systematically down one side of the hallway, then back up the other. By now, she had been in so many rooms she no longer knew with certainty what floor she was on.

During her wanderings she had developed a sympathy for the rooms. A vacant feeling had settled inside her mind and she felt like the hollowed-out husk of a locust. Her legs seemed to move of their own accord, while her willpower, which had been strong when she began, had faded until it was no more than the fluttering of a candle that had burned too long. Tiredness coated every fiber of her being. Nearing the end of the hallway, she could feel a faint draft and smell fresh air. Until that moment all the windows had been closed and Sharon Samuels wondered at the change.

She poked her head into another room as void of life as the others. Late afternoon sunlight striped the bed and for a moment she was tempted to throw her fatigued body across the faded green coverlet. However, visions of her daughter and son floated before her like disembodied souls, so she pushed herself off the smooth wood of the doorframe. Keep moving, she told herself, just keep moving.

The draft was stronger now and she could smell hay and overripe apples and horses. Suddenly a strange, fetid odor permeated the air. Sharon paused, sniffed, worrying the scent in her nostrils like a wild animal. In the dim hallway she paused, trying to place the scent. As she stepped toward the next room, the odor grew stronger. She had smelled it before, but not often, and not in a long time. Something in the odor made her hesitate; then she willed herself to go on. Three steps later she entered the next room.

It was exactly like all the other rooms she had entered. Exactly the same. Except for the body lying across the bed.

For a heartbeat she thought it was Bartlett, transferred from the dining room by some black magic incantation. For a second, she even thought that by some miracle he might be alive. Then she could see the flies, a thick green-black swarm hovering inches above the reddish trail. Her stomach turned over and then the burning started in her throat. Gagging, she stumbled across the floor and leaned against the wall next to the window.

Too many deaths. Too many deaths. She had seen far too many deaths. Her husband's alone had been too much. All the deaths and crying and shouting and bleeding rose up and smashed against her face, and she screamed until it seemed that the whole world would surely come running.

But no one came. Maybe they couldn't hear her for the gunfire, and shouting of men, and the prayer chanting of women, and the sobbing of boys with a bullet in their gut. Perhaps the violence at Yuscarana had rendered them numb. Maybe they had been numb inside for years and had only been pretending. Maybe they were all dead. Maybe she was dead and didn't know it.

After a time, her screams died and her crying eased to intermittent sobs. Peering through teary eyes, she cautiously glanced at the dead man. It was like looking up through water at something floating on the surface of a calm sea. The man looked familiar. Sharon Samuels blinked away her tears. They felt surprisingly heavy.

It was a man from the tour – the Oriental gentleman; she couldn't recall his name. Even if she heard it she might not recognize it. To be honest, she hadn't paid much attention to him, hadn't given a lot a thought to anyone on the tour, except her own family, of course.

The tears started again and she bowed her head and cried, praying about things that had once been beyond contemplation. When the second iteration of tears finally dried, she stood, wiped her eyes with the back of her hands, then walked out of the room without looking at the dead man. She had enough strength and time only for the living. She could not waste another thought on the dead, not even on her own husband lying in the restaurant below. For now, she must think only of the living. Time enough tomorrow for requiems for all the dead in Yuscarana. Today belonged to those who still breathed.

~ * ~

Captain Morales restricted his smile to a gentle curl of the lips, not wanting to display what would be judged by many his unseemly pleasure.

He had been waiting damn near forever for this moment. Waiting, ultimately, formed a major segment of any soldier's life. It was one of those mundane duties, neither pleasant nor unpleasant, that a soldier learned to accept. Some soldiers became adept at it, while others adopted a take-it-or-leave-it attitude that served them well. Then there were those who never quite developed any taste for it. They simply had to learn to endure.

Captain Morales was one who could endure. Over the years he had gotten adept at it. He had survived for thousands of hours, and he could survive for thousands more. He simply preferred action, however dangerous.

At least a different danger threaded through the action than suffering the waiting. Despite much reflection, Morales had never been able to decide which danger was more deadly. One way your body might die, the other way gradually destroyed your mind. The question was now moot.

Gunfire was coming from the front and the back, heavier than it had been all day, but still not what he had been expecting. Morales leaned a few inches closer to the window, risking a bullet for a quick peek at the street.

One man was running hard from one building to the next and shadows of other men darkened the ground. A bullet sang and adobe flew off the hotel to the right of the window. Captain Morales jerked his head back and shouted for some men to get to the walls and open fire. He looked around to see if they were coming. Everyone was moving except for one soldier. He looked too young and frightened to be in anyone's army. Morales fixed an eye on him and the boy blinked, swallowed, and ducked his head. Then he began to head toward the windows at a reluctant jog. He was crying. Morales was tempted to shout at him, but stopped himself. Why shout at a man who might be jogging to his death?

Morales pulled his pistol and maneuvered it into a firing position. It felt heavy. He must be getting old. None of the men were firing and he yelled for them to shoot at anything that moved. Then he squeezed off a shot, aiming where he projected the shadow throwers to be standing.

Now a few men were beginning to fire, but only sporadically and with looks of great hesitation on their faces. Captain Morales cursed under his breath and began to stride along the wall, moving behind the line of men, whacking one on the butt here, patting one on the shoulder there. Always he was encouraging them, telling them they had the advantage, that they were surrounded by walls and not out in the open, that the rebels had to cross the open road and when they did, they would be shot down like mad dogs.

A few of the men seemed to believe him, faint smiles moved on their faces, but many did not. For the most part they were a sorry lot. Hell, there were even civilians, foreigners at that, among them. *Mon Dios*, how did headquarters expect him to do anything with such a collection?

As he completed his round, he could hear gunfire coming more strongly from the back. He looked around for a sergeant, but could only locate a corporal.

"Hernandez, come here."

The corporal turned from his window and hustled over. With his droopy shoulders and skinny, bowed legs, he wasn't a great physical specimen, but he would obey orders and he had seen action. At the moment, he was the best Morales had.

"Yes, sir."

"Listen, Corporal. Do you hear all that firing coming from the back?"

Hernandez nodded.

The captain inclined his head toward the street. "And not so much from the front?"

"*Sí.*"

"*Bueno*, then I am going to go to the back and check on how the line is holding. Lieutenant Escobar may need reinforcements. You," he thrust a forefinger close to the corporal's face, "you are in charge here. Only hold the line. Do not try anything else. If they attack here with more force, send someone after me. I will not be gone long and you should have little trouble. Your position here is very strong." Morales let his eyes make a slow pass around the room, smiling for the benefit of Corporal Hernandez. "This hotel is virtually impregnable. You can hold it easily."

Morales knew he was lying, but, after so many years in the army, lying came easily. Waiting was not the only thing he had been practicing, and, besides, lying really required only confidence and the ability to think on your feet. Plus, enough actor's blood to carry off the scene. He didn't like to lie, but it had proven to be a necessary ability, and he did it when required.

Sensing the corporal's eyes on his face, Morales tightened his jaw and made his eyes as hard as rocks. The corporal saluted.

"Yes, sir, I understand." He flipped a hand back toward the lobby. "We will hold the line until you return."

"*Bueno*," Morales said. "Now go and make sure the men stay at their posts. They are to shoot at any target in the street, so make sure that they have plenty of ammunition. My gut tells me this is the big push. Rebels never like to stay in any one spot for long, and these have already been here longer than normal. Yes, corporal, this is the critical hour."

Taking a deep breath, Captain Morales closed his eyes. Without warning, images divebombed his mind, a multitude of faces: faces of friends, family members, teachers, priests, officers, and women who had passed through his life. Such images did not flow gently by. Instead, they flew at his face like a barrage of shooting stars.

In no way had he anticipated such a vision and he was stunned. He stood there, holding his breath, unable to move, his heart thudding like a pneumatic hammer in his chest. Then the storm of images passed and he felt a clear, chilling wind blowing through his mind. As the lobby of the old hotel stopped spinning, a great calmness settled over him. Every man in the room seemed to move in slow-motion. Morales felt very young and very old at the same time. A recollection of tales told by the elderly women of his village drifted across his mind, and the captain wondered if someone had just spaded up the first dirt from his future grave. Morales shook himself like a dog emerging from a river.

"All right, Hernandez, get moving. I will be back soon."

The captain turned and walked briskly down the hallway. Gunfire echoed off the dark walls, hammering at the mind of Morales.

~ * ~

He could hear Carlos yelling. But then, that was no surprise; Carlos was always yelling. No, the better word was shrieking – like a big cat with something hung sideways in its guts.

Speaking of guts, his was growling. These days he never seemed to get filled up. Leaning against the side of the building, Jesus eased his head around the corner. All those stores, he thought, my god, there must be food in some of them. Food, and other items he had a use for. He glanced across the street at the hotel, focusing on the windows, certain that soldiers with guns stood inches beyond the shattered glass. However, he could not see any soldiers, not even the glitter of their guns. Jesus took a deep breath, let it out, then flung himself around the corner. He jumped onto the low wooden sidewalk and started running, bent over as far as his protruding gut would allow.

He grabbed the doorknob and jerked. His back was to the hotel and it felt as big as a barn door. His muscles tensed, feeling the bullet smashing through muscle, nerve, and bone. In his mind, Jesus could see the blood spurting hot and red. He twisted the knob and pulled again, harder.

Damn, the door was locked—damn, damn, damn. He jerked one final time, then stepped to the window and smashed the glass with the butt of his rifle. Glass exploded like a rifle shot and his nerves screamed.

Glass skeletons still clung to the sides of the window as swung a leg over the sill, their razor fingers scratched at him. Ignoring them, Jesus pushed on, falling as his trailing foot caught on the window sill. He crashed against the wooden floor, getting an arm out and rolling as Carlos had taught him. He rolled across the floor and smacked against a counter. The room spun. He blinked and the world swirled back into focus.

Blood worms wiggled their way down his arms. He could feel stinging slices on his face and his left ear burned like it had passed through fire. Grumbling and cursing, he got his back firmly against the counter and pushed himself upright.

It was a dry goods store, with several small tables and crude benches covered with piles of clothing, blankets, towels, and sheets. Piles of clothing were arranged on separate tables. On the walls, lanterns, tools, and coils of rope hung from metal hooks. Shelves of canned goods, pots and pans, rows of candles and boxes of matches, along with a few glasses and cups stood between the hooks. At the far end of the room was a shelf of books. A brick at each end of the shelf served as bookends. The books were bound in leather.

At one time, Jesus had been a reader. He had especially enjoyed tales of the old American West. However, since he had joined the Revolución he had not picked up a book. He saw no reason to revert in Yuscarana. Instead, he stepped to a table covered with towels of various sizes and colors. Picking up a small white towel, he swiped and dabbed at the trickles of blood. He had to press the towel firmly against two to get them to stop. Throwing the towel on the floor, he began to evaluate the inventory.

All he could see was of no immediate value and he had started to curse when he spied the old, brass cash register. He marched around behind the counter and tugged on the drawer. It moved only a fraction of an inch, then came to an abrupt stop. Another damn thing locked, he thought. Bastardo owner must be security conscious as hell. Well, fuck him like a dog. Jesus hammered at the register, hurting only his hand.

He cursed aloud, then sucked his sore hand. Finally, he noticed a shelf holding plastic bottles of water. The bottles were clear with blue labels that looked like small lakes. Crossing the floor, he picked up a bottle, unscrewed the cap, and chugged the contents. The water was warm, but it was wet going down his throat. He drank two.

Still wishing he had some wine or whiskey, he leaned against the wall, his eyes scanning the street. Except for the carcass of a yellow dog, it was empty. Jesus could hear the intermittent rattle of gunfire, and, in the connecting silences, the shouts of men. Three or four times he was certain one of the shouting voices was that of Carlos.

Jesus the Pig stood in the store listening to the shouting and the gunfire, trying to decide what to do next. The voice of Carlos worried him. He could hear anger in the voice of the leader of the guerrillas. Twice he heard his own name called.

Jesus wished he had someone to talk things over with, someone to help him decide what to do next. There was always Carlos, of course, but Carlos was already angry, probably at him for not answering or being where Carlos thought he should be. With the attack not going as he had planned, Carlos would certainly not be in a good mood. Avoiding the man seemed a good idea.

Besides, he was tired of Carlos. These days, Carlos was always ordering people around, often for no reason at all that

Jesus could see. Also, he was always telling them about the new men who were going to be joining them any day, promising them reinforcements before every battle. However, few new men ever joined. And, when they did, they were little more than another handicap. Reinforcements seemed to come only after the battle was over, and they ate all the food reserves. No, he was going to give Señor Carlos a long rest.

If only Tony were here with me, he thought. I could talk to Tony. True, Tony was slightly demented, but over the years Jesus had come to the conclusion that every man went loco from time to time. He knew he had, and Jesus figured he was no crazier than the average *campesino*.

Yes, if Tony was with him, they could talk it all out, discuss their options, decide what to do. But Jesus had not seen Tony in quite some time. He tried to recall when he had seen him last. He wondered if Tony could be dead, but then decided such a thing could not be possible, for surely he would have felt it in his heart if it were so. They had lived in camp together for so long and fought so many battles together they were closer than brothers.

Sounds of gunfire grew louder and he could hear the shouts of men more clearly. Jesus could feel a pressure building inside of him. For a few seconds he thought of the yellow woman with the strange face, and a certain part of him wished he had brought her along. She was not pretty, but her body was an effective way to release tension. Nothing he could do about her now. After the fighting, he might swing by the sapodilla tree. He let out a long slow breath as he listened to fighting outside on the street.

A vision was forming in his mind. When the vision solidified, he walked back behind the counter. picked up a burlap sack he had noticed earlier and carried it over to the wall. Next, he grabbed a handful of candles and several boxes of matches, then pulled two lanterns off their hooks. Satisfied, he turned and jogged out of the store, moving swiftly for a fat man. He crossed the porch. jumped down, and ran low and hard across the street, curling away from the hotel, ignoring the sweat running down his face, keeping his eyes on the shadows, approaching his target obliquely.

~ * ~

No, no, not that way, Carlos started to yell at the man, but decided against it. The poor fool was confused enough. Fear painted his face. At least the man was moving and the attack was underway. Gunfire burst from the hotel and the fearful man dove for the shadows of a building.

Carlos sighed. To call this an attack was truly a stretch of the definition. After an hour, he had finally found seven men – none of the truly experienced ones – and done the best he could.

He had sent one man, the one who looked the most frightened, around the buildings in a wide sweep drawn to bring him out well in the rear of the hotel. There he was to hook up with the men Carlos had sent to that spot earlier, and get them going. Actually, their part was strictly to serve as a diversion. They were to fire many rounds, scream, yell, and keep moving so the soldiers inside would be certain that the real attack was coming from the rear. After all, that was the most logical approach, one they would be half-expecting anyway.

A bullet sang by his right ear and Carlos hunkered down behind a watering trough. Judging from the worn smoothness of the wood and the trampled earth, it had been in place for many years. Peasants living in the mountains and jungle that surrounded Yuscarana still counted themselves fortunate to have a horse, even a donkey.

The smell of animal dung was fresh and strong and he put his head against the wood well below the lip of the trough and stretched out until he was almost supine, listening carefully for the sound of the diversionary gunfire, trying to grasp how the attack was going. All he could hear were sporadic bursts of gunfire from the hotel. Purely for kicks, he turned, rested his pistol on the edge of the trough, and squeezed the trigger.

Carlos labored under zero delusions. Deep in his gut he had the bad feeling. The attack on Yuscarana had been fucked from the start.

For the moment he led only this small band of half-trained, poorly educated, nearly frozen-with-fear boys, but someday, when the Revolución was a great success, Carlos could see himself as a great general, important cabinet minister, even president.

Granted, that road was long and dark and winding, and at this moment, half-lying in the dust of Yuscarana with the smell of horse shit wafting around like perfume gone bad, he could not even see around the next curve. Still, he believed he would succeed to greatness. When or where, he could not say. His vision was not yet that clear, but succeed he would, and to no ordinary greatness.

~ * ~

When were they coming? He could smell them – they were that close. Even in the rotting, fungus infected jungles of Vietnam he had been able to smell the Cong. Smell the spices on their breath, the sourness of their sweat, and the stench of their fear.

Something was going on out there, just beyond his field of vision. He couldn't put a finger on it, but that did not change reality. Perhaps it was nothing more than a shadow moving when it shouldn't have, or the glitter of sunlight off metal where no metal was supposed to be, or maybe he had heard a sound so low it had been heard below the level of conscious hearing. No matter, something was coming down, coming down hard, and soon. Joe Moby checked his rifle, raised his eyes, stared across the sunlit ground.

~ * ~

A convoluted cacophony of voices speaking Spanish rose around him, the words flowing far too rapidly for him to follow.

His eyes, however, had no trouble following the running men. They ran to windows, fingering their guns and peering anxiously into the street. Kron turned and stared into the sunlight.

Movement caught his eye and he shifted his line of vision until he could see a shadow of a man moving across the ground. He moved his head trying to catch up with the man throwing the shadow. He squeezed the trigger and the rifle kicked hard against his shoulder. He blinked his eyes, opening them just in time to see his target drop down behind what looked like one of the watering troughs he had seen in old western movies.

Twenty feet to his left, voices rose. Cautiously, he turned his head. The captain was shouting at another soldier, giving him orders. Gunfire from the rear of the hotel was suddenly heavier. The captain and the other man both turned their heads and looked in that direction. Then the captain started to trot toward the rear of the building. The man next to Kron cursed and Kron turned to see what had happened.

~ * ~

At last, he could hear gunfire from the back of the hotel. Carlos smiled. The smile felt strange on his face.

His eyes searched for his men. Only two were visible. He waved his right arm, gesturing them forward. Then he rolled over twice and came out on the south side of the watering trough, stumbling to his feet, waving his pistol and shouting.

Carlos turned his head from side to side, trying to keep one eye on the hotel and, at the same time, see if his men were going with him. At first, he could only see two, then he saw another, and beyond him another. They actually looked like a small army and Carlos felt pride surge through him as he shouted and fired his pistol at a bluffy face on the far side of a hotel window. Not in a long time had he experienced pride like this.

Gunfire blasted from the hotel. In the brief silences, he could hear men shouting. Carlos grinned. Even Morales would be surprised.

He fixed his eyes on a small store to the south of the hotel. Women's dresses hung in the window. He put his head down and sprinted, driving with his legs and pumping his arms. Off to his left someone screamed. He kept sprinting. Ten feet away from the building he dove, tucking his body into a ball, hitting the wooden porch and rolling. He came up gasping for breath, his head against the wall of the shop.

Sucking air, Carlos looked back at the street. Two, no, three men were running in full retreat. Another man lay face down in the middle of the street, his left leg twitching as though electrical current was surging through it. Carlos could not see the man's face.

Heavy, hot anger boiled in his veins. Struggling to his feet, he leaned toward the street, curling his gun arm so the barrel pointed at the last window on the south end of the front of the hotel. His finger began to squeeze. Only when the clip was emptied did Carlos realize he was screaming.

Sixty-two

Tremors ran through her legs as she descended the wooden stairs. For a step, then two, Sharon Samuels wondered if the bones in her legs were going to crack. Already, her mind seemed cracked; in fact, she half expected to feel her brains oozing out with each step.

The handrail was darkly smooth beneath her palm, as though the wood had been polished every day for centuries. Beneath her feet, stairs creaked in protest. Thousands of uncounted steps had worn the wood smooth and she moved carefully, smelling dust and stale smoke, among a myriad of other, indecipherable odors.

Hearing voices, she paused. The voices were too faint and muffled for understanding. She moved on, more quickly. Soon she was on the landing, a space full of shadows, spider webs, and dust. Her body was exhausted; her mind was broken. Shadows moved. Unseen creatures made small sounds in the dark corners. She willed herself to go on.

"Momma."

The voice was so faint that Sharon wondered if it was only a memory-sound echoing inside her mind. Then, she heard it again and turned, frightened of what she might see.

Darkness covered the corner like a thin, ebony silk. Out of the darkness, the face loomed white and ghostlike, a face from an old celluloid moving picture, flickering and fading.

"Baby."

"Oh, Momma."

The girl threw her arms around the woman's shoulders, letting her body sag against the one person she felt loved her, honestly loved her. "God, Mom, I am so tired. This has been the most awful day."

Kristin Samuels lifted her face and kissed her mother on the cheek. "I want to go home. When can we go home?"

"I don't know, baby. Soon, I hope, real soon."

Sharon Samuels felt a wetness on her throat where her daughter's face had lain. She dabbed at it with her fingers. Tenderly, she maneuvered Kristin toward the door to the hallway. It was ajar, and shafts of light slanted though it. Her daughter's face was streaked with tear trails. Sharon pulled a tissue from her blouse pocket and leaned forward to wipe away the dampness. The closer she got to the girl's face the stronger the smell became.

"Kristin?"

"Yeah."

Sharon dabbed gently at the smooth flesh. "Have you been drinking?"

"Oh, Mom."

"Kristin?"

"What?"

"Have you?"

"Have I what, Mother?"

"Been drinking? Have you been drinking again? You know that liquor is off limits. Totally off limits, liquor and pills."

The girl jerked free from her mother's embrace and stared into her face. Kristin's eyes were glassy, with pinhole, black centers.

"Mom, I'm not a baby."

"You are also not a grownup. We've had this discussion before, Kristin. You know you aren't supposed to drink, or do pills. And I know you've been drinking. I can smell it on your breath."

"Only one," the girl thrust her face closer to her mother's, eyes bulging, veins prominent in her slender neck. "Only a little one."

"Right. Then what in the world is wrong with your eyes?" Sharon Samuels pushed the girl's hair off her forehead. "They look rotten."

"Mom..."

"My god, Kristin, how in the hell did you find pills in this godforsaken anus of civilization? And how could you take them with your father, with your father..."

"Mom..."

"Oh, Kristin, how could you?"

The two women stared at each other. Time moved with a heavy certainty. In the sudden quiet, they could hear gunfire. It sounded distant, as though it were coming from a neighbor's television whose volume had been turned down. As they listened, it grew louder.

Suddenly the air on the landing seemed very warm to Sharon Samuels. Her blouse clung damply to her skin and her hair fell damply against her forehead. There were words she wanted to say, but each was hard and hurtful and she did not trust herself to soften them.

She wanted to hug her daughter and, at the same time, slap the shit out of her. She loved her so much, and she knew she should tell her so, but she could not. Not at this moment. Too many times they had been through this same scene. Without, question, she had been through this too many times. Rather, they had been through this too many times. So many broken promises. Biting her lip, she willed an arm around her daughter's shoulders.

Her baby, her precious baby, her crazy, stupid mixed-up baby. Fighting back tears, Sharon started walking toward the shafts of light. For a second, Kristin resisted. Then she stumbled forward and they staggered together across the landing and into the growing luminescence.

Sixty-three

She came wide awake, excited, the way a child wakes from a sound nap. Sitting up, she blinked against sunlight that struck her eyes like an unexpected surprise.

For a moment she could have been anywhere in the world. Her reflection in the cracked mirror atop the sway-backed dresser stared resolutely at her and she remembered the old hotel and Yuscarana. She swung her legs off the bed and stood in the center of the room.

The air seemed suddenly full of quick, popping sounds, like firecrackers exploding in the night. Pop, pop, pop, the sounds grew closer. Only they were not the sounds of firecrackers – they were the sounds of gunfire.

As if a curtain had shifted inside her mind, she could see Joe as clearly as if he were standing across the room. She had not thought of him since before she'd fallen asleep. In the land of dreams, she had been a little girl again, and her husband had vanished.

She felt her body jerk. Amy Moby was surprised at herself, an event that did not often occur. She had been honest with herself for way too damn many years for such surprises. She stomped her right foot, then walked across the room to the dresser. A pitcher of water stood there and she poured water into the wash basin, then splashed some on her face. Eyeing herself in the mirror, she rearranged her lips, turned and walked out of the room without looking back.

Nearing the stairs, she could hear the gunfire more clearly. Then it died off, like a recalcitrant motorcycle shutting down. Gunfire came mainly from the back of the hotel, now and then a volley, but often a single shot. Snipers, she thought, or maybe merely a diversion. She thought of finding the captain and sharing her suspicions, but dismissed the idea almost as soon as it had been born.

No, the first thing to do was to find Joe. It felt like a week since she'd seen him, and the gunfire had set her nerves on edge. The need to see him was sudden, intense.

Two more steps and she could see the lobby. Gunfire erupted from the street in front of the hotel and then men were shouting and running. One soldier started firing his rifle. Instantly, it was too loud to even hear yourself think.

For a few seconds she stood, one leg extended, halfway between one step and the next. Then, she adjusted to the gunfire and moved on down the stairs, hurrying now.

Before she saw it, she smelled the blood – that quick nauseous feeling you get when you receive an unexpected smash on the nose rose, burning her throat. She put a hand on the railing to steady herself, caught her breath, held it, then let it out slowly. Her hair had fallen across her forehead and it felt heavy. She brushed it away as she stepped onto the lobby floor.

She paused, standing absolutely still while men swirled rapidly around her like horses on a turbocharged merry-go-round, screaming, shouting, crying out for ammunition, and help, and God. Guns seemed to be firing from all directions at once.

From the vicinity of the kitchen, she could hear women wailing. A great pressure was building in her brain, growing until she felt she had to scream to let off pressure or her skull would explode and her brains would fly across the room.

However, she would not allow herself to scream. Closing her eyes, she tried to think what Joe would do, or tell her to do. Too many distractions for it to be a clear image, but the momentary pause helped, and when she opened her eyes, her head was not hurting so badly and the lobby seemed less chaotic. Men were men now, and not running animals.

Joe was close by; the essence of his presence was there. Amy Moby was no New Age spiritualist, but there were times when she could sense her husband with unerring accuracy, though he had not spoken or stepped into her field of vision. More than being able to smell his cologne, there was a deep instinctive, animalistic knowing he was close.

Her plan was to cross the lobby, then go down the back hallway. If he was not in the lobby, he must be somewhere along the rear of the building. She knew he was alive, knew it in the knowing place of her soul. She took two steps before she saw the boy.

Technically, he was a soldier. At least he was in the uniform of the army of Morazon. But he was no more than a scared little boy with blood running down his right arm and chest. Amy Moby told herself to walk past him, that she needed to find Joe, that the army surely had medics. She told herself to walk past him, and she did, but only for a few steps. His face haunted her and she turned and retraced her steps. He looked up at her with dark brown eyes, blurry with shock. Smiling, she knelt.

Tears pooled in his eyes and his lips trembled. His head seemed too heavy a burden for his neck; it wobbled precariously as though it were an egg about to fall off the edge of a table. Crimson stained his upper right chest and arm; fingers of blood stretched down his arm. The soldier licked his lips.

"*Madre*," he said.

Instead of answering, she unbuttoned his uniform shirt, easing it away from the wound. The bullet had buried itself deep into the flesh. As gently as she could, Amy Moby pressed one finger against the boy's sweaty flesh. She could not feel the bullet.

His face was gray and his mouth worked without saying anything. His eyes were very dark and they moved slowly, as if the effort taxed him greatly. Pain flared in his eyes like a freshly stoked fire, then dampened down. His breathing was fast, shallow, reminding her of the way a hard-run dog breathes on a hot day.

Strands of black hair had fallen across his forehead, and she pushed them back. Cupping his face with her hands, she turned it so that his eyes were staring into hers.

"I'm only going to get some water and clean towels. I'll be right back. *Comprende*?"

The boy tried to smile. Neither recognition nor confusion flickered in his eyes, only pain. Amy eased his head back until the wall supported it. She let one palm rest against a cheek for a moment. "I'll be back soon," she said. "*Pronto.*" Standing, she stepped quickly toward the kitchen.

She looked back once to find the boy staring at her. Smiling, she lifted a hand. The boy did not respond.

Inside the kitchen, air was redolent with the aroma of garlic and peppers and onions. Meat was sizzling in a black iron skillet. A plump woman stood before the stove dumping sliced carrots into a bubbling kettle. Two younger women, obviously frightened, huddled in the far corner. One of them held a cigarette in a ringless hand. Smoke curled from the cigarette; the aroma mingling with the cooking odors.

The sizzle of the meat was loud. Amy Moby cleared her throat. "*Hola*," she said, raising her voice.

The woman whirled. Fear drained slowly from her face. Amy recognized the woman. She had seen her behind the check-in desk when the tour arrived, standing with the owner of the hotel. Amy had wondered if she was his wife. Amy smiled. After a second, the woman smiled back, but warily.

"One of the soldiers in the lobby has been shot. I need fresh water and clean towels. Please, he is hurting."

The woman only stared. Amy could hear time ticking itself to death inside her head. She wondered if the woman spoke English. Then she wondered if the woman was deaf. The smell of oregano was suddenly powerful.

Finally, the woman turned her head. She spoke rapidly in Spanish out of one side of her mouth, as if to keep the *norteamericano* señora from hearing. One of the girls in the corner, the one without the cigarette, left the kitchen through a door Amy had not seen. In less than a minute, the girl came back carrying two white towels. They looked clean. Without lifting her eyes from the floor, she handed them to Amy.

"*Gracias*," Amy said, but the girl turned away without responding. The woman who had been at the stove handed Amy a small clay bowl half-full of water. For several seconds, the woman gazed into Amy's eyes. Then she nodded and stepped back. Amy was tempted to try and express her emotions. However, her Spanish was rusty, English seemed inappropriate, so she smiled, turned, and walked toward the lobby as quickly as she could without sloshing the water out of the bowl.

The young soldier lay where she had left him, shoulders supported by the plaster wall. His eyes were closed and there was a smooth cast to his expressionless face. Arms and legs sprawled at angles more appropriate for a mannequin.

As she knelt, his eyes opened, glistening dully, like unpolished dark stones, fixed on a point that Amy Moby could not see. They did not refocus when she swung her face directly in front of the young soldier's.

For a heartbeat, she thought he was dead and her throat closed. Then she noticed a barely perceptible rise and fall of his chest. Letting her breath out, she felt her heart hammering against the walls of her chest. She felt silly for caring so deeply for a young man she had never seen until ten minutes ago, at the same time acknowledging the element of maternal caring that crossed all boundaries.

Dipping one corner of a towel in the water, she brushed it across the soldier's lips. Seconds later, his eyes flickered as his head shifted slightly. His lips moved slowly, as if they were arthritic. "*Señora?*"

Amy waited for words that did not come.

"Yes."

"Am I..." he paused, swallowed. The swallow went down hard, as though whatever he was trying to move down had lodged in his throat, too large to pass. "Am I going to die?"

She glanced at the boy's sallow, upturned face. He was about the age her son would have been and she did not want to lie to him. Joe advised always telling the truth. However, she had learned long ago that often there were many truths. The question then became which truth to tell. As truly relevant questions always are, it was a difficult one to answer.

Buying time, she wet the edge of the towel again and wiped at the sweat on his face. She smiled into the boy's imploring eyes.

"No, I do not think that you are going to die."

"But I have been shot, and the pain is intense." The soldier swallowed again. "The blood is still flowing. I can feel it." A faint trembling ran across his lips.

"You have been shot, that is true. However, the wound is not in a vital place. It is in your right upper chest, far away from any organs." She peered closely at the wound. "The bleeding appears to have slowed." She lifted the clean towel and pressed it against the wound. Blood was still flowing in a steady trickle. She hoped her words had not been false. She focused her eyes on the boy's face, slick and shining with sweat.

"Do you have something for the pain, señora? It hurts so bad."

Amy shook her head. "No, I have no medicines. Do you have a *médico* here?"

"No."

"What about medicines? Do your officers have any medicines?"

The boy shook his head slowly, with an undeniable degree of finality. Sweat covered his face and the lights in his eyes were very dim. "I know of no medicines, *señora*. Perhaps Captain Morales might." A spasm of pain worked its way across his face like a monstrous worm. "*Ay*, it is bad. Can you go, *señora*, and check and see if the captain has any medicine for the pain? Can you go now?"

Amy Moby pushed the towel against the wound in an effort to stop the bleeding. Wedging the towel in the triangle formed by chest, shoulder, and arm, she pulled his shirt tight across his chest and laid his arm across the shirt. From the street, more gunfire blared. It sounded very close to the hotel. A man groaned and she tried to shut her ears.

"Here now, hold that tight." She brushed a rogue strand of hair from his forehead. "I never asked your name."

"Tomas," he grunted, the pain working its way into the word.

"Well, Tomas, you must hold this bandage tightly in place while I go and find the captain. Think you can do that?"

"*Sí.*"

"*Bueno*, then I will go."

Fingers clawed at her arms. "*Señora?*"

"What?"

"If you cannot find the captain, try the lieutenant. His name is Escobar, and I think he is at the rear of the hotel. Promise me that you will find one or the other, the captain or the lieutenant. I am shot. I am hurt badly. Without help I will die."

The young soldier closed his eyes. "I do not want to die, *Madre*; I am too young to die."

She did not know what to say. After a few seconds, she bent and brushed her lips against his forehead. Then she rose and went in search of the captain.

~ * ~

All around him were gunfire and the shouts of men. Sounds came in broken echoes, as though they had traveled great distances and made many turns. A fuzzy effect ran throughout the sounds, making them seem other-worldly, unreal.

Trevor allowed his eyes to drift. Chairs were still overturned, dirty dishes still sat on uncleaned tables, flies still buzzed with a languorous monotony. Only the light had changed. It seemed somehow more diffused, as though it had passed through a series of powerful filters which had combed away much of the vitality. The light now possessed the quality of certain sepia-tinted photographs he had seen in the Hartford Museum.

Something about those photos – he couldn't precisely define it – had stayed with him. He wondered if he would always remember the light in the room.

A strangeness was woven through the light and he could sense it working inside his skin, transforming him in some way he could not define. In this bizarre tomb, he was undergoing metamorphosis; he would never be the same.

He knew that, and, in some instinctive way, he understood it. Trevor did not look at his father anymore. No longer did he have the sense that any part of the man or his spirit lingered in the room. Already the body was changing, so that even the face no longer resembled the father he had known.

He sat watching his mind rearrange the sepia photos stored there, standing somehow outside himself, looking down, observing his body the way one would a stranger on the street below from a second story window.

Trevor Bartlett sat in his quiet, sepia toned world, observing the shifting in his mind, saying goodbye in his own way, sensing the changing light, hearing gunfire as a final salute.

~ * ~

Shadows were falling too soon. Carlos pressed his back against the wall as he studied the darkening clouds moving in from the west, driven by a high, hard wind. Another storm coming? Surely God would not send another torrent like the day before. Truly, the rainy season was coming, but not so soon. A sense of urgency had been driving him all day and now he felt it shift into an even higher gear. Whipping his head around, he looked for his men.

He couldn't see any and panic rose in his throat. Then he saw a cap and a face beneath it. One of the new ones; he did not know his name or where he came from. He couldn't recount one moment from the man's life. And yet, he was asking him to die. Somehow that struck Carlos as obscene. He waved at the man, motioning him forward, onward to victory, onward to glory, onward to his death.

The man looked at Carlos as his body began moving reluctantly. Carlos tried to make eye contact with the man, but the man twisted his head to one side. Carlos shouted at the man, ordering him to attack, to come across the street, to fire his goddamn weapon, to fucking do something.

He could see the man's head turn and look down the street. Carlos let his eyes follow the man's line of sight. They settled on the body lying in the middle of the street. It was as motionless as if it were a statue fallen from a passing wagon.

Carlos spat his fear into the dust at his feet. "Come on," he shouted. "Come on, you son-of-a-craven-coward. Come cross the street and fight with me. Cross for the Revolución. Be a man.

"Show me your *cojones*. Show me you are a man. Shoot your rifle. At least shoot your goddamn rifle." Carlos waved his pistol in great sweeping loops. "Shoot your rifle before I shoot you, you dangerous fucking *hombre*."

Carlos lowered his pistol and pointed it at the man. He doubted he could even hit him in the chest at such a range, but this man would not know that. Carlos pointed it at the man's head. It was round like a casaba melon. The man's skin was the color of dried mud, and very smooth. His mouth was quivering like a pair of worms. Carlos cursed.

The man leaned toward the hotel. His legs were trembling. He raised his rifle and stumbled into the street, wobbling from side to side.

Carlos could hear the guns firing from the hotel. Twisting his body, he snapped off a shot at an open window. Carlos did not hope to hit anything. The angle was too great. He was trying only to provide cover. The guns from the hotel kept firing. Carlos turned and looked back at the street.

The man was still shambling forward, trying to sight over the barrel of his rifle as he ran. His finger squeezed the trigger and a shot spun harmless into the air. The man stumbled on. He was halfway across the street. Carlos held his breath.

The man's forehead blew apart. Skin and bone and blood and hair and brains flew into the air, raining down on the man as he lay on his back in the main street of Yuscarana. What was left of his face was turned toward Carlos. His gaping mouth echoed the crater in his forehead.

~ * ~

He could hear Gitano calling him. It felt horrible not to be able to respond. Lieutenant Manuel Escobar pressed his face against the smooth plaster wall as he peered across the open ground. If the angle had been better, he would have been able to see Gitano.

The horse called again and the lieutenant listened to the high, wild notes, letting the echoes rattle around the corridors of his mind. When they dissipated, he peered into the undergrowth. Only palm fronds and leaves of the wild banana plants appeared to move.

Earlier in the afternoon, there had been a spate of gunfire from beyond the rise of ground behind the barn. One or two feeble blasts had come from the other side of the courtyard in the vicinity of a large bush covered in pale yellow flowers.

The firing had tapered off to single shots coming at lengthy intervals. Eventually, even those had ceased. Lieutenant Escobar found the silence more unnerving than the gunfire. At least when the rebels were shooting, he was able to count rifles. He felt exposed, naked, vulnerable.

His eyes made a slow, careful scan of the perimeter. He shifted his gaze to the line of his men positioned along the back wall of the hotel. Not enough of them to properly man the wall, but he had spaced them out as best he could, trying to take advantage of the better defensive positions, setting up intersecting angles of fire.

They were a sad looking crew, leaning dispiritedly along the wall or, in the case of an especially lazy private from the Lake District, sitting on the floor with the back of his head against the plaster with his eyes closed. Lieutenant Escobar did not say anything. When the attack came, they would snap awake.

Only one man seemed to be maintaining a soldiery vigil, and he was the *turista*. His eyes were slit open, his face expressionless as his head moved in minute increments from left to right and back again. Something in the way the way the man held his body, and his rifle, told the lieutenant the man had undergone military training. Perhaps he had been a soldier when a younger man. In any case, the man looked as though he knew what he was doing. He could fire his rifle. Escobar had seen him do that.

This waiting was driving him crazy. He spat on the floor as he pulled a pack of cigarettes out of his shirt pocket. He lit one with a match commandeered from the kitchen and blew smoke out through his nostrils. Staring through the smoke across the open ground, he thought of the English *turista* who had been so loving. Lieutenant Escobar wondered if they would live to make love again.

Footsteps echoed off the walls and he turned to see a man jogging down the hall. Shadows were already taking possession of the hallway and it took a few seconds to recognize the man. Why was Corporal Hernandez headed for the rear of the hotel?

As he watched the man jog towards him, he was suddenly conscious of gunfire behind him. At first, merely a single shot, then another, then two more. Soon there was a small barrage. His own men began to return fire. Escobar swung around to face the guerrillas.

At first, he could see only the open ground covered by patchy sunlight, with the verdant jungle beyond. Then a flash of metal at the crest of the small hump of ground caught his eye. Seconds later, a bullet smashed into the windowsill inches from his head. Flying splinters stung his face. Blinking back tears, Lieutenant Escobar shouted at his men to keep firing. He glanced down at the revolver holstered at his right side. Knowing it was useless at the current range, he tugged it out anyway. Its familiar weight gave him comfort.

"Lieutenant?"

"*Sí*," Escobar said without turning around. He could not afford to take his eyes off the ground before him. Shots rang out with a disconcerting regularity. The corporal was breathing loudly.

"Captain Morales sent me to check on your situation. He was going to come, but an attack changed his mind."

"We are all right here, at least for now. They have been shooting on and off all day, but it seems to be more coordinated now. How are things at the front?"

"We, too, have only light action, but it seems to be picking up. Diego has been shot by a rebel sniper."

"Is the wound serious?"

Corporal Hernandez shrugged. "I am no *médico*."

The lieutenant was still looking out across the open ground. "I understand. I have lost one man, as well."

Escobar heard Gitano neigh again. Excited by all the gunfire, Escobar thought. All this waiting around and hiding behind walls and being shot at by men he could not see was not the lieutenant's ideal way to wage war.

Without turning his head, he gave orders to the corporal. "All right, Hernandez, go report to Captain Morales that Lieutenant Escobar and his men are under attack, but holding their position."

A bullet sang through an open window and smashed into the wall on the far side of the hall. Plaster fell like lime-green snow. "If this attack does not get any worse, I can spare one, maybe two men. However, that may change. My guess is they will attack in strength somewhere soon. Only a moment ago I heard thunder on the mountains. Another storm may strike yet today."

"Surely not after yesterday."

"No man knows what God has ordained. Let us hope he has ordained we will live to fight rebels again another day."

"Amen."

"Go now. The captain may have need of you."

The corporal's footsteps echoed down the hall. The echoes were interspersed with the gunfire and thunder. The trio of sounds stuck discordant notes which rattled around the lieutenant's brain like hot cinders.

~ * ~

He could hear Carlos yelling. No, screaming. Then he heard someone empty their gun. At least he assumed they emptied it; the shooting went on very rapidly for several seconds before stopping abruptly. For a moment, there was no sound in Yuscarana. Then Tony began to hear the soft sobs of the woman, whispering noises like a small animal makes. Then he could hear the song of a bird, clear, clean, three-noted. He glanced around, trying to find the bird that could sing such a song. A small, brown bird with a reddish head sat under the eaves of a building, singing to the world from the shadows. Tony was amazed that such an ordinary looking bird could sing with such splendid beauty.

Then he heard a rifle shot, followed by another more distant. Both sounded to him as though they had come from behind the hotel, near where he had been in the morning. He began to regret leaving.

Somewhere to the south, a dog howled and horses whinnied to each other, one louder than the rest. Horses were noisy animals. All night he had heard them moving restlessly in the corral below him, snorting, sniffing, pawing the earth, calling to each other. A decent night's rest had been out of the question. Tony decided he would shoot the next damn horse he saw.

A shadow fell across him and he looked up. Clouds were sliding across the sky. Turning, he looked back toward the mountains. Above the peaks they were massing, purplish-gray, going black around the edges. Another damn storm. Maybe this one will go around us, he thought, or rain itself out against the mountains.

Carlos shouted something, but gunfire drowned his words. Tony felt the adrenaline rising inside him. He needed to be moving. The woman whimpered again. Something had to be done about her.

Tony shuffled his feet and looked for the bird again, but it had flown away. Down the street, Carlos cursed loudly. Tony felt sweat break out along his hairline. His left leg was trembling slightly and his palms felt damp. He wished Carlos were here to tell him what to do about the woman.

One damp palm closed around the handle of his knife. Pulling it out of its holster, he ran toward the woman. The woman screamed as she struggled to break free from the ropes. The knife slid into the woman as though her skin was a ripe melon.

Blood splattered her body and his chest. He stabbed again, and again. Jerking the knife free, he stared at the blood on the blade before sliding it beneath his belt.

The woman lay in the dust, groaning. When she fell silent, Tony ran toward the main street of Yuscarana. He felt like a boy again, smiling as he ran, pulling his gun out, searching for soldiers to kill.

~ * ~

Lanterns banged against his legs as he ran. The candles kept working their way to the top of his pockets and he stumbled as he stuffed them back down. Reaching the last building on the main street of Yuscarana, Jesus leaned against the adobe. It was still warm from the sunlight, although now the sky was splattered with clouds. Jesus was not worried about the clouds. Neither was he worried about the citizens of Yuscarana. By now, all had fled or were holed up in their houses behind barricaded doors.

Shadows were playing silly games on the fronts of the buildings. He stuck his rifle out into the sunlight, purely to see what would happen. Only sunlight and silence greeted the metal. Jesus ran across the empty street, zigzagging as the instructor had taught, but only a little because he was too fat and carrying too much paraphernalia.

He ran until he was on the porch of the last store on the hotel side of the street. Pressing his back against the wall, he peered through the glass. All he could see was books. He spat the coppery taste of fear out of his mouth. By God, he could tell the world now that Jesus the Pig had liberated a library. Smiling, he turned and started jogging toward the hotel.

As he drew nearer, the gunfire grew heavier. He paused in the shadows, listening to the guns, trying to figure out what was happening.

At first, he couldn't see Carlos or any of his men. Then his eyes flicked down the street. Two men were lying there, unmoving, with shadows for shrouds.

What wasn't in sunlight was in shadows and he couldn't see a damn thing of value to him. Sweat dripped down his face and coated his body. Jesus cursed as he scratched his balls. Thunder rumbled high in the mountains behind him and he glanced at the sky, wondering if it was going to rain again.

Then he heard Carlos shouting at someone to shoot and he twisted his body and saw Carlos standing in a doorway only one building up the street from the hotel, so close to the building and so deep in the shadows that no more than his face showed, and then only when he moved. Carlos looked truly angry. Jesus decided staying away from Carlos would be a good plan.

Following the angle of Carlos' face, he was able to spot two men across the street. They were holed up in a store, only their heads poking up now and then above the windowsill like suspicious squirrels. Shifting his line of sight, he saw a man he knew slightly, standing three or four buildings up from Carlos, but on the same side of the street. The man's name was Hector and he looked like he was sobbing.

A fusillade of bullets poured out of the hotel windows and Jesus pounded down a narrow alley that hooked off to the right. Lanterns banged noisily against his legs. The alley ran straight for a few yards before curling back toward the hotel. Between the buildings it was narrow and dark. Sounds were muffled, as though the alley were a cocoon. Soon it became so quiet it seemed to Jesus he had entered another world. Buildings gave way to trees, then shrubs, then to open ground. Jesus stepped around a pile of rocks and paused to reconnoiter. A small path wandered off to the left. At the end of the path was one side of the hotel.

There was little cover, an overturned wheelbarrow missing the wheel, a pile of broken adobe blocks, a small garden of tomatoes and melons, bordered with red and yellow flowers. He ran as low to the ground as his gut would allow, sweating profusely, keeping an ear open for gunfire.

Twenty yards away from the hotel, he flung himself down on the ground behind a scraggly bush with long thin branches.

Only a few leaves grew near the outermost ends of the branches. Poor cover, but the only cover available.

Jesus lay on his back, refilling his lungs, analyzing the sky. Many clouds had grown darker and a strong high wind was moving them rapidly across the sky toward Yuscarana. Gunfire blasted from the rear of the hotel as he rolled over in order to unhook the lanterns from his belt.

Not all of the matches and candles had completed the journey with Jesus, but enough had survived to allow him get flames flickering. Once he had both lanterns going, he stuck two lighted candles in the softer dirt under the bush. In the rising wind the flames flickered among the lowest branches. Seconds later the bush burst into flame.

By then, Jesus was duck walking toward the window, a lantern in each hand. Gunfire was heavy now from the back of the hotel. Above the rising wind he could hear Carlos shouting orders.

~ * ~

In a pucker of silence, he heard a man shouting from the front of the hotel. The man sounded quite close. Then his own men began to shoot and he could no longer hear the shouts of the man. The voice had been full of frustration, anger, and another emotion the captain could not quite put his finger on.

Had it been the voice of Carlos? Yes, he decided, it had been the voice of Carlos, the voice of a leader. For many months, he had wanted to see Carlos. Morales admitted it was one of his small idiosyncrasies, this desire to see the rebel leaders. They were the enemy, yet the captain felt a certain kinship. After all, they occupied similar positions, faced many of the same challenges, dealt with roughly the same cut of men, put their lives on the same line of blood.

Morales had often thought, if the right moment could ever be found, if the proper space could ever be located, it would be interesting, informative, perhaps even pleasant to converse with men such as Carlos. Somewhere outside the hotel a man screamed in pain and Captain Morales realized this was not such a moment. "Hernandez," he shouted as he started crossing the lobby.

Sixty-four

His hands shook as he tucked the Bible under his arm and stuffed the half-empty bottle into his left pants pocket. Standing in front of the tall mirror, he patted his hair down as he tried a smile on for size.

His stomach was full of nervous acid – it gurgled faintly, like an underground stream. His legs felt as though he had just finished a hard race. He did not want to leave the comfort of his room, but he knew the people were expecting him. A man of God was always needed most in the turbulent times, and today certainly qualified as one of the turbulent times.

For the hundredth time, he wondered why God had allowed him to make this trip, to come to this dirty, hot, stinking, deadly hole.

"Oh God, why have You allowed Your servant Thomas Malloy to be brought to this hellhole of earth? What have I done to deserve this? Where have I fallen short? I have always loved You and worshiped You and tried to obey You in every way."

Closing his eyes, the reverend ran his fingers through his hair. "How long am I doomed to be held captive in this backwards country? How am I to do Your work here when all my flock is far away?"

The turning away of the Lord was too much for the right Reverend Thomas Malloy, especially when enhanced by several strong shots of whiskey. He began to weep, silently at first, tears sliding slowly down his cheeks as his body shook. Another barrage of gunfire erupted and he began to cry harder. He flung himself back on the bed, where he cried for some time. When the tears finally stopped, he poured himself another shot of whiskey and slugged it down. Then he struggled off the bed, washed his face, and began his journey back to the lobby on trembling legs.

~ * ~

"I am dying." The young soldier spoke softly, slowly, each word uttered distinctly, clearly, with finality. His eyes were pointed at Amy Moby, but there was a faraway look in them, as though he were seeing all the way to the other side of the universe. Then he blinked and his eyes refocused. Peering up at the woman, he murmured "I am dying, *Madre.*"

"No, you're not." She wiped a v-shaped line of sweat off his forehead. "I've got you bandaged up, after a fashion, and the bleeding has nearly stopped. You must be still and wait for a *médico.* Please, just be patient. Surely this insanity will be over soon."

The soldier groaned and slowly shook his head. "No, *señora,* no, no," he said, gasping between each word. "You are wrong. Never will there be an end to this." He gnawed at his upper lip. He had teeth like a monkey. "For as long as I can remember there has been fighting. It will go on forever." He coughed. Lines of pain stood out on his face as if they had been etched with ink. "I need a priest, *señor*a." Turning his head, he spat on the floor. His spittle was pink.

"Be still and I'll see what I can do." A volley of gunfire rattled against the hotel and reverberated inside her brain. The palms of her hands were damp. Her brain seemed full of nothing more than a tumbling jumble of inchoate thoughts. There was a wild fluttering beat to her heart.

She glanced around the lobby. Everything seemed to be tilting, spinning slightly. Panic rushed through her body. Her fingers fluttered like wounded butterflies.

Amy made herself stand still. Closing her eyes, she took a deep breath. This was not like her. Cool, calm, and collected was her favorite motto. She often quoted it to younger members of her Sunday school class, especially Melissa Tate. That woman became positively panic-stricken at the least thing. Even a harmless mouse that was more scared of her than she was of it. Thinking of such a familiar person calmed her mind and she opened her eyes.

Their tour guide was coming down the stairs looking around, an expression on his face she could not read. In addition to being a tour guide, he was a man of the cloth. Amy couldn't recall what denomination, but that didn't matter. He should be able to provide some solace to the boy. Say a few words about God's love and caring. He was the closest thing to a priest she had seen in Yuscarana.

Four or five steps above him were poor Mrs. Samuels and her daughter. Mrs. Samuels had an arm around her daughter, supporting her as they came down. Even from across the lobby, Amy could see they had been crying. Crying she did understand. It had been a horrible time for everyone, but to lose a husband, a father... That was more than she wanted to think about. Wiping her palms on her slacks, she started walking across the lobby.

"Reverend," she called.

Reverend Malloy turned and looked at her, and she waved at him. "Come here, Reverend, I need you." Not taking any chances, she started walking toward the bottom of the staircase.

Standing at the bottom of the stairs, he was leaning against the banister, staring at her face. Something like resignation worked its way across his as the gunfire fell off. The subsequent silence seemed loud. He rearranged his mouth into what might pass for a smile. "What can I do for you?"

She inclined her head toward the other side of the lobby, keeping her eyes focused on his face. "There's a young soldier over there. He's been shot. He needs a doctor and wants a priest. Apparently, there is no doctor, and I guess you will have to fill in for the priest."

"But I'm not a priest."

"I know. But that won't matter much. He's lost a fair amount of blood and shock seems to be setting in. The wound itself doesn't look terribly serious, but he's convinced he's dying. He wants a priest."

"I can't give him last rights or absolution."

"You can talk to him about God, can't you? Say a little prayer? That can't hurt."

Reverend Malloy opened his mouth. Then he closed it. Amy Moby could smell the whiskey on his breath. She merely blinked her eyes, and said her own short, silent prayer.

"All right," he said, "let's go."

~ * ~

The Bible lay in his hand like a stone. Squeezing it tighter, he ran his fingers along the pebbly grain of the leather, seeking assurances.

Gunfire had come again, heavier than ever, and they walked well away from the windows. Every other step, one of his legs trembled, and once his left one gave way completely and he stumbled against the woman, righting himself with effort, apologizing.

He turned his head toward the woman. "Suppose this little tour turned out to be even more exciting than you had counted on, Mrs. Moby?"

The woman tilted her head, glancing up at him out of the corners of her eyes. "Yes, I do believe it has."

Out on the street a man howled, a long, rising wail that made the hair stand up on the back of the reverend's neck.

From across the room the soldier had been a blur. Now, he was flesh and blood, way too much blood. The reverend felt his stomach go all queasy and he wished desperately for a drink. He tried to formulate the words he was going to say to the wounded man, but all he could think about was whiskey.

He stood looking down on the man. The soldier's sweaty face was upturned and Reverend Malloy could feel the force of the man's eyes moving across his face like brown searchlights. Strange to tower over the soldier, staring down at him, knowing the man was helpless. Reverend Malloy wondered if the way he felt was similar to the way God felt. The thought made him feel wicked, as though he had blasphemed. As he knelt, he smiled at the man in an effort to mask his thoughts.

"How are you, son?"

The man's tongue flicked out and moistened his lips. "Not so good, *Padre*. I have been shot and I am afraid that I might die."

"Surely there is a doctor in Yuscarana, and as soon as the fighting is over, we will get him to look at you." Reverend Malloy looked across the soldier at Amy Moby, who had also knelt and was checking the bandage. "Isn't that right, *Señora* Moby?"

She was holding the ends of the bandage. "Yes, of course," she said, staring into the reverend's eyes. "The rebels will withdraw soon. Their attacks are going nowhere. By now they must be low on men and ammunition."

She could hear the captain shouting at someone to hurry up and she talked quickly, raising her voice in an effort to cover the captain's orders. "We will get the doctor here." She pressed the bandage tighter against the wound, watching the soldier's face wince, but pushing down anyway. "He will give you something for the pain, then get the bullet out. After that, you will be all right."

Pain, infused with fatigue and fear, worked its way across the soldier's face. "I hope he comes soon. The pain is very great." He closed his eyes. When he opened them again, they settled on the face of Reverend Malloy. "Do you think he will come soon, *Padre*?"

Reverend Malloy still peered into the eyes of Mrs. Moby. Finally, he looked away. "Yes, undoubtedly this will all be over soon and then he can come. God will surely deliver us." The words sounded good. If only he believed them. Where had all his faith gone?

The young soldier coughed. Blood splotched the ends of the bandage. "Father?"

Reverend Malloy swallowed the lump that had been forming in his throat. He wanted a drink. He felt unworthy, unworthy of God, unworthy even of the boy. "Yes."

"Will you pray? Will you pray for me, Father? Father, what is the matter? Will you not pray? What is wrong with you?"

The reverend could not speak. Instead, he patted the boy on his uninjured shoulder. Then he stuck his hand into his pocket. He did not look at Mrs. Moby. He kept his eyes on the soldier. The man's face looked feverish. The reverend wondered if the man was going to die. Glass felt smooth and cool against his right hand. He still held his Bible in his left hand. He tugged the bottle out and sat the Bible on the floor. Then he unscrewed the cap and bent his head away from the boy, putting his body between the blood and the whiskey. He raised the bottle. He did not look at Mrs. Moby or the soldier. Capping the bottle, he stuffed it back into his pocket. Then he picked the Bible up. Gunfire was furious now.

He turned his face back to the young soldier's and gazed at him for a moment. Then he shut his eyes. He did not look at Mrs. Moby.

"The Lord is my shepherd," the reverend prayed. He went on praying for a long time, repeating words he had said a thousand times before, half-listening to the gunfire and the shouting, wondering, not for the first time, if any of them would survive.

After some time, the words began to ring hollowly inside his head, as though someone else was speaking and he was only listening. He was not even sure if he was speaking. He concentrated on his lips, actually feeling them move. Meanings of words hung beyond his comprehension – they were suddenly no more than stray syllables. He slitted his eyes open. Shadows striped the floor before him. Sharon Samuels was staring at him.

Oh, Lord, he said to himself, of all the people in the world I do not need to see right now. What am I going to say? All the comforting phrases he had learned as a young man studying the word of God from aged men of sanctified wisdom seemed old and worn out, no longer full of comfort or even mystery, banal.

His fingers worked like long white ants on the black leather of his Bible. All he wanted was to be left alone with the bottle in his pocket. Why did he continue these senseless charades? Gradually, he became aware of an enveloping silence. Perhaps I am going crazy, he told himself. Yes, I am going crazy. Maybe insanity will be better. Anything will be better. Closing his eyes as tightly as he could, he tried to imagine he was alone in the desert. The sounds of gunfire kept interfering.

A hand pressed against his shoulder. The reverend lifted his head. He rearranged his lips into what he hoped looked like a smile.

"Yes?"

"Have you seen my son?"

"Your son?" The words sounded hollow, but he could not think of anything else to say.

"My son, Trevor. I've been looking for him and can't find him. Have either of you seen him?"

Amy Moby looked up and shook her head. "Not for a long time."

Reverend Malloy placed the Bible on the floor, leaned his weight on it and pushed himself awkwardly to his feet. Away from the wounded soldier the air felt better.

"I haven't seen him in a long time, either. Where have you looked?" He stared at Mrs. Samuels' face as he spoke, careful to keep his eyes off the soldier and Mrs. Moby.

"We have checked every room on all the upper floors. I thought he might be in the lobby." The girl beside her sniffed and the woman put an arm around her and pulled her close. "Where could my son be?"

Reverend Malloy cocked his head and listened to the sound of gunfire. Out in the lobby, a man began screaming. If he did not move soon, he would start screaming, the reverend thought. I am going insane, he told himself. If I don't get out of this lobby, away from all this shooting and shouting and bleeding and dying, I will be certifiably crazy.

He leaned closer to Mrs. Samuels. "I'll go check and see if your son is in the kitchen. He may have gone there to get something to eat. I'll go check now." He was rambling, but he did not care. He started walking. Someone, perhaps Mrs. Moby, said something, but he kept on walking.

Lobby walls seemed to bend and arch before him. The floor swayed. His head felt hot and his mouth was dry. Inside his mind there was a roaring, like a whooshing fire.

Sixty-five

Hernandez's face was contorted, streaked with sweat. Morales walked toward him, keeping his ears tuned to the gunfire from the front. He couldn't tell if the corporal had been shot or was simply out of breath. Behind him, women were screaming. Shouts of men were bad enough, but cries of women, especially *turistas* were too much. Moving down the dark hallway, he could hear more gunfire from the rear of the hotel. This had to be the rebels' big push. Captain Morales wondered if he was going to finally get to meet the infamous Carlos.

Corporal Hernandez slogged down the hall, stumbling to a stop in front of Morales. Gasping for air, he saluted.

"Yes, Corporal?"

Hernandez panted like a hard-run race horse. "The lieutenant said to tell you he is under attack, but holding his position."

"Could you tell how heavy the attack was?"

"There was some shooting, all right."

The captain felt like shooting this panting fool himself. "How much shooting?"

"Plenty."

Captain Morales sighed deeply. And this man was a corporal. There were days when he despaired of the army of Morazon. "Was anybody hurt?"

Between pants, Corporal Hernandez nodded. "Yes, Captain, one man for certain."

"How badly was he hurt?"

"He is dead."

Morales closed his eyes and silently said every curse word he could think of. He said them silently for two reasons. First, he did not want to completely humiliate Corporal Hernandez, although at the moment choking him was tempting. However, he needed every man. The second reason for not voicing his comments was that he didn't want to waste his breath. Hernandez was Hernandez.

The captain jerked his head toward the lobby. "Get back to your post."

Standing in the darkened hallway, he watched the corporal trot slowly toward the lobby as he considered his options. Gunfire sounded equally heavy from the front and the back.

He permitted himself a few seconds to wonder about the reinforcements he had been promised for months. Then he shook his head in disgust at his wishful thinking. Daydreaming, that was all it amounted to. Morales whirled and walked back toward the lobby. Apparently, the rear line was in no more danger than the front, and Escobar was there. Better to divide the officers.

As he stepped into the lobby, he could see one of the *turistas* hurrying toward him. The man had a glazed look on his face. Morales couldn't remember for certain, but he thought the man was the tour leader. Then Morales noticed the Bible in the man's left hand and wondered if he was a man of God.

At the last minute, the man veered to the right and walked away, moving with a strange, stiff-legged gait. Whiskey clung to the breath of the man with the Bible in his left hand. Morales watched the man navigate unsteadily toward the arched entrance to the dining room.

A stray thought began gnawing at the back of Captain Morales' mind, chewing away like a skinny-tailed mouse. He leaned against the wall, trying to propel the nagging thought to the top of his brain.

The noise of the bullets peppering the adobe walls made him wonder if twenty years from now the *turistas* would come by and marvel at all the bullet holes the way they admired cannonballs still lodged in the walls of castles in Europe. Morales could picture the tour guide now, a great fat man with a Zapata mustache and slick-backed, oily black hair, standing in the middle of the main street, sweating like a pig in the sunlight, pointing at the pockmarked building. The captain felt his lips beginning to curl up at the ends.

The smile quickly faded. The dining room – he could not remember if he had assigned a man to the dining room. It occupied an out-of-the-way corner of the hotel. He had given so many orders it was impossible to recall each one. Yes, he decided, he could have forgotten. He started jogging toward the dining room.

The *turista* had already disappeared into the room and a feeling that he was missing something important washed through Morales. His right hand slid down his side and his fingers wrapped around the butt of his pistol. Gunfire from the street sounded more real somehow, as if all the shooting before had been so many firecrackers. Sweat beaded his upper lip and he jerked his pistol from its holster, praying at the same time for something he wasn't sure of.

~ * ~

No one was shooting at him, and he could not understand why. He was less than twenty yards from the hotel walls and even

Jesus acknowledged he was a large target. Plus, he was slowed by the lanterns. It had been a hassle to light them and he did not want to have to fool with lighting them again. Certainly not this close to the hotel. Lathered in sweat like an old horse who had been pulling a plow all day across a sun-soaked field, he moved steadily forward, looking like nothing so much as a gigantic, hirsute land crab.

Ten yards from the hotel, he stopped, crouching as low as the lanterns and his considerable belly would let him. The incongruous thought that he finally looked exactly like the baseball catcher he had always wanted to be flashed across his mind. He began to swing the lanterns, starting slowly, building momentum, keeping his eyes on the window directly above him. The glass was still intact, which he had not counted on. Why had Carlos not attacked this section of the hotel?

Every second he expected to hear the wham of a gun, the whiz of a bullet. Perhaps one would be the final sound he ever heard. Then he remembered you never heard the bullet that had your name on it and he felt better.

Jesus slung the lantern in his right hand toward the window. It tumbled slowly as it arched, reminding Jesus of a spacecraft he had once seen on television drifting through deep space, going end-over-end in a never-ending series of metallic cartwheels. It crashed satisfyingly through the glass and he slung the other lantern. For good measure, he fired a burst over his shoulder as he ran away from the hotel. Twenty seconds later he looked back. One side of the red velvet curtains was already blazing. Cackling, he headed for the jungle. Jesus felt quite pleased with himself – he had done his evil deed for the day.

~ * ~

The need was overpowering. All he could think of was getting out of the lobby, away from the begging, pleading, demanding people. He could not stand anymore. A man's face swam into view before him. It took a second for it to register;

423

then he realized it was the army captain. A doorway was on his right. He could not recall what room lay beyond. He stepped through the doorway.

Lighting in the room was poor, almost nonexistent, and he stood for a moment blinking, letting his eyes adjust. Gradually, he was able to see tables still littered with dirty plates and the overturned chairs, and he knew he was in the dining room. Back where all the insanity had started.

Reverend Malloy felt the adrenaline drain from his body. He sat down heavily on the nearest chair. An egg stared up at him with its one aged yellow eye. He tried to recall when he had last eaten. Certainly, he was not hungry. Thirsty, however, was another matter. Pulling the bottle out of the shelter of his pants pocket, he twisted the cap off.

For a moment, he made himself gaze at the amber liquid sloshing gently inside the bottle. He held his desire in check, keeping it under control, serene in the knowledge he could satisfy the urge at any time. It seemed forever since he'd had a drink, although he knew perfectly well he had sneaked a nip only moments before.

Playing mind games with himself. Crazy to play those games. They were dangerous, and led down roads of no return. Still, he played them. Even prayer did not help.

Oh well, as he had told a thousand parishioners over the years, God doesn't answer all prayers immediately, and when He does, He sometimes answers no. Rasing the bottle, Reverend Malloy asked God for forgiveness.

As the whiskey slid slowly across his tongue, he casually glanced around the room. He wasn't looking for anything, merely surveying his surroundings. In a second, he would close his eyes and savor the moment.

In that final millisecond before his eyelids came together, he saw the body. It was all the way across the room, sprawled on the floor, half-hidden by table legs. He couldn't say why he had happened to glance at that particular segment of the room, unless at some subconscious level he had heard the somnolent droning of the green and gold flies.

The reverend spluttered, coughed, and spat precious whiskey in a dozen directions. Finally, he got his throat under control and set the bottle down on the table. His hands were trembling. Wiping his eyes with the back of his hands, he asked God why.

In the midst of his meditation, an awareness began to seep into his consciousness. At first it was no more than a tickle at the bottom of the brain pan. Reverend Malloy forced himself to sit still and listen. He could hear nothing beyond the frightening burps of guns and the vulgar shouts of men. Still, somehow, he sensed he was not alone.

God had been so recently on his mind that for a few heartbeats he was almost certain the Holy Spirit was in the room with him. The reverend could feel a presence – no doubt of that. He began to look around the room, searching for a manifestation, endeavoring to keep his hopes from rising too rapidly.

Could this be the moment, the moment he had been praying and waiting for his entire life? His eyes flickered from table to table. His heart was beating rapidly and he could feel the sweat sliding down his face and pooling on his chest. A nerve jumped below his left eye and both legs trembled. Would he be worthy? He remembered the whiskey and, in that instant, regretted every drop that had passed his lips.

Yuscarana? Well, he told himself, remember Bethlehem. Fingers gripped the table, pressing against the wood. He half rose from his chair, ready to receive the Glory.

Movement. Against the inner wall a shadow moved, or something deeply imbedded in the shadow, and he turned his head slowly, not knowing what to expect. In his imagination, he had always envisioned a great celestial glowing, holding back the eternal dark, lighting the way for all of mankind.

Reverend Malloy rose very slowly. His body seemed to weigh no more than a parrot's feather. His arms reached heavenward. His lips stretched in smile until he began to wonder if his face was going to rip apart.

The room was only shades of darkness. Then he saw another flicker of movement. Reverend Malloy nervously eased the angle of his head to the right and squinted.

He looked for the Lord. He saw a boy.

"And a child shall lead them." The verse vibrated through his mind. Was he, Reverend Thomas Malloy, old Doubting Thomas, going to be allowed to see the Christ Child? A prodigious trembling wracked his body. His lips parted. His eyes felt like they were on fire. He stepped toward the Being.

Doubt ran in torrents through his mind. The boy did not look like anything like even his most outlandish concept of the boy Jesus. In fact, there was something familiar about the boy. He took another step. Why, it was the boy from the tour, the Samuels kid. The one whose father had been killed. Reverend Thomas Malloy sensed a great lessening within, as though an unbelievably potent life force had departed. Anger replaced the force. He had been duped by that stupid boy. What was he doing here, sitting all alone in a darkening room with the body of his dead father? The reverend began to walk more quickly toward the boy, uncertain in his mind whether to comfort or choke him.

Blinded by the disillusion of his vision, he banged his leg against a chair. "Curse the Pharisees, that hurts. Boy, what are you doing here? You almost frightened me to death, you know."

The boy pointed his chin at the man, staring at him with dark eyes that reflected light.

The reverend rubbed his shin. "You ought not to do that to an old man." He was going to say something about politeness, but then he remembered the boy's father and swallowed the fine advice as he endeavored to make his face more pleasant. Hobbling, he crossed the room and sat on a chair at the boy's feet.

He felt horribly foolish, deflated. Yet, at the same time, somehow relieved. It would have been a great, grand, glorious moment, but an incredible responsibility. Reverend Malloy was not sure, in the depths of his soul, that he wanted to bear that particular burden.

He bowed before the boy. "Why are you here, son?" He asked the question in as gentle a voice as he could muster. "Don't you know that your father is no longer with us? Only his body is here in Yuscarana. I feel certain his spirit is already in Heaven."

Reverend Malloy peered into the boy's eyes, trying to get a sense of what was working behind them. He felt a smile spread across his face. It felt genuine. "Isn't it a glorious, comforting feeling to know that a better place than this tired old earth awaits us, and our loved ones, when our race is run?"

The boy stared at him as if the reverend had just arrived from Uranus. His gaze was strangely powerful, disconcerting even. A nasty doubt began to blossom in the reverend's mind.

"You do believe in God and Heaven, don't you, son?"

The boy tilted his chin. His eyes were locked on the reverend's. "I don't believe in anything."

"Surely you believe in God."

"Nothing."

"But..."

"I believe in nothing."

Reverend Malloy rose from his chair and put a hand on the boy's shoulder. His intent was to provide comfort. The boy shrugged the hand away.

"Son, let me help you. I am a man of God."

"There is no God."

"Don't say that. Of course there is a God."

"Then why did my father have to die?"

Reverend Malloy pursed his lips. "God's ways are sometimes difficult to understand."

"There is no God." The boy's eyes had turned opaque and his voice was hard and flat, imbued with a brittle quality.

"Don't ever think that."

"Go to hell."

Reverend Malloy knelt beside the boy. At that moment, he very much wanted a drink. Instead, he closed his eyes and thought of a short prayer. It was one that he had often said before. "Listen, son..."

"I am not your son, you old drunk. Yes, I can smell the alcohol on your breath. I've smelled it on there ever damn day of this damn tour. That's my father lying there on the floor, dead. Why did he have to die, huh? Tell me that. Where was your so-called God yesterday morning? Well? Well?"

The reverend licked his lips. His eyes felt hot. "I know you are hurting. Pain in such moments is only natural. But if you will simply go to God in prayer..."

The boy put his hands on the reverend's chest and shoved. "There is no God," he shouted, his spittle dampening the reverend's face like a Methodist baptism.

"There is no God. Not for me. Forever."

Bullets rattled as hard as summer hail against the walls. Involuntarily, the reverend jerked, imagining for a second he had been shot. Then he twisted his body and looked toward the windows. At the right edge of his vision, he saw the face of a man. Guerrilla was the word that flashed across his mind screen, and he stifled a scream because of the boy. He made himself turn his head with deliberate slowness. Reverend Malloy found himself staring into the face of Captain Morales.

~ * ~

"What are you two doing here?"

Morales could hear the roughness in his voice, a roughness that actually reflected anger at himself. He should have had a man posted here. He couldn't blame Escobar for this. The officer in charge always had the responsibility. He should have covered this room. Making his face hard, Captain Morales started walking across the room.

He was looking at the boy's face, trying to see his eyes, trying to read him. The man he knew. Lots of talk, with plenty of drink on the side; he wasn't an issue. The boy, though... that must be his father lying on the floor.

Morales had always had a soft spot for young men. Once, a long time ago, he had been one. It was an effort, but he remade his mouth into a smile. He could not imagine what to say to the boy.

The *turista* was saying something. Morales did not want to talk to the man and didn't listen. His interest was in getting the boy out of the room, back with his mother, perhaps, and getting a soldier into the room. So far, the attack had not been as vicious as he had expected. Carlos must be short of men. He could spare one man from the lobby.

The gunfire did not seem as heavy now. Thunder rumbled between the mountain peaks. Perhaps they had weathered this wave. Another storm might drive the guerrillas away. The air in the room seemed heavy, close, full of foul odors: decaying food, drying blood, death.

The *turista* who drank was still talking about God and deliverance, deliverance from Yuscarana. It sounded like a prayer. Captain Morales wished the *turista* would pray silently.

Suddenly there was an explosion of glass, followed by a great whooshing sound. Morales whirled and faced the window. Flames flickered at the heavy red velvet draperies. They were firing the hotel. Goddamn Carlos was firing the hotel. Shouting, he ran toward the flames, dodging tables and overturned chairs.

One side of the draperies was already ablaze. Wind rushed in through the broken glass, fanning the flames. Behind him, Morales could hear screams. Then, above the screams he heard a monstrous clap of thunder. Beyond the flames the sky looked dark.

Ten feet away he could feel the heat. Damn drapes must have been as dry as the desert. He could see the problem now;

fire flickered from two old fashioned lanterns that were still in heavy use in this territory. One set of draperies was in full flame. He slowed, moving sideways, trying to find a way around the flames.

His face was awash with sweat. He tried to reach a section of material not yet on fire, but the flames drove him back. He willed himself to reach again and fire seared his flesh. Morales whirled, looking for something to cover his arm. Waiting for help was no good. Every second was critical. A wall of flames seemed to rise behind him. Morales ripped a tablecloth from the nearest table. Glasses, plates, and silverware clattered against the floor.

Wrapping the tablecloth around his left hand and arm, he stepped into the intense heat. Hell must feel like this, he thought. Thrusting his wrapped arm, around the drapes, he jerked with everything he had. Flames showered around him and licked at his face.

Roaring with pain, Morales flung the burning drapes on the floor, ripped the tablecloth off and threw it on top of the flames. It was already on fire. He stomped on the burning drapes like a man gone mad.

The fire did not want to go out. His boots were so hot it seemed the leather must melt. A jug of stale water sat on a nearby table and he grabbed it and dumped the liquid on the flames. Slowly, he brought the fire under control.

A man was screaming. He kept on screaming. Morales risked a quick glance across the room. The *turista* was screaming and pointing over Morales' right shoulder.

He turned and looked. His heart sank to the bottom of his stomach. He felt as if his guts were being ripped out.

The other panel of drapes was blazing. Fingers of fire had found their way to at least two tables. Napkins and tablecloths were burning. As he watched, the burning drapes fell with a slash of fire and a great whoosh to the floor. It seemed to

Morales as if it were the sound of all the air being sucked out of the world.

Morales thought he was going to puke. Then he wanted to cry. Crescents of fire were consuming the room, ravaging it in fervid gulps. Already, flames from the drapes had torched two more tablecloths.

Captain Morales turned and looked at the man and the boy. Rigid as wax figures, their eyes were fixed on the fire. He made pin-wheeling motions with his arms. "Run," he shouted, "run!" Cursing, he started pounding for the lobby. At the edge of his peripheral vision, he saw two moving figures, the larger tugging the smaller along behind him.

Sixty-six

His fingers trembled as he reloaded. Carlos wasn't sure if he was exhausted, or experiencing a case of nerves. He flicked a glance at the street. Bodies lay sprawled like dark bundles of dirty clothes. He would take fewer soldiers of the Revolución back to the jungle.

Thunder rippled in the mountains ringing Yuscarana like the farts of a fat man. Carlos shifted his eyes to the sky above the mountains. Blue in the morning, it had changed to indigo, then to a gray streaked with purple. Now it looked black. Lightning stabbed inky clouds and highlighted the naked mountain peaks.

Carlos spat with disgust. Granted, it was the season for storms, but two days in a row? Clouds were building now, piling on each other like massive stones. Living outdoors for many years had trained his weather eye. This storm was taking shape. If it continued to develop, it might prove worse than yesterday's, and that had been as bad a one as Carlos could recall.

Thin, cobalt-blue streaks of despair raced around the contours of his mind. There were moments when even he despaired of the *Revolución*. Too few men, too few guns, too few supplies, and never enough money with which to buy them. Disease and desertion and death. All that he had learned to live with, but now even the good Lord seemed to be against him. Two terrible storms in two days – no way could that be interpreted as a good omen.

The storm was moving in from the southwest and only a narrow crescent of sunlight rimmed the far northeastern horizon. It was as though a giant curtain were being pulled across the sky, bringing the day to a close.

Carlos finished reloading and took a careful look around. It was only the middle of the afternoon, but already the daylight was dying. Wind blew dust and yellowing newspapers among the dead on the main street of Yuscarana. Decisions must be made.

He peeked around the corner of the doorway. From the start, it had been obvious a frontal assault of the hotel would be dangerous, perhaps disastrous. Attacking armed men holed up inside a solid fortification was never pleasant. Even with the diversion in the rear, the attack had been a failure. Another attempt would undoubtedly yield the same results, unless they could somehow catch the men inside off guard.

With a leader like Morales, Carlos did not see that happening. For many months, he had studied Morales. While the captain might not be the boldest of battlefield tacticians, he was an experienced soldier who did not make stupid mistakes.

No, another frontal assault would be useless and Carlos did not think he could starve out the soldiers of Gutierrez, not when they were inside a hotel with a well-stocked kitchen. Besides, Morales might well have gotten through a call for reinforcements. Carlos still was not certain how the attack on the communications shack had gone. Either the men who made it were dead, or they had deserted. Since Felix had not returned, he was inclined to favor dead. The boy had proven little more than an adequate soldier, but he had been loyal. Carlos ran the fingers of one hand through his hair, closed his eyes, and tried to think.

Logic dictated that he should simply pull back under cover of darkness or the storm, whichever got to Yuscarana first. Yet, there was an innate stubbornness to him that would not allow him to retreat, not just yet. Pulling his head back behind the wall, he closed his eyes and listened to the thunder that was now rolling almost continuously, trying to make up his mind. God, but he was tired; what he wouldn't give for a good night's sleep.

Another sound reached his ears, a crackling sound which sounded familiar, yet unnatural. His mind worried with it for several seconds. Then he heard men and women shouting and screaming. He opened his eyes.

Thunder had become almost continuous, and lightning flashed like a fireworks show at Fiesta. He could smell the electrical discharge and the rain that was coming. Already, it had moved down from the mountain peaks and crossed the flanks of the mountains. Even now it must be pounding across the great, green, living jungle.

In a small dark cavern of his mind he usually kept sealed, even from himself, Carlos knew that at least a part of him was no longer comfortable anywhere except the jungle. He had lived there for so long it had become a part of him, and he of it. Merely by closing his eyes he could hear the hum of insects too tiny to be seen, the drip of water from the broad leaves, and the slithering, rustling sounds small animals made as they moved. He could hear the whistles and cooing and twitters of birds, and the howl of monkeys.

As the rumble of the thunder faded, a crackling sound reached his ears. Seconds before, he had heard it, and this time he placed it. Without question, something was burning. No, make that something big was burning – the smell of smoke was growing by the second. Carlos sniffed the air like a dog. Perhaps the lightning had started a fire. He looked around to make sure the old building in whose doorway he crouched was not on fire. He was very curious about what was burning in Yuscarana. Curious enough to poke a nose around the corner of the doorway.

Every second the smell of smoke grew stronger and now he could clearly hear the shouts of excited men from the side of the street where what was left of his band waited. Carlos glanced across the street. The rapidly falling darkness looked like a broad, dark river, and he felt extraordinarily vulnerable. Two of his men still lay dead in the middle of the road and he did not think any of the soldiers of the Revolución were on his side of the street. Carlos felt like a man deserted on an island. Although he was not a particularly religious man, Carlos said a short prayer. He needed a miracle; the Revolución needed a miracle. Today was the day for a miracle.

~ * ~

Smoke. What in hell could be burning in the middle of the afternoon in Yuscarana?

Tony poked his nose out around the foundation of an empty building so dilapidated it did not look as if it would last the night, let alone survive the coming storm. His fingers were spiders along the trigger of his rifle. He smelled the rain falling on the mountains; then he caught a scent of smoke.

Wind whistled around the corner of the old building, reverberating in his ears. Even with the wind, he had begun to hear shouting and screaming from the direction of the hotel. He stuck his face out into what was left of the daylight.

At first, he saw only the main entrance of the hotel. Doors were still closed and the walls still solid. Glass was piled up in glittery mounds below the windows. Easing further into the street, he looked left. Nothing. He looked right and saw smoke.

It took a few seconds for him to comprehend. Tony had never imagined the hotel itself might be on fire. But one wing was in full blaze. Yellow flames leaped through the window, pointing hot fingers at the gathering darkness.

Dozens of voices shouted and screamed at once, rising and blending with the burning sounds until the hotel seemed a solid wall of sound. Inside the structure, someone began shooting. It sounded like a machine gun, and it sounded as if their finger had gotten stuck on the trigger.

Tony scrambled to his feet. No way the soldiers inside the hotel were going to be able to put out the fire. Their only water would be bucketfuls hauled from the kitchen. Any hoses would be coiled outside, and the minute anyone stepped outside the door they would be shot. Tony started running toward the hotel. The people inside could not put out the fire, and yet they could not stay inside. Smoke and heat would soon be too much. Already, the fire had climbed to the second floor and was working its way down the hallways. If it was not stopped, it might burn all of Yuscarana.

As he ran, Tony could feel the wind rising, whirling dust and debris against his face, howling like a lost child. Particles of dust smashed against his cheek, stinging like tiny pellets of ice. They blew into his eyes, making them water, rendering him half-blind.

At any second the people inside the hotel might be forced out into the open by the fire. They would be running out coughing, choking, temporarily blind. It would be like shooting ducks floating down a slow flowing river. Tony ran as hard as he could. Such a glorious moment he surely did not want to miss.

~ * ~

"Listen at all that shouting. What in the world is going on?"

Maria shifted her head from the pillow, trying to catch the words, but all she could hear was the shouting of men. Then she heard a woman scream.

She allowed her eyes to drift over the naked body of the English *turista*. They traveled over the small breasts with the extraordinarily large nipples, down the side with the ribs prominent beneath the skin, and across the flat stomach to the thick triangle of hair below. Maria felt funny looking at a naked woman. She had been taught it was wrong to do so, and those teachings lingered in her mind, scolding her like a frantic mother. Perhaps what she had done was wrong, although how anything that felt so good could be wrong was something she could not understand.

For the first time since she had left her village, she felt warm and safe and at peace. She ran a finger down the jaw line of the English *señora* and made circles on the point of her chin. Then she pushed it up to the surprisingly full lips and traced them. In the middle of the second lap, the older woman softened her lips, spread them, and sucked the finger into her mouth. Maria remembered then where that finger had been and she wondered what the English *turista* would do. All she did was to suck it harder, the way a hungry baby sucks a nipple.

"Perhaps the rebels have gotten inside."

"I don't think so," the woman mumbled. "There would have been more shooting." Pulling her mouth away from the finger, she urged Maria's face closer to her own.

Maria could see the reflection of her face in the mirror of the woman's eyes. She could smell her breath, a strangely comforting mixture of coffee, cigarette smoke, whiskey. Running through them, connecting the elements, was the faint scent of her own womanhood. Above the woman's steady breathing she could still hear the shouts and gunfire. The shouts sounded louder than ever.

"Maybe we should go check and see what is going on. It does not sound so good."

"Maybe we should stay here and take care of more business."

The woman's hands drifted through the still air and cupped Maria's breast. She rubbed a nipple between each thumb and forefinger. Maria felt her nipples grow hard and she sighed and closed her eyes. Never had she felt anything like this. Even her own hands had never accomplished such a touch. The woman's breath was warm against her face, and then the woman's mouth surrounded hers. Maria could feel the tongue of the English *señora* softly licking her lips, then it was poking at her teeth, and then it was inside her mouth, licking her tongue.

Again, Maria felt the great soft helpless energy flowing, her body going spongy, yielding, with her legs coming apart as her arms tightened around the neck of the English *turista*. A small, soft moan of pleasure escaped her lips. She could offer no resistance. Never had she been so helpless. She cried out with gratitude when the long, slim English fingers entered her. Her breath rasped in her ears and it seemed as if an internal fire was consuming her body. For a second, she thought she smelled smoke. But, of course, that was only her imagination. Sounds of gunfire and shouts began to fade. Again, she moaned, finding pleasure in her utter helplessness.

~ * ~

He had listened to the sounds of guns being fired for so long it had become no more than background music, Musak for the Revolución. He had been reading Somerset Maugham and now his eyes were tired. Turning the book over so that its spine faced him, he laid it across his lap. Lord Threlkeld picked up his glass.

For a moment he held it, admiring the smoothness of the glass and the lovely color of the liquid, amber with a reddish tinge when the light hit it just right. Once, he had won a good deal of money betting a steeplechaser that very color.

Lifting his glass, Lord Threlkeld toasted that horse. Then he took a long sip and listened to the guns. Damnation, there seemed to be an extraordinary amount of shouting going on and now some bloody woman had started to scream. Maybe, he thought wishfully, it was his wife. Then he shook his head; might as well forget that fantasy. That bitch was so cold and calculating that screaming wasn't even part of her vocabulary. Lord Threlkeld sat his glass down carefully, placed his book on the floor, and, with a deep sigh, pushed himself up from his chair. A spot of reconnoitering was in order. He tottered on rather unsteady legs to the window.

Leaning against the windowsill, he peered out. With all the gunfire, shouting, and now the screaming, he wouldn't have been at all surprised to see a horde of Che and Fidel look-alikes running up and down the main drag of Yuscarana, waiving machetes and bolo knives, with ammo belts crisscrossing their backs, slaughtering soldiers, raping women, firing the town.

Instead, Lord Threlkeld saw an almost empty street. Two bodies sprawled on the asphalt, their arms and legs flung out as if they were striving for the Promised Land.

Lord Threlkeld twisted his body. turning his eyes toward the peaks that rimmed the town. Floating only a few meters above them were the nastiest looking clouds he had ever seen – clouds the color of ripe eggplant.

Streaks of lightning lit up the skyline, highlighting the jagged range of mountains to the northwest, making their bare peaks look like animal teeth. Rain was rolling down the flanks of the mountains. He could see the silvery curtains shimmer in the remaining light and smell the coming dampness. He could also smell another aroma. Something was burning. Surely that was only his imagination, a suggestion from his unconscious mind. Lord Threlkeld drew a deep breath in through his nose. No, by God, something was actually burning. No confusing the pungent scent of wood on fire.

Pulling his head back in, he surveyed his surroundings. Satisfied his room was not on fire, he looked out the window again. No flames, no smoke.

Somewhere below, that damn woman was screaming again – the sound grating on his nerves. He began to make his way to the door. The door knob was faintly warm, and he eased the door open cautiously.

The air was warmer in the hallway, the smell of smoke stronger. Coughing, he pulled his handkerchief out of his inner coat pocket and pressed it over his nose and mouth. It smelled faintly of Dianna. Always an essence of lilacs about her.

The smoke smell seemed stronger to his right, toward the end of the building, and he ventured that way. Something in the hotel was most definitely on fire. The smoke had a sobering effect and he turned, retraced his footsteps, collected his bottle, then headed for the lobby.

A thin line of smoke was visible in the hallway, as if a fine gray cloud had infiltrated the building. The air had grown significantly warmer and he felt sweat begin to form on his skin. Lord Threlkeld propelled himself along more quickly.

Seconds before he reached the central staircase, he wondered where Lady Threlkeld had hauled herself off to. Some little love nest, undoubtedly. Well, she had always liked a good time. Bless her nymphomaniac soul, she ought to really be having a hot time this afternoon. Chuckling at his own humor, and clutching his bottle firmly to his chest, Lord Threlkeld began a careful descent.

~ * ~

He was more scared than he had ever been in his life, and yet... Kron let the thought trail off as he took a quick peek at the slice of the street visible from his vantagepoint. All afternoon, guerrillas had been sniping away and it wasn't safe to keep an eye pressed to a window for long. A tall man who appeared to have borrowed the face of young José Ferrer had found that out about an hour ago, the hard way. His body lay sprawled on the lobby floor where it had fallen. He was looking up at the ceiling. His eyes were open, all three of them.

Outside the hotel it was dark as dusk. Kron glanced at his wristwatch. A great rumbling, louder and stronger than any gunfire, shook the building. One hell of a storm must be brewing. After the day before, he would not have believed the clouds could hold more rain. Thunder rumbled again as lightning popped at close range.

There was a wild burst of gunfire, and the soldier to his right cursed and jerked away from the window. Blood streamed down his face. He looked at Kron, rolled his eyes and started picking glass out of his skin.

The floor seemed to move beneath him. Glancing down, Kron could see it was only his body trembling.

He felt like crying, only he was too old and the lobby too public. As thunder rolled like the end of time, Kron started to laugh. You sad son-of-a-bitch, he thought. You said you wanted to experience life in order to become a real writer. Well, you sure as hell are experiencing it now. Only all you can do is be scared as a baby, when you ought to be chiseling every mad image into your mind so you will finally have something real to write about when you sit down before that empty screen. Chicken-shit. Before Yuscarana you were a presumptuous bastard.

Kron laughed until the soldier to his left, who vaguely resembled a bullfrog, started staring at him. Turning his head, Kron kept laughing. He laughed until his sides hurt, wondering if he were going crazy.

Eventually, the laughter began to subside. The pressure of the air told him the storm had to be very close. Kron risked another quick glance. Across the street, dust devils danced and scraps of papers and strips of rags blew about like rambunctious confetti.

He could smell the rain. Kneeling, he looked toward the ring of mountains. Silvery curtains were sliding down the flanks of the mountains.

Remembering the guerrillas, he turned his head and looked as far as he could up and down the street. He couldn't see a living soul. Darkness pressed down on Yuscarana. Lightning struck the top of a sapodilla tree across the road. The smell of electrical release was strong in his nostrils. Gradually, it was replaced by another odor. It took him a few seconds to place it – October campfires and Betty McAllister – the scent of wood smoke.

Turning, Kron sniffed and looked across the lobby. Two men and a boy burst out of the dining room. One of the men was the leader of the soldiers. Then he saw the other man was the tour guide. He seemed to be pulling the boy along. The boy was the one whose father had been killed. The captain was shouting something, but Kron couldn't decipher the words.

Smoke billowed through the dining room door like a lost cloud. Now he could place the smell. Stunned, he stood, unable to speak or move. Then he shouted: "Fire!" and started running.

Halfway across the lobby, he realized he had no idea where in the hell he was going and slowed his pace. Smoke was beginning to fill the room. Soldiers were pointing and shouting. Kron didn't know what to do. If he went outside, the rebels would shoot him. If he stayed inside, he would be barbequed. He wanted to scream.

A woman from the tour was screaming. Screaming a name. After a couple of screams, Kron figured out she was calling her son's name. He recognized her now; it was her husband who had been killed. The vacant-faced girl beside her must be her daughter.

Kron glanced back at the boy. He had stopped running and stood stiffly beside some soldiers, leaning away from the men. There was no more expression on his face than was on the side of an unpainted barn.

His mother rose, pulling the girl with her. The girl moved clumsily, as though her legs were filled with sand. She stumbled and the woman jerked at her, pulling her erect, shouting words Kron heard only as another noise. Something tugged at his leg and he looked down.

Another woman from the tour stared up at him. He remembered her face perfectly, but couldn't recall her name.

Her eyes were calm. A soldier lay on the floor beside her. Kron thought he was dead. Then the young soldier's tortured mouth moved and a moan the sound a small animal makes when it is dying squeezed out between the pressed lips.

"Help me," the woman said. "He's been shot. He's badly hurt."

Kron looked over his shoulder at the smoke. "The hotel is on fire," he said.

He watched her turn and stare at the smoke. Then her eyes came back to his face. "We have to hurry."

"He can't walk."

"You'll have to carry him."

There was a smooth, soothing quality to her voice, yet it carried far more weight than a suggestion.

Kron stared at the gun in his hand. It felt like a reptile to him, smooth, slick, nasty. He let it fall to the floor where it clattered like a sack of broken bones.

He knelt beside the solider. His fingers touched the skin on the soldier's face. It felt fake, wax-like. Nausea rose in his throat, a great acidic clot. He turned his head and swallowed. His throat burned.

"Pick him up. Hurry, please."

Gagging, he slid his arms beneath the soldier's body. He could smell the man's sweat and felt warm blood worming across his own skin. Kron felt like puking. He did not want to do this. He did not want to be there. Why in the hell had he come to Yuscarana anyway? His brain felt feverish. Grunting, he began to lift.

The weight of the wounded soldier stunned him. The man, who seemed hardly more than a boy, looked as though he could weigh no more than a few pounds. Yet, his inert body was heavy, like a large bag of wet sand. Kron peered down at the soldier's face. The man's eyes were closed so tightly they appeared to be screwing themselves into his face. Now and then a moan too strong or slippery to be contained escaped between his lips.

Kron bent his knees, then thrust upward, shifting the man's weight so that some rested on his shoulders, curling him in against his chest, stumbling like a punch-drunk boxer. The hot animal smell of blood was powerful. A sweet sickness ran through it, and he gagged against the bile rising in his throat. Kron spat and stumbled on.

All around him he could hear shouts and screams and, from the far end of the room, the crackling of burning wood. Underlining it all, like a river rumbling just beyond sight, was the thunder, rolling, rolling, rolling. It kept rolling closer and closer – a locomotive highballing down the tracks of Yuscarana.

The soldier lay like an iron bar across his arms. Kron could feel his muscles harden, then burn, then start to tremble. Where was he going? He couldn't stay in the lobby. Already a veil of smoke was rising, spreading, coloring every corner of the lobby. Where was he going to go? The man was so heavy, so damn heavy.

He looked up into the face of the woman whose husband lay dead somewhere in this hotel from hell. Her daughter trotted behind her. The woman's eyes were open and dark and vacant. The girl was crying.

"Where," he asked out of the corner of his mouth, "where are we going?"

The woman only stared at him.

Smoke had grown thicker and he could feel the heat from the fire. Kron stopped, shifting the soldier again and looking around, trying to get his bearings. The check-in counter was only a few feet away, and he staggered over to it and eased the soldier down on the smooth, polished wood. The man groaned and his eyes flickered open. Spit dotted his lips. Then he subsided, the back of his head thumping against the countertop. Kron felt a tug on his left arm. He turned his head.

"Let's go out the back," the calm, brown-eyed woman said, nodding toward a hallway Kron had not noticed. "I don't see smoke down there."

"Where does it go?"

The woman shook her head. Her face was hard and set, but calm. "I don't know, but we can't stay here. There's got to be a back way out of here. Anyway, it's worth a try."

Kron nodded, coughed, then lifted his head and surveyed the lobby. The smoke was noticeably thicker. "You're right about one thing, we can't stay here. Just hope we aren't going into some dead end."

"Do we have a choice?"

"No," he said, slowly, "no we don't. Let's go."

He bent, sliding slid his arms under the man's shoulders and torso. The man's breath was warm and moist on his face. The man's lips moved.

"Brother?"

"What?"

"I am hurt. I am hurt bad."

"I know."

"Do not move me, *por favor*. I cannot stand the pain."

"Sorry, but I don't have any choice. The hotel is on fire."

"On fire?" He opened his eyes. Pain flickered in them.

"Yeah, the damn place has caught on fire." Kron coughed and lifted. "We've got to get out of here, and fast."

"Oh," the man groaned. "You are killing me."

"We're all going to die if we don't get out of here," Kron grunted. The rest had been too brief and the man seemed heavier than ever. The man's lips kept moving. Sometimes words came out, sometimes merely sounds, sometimes the lips simply moved.

Kron did not respond – he couldn't spare the breath. Just carrying the man was a strain. His legs trembled and he stumbled once, but the calm woman got a hand on his elbow and steadied him. He sucked in air shallowly, trying to keep as much smoke out as possible. The lobby air was thick with it now, a moving white curtain, and he kept his eyes focused on the darker hallway ahead.

The brown-eyed woman on his left was saying something, but Kron was no longer listening. He was focusing solely on the getting to the hallway. The soldier was so heavy and the blood running from the wound made his hands slick. He prayed he would not drop the man and that he would make the hallway. Then he prayed he would live.

The girl with the woman on his right was still crying. Her sobs sounded faint, far away. He didn't look at her. He did not care. He could not care. His job was to keep walking. The soldier in his arms was heavy and bloody, but the hallway was close. Kron kept putting one foot in front of the other.

Sixty-seven

The president of Morazon jumped as if he had been bitten by a snake. Breathing rapidly, he twisted his neck and stared down his nose at the offending instrument. Its coiled cable reminded him of a forked-tongued serpent. President Gutierrez despised snakes, despised them and feared them. The phone rang again. With a noticeable reluctance, he stretched out a hand. The receiver was slick against his flesh.

"Yes."

"This is Colonel Mendoza. We have heard from our reconnaissance plane."

"And?" He tried to keep the impatience out of his voice.

Colonel Mendoza sighed on the other end of the line. Gutierrez sensed reluctance; that could only foretell bad news.

"Speak, Colonel. Tell me the news. If it is bad, it is bad. Telling me bad news will not alter the facts."

"It is not so much that the news is bad, El Presidente."

"Then what is it?"

"You see, there was much turbulence and the reception was very poor. Apparently, there is a storm brewing in the mountains around Yuscarana..."

"So there is a storm? Maybe it will drown the damn rebels. Would that be so bad?"

"No, no, of course not."

"Then tell me the news, Colonel."

"Certainly, El Presidente, I was only telling you about the storm because it interfered so with the radio that the reception was very poor. We could not hear every word, not for certain."

Gutierrez sighed. This day had turned into a night from hell. Shouting at the colonel will do no good, he reminded himself. He made himself count slowly, *uno, dos, tres...*

"Okay, Colonel, you have explained about the storm, now kindly tell me what the pilot saw."

"Yes, sir. It seems that Major Borres, Major Borres is one of our best men, reported something about a fire."

"A fire? A fire in Yuscarana?"

"Yes, we are certain of that; he repeated the word fire several times."

"What sort of a fire? What was burning?"

"That is one of the things we could not quite catch, even though the major did repeat it. Corporal Estrada, the radio operator, thinks Major Borres spoke of a burning hotel. Does that make any sense to you?"

"Colonel, very little makes sense to me these days. However, I do believe there is a large hotel in Yuscarana. In fact, some years ago, if memory serves, I stayed in a hotel there. If I recall correctly, that hotel was the largest building in the entire town."

In his mind, Gutierrez could see the hotel quite clearly. As clearly as though he had been there only the day before, he recalled the high-ceilinged room, the wide brass bed, and the tall narrow windows with the glass pushed up and the cool night wind blowing the gauzy white curtains aside so that slabs of moonlight the color of fresh milk fell into the room and caressed the brown skin of the woman lying in the bed beside him.

She had said his name over and over and over, each time with the same faint lisp, while her fingers had played his body like it was an organ in a church.

I should have married that woman, he thought. The president of Morazon sighed. But I was young and foolish and thought I had all the time in world. And that I could return at any time. About that I was wrong, he admitted to himself, although he had never done so to another man. No man can ever go back.

The voice of the colonel crackled on the line and Gutierrez shook off the memories.

"Did you know, Colonel Mendoza, that, at one time, Yuscarana was considered quite the town? Much mining took place in the surrounding mountains, and truckloads of timber were brought out of the jungle each day. Every store on the main street did a booming business and families were moving in almost every day. Money flowed in and out of that town like water. There was even talk of a university."

"What happened?"

"Who can say, Colonel? Events took place, events long forgotten. Even I, the president of Morazon, do not perfectly recall exactly what happened. It seems to me as if the mines played out and there was a glut on the timber market. And was there an earthquake? No, that was near Minora."

Gutierrez stopped speaking and glanced out the window. Streetlights had popped on and he could see the evening breeze gently blowing the leaves, creating new, holy patterns of light. Watching the ever-changing light, he spoke softly into the receiver. "And, of course, there was the Revolución. Always in Morazon there is a Revolución."

After a silence that seemed painfully long to the colonel, Gutierrez spoke. "Did the major have anything else to report?"

"Only that the storm was coming so close to his plane that he was turning back. That, and if the storm did not reach Yuscarana soon, the entire town would undoubtedly burn."

Silence drifted along the phone connection. It was so quiet for so long the colonel began to wonder if the president had disconnected. He even debated within himself whether or not to hang up the receiver. A moment later he was extremely glad he had not.

"Is that all, Colonel?"

"Yes, sir."

"Then, goodnight."

Without speaking again, Gutierrez hung up the phone. For some time, he sat quietly in his dimly lighted office, thinking. The president thought slowly, carefully, in great detail. He wanted to be absolutely sure. As sure as he could be, anyway. A wrong move, he could not afford.

After many minutes, he glanced at his watch. The hour was late. Picking up the phone, he dialed the number for his personal pilot. Following a brief conversation, he walked quickly to his bedroom where he began to pack a bag. Traveling light was the plan. He had money sequestered in private accounts under different names in different banks in a dozen countries. Gutierrez did not take the time to call any of his mistresses. Like designer clothes, fine crystal, original paintings, vintage wines, and fancy watches, there were thousands of women in other countries.

Gutierrez packed quickly, taking only what could not be replaced. The final two things he packed were a photograph of his mother and father on their wedding day and the last letter his mother had written him – dated the day before her fatal heart attack. Then he glanced at the full-length, gilt-framed mirror, decided to dye his hair silver when he landed, and picked up his suitcase. He left his chambers by the back door.

Sixty-eight

Joe Moby felt a hand fall on his shoulder. Turning, he found himself staring in the face of the lieutenant.

"You are brave to be fighting with us. *Mucho hombre.*" The lieutenant patted his shoulder.

"Not really. The rebels will come whether I am here or not, and I can still handle a gun."

"*Sí, sí*, you are correct; every man is important in such an engagement. Captain Morales sent a request for reinforcements, but there is no certainty it got through, or if it did that headquarters would have men to send."

"I understand about headquarters."

"You have been in the military?"

"I served a tour."

"Were you an officer?"

"Never more than a non-com."

"The backbone of an army."

"So they say."

The lieutenant leaned forward. Moby could smell the remnants of the man's cologne, his sweat, and the odor of stale cigarette smoke. The lieutenant rubbed his jaw with the palm of a hand; the rustle of his stubble was audible between thunder rolls.

"Damn," the lieutenant said, "it is getting dark early."

"Big storm rolling in. Been watching it move down the sides of the mountain for the last hour. It'll be here in thirty minutes, or less."

Lightning flashed, lighting up the open ground. Half-blinded by the sudden burst of light, Joe Moby strained his eyes, trying to see into the perimeter of the jungle. All he saw was open ground and jungle. God, how he hated the jungle. In 'Nam, he had experienced enough jungle to last him a lifetime. Nasty wet, noisy, stinking, rotting, insect-plagued, disease-breeding, gook-hiding, motherf'ing jungle. Nothing but trouble came out of the jungle. Why in the hell had he allowed himself to be talked into coming to another damn jungle? Then he thought of Amy, and he knew the answer to his own question. Certain things were worth a great sacrifice. Not that it was ever really a sacrifice to do almost anything for her.

Thunder rolled; as it faded, he could hear a new sound.

"Sounds like a thousand men drumming," the lieutenant said.

"Sure does," Joe said. He listened carefully for a few seconds. "Still some distance off, but it's raining like hell out there in the jungle. Can't be long until it reaches us."

"*Bueno*. I hope it drowns Carlos and all his men."

"Better them than us."

The lieutenant laughed, the sound like a chopped-off dog bark.

Something glittered metallically near the old barn. Joe moved his eyes fractionally, trying to pick up more metal. All he could see were shadows and darkness. He waited for the lightning.

"Thought I saw something, Lieutenant."

"Where?"

"Over by the old barn, just to the right."

"I don't see anything, except maybe a few shadows moving."

Joe sniffed the air. "The rain is so close I can smell it."

The lieutenant sniffed. "Yes, I can smell the rain, and the horses in the corral, and the coffee brewing in the kitchen, and the sweat of the men, and…"

The voice of the lieutenant stopped. In the vacuum, Joe could hear the rain striking the leaves, mingling with the nickering of the horses, overridden by the rumble of thunder. Then he could smell a surprising scent. He wondered if that was what the lieutenant had smelled. He sniffed.

"What else did you smell, Lieutenant?"

"Blood," Escobar said, "I smell the blood of my men."

"Think I smell something else."

"What else do you smell, *señor*?" The lieutenant spoke slowly, emphasizing each word.

Thunder smashed the sky, a monstrous clap that rattled glass and left hollow echoes. Joe Moby felt a single bead of sweat slide down his right ribcage. An unexpected dryness had invaded his throat. He swallowed. The sound of rain on leaves sounded very close. He heard another gunshot; a man screamed, followed by shouting from the lobby of the hotel.

"I smell smoke," he said. "And it's close."

The acrid smoke scent was growing steadily stronger, but he still couldn't see it. Then the lieutenant touched his shoulder and Joe turned his head, letting his eyes follow the line of the lieutenant's pointing finger.

Like the fingers of an elderly ghost, wisps of gray smoke drifted from the far corner of the hotel. Orange and blue lights flickered. Then a great sheet of yellow flame enveloped one wall.

The damn hotel is on fire, he thought with a kind of stupefied wonder. Then he thought of Amy. The lieutenant shouted at him.

Joe could hear the sound of the words, although they did not register except as an addition to the cacophony of noise. He was already running. Her name rose in his throat as he ran down the hall, but he knew it was useless to call it. Lowering his head, he drove forward, running toward the wall of sudden fire.

~ * ~

For the first time in his entire life, he had been granted a stupendous, glorious opportunity. He could not believe his good fortune. Never before had such a wonderful occurrence happened for him. Never; not even in his wildest dreams.

At first, he thought it must have been a vision, like seeing the face of the Virgin Mary. Or a mirage such as men in the desert saw when they had gone too long without water. Then, as flames began to shoot out of the windows and gray smoke started to fill the sky like a dirty fog, Carlos realized the hotel was truly on fire.

He could hear the frenzied shouts of men inside the hotel, punctuated by the screams of women. Thunder rolled as he started to run.

Carlos ran toward the hotel. He could see the fire more clearly now; the entire right wing of the hotel was engulfed in flames. He held his gun before him as he ran. No way for the men of Morales to stay inside the hotel with such a blaze.

No man could stand up to fire. They would have to run directly into the range of his guns. It would be like shooting a pack of dogs. All the soldiers of Gutierrez in Yuscarana were going to die this night.

Close enough now to feel the heat, he glanced around him for his men. He could see no one—the cowards. Let them stay behind their buildings, that would only mean more killing for him.

Thunder rumbled like the herald of doom. He would cut them down; slaughter them as they ran out of the hotel; slaughter them like cattle in a holding pen.

Scents of victory were sweet.

~ * ~

Out of the corner of his left eye he could see the man and the boy running. The man's face was flushed, his chest rose and fell, and his breath came in great gasps, audible even to the captain. The fingers of his right hand were locked around the left wrist of the boy, who jogged easily along behind the man. The boy's face was as expressionless as an old hound's.

They were going to be all right, Captain Morales thought. At least until they step through the door. That was the problem all would have to face. The fire was going to burn the hotel down. Already, it was out of control, and he had no firefighting equipment. If he pulled men from the walls, he would not be able to keep the rebels out, although why they would want to capture a building being consumed by fire he could not imagine. All the rebels would have to do was wait where they were and shoot the people from the hotel down like chickens running from the coop. It would be so damn easy; his men would not have a chance.

Morales peered over his shoulder toward the kitchen and the back hallway. Smoke was already rolling in a thickening gray cloud behind him and one wall of the kitchen was burning. He could hear the crackle of burning wood, and above that the shrieks of frightened women. A veil of smoke covered the hallway and the captain wondered what Lieutenant Escobar was doing.

All Captain Morales cared about was getting himself, his men, and the aggravating *turistas* out of this mess alive. He did not really expect to get everyone out, not alive, anyway. The lobby was suddenly full of people, people he was responsible for. *Mon Dios*, but there seemed a great number of them. Some of them sniffed the air, but panic had yet to settle in.

All the faces of the people of the lobby, soldiers and *turistas*, those too frightened to think and those too beaten down by life to care, they all seemed to turn toward him in slow motion, their eyes swiveling in their faces like miniature cameras settling on his face. He made his face hard.

Captain Morales did not focus on the eyes of the lobby people. He was looking for ways out of the damn hole they were all in. They might not all get out of it together, but they were in it together. It simply happened to be his job to get them out of it.

Morales stared for a second at the windows. There were many of them. Perhaps if the soldiers and the *turistas* went out different windows all at once, perhaps they would have a chance. Morales took a deep breath before he began to call out instructions.

"Fire, fire," the voice behind him screamed. Morales cursed as he twisted around.

The *turista* ran into the lobby screaming fire in a loud voice that gasped for air. He was still dragging the boy behind him, but as the man turned to point at the flames, the boy jerked away and ran across the lobby.

"Run, run, the hotel is on fire," the *turista* shouted.

"Remain calm," Morales shouted in his best parade ground voice, but a woman screamed and a dozen men shouted all at once, and his words were drowned. Then there was a great whooshing behind him and Morales felt a wall of heat against his back. Without thinking, he turned to face a curtain of flames. More shouting behind him now and he whirled around in time to see the stampede. Men and women, soldiers and *turistas*, all running for the front door. Those who could not run, limped. One soldier who had been badly shot in the upper thigh crawled, a spoor of blood trailing behind him. They have forgotten about the rebels, Morales thought. The fire has driven them insane.

"Wait," he shouted, but the word was nothing more than a pebble falling in an ocean of sound. He started running as hard as he could, the barrel of his gun preceding him.

Madness, this was madness. Captain Morales could see quite clearly there was no use in trying to stop the people. They had crossed the line beyond which reason ceased to matter.

If he could not stop them, he thought as he ran, at least he could lead them. He had the angle on most of them. Morales ceased thinking, ducked his head, focusing solely on getting to the door first. He could lead them, come out firing and yelling, and maybe the sheer force of their onslaught would allow a few to break through the rebel lines.

Morales could feel his heart pounding. Pounding so hard it was starting to hurt. His breath came in great ragged gasps. He was in horrible shape, and he wasn't that old. The captain promised himself that if he got out of this disaster alive, he would take much better care of his body, get in shape and stay there. It was not a promise he felt confident he could keep.

~ * ~

It looked like a scene from a movie about the siege of Carthage he had seen years before in London. Standing on the fourth stair from the top, he could see dozens of people, civilians and soldiers alike, running for the front door of the lobby. What was wrong with these people, Lord Threlkeld wondered fuzzily. Didn't they know that armed guerrillas waited for them just outside the hotel, ready to shoot them down?

He was dumbfounded. Why were they all running so hard for the door? Why leave a moderately safe fortress to go rushing like frightened rabbits into the street? Insanity? Surely not all at once. Moving cautiously, he began to descend the stairs.

He had been seeing and smelling smoke long before he saw fire. He had always been blessed with a keen sense of smell. As a boy, he'd been able to smell two-day old cigarette smoke on his chums at school, or whiskey on the chauffeur's breath, or the secret scent of the parlor maids when they became aroused. Ah, those had been the days, he told himself. Oh, to be young again...

Two steps from the bottom he stumbled, but righted himself and kept going. He could see the fire now, flames consuming furniture, draperies, magazines and newspapers, and whatever else got in its way. Easy to see it was too far gone to be stopped. Far worse than he had imagined.

He glanced at the flames only once, then turned his head and kept walking, not breaking into a run. That wouldn't have been seemly, it didn't appear necessary and, anyway, he wasn't absolutely certain he was up to such an effort.

The fire sounded hungry, crunching wood and slurping up paper. The sound reminded him of the old train he had ridden back to school after summers and holidays, cracking and popping, belching thick, stinging smoke. Smoke had burned his eyes and the food on the train had been lousy, either soggy as a bog or dry as years-old paint. Not that he could have eaten anyway, what with all the motion. Nobody from Kings had ridden with him and the train had always been crowded, so he had been forced to sit with fat, balding men who smoked cheap cigars, and middle-aged women with layers of face powder and more parcels than brains, and younger children who invariably suffered from runny noses and flatulence.

Stepping onto the floor of the lobby, Lord Threlkeld could feel the heat against his left shoulder. A great roaring rose behind him and he felt as if his back would soon be roasting. Before him, all the people were running toward the door as though they had a death wish. Angling across the lobby, he headed for a side window, walking as quickly as he dared on questionable legs. Crossing the lobby, he could hear thunder and, more ominously, the sound of gunfire.

Between the fire and the guerrillas, it was damned if you do and damned if you don't. The way he looked at things, the fire was for damn sure; a man stayed in the hotel and his testicles got fried to a crackly crunch. At least with the guerrillas he would be out in the open, with a chance to move and, who knew, maybe the bastards would miss. All in all, he'd been quite lucky on numerous occasions over the years.

Ignoring the chaos, he pushed open the back window on the far side of the hotel from the registration counter. It seemed the quietest and safest, and, besides, he didn't have much of a choice. Wobbling, he swung one leg over the windowsill, stepping unhesitatingly into the growing darkness.

Beneath the window, the ground sloped away and his foot found only air. Then he was falling. Hitting the ground unceremoniously, he forced his body to keep rolling, ending up on his back in a small depression, half out of breath, staring up at the blackest damn clouds he had ever seen, smiling like he had just broken the bank at Monte Carlo. A big, fat, juicy raindrop splattered squarely between his eyes and Lord Threlkeld started laughing.

~ * ~

In the gaps between the running men, she could see the orange mouth of the fire and once, in a surreal moment, she glimpsed the English man who had been in a state of perpetual, yet never total, drunkenness the entire trip, walking quite nonchalantly down the stairs, walking as though he had all the time in the world.

Such luxury, they did not enjoy. "Come on," she said, "we've got to get out of here. This hotel is going to burn down, and quickly." Her left knee tried to give way on her and she shifted her weight until she regained balance and the knee slipped back into place. Getting old was hell. "Deal with it," she admonished herself.

Even with the billowing smoke, Amy could see Mrs. Samuels was trembling. "Let's go," she said, trying to infuse calmness into her voice. Deliberately, she hardened her face. "Come on, now."

"I can't."

"Yes, you can. Let's go," she grunted and began to move. The man carrying the wounded soldier trudged on, a few steps in front of her.

Gunfire again, and she thought of Joe, what he was doing, hoping rather desperately he was all right. With her eyes wide open, she said a brief, though heartfelt, prayer.

The door seemed a long way away. Fire burned closer every second. Only one thing to do. Amy could hear Joe's voice as though he were standing beside her. Nothing for it but to do it, and no time like the present to get started, he would say. Yes, that is exactly what he would say. They had been together for so long she was absolutely certain. In that certainty was comfort.

Coughing in the thickening smoke, she nodded at the girl slogging along beside her. We must look like three drunks. Amy thought. She tried to ignore the flames and focus on the doorway.

Soldiers were already running through the door. Out in the street, a barrage of gunfire greeted them. Shouts and screams of men rose above the gunfire. My God, Amy Moby thought, it must be pure, unadulterated hell out there, and they're walking right into it. Fire crackled. It had reached the check-in counter and the heat was tremendous. They stumbled on, angling away from the flames, making for the back of the hotel. A soldier lay sprawled face down on the floor, as still as yesterday. Breathing a sigh of relief that it wasn't Joe, she kept moving. Down the hallway the dark world looked foreboding.

Sixty-nine

Steam rose from the kettle on the stove. Inside the kettle a reddish-brown liquid was coming to a boil. Bubbles dimpled the surface where they broke open. Above the pot, the air was redolent with the scents of onions, chilies, and peppers. Somewhere beneath the surface of the liquid was a long bone with stringy strands of meat still attached, along with a few potatoes and the last of the carrots. Today, this blend was what passed for soup at the hotel.

Señora Herrera stood beside the stove, stirring the soup absentmindedly. From time to time, she allowed her eyes to wander across the kitchen where the maids were huddled in a corner. All wore worried expressions and their eyes were reddened from crying. Looking at them depressed her, so she did not do it often.

One of the maids sobbed gently into a handkerchief. At first, they had cried frequently and loudly, but, as the hours passed and the rebels did not go away, their crying had come less frequently and with a steadily decreasing intensity, as though they were gradually becoming resigned to accept whatever happened.

Señora Herrera was not ready to go that far. Granted, things did not appear to be going well at the moment. These rebels were certainly more persistent than most. Usually, they made a surprise attack, often moments before dark or in those first few minutes of predawn light when most of the world still slept, then slipped away as quickly as they had come, blending in with the darkness, or the jungle, or the people of Morazon. For they were the people; they looked like them; they talked like them; they ate and played and loved and died exactly like them. There were days when Juanita Herrera wondered if, deep in her secret soul, she wasn't a rebel, too.

Señora Herrera was not thinking of the rebels as she stirred the soup. Nor was she thinking of the soldiers.

It was her husband, Poncho, who was on her mind. When had she seen him last? Her mind was so cluttered with images of bullets, bodies, blood, and broken dishes she could not remember.

For Poncho to slip away for a few hours was not unusual. After all, he did like his liquor and, after a long night, a nap. Señora Herrera had also noticed, on more than one occasion, a maid looking rather flustered, guilty even, as she entered a room unannounced. Such things she could understand. This, however, was different.

For one thing, he had never been gone so long, at least not without an excuse she could believe if she were willing to be open-minded. Usually, his tales involved some rather disreputable friend and a trip to the next town for a certain item not carried in Yuscarana, or the lake where the big fish always were, or a journey to visit a certain cousin who owed him money. Not that the tale mattered; he never came home with the special item or the fish, certainly never with any money. At least not any he shared.

Still, if he were going to be gone for more than a couple of hours, he had always told her some tale. This time he had said nothing. Nor had he said anything to the maids. She had asked them all, except for Maria, who had gone to take coffee to the demanding English *señora*.

Señora Herrera glanced at the clock on the wall. Maria should have been back well over an hour ago. When she did return, that girl could certainly count on a harsh lecture. Señora Herrera stirred the soup.

Where was Poncho? She had imagined everything: him lying somewhere hurt or dead, or knocked unconscious, even taken prisoner by the rebels. Poncho always believed he could talk his way out of any situation. Perhaps this time he had not succeeded.

It was also, in her mind, not beyond the realm of possibility that he had run away. She did not see how he could have done it. Yet, in his own way, Poncho was a very clever man.

Where was that man?

Where was Maria?

What did she smell?

For some time, she had been vaguely aware of a new scent. A scent so light and nebulous she had paid little attention to it. Stirring the soup, Señora Herrera sniffed, drawing air in through her wide nostrils.

Ah, she had it now – smoke. A smell she knew well. Something was burning. Quickly, she glanced at the stove, then around the kitchen. Except for the soup and a percolator of coffee, there was nothing to burn. Sniffing as she went, she walked across the kitchen.

As she reached the swinging door, a woman screamed. A thousand spiders seemed to crawl across her body at once.

Near the door the air was much warmer. Nervously, she pressed the tips of her fingers against the door. The wood felt unnaturally warm. Cautiously, she pushed.

Smoke, thick and gray, slid through the opening, accompanied by an unmistakable heat. For a moment, she merely stood there, smelling smoke, half hearing the rising babble of the maids, not knowing what to do.

Then one of the maids screamed and she felt a hand in her back, pushing her, and she fell against the door and it swung open. She stumbled against a wall. To her left, the fire was burning. At a glance, she could see it was beyond control. To her right, soldiers and *turistas* were running for the front door. Suddenly, the maids were brushing past her, screaming and running. A huge support beam crashed to the floor and Señora Herrera started running, too. Her plump buttocks wobbled dangerously and within three strides her breathing was labored. Truly, she had not run since she was a little girl.

~ * ~

Stretching her naked body luxuriously, Lady Dianna Threlkeld closed her eyes and sighed. She couldn't remember when she had last felt so good. Her stomach growled with the good emptiness that, according to Hemingway, promoted beauty in paintings, gardens, and love-making. Thunder clapped and the glass in the windows rattled. She opened her eyes in time to see lightning jag across a dark sky. Lady Threlkeld snuggled closer to the woman beside her.

The curves of the younger woman's body were wondrously soft and plentiful. Lowering her head, she pressed her lips against the hollow of the girl's neck, while her right hand curled around the girl's left breast. She squeezed it ever so gently, then a little harder, tweaking the nipple between her thumb and middle finger, making it hurt just enough.

"Uumm," the girl moaned deep in her throat. As if in answer, thunder rolled again, echoing off the walls of the surrounding buildings as if they were sides of mountains." Ooohh..."

"You like that don't you, you plump little pussy."

"Umhum."

"And do you like this?" The long fingers of her left hand worked their way down the pronounced curve of the girl's belly, burying themselves deeply into the crevice below, sliding like hungry snakes across the moist smoothness, again and again and again.

Her fingers found a rhythm. Outside, thunder rambled like a long freight train rolling through a tunnel, while inside the younger woman moaned and jerked as helplessly as a harpooned salmon.

After a considerable time, the spasms abated, dying a slow, natural death, and the younger woman buried her face against the English *señora's* breasts, snuggling close like an exhausted child.

"Oh, I never knew," she whispered in a soft, muffled voice that rose from the back of her throat.

"Never knew what, baby?"

"That it could be so wonderful."

"Yes, sometimes it is very wonderful. Doesn't always happen, but when it does, well, let's just say that you will remember this day for the rest of your life." Lady Dianna began to kiss the girl's face, working her way steadily lower, inhaling the girl's scent.

She sucked and smelled for some time, listening to the purring of the younger woman playing counterpoint to the orchestra's thunder and lightning. Occasionally she heard muffled, faraway shouts of men and the hard, metallic twang of gunfire, but she ignored them and concentrated on the opulent flesh between her lips.

Quite slowly, as if emerging from a dream, she grew aware of another scent, the unmistakable odor of something burning. Reluctantly, Lady Dianna Threlkeld lifted her head and sniffed. Her nostrils were still saturated with the woman scents of Maria and for several seconds the odor of smoke seemed scarcely more than an illusion. Then her nasal passages began to clear and she clearly smelled smoke.

"Baby... "The older woman bent her long, graceful neck and kissed the soft full lips of the younger one. "Baby..."

"Yes."

"I hate to say this, but I am afraid we are going to have to get out of here, and rather quickly."

"Why?" Maria purred.

"Because, you sweet, sexy creature, this old hotel seems to be on fire."

"On fire?"

"Yes, dear girl, on fire." Lady Threlkeld caressed Maria's lips a final time before pushing with her palms against the back of the couch.

"But I don't understand."

Lady Threlkeld pulled on her blouse; she did not worry about her bra. "Actually, I smell smoke quite strongly and I'm virtually certain I hear shouts of fire."

She stretched out an arm down and ran one palm very gently across the girl's face. "Think we had better be getting a move on, don't you?" She picked up the girl's white blouse and tossed it to her. "Come on, get dressed."

Before all the buttons were done, they could hear a strange crackling sound, as if a giant were wrinkling all the tissue paper in Morazon. Already, the air in the room had grown warmer. Lady Dianna wiped a thin line of sweat from the base of her neck. Smoke was sliding in under the door. Maria coughed. Lady Threlkeld could feel her eyes burning.

"Dear, I really don't think we have time to put on any more clothes." Tiptoeing over to the door, she pressed the tips of her fingers against the wood. The wood felt far too warm. Smoke hung thickly by the door. Twisting, she looked across the room.

"We'll want to use the windows—this door is way too damn hot."

"But I'm not even half dressed."

"No time for modesty now, young lady." Lady Dianna Threlkeld walked across the room with quick, short steps.

Behind her, she heard the crackling of wood as the fire licked at the door. Maria gasped, but Lady Threlkeld ignored her. She was concentrating on getting a window open. She tugged and pushed on the first one, but it would not budge.

Pearls of sweat lined her forehead. Sweat slid down both sides of Lady Threlkeld's nose. She glanced at the second window. Silver nail heads shone dully against the sill in the fading light. Her eyes roved along the desk. Moving quickly, she picked up a bookend that looked heavy. It was shaped like an Indian elephant. She carried it back to the window and began smashing glass. Seconds later the shards lay like shining, but broken, dreams on the floor. Aiming carefully, she smashed at the wooden framework, and, using the elephant as a scraper she swiped off as many of the remaining glass shards as she could.

Turning, she gave Maria a quick hug. The poor girl was trembling with fear. From the hallway there was a tremendous smash, as if half the world had fallen. The girl screamed and gave a little jerk, and then there was a stream of yellow running down her leg, collecting on the floor in an acrid, pungent pool.

Lady Threlkeld shook her head. Then she kissed the girl's cheek, put an arm under her elbow, and helped her step over the sill. As soon as the girl was outside, Lady Threlkeld slid a long, slender leg over the sill. Halfway out, she glanced back. The door was a flaming rectangle and streams of fire ran across the floor. Someone was screaming. She could not tell if it was a man or a woman, only that they were in pain. For one second, maybe two, she wondered about Donald. Then she swung her second leg out the window.

The ground below was a flower bed and the soil was loose. She stumbled, but the younger woman steadied her. Holding hands, they started running. All around them was darkness. The only light was from the fire. Near the hotel the air was hot, full of sparks and hot ashes. Shadows gyrated against the outer walls of the old hotel, but the women did not stop to watch. They ran for the vast darkness before them, clutching tightly to the other's hand, trying to keep their emotions and bodies under control.

As they ran, stumbling now and then – staggering when the ground fell away or vines reached up to trip them – the first few pregnant raindrops fell. The cool wetness felt good against their exposed flesh. They were less than half-dressed, and the girl, at least, was grateful for the darkness.

She squeezed the older woman's hand more tightly as she struggled not to fall. She did cry a little, although she was not certain exactly why.

~ * ~

It was imperative that he get to the front. A leader must lead by example. Captain Morales signaled his legs to move faster. Only three or four men were still in front of him, and all were all soldiers. Good. He did not want any of the *turistas* to be in front of him. He and his men were here to protect them. He should be first out the door. That was only fitting. Besides, he was eager to get the first look at Carlos.

He was not going to be first. He could see that now. One of his men, he could not tell which one, was already at the door. Another was close behind. Morales seemed encased in a capsule of sound. Screams and shouts assaulted his ears; the roaring crackle of the fire seemed everywhere. Thunder rolled, echoed, rolled again. Morales knew that to shout at the man was useless.

For a second, the man hesitated, then he stepped through the doorway and disappeared. Morales heard the sharp report of gunfire and the scream of a man in pain. He flung himself to the floor and rolled against the wall, keeping his gun off the wood, trying to suck air down his lungs. Blinking away stars, he found himself staring at the legs of a soldier. For a moment they were still and straight. Then they began to lean backwards, and then they were falling like a tree that had been cut.

The man fell, slowly and heavily, smashing down on Morales, sending his gun sailing. Morales could hear it clatter on the floor. Then he heard a low moan and the man rolled over. Liquid dripped warmly against the captain's face.

Morales grunted and shoved. The man rolled off and fell heavily to the floor. He landed on his back, vacant eyes staring up at Morales. Captain Morales knew the soldier. A private, he came from a family of ranchers in the north. His name was Benito Santiago, but the men had all called him El Rojo, after his perpetually red nose.

Something else was red now – his chest. An area the size of an immature breadfruit had turned crimson. The crimson spread in a silent flood. Morales had liked the man, a decent enough sort, relatively honest, if not overly bright. The captain spat the bitter taste out of his mouth and felt furiously for his gun. Grabbing it, he started for the door, crawling like a scared dog. Mixed with the blood scent was the smell of rain.

~ * ~

One entire wing of the hotel was fully engulfed in flames. Carlos grinned: it was just like the time the fireworks stand had exploded during festival. He could not believe his good fortune. In his wildest dreams he could not have imagined. Although, if he got out of Yuscarana alive, he was going to claim the burning of the hotel for himself. Crouched in the doorway, he could not understand why he had never thought of firing the hotel.

Carlos strained to see through the darkness. He could hear much yelling and wailing from inside the hotel. Any second now, more soldiers and *turistas* would burst through that door. He wanted to call to his men to be ready, but he knew that with the rising wind and the crackling fire, plus all the shouting from inside the hotel, it would be a waste of breath. He could only hope they were still out there in the darkness, ready to fire. Most of them he did not know well enough to trust. Rarely had Carlos felt more alone.

He shook off the loneliness as if it were a shower of dying leaves. Noises from the hotel grew louder. Any second, he told himself, fresh targets will come bursting through that door. His finger tightened on the trigger. His grin grew even wider. Bring on the soldiers of Gutierrez. Bring on the famous Captain Morales. Bring them all on, the mother-fuckers, the assholes, the sons-of-bitches, the *bastardos*. He was ready for them. He was ready for all of them.

Seventy

Raindrops splattered against his nose. His nerves were so heightened that for a millisecond the drops felt like bullets. Jerking instinctively, the captain banged his head against a wooden post and stars exploded behind his eyes. A man pushed past him and stepped into the street, turned right, and began to run. Three strides later, a bullet smashed into his back. If he cried out, Morales did not hear the sound. All he could see in the poor light was the man's arm flung skyward. For a heartbeat, two, three, the man was silhouetted against a lightning flash, legs bent and leaning forward, arms apart, thrown back with the palms up, his face pointing toward God as though he were impaled on an invisible cross. Captain Morales felt like a voyeur at a crucifixion. Then the main body of the herd reached the doorway and there was no longer time for thinking.

Men and women and children, soldiers and civilians alike, were pushing past him, panting, crying, screaming, running, heedless of what lay waiting in the darkness. No use trying to stop them; such an action was beyond his capabilities, beyond the capabilities of any man or woman. Besides, there was the fire behind them, roaring, consuming the hotel in great hot gulps.

A few of the soldiers at least had the presence of mind to fire their weapons as they came out, dropping to the ground after they fired, rolling for greater darkness. He could hear the high twanged pitch of the return fire and he knew that with the people running directly toward them, backlit by the fire, it was nothing more than live target practice for the rebels. Morales scrambled to his feet and began to run.

Most of the gunfire seemed to be coming from his left and from directly in front of the hotel, so most of the people were turning and running right, searching for a darker sanctuary. He turned and ran to his left, crouching low, heading down the wooden sidewalk, hugging the adobe walls.

~ * ~

His own laughter was echoing inside his head. He clung to reality by only the thinnest of strands.

This was incredible. People were running in a great wild herd out of the burning hotel. Splendid targets. Only if they had been standing still would they have been easier to kill.

At first, they had come out one at a time, and picking them off had been ludicrously easy. Now they were pouring out in such a mass he could not kill them fast enough to prevent some from reaching safety in the deeper darkness.

"Shoot, shoot, you fools," he screamed at his men. "Kill them all. Kill the *bastardos*. Kill them now." Enough sanity remained that he realized the thunder and screaming *turistas* drowned his words. Yet he screamed them anyway. In his ecstasy he was incapable of coherent thought. Words drifted away with the wind to where all spoken words go to die.

So excited his hand was quivering, he could not stay still. Stepping out of the doorway, he began to jog down the sidewalk, shooting as he moved. Carlos no longer watched to see if his shots were hitting targets or spinning off harmlessly into the night. Passion he could not contain was driving him forward, fueled by a wanton desire to stare into the eyes of Morales as he blew him to hell.

In the half-light of the fire and lightning, he could see the herd turning away from him, running hard through darkness toward greater darkness. The thought he might miss Morales in the crowded dark drove him forward. Only two small buildings stood between him and the hotel. As though it were an apparition, Carlos could see a lone figure running toward him, moving out of the shadows into the firelight like the night specter. He lifted his gun.

~ * ~

In an oddly comforting way, Captain Morales felt happy running down the sidewalk. He could no longer command. All his troops had been swallowed by the great nocturnal maw. No longer was he an officer asking men to die for him; he was simply a soldier doing his duty.

As he ran, he snapped off a couple of shots, aiming across the street at roughly the spot where he had fixed rebel fire, letting his instincts guide him, praying a little, trusting to chance. He heard no screams and there was no return fire, but a dozen different explanations could hold truth.

He ran on, moving slower now, watching his footing in the quivering light thrown by the flames, planning to circle behind the rebels. Crossing from one shadow to the next, he saw a man running toward him. Morales was not surprised; Carlos would be too smart not to attack from multiple angles. His stomach was suddenly sour. So it came down to this. It always did. One man had to kill another man, or be killed himself. A quiet, icy aloneness began to flow though the captain's veins, colored by a faint sadness for mankind. He lifted his gun.

Lightning painted the mark of Zorro across the sky as thunder smashed louder than all the thundering that had come before. Surely, it must be the sound of the night cracking open. Rain pummeled the earth so hard and fast no single drop could be distinguished from its brother. In the darkness, raindrops smashed against trees and grass and earth and mortar and machines and men. Smashed as if they were small stones thrown by an angry God.

~ * ~

Carlos and Morales ran toward each other through the deluge, each seeing the other only as a dim, mystical figure, disappearing and reappearing like a mirage.

Neither man could know with certainty who the other was. Yet, they both sensed identities long dreamed of in the firelight of campfires and the darkness of nocturnal barracks. Twenty yards away, in the same heartbeat – as if obeying the same demon – each squeezed the trigger of his gun. For one stride, two, they stumbled on. Then they fell in synchronicity into the darker shadows, mouths open – saying nothing, eyes open – seeing nothing, reaching with outstretched arms for each other.

Seventy-one

In a wild stampede they ran, all the soldiers and *turistas* and hotel staff who could still run, the incredible heat of the fire driving them on. They did not stop to grab their clothes, or their cameras, or their cash. Such things were no longer of importance. Most of the soldiers carried their rifles, but that was only because they had them in their hands at the instant flight became imperative, and in their overwhelming terror their weapons had become nothing more than appendages to their body. One of the kitchen maids ran with a dish towel, another still grasped a mango in her left hand. Señora Herrera carried a soup ladle as she lumbered near the back of the pack.

What they primarily carried were their fears of dying (dying too young, dying before their time, dying with their music still in them, dying a virgin, dying an old maid, dying alone, dying in a fucking hellhole code-named Yuscarana, dying before salvation, dying with doubt), and their multitudes of regrets (unconsummated loves, loves never spoken, sins of commission and sins of omission, goodbyes unsaid, hurts unforgiven, songs unsung, stories unwritten, dreams unfulfilled, prayers never voiced).

Every person ran as hard as they could, fleeing the fire, and whatever unnamed demons chased them. Knowing that, while they might outrun the fires of Yuscarana, they could never outrun the demons who cried their names in the language of the damned.

They ran to live, knowing they were going to die. Only not this day, Lord, not this day. Let me live a little longer and I will be so good my sins will be transformed from scarlet to the white of falling snow, and my countenance will reflect Your glory, and people will call me saint. All right, all right, at least let me live until I have made love to the widow with the long legs and the breasts like hills.

They ran like hell.

They ran from hell.

They ran straight into hell.

~ * ~

His tongue flicked out and licked away the drool at the corners of his mouth. He almost pinched himself to make sure he had not died and gone to heaven, but then the first slanting sheet of rain struck him full in the face and he knew he was still in Yuscarana. Tony, known as The Demented, grinned. Heaven, as described by the priests, had always seemed a rather dull place to him, what with all those harps and clouds and angels. Yuscarana promised to be a more enjoyable locale.

Excitement trembled his hands as he raised the gun to his shoulder and his finger fumbled with the trigger. Never, never, never in all his life had he had so many easy targets. Men and women lumbering like cattle down the main street of Yuscarana, their bodies outlined in flames. Other guerillas were shooting. Short sharp barks of sound reverberated against his eardrums. However, they were few in number and infrequent. Tony would fix that. His finger wrapped around the trigger.

In the final second before he squeezed, he caught sight of movement out of the corner of his right eye. He shifted his line of vision in time to see two men running down the wooden sidewalk toward each other. One ran from the hotel, the other toward it. Something in the movements of the man running toward the hotel was familiar. Lighting lit the street until he could see that both men had drawn their weapons. The man running from the hotel was dressed in the uniform of the soldiers of Gutierrez. The other man was Carlos.

Fascinated, he watched. The men kept running. Then, in the same heartbeat, they fired. Transfixed, Tony watched both men stumble and fall. They lay without moving. He could not believe Carlos was dead. Then he saw Carlos lift his head and began to drag himself across the sidewalk. Good, Tony thought, I will tend to him later.

He whirled, brought the gun up and sighted down the barrel. A long-legged soldier ran into view. The man ran with a herky-jerky stride that covered ground surprisingly quickly. Letting out the breath he had been unknowingly holding, Tony squeezed the trigger.

Herky-Jerky broke stride and fell off the sidewalk onto the wet pavement. If he screamed, the storm drowned out the sound. The man rolled and came stumbling up, his legs unsteady, gripping his right shoulder with his left hand. He stumbled on, deeper into the night. His gun lay in the rain on the road that ran through the belly of Yuscarana. Tony shrugged and let him go.

He swung the gun along the crowd until he came upon an older man dressed in civilian clothes. His white hair reflected the firelight and his face strained with the effort of running. To Tony, it appeared as if his lips were moving in prayer. Just as the man known as The Demented squeezed the trigger, his target stumbled, throwing up his hands as if in supplication. Although Tony never knew it, the bullet cut off the little finger of the man's right hand as cleanly as if it had been amputated by a surgeon's scalpel.

The herd was breaking apart, running in forty different directions, running into the blessed darkness, running away from the light, and the fire, and the guns. Rain had begun falling harder, great silver sheets of water blowing across Yuscarana. Smoke rose in thick, choking columns as flames flaunted the rain. In the hellish light, the running people had been transformed into ghosts. Fear tickled the throat of Tony the Demented, but he spat it out as he fixed his sight on the fat, wobbling rump of a woman. He knew he was seeing visions; she seemed to be carrying a soup ladle. Never before had he shot a vision. He squeezed the trigger.

The woman appeared to jump three feet straight into the air. Then she fell heavily onto the pavement, landing face down, her right hand grabbing the fat right cheek of her ass, her legs kicking like gigantic scissors.

When Tony got his laughter under control, he placed the sight of his rifle squarely in the center of the woman's left buttock and squeezed the trigger. Even above the storm, he heard her scream. She gyrated in the middle of the street like a sow in the throes of an orgasm.

By the time Tony was able to drag his eyes away from the convulsing woman, the rest of the people had disappeared into the shadows. Enraged, he simply pointed the end of his rifle in the general direction of the street and began to squeeze the trigger. Only when the empty click of the hammer finally penetrated his brain did he stop firing. He knelt in the rain, getting his breath, silently saying the only mantra he knew. Then he pushed himself erect and walked across the street to help Carlos. The rain was beginning to abate and his legs wobbled as though he were walking on stilts.

Seventy-two

Blood flowed in the darkness, merging with the water running down the sidewalks and streets of Yuscarana, tingeing the brown with red. Rolling thunder blended with the blasts of guns, the cracking of lighting, and the roaring fire until the sound was so bizarre, so primeval that even the women and men who survived that ordeal could never find words to adequately describe the sound as unique as it was deadly.

Carlos looked at his left leg with a sort of medical curiosity. He could feel no pain. Shock, he supposed. However, in the uncertain light cast by the flickering flames, he made out the gaping hole and the red pulp, peppered with bone, that covered his knee. Someway, he could not remember how he had done it, he had drug himself up under an awning and collapsed against the side of an empty building. Now, all he could do was rest his head against the wet adobe and stare at the bloody vulgarity that had been his leg, and, beyond, to the man lying on his back in the street where he had fallen, the rain baptizing him without ceasing.

Most of the time, the man was no more than a uniformed skeleton. When lightning flashed or flames flared, he could see the face of the man. It looked strangely calm and at peace, almost youthful in the smoothness of the brow. Carlos wondered if the man was the great Captain Morales. As his own pain grew, he decided the identity of the fallen man no longer mattered, if it ever had.

Closing his eyes against the pain, surrendering to the weakness that was consuming him, Carlos wished the man well. He had fought like a man, and if he lived, he could live with pride and honor. If he died, well, let him go quickly, Carlos murmured to himself and whichever god happened to be listening.

~ * ~

In the street, Morales lay on his back, not moving, drifting in and out of consciousness, trying not to think about the metal lodged inside his body.

At times, he could feel only the pain. It came in long series of waves, each more full of pain than the one before, until his mind could not bear it and he slipped into a welcome darkness. After some time, the waves subsided and he came back to himself.

In the sweet, lucid moments that followed, the captain knew he had been shot. The bullet had smashed with paralyzing force into the upper quadrant of the left side of his chest, higher than his heart, lower than his shoulder, ripping flesh and smashing bone before it buried itself against the scapula. Of course, he could see none of this, but he knew, oh how he knew.

At times, he wondered about the other man. As he had pirouetted from the force of the bullet, he had seen the other man stumble and fall. In those seconds after the first awful pain there had been a brief interlude of peace and Morales had pictured them both as puppets, falling when their strings had been cut.

Now, he lay on his back with the rain in his face, wondering, when his mind decided to cooperate, if the other man were alive or dead, or, like himself, in that twilight state between.

Morales did not mind the rain. It had slackened until it felt to him like the cool showers he had enjoyed at fancy hotels while on leave. Even the water running brown against him in the street felt good. At least when he could feel the wetness he knew he was still alive.

As Captain Morales listened to the slow, rhythmic thumping of his own heart, it seemed of paramount importance that the other man lying in the rain falling on Yuscarana should live. As the gentle rain kissed his face a thousand kisses, Captain Morales stared up at the lightning zigzagging across the ebony sky, a pleased expression fixed on his face.

And the rain, like tears from a mystified god, fell as a blessing and a curse, unrelenting, with mercy and without condemnation, on the living and the dying and dead of Yuscarana.

Seventy-three

"You are very beautiful," Poncho murmured.

For over an hour he had been drinking steadily and his words sounded slurred to him. He peered into the woman's face, anxious to see how she had taken his compliment.

She stared back at him with lizard eyes, golden in the uncertain light of the cantina. With her narrow beak of a nose and close-set eyes, she was not a pretty woman. But in the right light, after several whiskeys, she had a certain appeal. Poncho rearranged his lips into what he hoped was a more pleasing display.

The woman's cool, steady stare made him nervous. He searched his mind for something clever and amusing to say. Usually, he was a marvelous conversationalist, if he did say so himself. He read the papers, kept up with the news bulletins from the radio, and talked with the travelers who stayed at his hotel, so he was well versed on current events. Furthermore, he was not an uneducated man. Six years he had gone to school. Once, he had even taken an art appreciation course by correspondence.

The woman continued staring at him with eyes she had stolen from a lizard. She did not speak; she only stared. She stared at him as if he were something that had once been alive but was now lying on the jungle floor. She stared at him for so long Poncho began to wonder if she was deaf. Finally, she shifted her gaze down to the glass on the table before her. Scarcely a quarter inch of liquid remained in the glass. She did not speak, only turned her head in the direction of the bartender and made a motion with her right hand.

After some time – time had become an elastic element – a short, fat waitress brought another drink. She set the glass in front of the woman. A look passed between them and the waitress turned and stretched an open palm before Poncho. She named an amount that seemed exorbitant. Fumbling in his pocket, he pulled out the bills he had stuffed there, holding them tight against his body in an effort to shield them from prying eyes. His hand became momentarily entangled with his belt and several bills fluttered to the floor. He bent quickly to pick them up, almost tipping himself onto the floor. Just in time, he grabbed an edge of the table. The waitress helped him pick up the bills.

Swiping at the line of sweat stretching across his forehead, he smiled at the woman across the table. "It is getting warm in here."

She sipped her drink. "*Sí*, a little."

"Do you come here often?" Poncho arched his neck and let his eyes sweep the room. He was surprised at how small and dark and full of hard-faced men it was.

She shrugged, a movement which meant less than nothing. "Sometimes."

"I have not been here before. Is this a nice cantina?"

"It is all right. Do you have a cigarette?"

"No, I have cigars only."

The woman wrinkled her nose. "If that is all that you have, then I will take one of those."

Poncho dug a fresh cigar out of his shirt pocket. Only two others were left, and one of them was little more than a stub. He offered the fresh cigar to the woman as though it were a birthday present.

"Do you have a match?"

He lit her cigar. "My name is Poncho."

"Esmeralda." She blew smoke out her nose.

"Esmeralda, that is a pretty name. I do not think I have heard it before."

"It is the name of my mother's sister."

Lifting his glass to his lips, Poncho studied the woman. She appeared bored. He shot a quick look around the room. Only three or four other women were in the cantina and they were all either older or uglier than the woman with the eyes of a lizard. He drained his glass, then waved it at the short, fat woman leaning against the bar. Poncho unbuttoned the top button of his shirt, wiping at the dampness on his chest, then that on the back of his neck.

"It is very warm in here."

The woman shrugged. Her reptilian eyes made him nervous. Sweat began to roll down his back. It pooled in the hollow of his chest.

"I suppose it is warm in here. Here is Conchita with your whiskey. Pay her, and drink the whiskey. Then you will feel better."

Poncho tried to keep his money hidden, but ends of the bills kept poking out between his increasingly thick fingers, and when he tried to pull one out, two fell on the floor. When he bent to pick them up, he rocked his chair, flinging his free hand out for support. It landed on the woman's left knee. She did not bother to remove it, and Poncho felt urges rising.

As he pushed himself back into his chair, his eyes, of their own volition, settled on hers. They glowed, hot and golden. He wanted to say clever words to make her like him. All he could think of was to again ask the woman if she wanted a drink. It must be the heat, he decided. All that heat is making my brain fuzzy, he told himself. Golden eyes kept staring at him. A drop of sweat rolled into his left eye. He rubbed it away with fingers which felt like sausages.

"Would you like another drink?" His voice sounded loud to him, decibels rattling around in his head like atomic marbles.

"Certainly."

"*Bueno.*" Poncho waved a hand at the fat waitress who had crossed the room and was talking to a tall man wearing a black serape and a white sombrero. She did not notice him, so Poncho began to push himself out of his chair. He felt the woman's hand on his arm.

"Sit still, señor; I will go." Smiling, the woman rose. Her lips were quite thin and she seemed very tall to Poncho. Her head seemed to float among the dark beams that formed the ribs of the low ceiling. "I need to powder my nose, anyway." Patting his hand lightly, she turned quickly, her skirt swishing against his legs.

Poncho settled back in his chair and watched her hips sway in the dim light. Putting his head in his hands, Poncho dropped his elbows onto the table as he tried to steady the world. The room seemed to undulate and the whirling movements made Poncho nauseous. He closed his eyes until the whirling lessened.

It seemed to Poncho that for some time he floated on a dark sea, drifting in and out of a state between unconsciousness and reality. Still, he was not asleep. That he knew, because he could think of being awake. Yet, he was not fully awake either. I am in limbo, Poncho told himself. Something began to shake him, and continued to press and pull his body until he opened his eyes.

The woman with lizard eyes was standing beside him. He shook his head the way a dog shakes its body after a swim.

"All right, all right, what do you want?"

She stared at him for several seconds, her face as expressionless as the table top. Then she stretched out a hand. Her fingers were long, curling slightly at the tips. "I must pay for the drink."

Grumbling, Poncho fumbled for his money. It twisted in his hand like a fat, slick worm. Peeling off a bill, he handed it to the woman. He was not certain of the denomination. He watched her pull the bill from his fingers and walk across the room where she whispered in the ear of the fat waitress. Then he watched her walk back. She seemed to be walking in slow motion.

Poncho sipped his drink.

Unbuttoning another shirt button, he twisted in his seat, trying to find even a hint of a breeze. The air in the cantina was stifling, as though all the oxygen were being slowly sucked out of it. Poncho set the glass on the table and, grunting, pushed himself to his feet. It took him a moment to locate the door in the dimness and, as he stood by the table, swaying gently, he felt a hand on his arm. His drinking companion was peering at him. Through the odors of smoke and sweat, he could smell her perfume. She smelled like stale flowers.

"You are not going?" Her hand rubbed his arm as though she were polishing brass. Above her shoulders, he could see the open doorway. Darkness covered the street, but he could no longer stand the cantina. The room was smothering him.

Poncho pushed the woman a few inches to his left and began to walk. At first, his legs were unsteady and he concentrated solely on walking. The woman walked beside him, talking in a rhythm that rose and fell with the movements of her body, but he ignored her. By the time he was halfway to the door his legs were working better and the woman's words began to penetrate.

"If you do not mind, I will walk with you, *señor*. It can be dangerous to walk alone after dark in a strange town."

Her words made much sense to Poncho, and he nodded. One of her arms slipped through his and they marched across the cantina floor, stumbling only once. Poncho did not look at any of the faces that swam out of the dimness. His eyes, he kept focused on the door. The hands of the woman were alive on his arm.

Like lost Legionnaires, strange men stood along the bar. Some leaned against the bar for support, their tired faces turned inward, tilting toward the shadows. Others stood with their backs to the high wooden bar, their hungry eyes searching the smoky room. A few simply hunched over their drinks like disturbed monks, shielding themselves from the world. One man sat on the floor, his head bowed over his knees, eyes closed.

Words murmured in the still, pure air, too loud to ignore, too soft to understand. Trekking toward the darkness, Poncho wondered if they were talking about him.

Night air rushed against his face, cool and sweet. Poncho could feel it working inside his head, blowing away some of the cobwebs and smoke. In the sudden clarity he did not know where he was. Then he felt the woman's hand on his arm.

One of her breasts was soft against his side and desire began once more to rise within him. His legs again felt as if they belonged to him. His stomach gurgled and he realized it had been a quite a long time since he had eaten. For a few steps, he thought about Juanita. One thing he had to praise the woman for was her cooking. Her stews were wonderful, and her mango pie was to die for. Briefly, he wondered how the battle was going in Yuscarana. Then, he wondered if Juanita were still alive. Fragrances of the woman walking beside him caressed his nostrils and thoughts of his wife dissipated like a thin summer fog.

They were walking down a narrow alleyway. Adobe buildings rose on either side, slanting inwards, like an early painting by Dali he had seen once in a museum. Buildings seemed to sway in the murky light. Poncho peered up at the sky. No moon, only a few stars, faint and distant.

In the quiet of the alleyway, he could hear the hollow ringing of their footsteps and, beyond the alley, the twittering of unseen birds in trees that were no more than dark patches in a greater darkness. Somewhere in the encompassing night, a dog howled, a high, thin, lonely call that rose, fell, and went unanswered. Unease smeared itself across his mind.

"Where are we going?" The sudden loudness of his own voice startled him and he jerked his arm the woman was holding. Her hand moved with the arm, fingers gripping like talons.

"You looked tired. I know a place."

"To sleep?"

"But of course." Her fingers played a lullaby on his forearm.

"I am hungry, too."

"Food can be arranged."

Poncho grunted and kept walking. Yes, food sounded good, a real meal for sure, followed by a real bed. Ah, what a marvelous combination.

As they moved deeper into the alley, the light faded. Their footsteps thudded in the thickening darkness. When they paused to allow Poncho to steady himself, he could hear a new, elemental sound, the sound of his own breathing. Poncho felt fatigue seeping into his body.

"Are we close yet, woman? I am tired and hungry."

"*Sí*, only a little farther." Her fingers slid from his arm and he heard a faint rustling. "Here, would you like some refreshment?"

Glass glittered in a stray band of light. Poncho eyed the bottle. One corner of his mind recognized he was already rather drunk. Yet, a powerful thirst swept through him.

"I stole it from the cantina," she whispered against his face. "I thought we might need refreshment during the night." She pressed her lips against the side of his neck.

Poncho felt his fingers close around the smooth glass. He lifted the bottle from the woman's hand and held it before his face, faintly surprised, for he had not been conscious of the movement of his own hand. Holding the bottle steady, he pulled at the cork with his teeth. The label, an idealized painting of a black fighting bull, was faintly visible. The bull's face looked fuzzy; his horns disappeared into the night. Cheap bar whiskey, but Poncho did not care.

Poncho maneuvered the bottle to his lips, closed his eyes, and pointed the bottom of the bottle toward the brightest visible star. Whiskey burned the lining of his throat. The woman's fingers worked the length of his torso. Cool air kissed his chest and belly as his shirt swung open. Suddenly, Poncho felt young and macho, a real hombre as he drank stolen whiskey bare-chested in the fallen lights of stars while a strange woman rubbed his chest and kissed his neck. Animal urges surged within him. He wanted to howl like the dog. Instead, he tilted the bottle again and took a longer drink.

"Follow me." Her words were scarcely more than heavy starlight against his ears.

Poncho gripped her right arm tightly, holding her prisoner as he drank. Then he swallowed, belched, and began walking, leaning against the woman, allowing her to lead him into a darkness that seemed heavier, thicker, blacker with every step. Scattered stars undulated on an ebony sea. After every three or four steps, Poncho paused and took a swallow, but only small ones now. The whiskey of the bull tasted good and he wanted to make it last.

The alley zigged, zagged, and narrowed. Poncho was very tired. In an effort to keep himself going, he sipped with each turn. Only the whiskey and the allure of the woman's perfume enabled him to go on.

Now and then, she spoke to him. Sometimes he understood the words and sometimes he only heard the babble of her voice. Sometimes, he did not even hear that. Walls began to look familiar as though he had traveled by them before, perhaps in another life.

Turning again, they twisted deeper into the darkness. A wall leaned out and brushed his left shoulder. Poncho rested against it.

"Halt for a moment, woman. How much farther is this place we are going? We have been walking for a long time and I am weary."

"Only a little farther. You are so big and strong. I know you can make it."

Poncho shook his head. He felt like the way bulls looked in the bullring after the matador had made many passes. "I do not think so. I am tired, so very tired. You do not know how tired I am. For many days I have been walking."

The woman ran her fingers across his face, rustling his stubble. "Have you come far?"

"*Mucho* kilometers."

"From where did you come?'

"I came from Yus... Never mind where I came from. Simply tell me how much farther we have to go."

"Only a little ways, but perhaps we should rest for a moment."

His legs trembling beneath him, Poncho felt a sudden sympathy for fighting bulls rising in him. He vowed never to go to the bullfights again. Seconds later, he decided he would go, but only to root for the bulls.

"*Sí*, let us rest." There were other words he wanted to say, but the last of the strength left his legs and he slid down with his back pressing against the wall. He sat down faster than he would have liked and the rough landing jarred him. He sat staring straight ahead, seeing nothing, blinking steadily.

"Take a drink. You need to build up your strength."

"*Sí*," Poncho said, speaking slowly and deliberately, signaling his lips to shape themselves with precision. "Let's take a big drink. You are right. I do need strength."

In the stillness of the night, the words sounded thin and faint, as if they had been spoken at some great distance and carried to him on the wind. The woman's face swam before him, a dark, deformed moon. Behind her, the alley wall swayed in the gentle breeze. He rubbed at his eyes with his knuckles. The wall grew still again.

"Take a drink," she said. "Take a big drink.

He tilted the bottle and swallowed. The earth moved beneath him. He looked up and all the stars were whirling across the black sky. The bottle had grown heavier during their journey. Poncho nodded at the woman's face, at least the one on the left; she seemed to suddenly have two faces. He could feel his face coming apart, crumbling like old, dry adobe.

Soft hands cupped his head and lowered it to the ground.

Bless you, Christ, he thought.

High in the night a bird whistled.

Poncho closed his eyes. Beneath his body, he could feel the world was turning on its axis. His arms and legs felt as if they belonged to someone else. He could still hear the bird, but only faintly. It sounded as if it were laughing.

Stale perfume filled his nostrils. The woman was talking to him in soft, low murmurs. He tried to speak, but his lips had gone numb.

Soft hands worked across his body like giant ants. He could feel them against his chest, then on his legs, finally in his pockets. After a time, he could no longer smell the woman's perfume.

Poncho lay very still with his eyes closed. If he moved at all, if he even opened his eyes, the world spun and dipped and shivered. He was too tired to struggle, and a man with a hammer had somehow crawled inside his skull and was steadily pounding away against the walls. This was one very strange town, Poncho decided. Next, he decided to simply lie very still. When his stomach began to churn, he decided to go ahead and die.

Sometime during the night, he heard the voices of children, talking very fast. A dozen hands pulled at his clothes. His boots were tugged from his feet and his shirt jerked off his back. He giggled as his pants and underwear slid down his legs, but he did not open his eyes. Never did he want to see another night.

Eventually, the children's voices went away.

Poncho grew cold.

Then his stomach turned over and he vomited into the darkness.

For a long time in the shrouding blackness he lay shivering, smelling his vomit, praying when his mind swirled briefly into focus.

With great fervor, Poncho prayed to die.

Seventy-four

Darkness fell on the small village of Carbajal, no more than seven or eight houses and a modest store that sold foodstuffs, work clothes, petrol, and whiskey. An outpost in a small clearing in the great green jungle, no more. One of a hundred, all more or less the same.

This one had been created twenty years before by two cousins. Their plan had been to harvest some timber, then clear the land and graze fine black cattle. However, before the venture was even two years old, one cousin had stolen the other's wife, his U.S. Army surplus jeep, and virtually all his money, driving away before dawn one day with the trophy wife and the payroll for the next two months.

The remaining partner had tried to carry on, but the struggle rapidly wore him out and he died nine months later of either a broken heart or monkey fever. As there was no doctor in the village, no one could say for certain. Some of the workers had stayed on to do light timbering or subsistence farming, while the others had gone, disappearing into the encroaching jungle.

In two months, the two men and their employees had largely been forgotten. In six months, it was as though they had never existed. Other men, needing shelter, came and occupied the abandoned shacks. Some of these men scratched a living from the jungle. Each day, others made the long, rough drive back to other outposts to work long hours at low pay. One of these men drove a bus, an elderly, noisy, violently yellow bus festooned with toucan shit. His nickname was El Cartero. No one in the village except him knew his real name, and he never used it.

El Cartero sat on the shallow porch that fronted his shack. He sat on a straight-back chair which he had tilted so his head rested against the front of the house and his feet were up on the railing that formed the perimeter of the porch. The house had needed a coat of fresh paint since before El Cartero had moved in. The prior occupant had been more concerned with members of a rival drug cartel than peeling paint and El Cartero was not overly domesticated.

As he digested his evening repast of rice, beans, and tortillas, El Cartero smoked a cheap cigar, staring into the purple darkness, listening to the night come alive, wondering who still lived in Yuscarana.

Sufficient light lingered for him to make out the dim, yellow outline of the bus. El Cartero sucked in a lungful of smoke, held it for a moment, then blew it back out in rings that faded almost immediately into the thickening dusk.

He liked his evening cigar. Many days, thoughts of it kept him going. Actually, he would have liked to smoke more expensive cigars throughout the day. However, with a wife and three children, a single cheap cigar a day was all he could afford. That might soon change. There was talk that Señor

Bigela, who ran the bus company, might give him a bonus for rescuing the vehicle from the destruction in Yuscarana. Drivers were plentiful and worked cheap; buses were few and cost much money. Yes, El Cartero decided, surely he would get a bonus.

Taking another drag on his cigar, he held the smoke for a few seconds. Behind him, he could hear the rustle of domestication as his wife cleaned the kitchen while his children chattered, arguing over who could run faster. From out of the encroaching darkness, he could hear the screams of howler monkeys and the cries of birds who hunted in the night. Deeper in the jungle, he heard the harsh, deep cough of a great cat.

El Cartero blew smoke out his nostrils in the direction of the cat. Then he began to whistle a tune. It was an old tune, a happy tune, a tune he had learned as a boy. He had learned it so long ago he had forgotten the name of the tune. He whistled it all the way through, twice. Then he eased the chair down, stood, and stretched. Stepping to the railing, he leaned on it, gingerly.

The cat coughed again, deep in the great alive jungle, and El Cartero grinned. All dangers, the great cat, the bullets of Yuscarana, poverty, had been swallowed by the benevolent darkness. He peered through night at the old yellow bus. Yes, he was clearly a hero for rescuing that fine vehicle from certain capture or destruction. Surely his bonus would come soon. Perhaps even with the next check. El Cartero's grin widened. In the night his teeth shone white.

Seventy-five

Moments after daylight, the trucks arrived from the headquarters. They were filled with soldiers anxious for battle, and the men rolled out of the back with rifles raised, ready for action. Only smoke rising from the blackened skeleton of the hotel greeted them.

The sun was out, burning off the mist, drying up the shallow brown puddles that still lingered. Birds and old dogs drank from them. Bodies lay in the street, face down and face up, on their left side and their right. Arms and legs sprawled at odd angles, pointing to the empty store fronts, or the chiseled edges of the mountains, or the smoldering ruins of the hotel. Each face wore a different expression. Some looked surprised. Others reflected pain they had been unable to bear. Some bore no expression at all. One actually revealed a trace of a smile. All had one thing in common, however; they were dead.

Kron meandered among the bodies, taking a serpentine route with no preordained destination. At first, he had told himself he was simply checking to see if he knew any of the faces. Since the first blush of dawn, he had been trying to locate members of the tour. Of course, he knew Mr. Samuels was dead, but all the others?

He had found most of them, but not all. He had still not located the Oriental couple, nor had he found Reverend Malloy, and that man was supposed to be the tour leader. Surely, he would have shown up by now, unless he were hurt or dead.

Sunlight was warm on his back and steam rose from the black pavement. Smoke still drifted from the charred timbers of the hotel, stinging his eyes. Some had settled in his throat, and he coughed and spat, being careful not to come too close to a body.

Kron caught a glimpse of the Samuels boy, sitting on an upturned wooden box. The boy's face was as flat and vacant as the side of the box. Kron smiled at the boy – strange – but he couldn't think of the kid's name, and lifted a hand. The boy's eyes were open, but he seemed to stare right through Kron, as though he were looking clear to the other side of the world.

Turning, Kron walked away from the hotel, heading toward the edge of Yuscarana. Sunlight shone into his eyes. Bareheaded and half-blind, he had lost his sunglasses somewhere along the way, he stumbled down the morning road, telling himself he truly possessed the story of a lifetime. All he had to do to was tell it straight and true, craft the storyline so Papa Hemingway would be proud.

At the edge of town, where the jungle grew tight against the adobe, he saw the Reverend Malloy kneeling by the side of the road in a patch of damp earth. All about him were the sounds of the jungle: screams of parrots and macaws, chattering of monkeys, buzzing of five hundred insects.

The reverend paid no attention. His hands clasped each other and his eyes were screwed tightly shut against the light. His head was bowed. Kron stood silently, watching him, wondering. When sweat began to roll down his back and slide into the crack of his butt, Kron turned and strolled back to town, words forming mosaics in his mind, his fingers restless for his pen.

The drivers of the trucks began to blow their horns. A truck with the wounded, including the only two guerillas who the soldiers had discovered, along with Captain Morales and Señora Herrera, rolled by. Morales' face was open to the sky. His eyes were blurred with pain, or thought. An unlit cigar was jammed into one corner of his mouth. Señora Herrera lay on her stomach. Kron could see she had been crying.

Another truck had been cleared of military gear, and soldiers and all the members of the tour who had been accounted for were being loaded onto the truck. Lord Threlkeld struggled to climb aboard with a glass half full of liquid in one hand. A soldier helped pull him up, while a second soldier took care of the glass.

Lady Threlkeld was already on board, sitting on the right-hand side, leaning over the wooden slats that formed the sides of the truck. She was talking to one of the maids. While Kron watched, the English woman inclined her head and kissed the dark-haired girl on the mouth.

Some of the people of Yuscarana were leaving, as well. Two tall, well-muscled privates were helping push them up into the back of the truck. A narrow wooden bench ran the length of the truck bed on each side. A few members of the tour were already seated. The rest were searching for a spot. Most of the faces had a glazed-over look, like the look on the face of the woman whose husband had been shot that first morning. Her daughter sat beside her. In the holy morning after, the girl was shivering.

The Samuels boy swung easily aboard. Then he turned and looked back as if he were committing Yuscarana to memory. His eyes halted as they reached Kron and he briefly raised a hand. Kron waved back, but the boy was already moving toward the bench on the left side of the truck. Kron watched him until the boy sat down. Then, he walked across the street and got in line.

He found himself standing behind the tour leader. One of the man's hands was heavily bandaged. As Kron's shadow fell across the back of his neck, Reverend Malloy turned and smiled at him. The reverend's face looked exceedingly tired, yet sweetly peaceful. Wondering how his own face looked, Kron smiled back.

Kron studied the truck. There was one noticeable dent on the right side and what looked to be three bullet holes just above the dent. Still, the vehicle appeared sturdy and dependable. However, in his eyes that morning, it lacked the character of the old yellow bus with the toucan shit running down the windows that had delivered them to Yuscarana.

Kron put one hand on the bed of the truck and started to swing himself up. A hand pressed against his backside and gave him a firm shove. He sat down by the older American couple from the tour. They looked tired as they leaned gently against each other, smiling faintly. Kron wondered where the rest of the rebels had gone. They seemed to have vanished into the jungle. As he gazed down the street that led to tomorrow, he wished he were leaving the way he had come in, riding the old yellow bus on a cracked, vinyl seat with his face pressed against the rattling window glass, half-dreaming, watching the great, green, alive jungle growing closer with each revolution of the wheels. Maybe I'm finally starting to come out of the cocoon, he thought.

He grinned and grimaced, happy and sad at the same time, not caring if someone were watching. The driver tooted the horn twice and the truck jerked into gear and began rumbling down the main street of Yuscarana, taking them back the same road they had traveled only days before. Yes, Kron thought, as he watched the green blur of the jungle slide by, they were traveling the same road; only they were headed in the opposite direction and they were no longer the people they had been – not a single one of them.

The truck jolted over a rough patch of highway as Kron glanced at a sky so blue it looked as if it had been painted by Picasso during his blue period. A bird, black against the blue, soared high above the truck in silent, endless spirals.

Seventy-six

High above the hillside, a great bird soared. This bird was midnight black and its wingspan was as wide as a man is tall. Slowly it circled, each orbit dropping it closer to the earth.

On the hillside, a man lay on his back. He lay extraordinarily still. For several hours, he had not moved. Only the faint rise and fall of his chest revealed life. All around him the verdant grass was stained the color of copper. The man's eyes were open, but they no longer saw.

Actually, the man was merely a boy and he had lain on the hillside for days, unable to move. Able now only to listen, in the brief moments he was conscious, to the ceaseless murmurings of the jungle.

The shadow of the great bird swept across the man, cooling his face for a fraction of a second. The shadow seemed, to the tiny sliver of mind that the man had left, a dark angel, a harbinger of death.

Once he had dreaded such a concept, but no longer. Pain had gripped his body for far too long. If he had been able, he would have opened his arms in welcome. But he had no strength. He could only wait for the shadow to fall again and listen to the ceaseless murmurings of the great green alive jungle – the jungle that had lived long before the boy first heard the name of Yuscarana, and would live long after he dreamed of Yuscarana no more.

Meet Chris Helvey

Chris Helvey is an award winning short-story writer, a poet, and a novelist. The author of more than a dozen novels and multiple short-story collections, Chris' latest novel, *Afghan Love Potion*, was recently released by Wings ePress, and is available in both paperback and e-book formats on Amazon. A founding member of the Bluegrass Writers Coalition, he is also editor-in-chief and publisher of *Trajectory Journal*.

Other Works From The Pen Of
Chris Helvey

Yard Man - A lonely man simply trying to survive the Great Depression, suddenly stumbles into a job he doesn't want, falls in love with a prostitute who doesn't love him, and incurs the wrath of the most dangerous man in Mississippi.

Dancing On The Rim - The story of one man's journey across a violent wilderness; a journey of revenge, retribution, and a search for redemption.

Violets For Sergeant Schiller - A young German poet is swept up in the maelstrom of World War I, facing fear, bullets, and the prospective of an early grave.

The White Jamaican - A private eye is hired to find a husband who has mysteriously disappeared, only to fall in love as he faces death and struggles to save his soul.

Into the Wilderness - A middle-aged man's life ruptures and he returns to his hometown in a search for peace, happiness, and a place to belong.

Last Train to Miami - A Mafia hitman from Philly is sent to Miami by his Boss to do a hit for the Miami boss. Only when he arrives, he discovers that even among the Family truth can be an elusive creature.

Looking at Kansas - An aging Missouri sheriff must fight a fentanyl epidemic, his most dangerous enemy who has vowed to kill him, and his own weaknesses.

Bayou - Crime, revenge, love, and death interconnect in this fast-paced novel set deep in the bayous during the Great Depression.

Afghan Love Potion - An honest, detailed look at the blows both life and war can and often do deliver, and how people are forced to respond, positively or negatively, to the damages inflicted.

Dear reader,

I hope you've enjoyed reading this story of the horrors of
revolution.

Your opinion is valuable to other
readers like you,
who may be looking for books like mine.

Please consider taking a few minutes to post a review,
however brief,
on the site where you purchased this book
or on the Wings ePress web page.

You may also want to visit my author page
at the Wings' website where you can find the

Thank you!

Visit Our Website

For The Full Inventory
Of Quality Books:

Wings ePress, Inc

Quality trade paperbacks and downloads
in multiple formats,
in genres ranging from light romantic comedy to general
fiction and horror.
Wings has something for every reader's taste.
Visit the website, then bookmark it.
We add new titles each month!

Wings ePress, Inc.
3000 N. Rock Road
Newton, KS 67114